THE ROAR OF THE THUNDER GOD

A 1997 VALCO TRUST FUND
LITERARY AWARD-WINNER

LARRY D. KUMASSAH

Sedco

9964 72 156 0

Sedco Publishing Limited
P. O. Box 2051
Accra

First published 2000

ISBN 9964 72 156 0

Typeset in Ghana by Frank Publishing Ltd.
P. O. Box MB 414, Accra

Printed by
Sedco Enterprise
P. O. Box 2051
Accra

The events and characters in this novel bear no reference to any real person or persons, living or dead. They are figments of the author's own imagination.

TABLE OF CONTENTS

Page

Acknowledgement.. ix
Prologue.. xiii
Chapter One... 1
Chapter Two... 11
Chapter Three.. 26
Chapter Four.. 41
Chapter Five... 56
Chapter Six... 69
Chapter Seven.. 88
Chapter Eight... 100
Chapter Nine.. 112
Chapter Ten.. 131
Chapter Eleven.. 156
Chapter Twelve.. 167
Chapter Thirteen... 185
Chapter Fourteen.. 201
Chapter Fifteen.. 225
Chapter Sixteen... 244
Chapter Seventeen.. 265
Chapter Eighteen... 285
Chapter Nineteen.. 312
Chapter Twenty... 334
Epilogue.. 350
Glossary of Words... 354
Glossary of Songs.. 360

The Roar Of The Thunder God won the 1997 Valco Trust Fund Literary Award. Another novel by the same author, *Count Yourselves Among The Dead,* also won the 1995 Valco Trust Fund Literary Award. It is yet to be published.

This novel is dedicated to the memory of my mother Norviegbor and my aunt Akumansa, and to the Medical Superintendent and staff of Keta Hospital, March 1995–March 1998.

Acknowledgement

My gratitude goes to my wife, Roberta, for her patience during the long nights while I worked at my desk, and to Kofi Bonuedi and George Gbemu for our long conversations. This book owes a lot to those conversations.

...From the direction of the marketplace which lay about a hundred metres from the square, the lonely figure of a man approached the square...

The owls set off a cacophony of hoots and the man shuddered. Tales of witches perching on the durbar ground's shady trees to devour their human victims flashed through his mind, but he resolutely pushed them away. He began to sing a war song to bolster up his faltering courage...

The adrenalin began to pump up in his blood and he took a few steps of the war dance. He reached the trees, no more afraid, and leaning against an electric pole that rose through the foliage of the trees, he began to wait. Soon after another figure loomed out of the darkness...

The man disengaged himself from the electric pole. "You are very much on time," he said as the figure came to stand before him.

"So are you."

The man stretched forth his arms and the two people fell into an embrace. "Ah..." the man sighed.

"Did you tell anybody you were coming here?" the figure in dark clothes asked.

"Not at all," the man said. "I am not a woman."

The arms of the figure had been thrown around the man's neck in the embrace. Now one arm disengaged itself and from the pocket of its trousers, the figure pulled out a long knife. The arm drew back and in swift movements drove the knife repeatedly into the man's stomach.

"*Adzei!*" the man shouted, his arms flying off from the embrace to clutch at his stomach. The figure watched as the man tottered back and fell on the ground with a thud. Carefully, it cleaned the knife in the man's clothes. Then it turned and left the scene as silently as it had come.

PROLOGUE

The ruins of Fort Prinzenstein stand on the beach at Keta like the remains of the destruction on the battlefield after the looting. The fort was built in 1784 by the Danes in the then Gold Coast as a station for their trading activities and as a stronghold against the rivalries of other marauding European nations. In the years before its present state, Fort Prinzenstein had looked formidable and exuded power and strength. After independence when the colonialists had left our shores and the Gold Coast became known as Ghana, the fort served a myriad of purposes. It once served as a court-house, a prison yard and district headquarters of many departments like Fisheries, and Water and Sewerage. Now, it lies abandoned, save for a few tramps who have found home here, its huge metre-thick walls tumbled down by the violent waves of the sea like the plastic bricks of a child's game.

The Keta township lies in the middle of the southern end of the Volta Region forming part of a littoral between the Atlantic Ocean and the Keta Lagoon. This littoral runs from Kedzi in the east to Anloga in the west. Fort Prinzenstein and Keta and its surrounding areas had long been known to be built on a sand-bar far below sea level. It had been only a matter of time before the sea started repossessing the land it had receded from, thousands of years ago. At first the inhabitants of Keta took the sea erosion as an interesting natural phenomenon. The town was a large and vibrant commercial centre with large departmental stores, hotels and other entertainment spots. The complacent attitude of the inhabitants changed when the sea entered the town and started smashing up everything. Sea defences built hurriedly could not hold back the roaring sea. It ate away everything from Keta running through Hagbanu, Adzido and Kedzi to the east. The remnants of these villages are now only little patches of buildings where the die-hards among the inhabitants left behind, huddle in fear of their lives and property, unable to abandon the sinking ship of the land of their birth. Those who fled into the arms of foreign lands sometimes come back, furtively, to the remains of the battered land and with tears in their eyes, they will point out to friends, far out to sea, the spots where their ancestral homes once stood.

Beyond the township of Kedzi, still to the east of Keta, lie other towns and villages no less damaged by the sea erosion— Horvi, Blekusu, Agavedzi, Salakope and Amutsinu. These link up through Adina, Adafienu and Denu right to the Ghana-Togo border at Aflao. In the days when the road linking Keta and Aflao was still intact, the journey from Keta to Aflao took just a few minutes. Now to get to Aflao from Keta over this route, you have to take a boat from Keta to Kedzi where you board a car to take you over the rest of the distance by road to Aflao. If you want an uninterrupted journey by road, you will have to turn the other way, going west through Kedzikope, Abutiakope, Dzelukope, Vui, all suburbs of Keta, then Tegbi, Woe, Anloga, Srogboe, then turn north and go clockwise through Dabala, Akatsi, Abor, Afiadenyigba, Agbozume and Denu to Aflao. So that the journey of about twenty-five kilometres is now over a hundred and twenty kilometres.

Until the government's two-pronged and time-worn promise of building a permanent sea defence and reclaiming the lost land materialises, Keta remains perched on its last leg on a sand-bar and whether help reaches it before it finally collapses into the Atlantic Ocean, only time can tell.

Though the reason for the rape of Keta may seem obvious to the outsider, a sizeable number of natives attribute it to supernatural forces, the result of the sins of the inhabitants.

Sena Akakpo, a primary school teacher at Keta believed the obvious — that Keta was built on a sand-bar far below sea level, so the sea was simply striving to achieve a level commensurate with its height. He insisted that the Europeans who contributed in no small way in founding the town knew very well the town did not have long to live, but since they were not planning to make Keta their permanent home, they finished their self-assigned jobs in a hurry and left the unwary natives to their fate.

Sena was a very pragmatic teacher who saw things as either visible or non-existent, with the exception of the air he breathed. He believed in evolution with a Divine Hand guiding the development of species from one stage to another, thus leaving some room to explain his occasional church-going.

Sena liked his job as a teacher because it gave him a ready audience for his garrulity. His only regret was that he taught a primary four class and the children often lost track of his expostulations. The minds of the poor children very soon wandered off, longing for their salty playgrounds.

The unceasing song on the lips of most salaried workers in the locality where Sena worked was the inadequacy of their monthly salaries. Fortunately for Sena, he never worried if his salary would be able to take him from one pay-day to the next. He had a fairly rich fiancée, Cathrina, a trader, who prepared his meals on time and never asked for remittance.

On this May night, the moon was out but partially hidden by large clouds that floated across the sky. It played hide and seek with the clouds, its soft light sparkling off the soft sand on the beach. Sena and his fiancée on this night, walked hand-in-hand along the beach, picking their way through the little shadows thrown by the undulations in the sand. The noise of the sea waves pounding the beach was less intense at this time but their muted strength that had slashed away large portions of the land could still be felt by the lovers.

Both Sena and Cathrina had never before walked on the beach in the night. They found the serenity and the quiet in the midst of the muted noise of the sea waves unnerving but at the same time very pleasurable. Wordlessly, they wondered why they had not been there before.

Sena was a sprightly young man with a huge moustache which rather emphasised his slight structure, like a puppy carrying a bone too big for its size. He had a well rounded forehead and piercing eyes that easily gave him a domineering look, and when he launched himself into an argument he was like a hellcat let loose among attacking dogs.

"If it were not for some wicked fishermen," Sena said, "I think a lot of people would come to the beach in the night to enjoy the atmosphere here."

"Do you still believe those stories?" Cathrina asked as she missed a step and leaned her weight against Sena. He feigned imbalance and fell in the sand. Cathrina fell on him. Sena held her and would have loved to continue holding her but the angle at which his leg lay was uncomfortable so he pushed her up to re-adjust his leg but she misunderstood him and stood up.

He stood up too, regretfully, and picked up the conversation where they had let off. "Didn't you hear about the dead man that was recently washed ashore?"

"What proof was there that he was murdered for any ritual purpose?"

"Who made the gash on his neck, the fish?"

"Did you see the body?"

"I didn't."

"People could be making that up, you know."

Cathrina believed in the goodness of man and even though she recognised that there were bad men and women in society she thought this an exception rather than the rule. She came from a family whose forebears belonged to the cult that worshipped the *Yeve* god. Some of her uncles and aunts still indulged in the worship of this god, albeit not as intensely as had been in the past. Cathrina's parents were Christians and she herself had also been baptised into the Catholic faith but the shadows of *Yeve* worship were never far from the fringes of her mind, moreso when the house she shared with her parents was not far from the main family house where the drumming and singing of *Yeve* songs were done on occasions when sacrifices were made to the god. She regarded these practices with amusement and sometimes hummed their songs but only in the privacy of her room. Her mother who abhorred the *Yeve* rites would literally kill her if she heard her sing those songs.

"Well, if what we hear is true then it is very sad. Look at all this stretch of pleasure," Sena said, stretching forth his hands.

"We can come here every day if you wish. In fact, I want us to come here every day, that is when the moon is up." She took his outstretched hand and clasped it behind her. "There is nothing out here to hurt you." But Cathrina was just about to receive the rudest proof that it takes all sorts to make up society, that every type of unusual behaviour exists under the sun.

Their steps now appeared aimless as they began to veer sometimes towards the sea and at other times away from it. They were returning from the Keta market where Cathrina had gone to sell her wares. On market days as today, she closed late. By a slight misunderstanding today, her householp, an eighteen-year-old girl, had left without her, with her unsold goods in a taxi. When Sena arrived to take her home as he sometimes did, he suggested they walk, and on an impulse they decided to walk across the beach to Cathrina's house at Abutiakope, a suburb of Keta, a distance of about one and a half kilometres.

To their right, the lights of Kedzikope, another suburb of Keta, shone brightly, reassuring them against the silent fear of evil in their hearts which they both refused to acknowledge. They had now moved quite close to the crest of the sand bordering the sea and could now distinctly feel on their faces the salty mist from the waves. Suddenly, Cathrina stopped short, dragging back Sena with her. He looked in her eyes inquiringly and seeing the terror there, his eyes followed the direction of her gaze. Two men who appeared to have been defecating were now dragging up their pants. The men appeared to be conferring with each other and from the furtive glances they gave Sena and Cathrina, it was obvious the lovers had become the cynosure of their attention.

The whole air began to smell of evil; suddenly all other things lost their relevance as the presence of the two men loomed over them like a woollen blanket of darkness about to envelop them. The two lovers began to make a bee-line back towards the safety of the lights of the town, constantly looking over their shoulders at the two men who had started walking purposefully after them. Their steps quickened to the brink of breaking into a sprint. So intense was their concentration on the men after them that they failed to see a second pair of men walking briskly up the beach towards them.

Cathrina uttered a thin cry of alarm when they almost ran into the two men. She pulled Sena's arm with a jerk and together they broke into a run at an angle towards town. Almost simultaneously the four strange men shed every pretence and began to run after the lovers. Cathrina's long slacks made the going difficult and Sena had to practically drag her after him. It did not take long for their pursuers to catch up with them and encircle them.

"What is it? What have we done?" Cathrina asked breathlessly as she turned to each of the strange men around them.

Sena appeared to have lost his voice; with Cathrina's hand still clutched firmly in his, he moved within the human circle like a trapped animal, looking for a way of escape. Suddenly, he dashed against the wall of men, pulling Cathrina after him. A muscular leg flew across his path and he fell down heavily, bringing Cathrina on top of him. They scrambled in the sand to get up as the men quickly formed a new circle around them. They sat up, looking up at the sinister faces that glared down at them.

"What do you want from us?" Sena asked, at long last finding his voice. "What have we done?"

A stout man among the group who appeared to be the leader spoke. "We are taking you somewhere very near," he said. "Just remain calm and come with us quietly. No harm will come to you."

"Where?" Sena asked.

"Somewhere very near. Get up."

The young couple were dragged to their feet and shepherded back towards the sea. As they walked, Sena's mind began to record the features of their captors. He kept looking back, taking mental notes, the moon providing ample light to identify the men who were now a huge barrier between him and all his dreams — the happy marriage he foresaw with Cathrina and a secret ambition to run for membership of the local District Assembly. Were all these about to fizzle out?

They reached the crest of the beach, the two lovers continually turning to look at the men who were crowding them towards the sea. The stout man who led the group carried a metal rod in his hand.

"Look forward!" the stout man said.

And in the instant in which Cathrina and Sena's head jerked forward in obedience, the hand of the stout man flew out in a flash, hitting Cathrina on the back of the head with the metal bar. The girl's shrill cry rang out across the deserted beach. She began to whimper, "*Torhonor* will avenge me, *Torhonor* will pay you back..."

Torhonor was the fearful god of thunder of the *Yeve* cult. In the moment of her anguish, Cathrina deserted the Christian path laid down for her by her parents and called on the primeval faith of her ancestors for help. The metal rod descended again, this time on her forehead and she slumped against Sena and flowed to the sand at his feet.

Sena watched his fiancée fall to the ground like someone in a dream who had no control over the events unfolding around him. Then in a flash he was on the assailant of his fiancée like a mad dog. He grabbed the metal rod and swung it, hitting the man nearest the stout man behind the ear before the other men fell on him and disarmed him. The leader of the group took the rod and calculatingly brought it down hard on the base of Sena's skull. The young man went limp.

"Quick!" urged the leader of the group.

Sena was stretched out on the ground, lying sideways. One man pinned his legs into the sand and another his arms. The third man pulled back Sena's head, making his thin neck taut. Their leader pulled out a sharp butcher's knife and a plastic container. He knelt in the sand and with the container held beneath Sena's neck, he slit his throat in one deft movement. The young man's body jerked mightily as blood sputtered into the container and on the sand. He began to struggle violently, his windpipe making gurgling noises. The men struggled to hold him still and catch as much of his blood as possible.

The sputter of the blood reduced to a dribble and the young man's body began to relax. The man with the plastic container caught as much blood as he could, then stood up and screwed on the lid of the container. The other men let go of the body which was now producing only sporadic twitches. One of them produced two sacks, one of fibre the other of polythene and with the help of the others, Sena's body was first bundled into the fibre sack and then into the polythene. The polythene was to stop tell-tale trickles of blood dropping onto the beach. Then the mouth of the sack was tied up with a piece of string.

They were now covered with blood and sand. They worked clinically and methodically and did not appear to be worried about the danger of someone chancing upon them, as if this was something they did every day. They seemed to have forgotten all about the girl until one of them said "What do we do with the girl?"

They left the sack and moved over to Cathrina who lay on her side with her head resting on an outstretched arm as if in sleep. One of the men bent down and felt her pulse. "She is still alive," he said, stretching up.

"I wish she were a man too," the stout man said. "Then it would be a double coup; we are already in the mood."

"What do we do with her?" the first man repeated.

The leader turned the girl over and with the metal rod, he beat her repeatedly about the throat. Then he said, "Come on, throw her into the sea."

They grabbed her limbs, waded far into the water and threw her out into the angry sea, the splash of her body lost in the sound of the waves. They came out of the sea, dripping water. Then systematically, they scooped up the blood-soaked sand and threw it into the sea. After that they covered the spot with clean sand. At a sign from the leader, two of them picked up the sack containing Sena's body and then all of them began to run along the edge of the water. They ran for a short distance and then climbed the crest of the beach. With the feet of those carrying the sack sinking into the soft sand, they could now manage only a quick walk. Above them the moon continued to play hide and seek with the clouds and little crabs on the beach scurried out of the way to stand at a distance to watch the impatient men walk past.

The men hurried along until they reached a patch of

reeds growing on the beach. Their bodies rustled through the reeds until they got to the edge of one of the little lagoons on the beach. The two men carrying the sack dropped it carelessly to the ground, huffing and puffing. Just on the edge of the lagoon, a deep hole had been freshly dug with earth piled up on its sides. By the hole was a plastic bucket. The polythene sack was pulled off from the fibre one and Sena's body was pushed into the hole by the stout man who then pulled some leaves from his pocket and threw them into the hole followed by the sprinkling of some dark powder. Then he recited some incantations ending with, "...We don't know you and we don't have anything against you; we are only doing a job. When you go, go with your eyes closed and don't look back at anyone..."

Working quickly with their bare hands, the men filled up the hole with the loose soil. They stamped on the soil to make it level with the surroundings. With the rubber bucket, they fetched water from the lagoon and watered the loose earth. Then they uprooted some reeds and strewed them over the filled hole.

From the reeds nearby, the stout man brought out a stuffed polythene carrier bag. From this, he pulled out several clothing. The men quickly looked through, each man taking his fit. They removed their blood-soaked clothes and changed into the fresh clothing. They stuffed their soiled dresses into the polythene bag and then moved to a distance.

The leader of the group then brushed each man with some leaves, muttering incantations, "...Nobody has seen anything, nobody has heard anything, nobody has done anything, nobody has touched anything... He who says he has, let his face be twisted to the back of his head, let him lose the power over the use of his limbs, let him and his family perish without a trace from the surface of the earth..."

The head of the man who had been attacked by Sena was now throbbing with unbearable pain. "Hurry up so that we can find some medicine for my head," he said.

The leader examined his head and said, "I have some herbal preparation that will solve your problem." He then turned to the other men. "Has anybody forgotten anything?"

"No," they answered in unison.

The leader took the container of blood from the ground where he had placed it and wrapped it carefully in a piece of cloth. Then they set off at a fast pace towards town, each engrossed in his own thoughts. The moon had journeyed across the sky and was now almost vertically overhead. Its glare followed the men right into town as it struggled to peep through the dark clouds. Then the men entered the narrow alleys at Abutiakope and were lost to the moon.

The following day, Cathrina's body was found washed ashore on the beach. The police took her to the Keta Hospital mortuary and the next day, a doctor performed an autopsy on the dead body. His report read, "...Body found to have central and peripheral cyanosis, foaming at the mouth and nose with scalp laceration at the right temporal region. Dissection of the body showed both lungs full of water, fractured skull at right temporal region with massive right temporal subdural haematoma. Cause of death: Asphysia due to drowning. Significant contribution from head injury due to possible assault."

The disappearance of Sena made him a prime suspect and the police sent out an arrest warrant for him. Cathrina's body was then released to her parents for burial.

CHAPTER ONE

When the rain falls at Keta, it falls like a parent beating up a helpless child lying prostrate on the ground. In forest areas much of the rain falls on trees and bushes before falling onto the earth, the impact of its fall lessening considerably. But at Keta, the rain beats a tattoo on the bare sand and roofs. No wonder when it rains it does not take long for many parts of the town to be flooded.

There is a popular belief in town that during the rainy season, the rain prefers to fall on market days. This market-day was no exception. It first started with dark clouds covering the sky, blocking out most of the sun's rays. In the big market at Keta, those traders who had displayed their wares outside the stalls provided for them, quickly started gathering their wares and moving under the protection of the stalls. Shoppers hastily concluded their purchases, the dark clouds above cutting short the normal haggling and heckling over prices called bargaining. Some of those who had somehow finished their purchases rushed to the lorry park hoping to reach home before the rain started. Others took refuge under the numerous sheds.

On days like this, dogs, goats, chickens and crows which were also regular visitors on market days, had a field day. Traders and shoppers alike in their haste dropped pieces of food items which these animals fed on gleefully. Some of these animals also made quick dashes at food items on tables and even in baskets. With the threatening clouds above, they knew that not much effort would be put into chasing them away. They so harassed both traders and shoppers that these seemed to be

1

running away from two evils at the same time.

That, maybe, was why on sunny market days when the traders and shoppers got a good opportunity, they put their whole strength into the whacks and blows that they delivered to various parts of the bodies of these animals. Most animals around the Keta market with deformities were not deformed from birth — they were casualties of the war of survival between them and the market women.

The dark clouds moved gently across the sky and everyone knew this was going to be a very heavy rain. Across the town people hurried home or looked for places that offered more than temporary shelter from the rain. From the numerous drinking bars both men and women dashed out, the women more surreptitiously, towards their homes. The habitual drinkers who had put off their daily dose of liquor until much later during the day now rushed out to fortify themselves against the coming cold. Some of them would spend the entire time of the rain inside the drinking bars using the rain as an excuse, so that after the rain when they came out they would be so soaked you wouldn't know the difference between them and those who had been beaten by the rain.

The dark clouds also drove out hordes of school children onto the streets. The wise teachers foresaw that this was no ordinary rain, it was a rain that could go on for the whole day, even into the next day. So they dispersed the school kids to run to the safety of their homes. They had always been beaten by the rain which leaked through the dilapidated roofs of their classrooms. With the school kids gone, the traders among the teachers quickly counted the proceeds from their daily sales of ice water, *kenkey* and fried fish, cooked rice, biscuits, etc., and made plans for business for the next day. They

2

worked in haste so as to reach home before the rain started; but should the rain catch up with them they hoped to walk home through it under the protection of flimsy umbrellas they had bought on their numerous trips to the Makola Market in Accra, the capital city.

It was on days like this that commercial vehicle drivers did good business, albeit briefly. People were ready to jump into any machine that moved on wheels. The drivers charged them exorbitantly, especially in times like this when the Ghana Private Road Transport Union had yet to come out to fix transport fares after the recent annual hike in the price of petroleum products. Those with loads like they were moving house suffered more — they were charged fares that made them grumble all the way to their destinations.

Some of the vehicles you see at Keta are so wretched that it is a wonder they even move at all. The salt element in the air at Keta has wreaked so much havoc on these vehicles that when some are parked you would think they were metal scraps waiting to be towed away. They have very little paint left on their bodies, some have no windshields and others have leaking roofs. It is not unusual to see people riding in vehicles with umbrella's opened over their heads. This often brings quarrels because the water drips from the umbrellas onto the other passengers.

There was a funeral procession moving towards the most popular cemetery in town. When the procession had left the chapel, it was with the usual decorum of slow steps and mournful songs, the pall-bearers, descendants of the old man in the coffin, looking sufficiently solemn and important in their task. Half-way to the cemetery, with the sudden appearance of the dark rain clouds, the procession was thrown into confusion — should they run or should they continue at the slow pace? The catechist solved the problem when he moved to the head of the procession and ordered the pall-bearers to hurry up. Everybody promptly broke into a pace between a fast walk and a trot. The dead old man was destined for a fast burial service at the graveside not usually witnessed in this area where the dead were given elaborate burials.

The long corridor of land between the large Keta lagoon and the main road running from Tegbi to Anloga produced the shallot requirements of the whole country and some even for export to neighbouring countries like Togo, Benin, Nigeria and Cote d'Ivoire. This long stretch of land was meticulously divided into well tended beds of almost identical sizes, and throughout the year these beds were covered with one food crop or another. If it was not shallot, then it was cowpeas, if it was not cowpeas then it would be maize or some other crop like cassava, pepper, okro or tomatoes. The beds were carefully fed with manure to sustain this kind of regimen.

A tacit agreement reigned among owners of this stretch of land. No portion of it was used for building purposes. The low level of the land even discouraged people from using it for building purposes. That was why people could buy or sell land here, the total area of which could be two by five metres.

Rain clouds were often greeted with shouts of joy on this stretch of land, except when the fields were in danger of becoming water-logged. A sizeable number of shallow wells dotted these fields and from these, water was drawn to water the beds. It was a tedious process even though the ease with which the farmers did it made it look effortless. Small buckets with cords attached to them

4

were thrown down the wells and pulled up by the cord, then with one hand holding the handle of the bucket and the other the bottom, the water was thrown out forcefully depending upon the distance it was intended to travel. It rolled out of the bucket then spread out covering the beds in a soft spray.

The shallot fields offered considerable employment to the working population. Most people had something to do one way or another with the shallot fields. If it was not your husband who was into it, it could be some of your other relatives. Hordes of school children also found employment over here. They came in droves especially during vacation. Some of the children actually depended on this for paying their school fees; to others it was just another source of fun. Most of the farmers gave their hired workers breakfast. This usually consisted of *abolo* or *kenkey,* meals made from maize, and fried fish with some ground pepper, shallot and tomatoes. These meals often turned out to be very competitive; the meek and humble came away from them still hungry. There were boys who could make adult-fist-size balls of kenkey disappear down their gullets in a matter of seconds. These boys were held in awe by the younger ones and regarded as 'champion boys' because by some strange coincidence they didn't just eat, they also worked like bulls.

This rainy day was no different in the shallot fields. When the dark clouds appeared, whoops of joy rang out among the farmers. This year had been a particularly dry one and scarcely any meaningful rain had fallen. Those who were already very tired from watering the fields threw down their watering buckets and started preparing hastily to go home. Those who believed that not every cloud in the sky would bring rain continued watering

5

their fields, albeit at a slower pace.

Along the grey area between the towns of Woe and Anloga, where one was never certain whether one was in one town or the other, two brothers worked on their field. They were not watering shallots. With a pointed stick, the younger brother, Besa, was making holes in the beds and the elder brother was planting pepper seedlings. They worked in silence and appeared unmindful of the dark clouds gathering overhead, each one humming the same tune under his breath. It was a popular *agbadza* dance tune that said:

Ne 'tso tu ha;
Malee ko'ko;
Ne 'tso 'hε ha
Malee ko'ko;
Amekpui ne d'ehε he
Adzogba!
Amekpui ne d'ehε mikpɔ...

At times each man appeared to be singing a different part of the song but somehow they managed to end the song on the same note and words. They talked little but worked in perfect understanding of each other. When Besa finished making the holes on the beds he proceeded to fetch water from a nearby well to water the seedlings just planted by Gbagbladza, for that was his elder brother's name.

Gbagbladza literally translated meant cockroach but the one who bore the name was not in the least bothered by being identified with this orthopteron. Indeed he took pride in the name for it was one attribute about the cockroach that he displayed in a fight that gave him the

6

name.

In the coastal suburb of Woe where Besa and his brother lived, when two boys of about equal strength fought, they were often left to fight on until one gave in. But it was unusual, when four boys attacked one boy, to allow such a fight to go on. That was what happened to Gbagbladza when he was barely into his teens. The fight was started by an argument over the ownership of some catch from the sea. The four boys attacked Gbagbladza in a wave and he fought back. He was very strong for his age, fast and stocky, a structure he retained to this day He fought the four boys to the admiration of all those who had gathered to watch the fight. That was the main reason the fight was allowed to go on. He threw a fist here and a leg there and butted them with his head. The boys still kept attacking him and after some time Gbagbladza began to tire. Like mad dogs going in for the kill, the boys fell on him pulling him to the ground. They rained blows on him, but just as the onlookers were about to move in and separate them, a miraculous thing happened. The body of Gbagbladza which seemed to be pinned to the ground began to vibrate violently. The boys on top of him felt the sensation too and for a moment became still. Gbagbladza rose from the ground, some of the boys still clinging to his arms. He took hold of the throats of two of the boys in each hand and began to squeeze with all his might. The other two boys fled for their lives when they saw the sudden turn of events. It took the combined strength of several men to free the hapless boys from Gbagbladza's grip. From that time onwards he began to be known by his new name, Gbagbladza. It was believed that even when you cut off the head of a cockroach, it continues to live for a long time kicking its legs in the air sometimes to the following day.

There was a tight bond of friendship between Besa and Gbagbladza. One man was seldom seen without the other. Besa was the third-born son of his father, Gbagbladza being the second. The first, a boy, was still-born. When Besa was born, Gbagbladza followed his mother anytime she was carrying Besa. When he was allowed to start carrying the child, he allowed none other than his mother to do so. He refused to go to school and played truant most of the time until Besa was old enough to go to school with him, so that even though one was older than the other they were both in the same class. At class six, they dropped out of school, preferring the life on the beach. Later on they started farming too. Gbagbladza was married with two children, Besa with three.

One strange thing about the brothers was that they hardly interacted with any other person unless it was necessary, either in a business transaction or any other situation. And when they were alone they did not appear to talk much among themselves just as they were doing on the farm now. Unlike his brother, Besa was slim and of a soft countenance.

"It looks like it's going to rain," Besa said looking up.

"Is that so?" his brother asked. He rose up painfully and with his hands on his waist let his gaze run across the sky. "Let me finish this bed and we will go home." They stayed in the same house with their families together with their aged parents. From their toil they fed their parents too.

Besa walked idly behind his brother watering each seedling as it was planted. He removed the occasional weed from the freshly prepared bed. He loved farming but Gbagbladza was more at home with the sea. It wasn't

8

something that they talked about. Besa had never been able to overcome the terror that the sea held for him. Even though he could swim very well he always had the sensation of being squeezed in from all sides any time he was submerged in the sea.

The rain began more suddenly than they had expected. They quickly gathered their buckets, hoes and cutlasses but realised it would be hopeless to attempt to run home without getting very wet. Without a word to each other, they headed for a plantain grove in a depression below the street. The wind blew from seaward so they were adequately protected from the driving rain.

As the rain fell, the clouds seemed to grow more intense, darkening the sky. The wind driving the rain picked up speed and now blew in gusts, changing direction intermittently. It picked up rubbish and hurled it into the air. Trees shook to their roots and several branches came crashing to the ground. The rain beat about the heads and other exposed parts of those who were out and running hard for shelter. It fell in a hail and was painful to the skin. The children called it pebble-rain and on more cheerful rainy days they would run out to pick up the crystals of ice that fell from the sky. They would put them in their mouths, enjoying the cold that it induced in their mouths, and those of them who had heard of countries where snow covered the ground would imagine how delightful it would be to live in a country where you could pick ice from the ground anytime and put it into your mouth. But on this day no child needed to be told to stay indoors.

The rain fell with an intensity as if it wanted to inundate the earth in a hurry. The few people still out ran like they had the devil right on their heels, and on the beaches the brave fishermen secured the long twines on their nets to stumps of coconut trees and ran for shelter. The rain fell along the littoral from Vodza through Keta, Woe and Anloga right down to Anyanui on the banks of the Volta River, and beyond.

Thunder began to rumble in the sky and streaks of lightning pierced the gloom, inundating large areas in blinding white light. In several places the thunder sounded like giant crackers thrown into the fire. In many homes old men and women uttered mournful sounds and nodded their heads as if privy to some secret knowledge.

Then the wind died down as suddenly as it had started and the sound of thunder became only a distant rumble, like the angry mutterings of an offended father after he had dealt out enough punishment to a disobedient child. The rain now beat a steady staccato on the corrugated roofs. Night had begun to fall and those who had taken refuge with friends and relatives began to come out cautiously and head for their homes. There was no haste in their movement now because they were already wet to the skin.

CHAPTER TWO

The morning after a downpour at Keta was always a pleasant one. A cold breeze swept over the land and people huddled in their sheets for a last snooze before getting up for the daily hustle and bustle. The sun rose slowly from behind the sea and when its rays broke over the land they added some warmth to the air making it not too cold and not too hot either. The rain of the previous day left many places in the town inundated and a lot of people had to wade through water getting in and out of their homes.

The daylight revealed the havoc caused by the storm. Leaves and other garbage littered the streets and tree branches lay on the ground, some of them many metres away from the trees they had broken from. The roofs of two houses had been ripped off but the cries and wails of the inmates had been drowned by the fury of the storm. The inmates could now be seen salvaging what they could from their damaged buildings; fortunately no-one was hurt by the flying roofs.

Like bees going for nectar, people started trooping out to their places of work. Traders, farmers, fishermen and artisans in their own employ rose earliest; government workers reached their work places much later, some more than two hours late. But this did not affect their end-of-month salary in any way. Government workers' salaries in Ghana were not affected by how much work they did or did not do. Some could do no work at all during the entire month and still collect their salaries intact at the end of the month.

Samson Gbetor was a government employee turned full-time farmer overnight. He bore a huge grudge against the government of Ghana and his superiors at his former place of work; he had been retired at short notice from his work as night watchman at the District Administration offices. When he protested he was told he had reached the mandatory retirement age of sixty. Why wasn't he informed well in advance? He was told he had given two different dates of birth; his birth date at the regional office was different from that at the district office. That was, why the regional office had written a retirement letter to him dated twenty-third of March which he received two weeks later. They didn't even have the courtesy to pay him for the month of March even though he had worked throughout the month. He had protested vehemently against this but that sleek-tongued administrative officer at the District Administration had assured him he was in contact with the regional administration to find out what the problem was and that he would make sure he was paid. But to date he had not received a pesewa from his March salary. His only hope now was that, by some miracle, the usually slow process of paying social security entitlements would be hurried up so that he could be saved from the financial gloom that he saw right in front of himself.

Samson Gbetor was tall and had overly long fore-limbs. He had a long face and always wore an expression that made people wonder if he was not going to say something stupid anytime he opened his mouth to speak. His father called him Sepa when he was born. It was only when he was employed into the civil service as a night watchman at the age of forty-two that he got baptised and took the name Samson. He did this to be more acceptable in his new environment where everybody seemed to have an English name. The exploits of the biblical Samson also

12

impressed him a lot, especially where the young man killed a lion with his bare hands. But most people still called him Sepa. Anytime somebody said "Samson" and he turned to realise he was the one being referred to, he felt like being clothed in borrowed robes.

Sepa was a native of Woe but when he got employment at the District Administration offices at Keta he moved to stay at Keta. With his retirement he was now thinking of moving back to Woe to be closer to his few beds of shallot which he tended meticulously. Every morning he took a bus to his farm which was about eight kilometres from Keta.

Today Sepa did not feel very well, but what would he be doing in the house all day if he did not go to the farm? He arrived at the farm a little later than his usual time of between six and six-thirty. He collected his watering bucket from a nearby house where he kept it and started watering his beds. He felt pains all over his body and decided he would have to go back home early today.

"Sepa!"

He turned round to acknowledge the waving from a man who had just entered the fields. He was Tsatsaklitsa, a veteran of the Second World War who, as age crept on him, seemed to remember more and more stories of his exploits in the war in the Congo. When spurred on by enough local gin, he could throw about such fantastic ones as it was he who killed Adolph Hitler at the orders of the American president.

"How are the people of your house?" Tsatsaklitsa said, launching into the long traditional Anlo greeting, and even though Sepa hated to respond because of the long distance between them, he let his watering can hung by his side and answered back.

"They are well."

"My relatives?"

"They say they are well."

"Everybody?"

"They are fine."

"The children?"

"They are well."

"The obedient ones?"

"They are okay."

"The disobedient ones?"

"They are very fine."

"My in-laws?"

"They are well."

"Our enemies?"

"They are well."

"Our well-wishers?"

"They are okay."

"Ah..." This was where the other party was invited to take over the catechism.

"The children?"

"They are well."

"Everybody?"

"They say they are fine."

"Have a good day."

Sepa turned away to resume his watering. He knew if he gave Tsatsaklitsa the slightest hint of invitation the man would come nearer and that would mean a long bout of conversation which he was not prepared for at the moment. Tsatsaklitsa walked away regretfully; he liked talking to Sepa because he was a good listener and was easily impressed. Soon after that Sepa slung his watering can over his shoulder and headed for home. He picked his way carefully between the beds. Walking in these fields was an art in itself; the passages between the beds were so narrow you couldn't put your two feet side by side. While you walked, each foot had to be carefully lifted and put in front of the other and when you stood still it had to be in the posture of standing at ease sideways. The non-initiated often tumbled down damaging the carefully tended crops.

Sepa walked until he reached the foot of the steep incline that would take him up to the street to wait for a bus home. Just as his heels were straining to tackle the incline, a frown jumped into his expression and he came to a slow stop. To his right was a growth of nim trees and some plantain plants. He had often taken shelter there from the hot sun when the owners of the adjoining farms were not already occupying it. Now it appeared to him he had seen something sticking out from the nim and plantain grove. He retraced his steps, stretching his neck to peer into the thicket. His heart pounded against his chest as his excitement mounted over the prospect of being about to make an important discovery. He stumbled and fell to his hands but he quickly got up and came closer to the thicket.

What appeared to be a crop of hair lay in the bush and a faint buzz could be heard as flies hovered over the object. Sepa bent down and parted the bush. The bush fell apart to reveal a human head. Sepa jumped back and screamed, his shout not so much out of fright as an invitation to others to come and see what he had discovered.

"An abomination has befallen us!" Sepa shouted beating his chest. "Come to my aid! Come and witness this with me. I can't bear this alone!..." He jumped about, no longer mindful of where he put his feet.

From across the fields, people stopped what they were doing and watched Sepa's antics with interest. As his gestures increased, his huge arms flying about like a windmill, some of the farmers including Tsatsaklitsa started walking towards him; soon some started running.

"What is it?" they enquired.

By now Sepa was several metres away from the reason for his agitation. "Just look at what I have seen! Just watch it!"

"Watch what?"

He led them back to the thicket, bent low, his forefinger jerking in front of him like an independent part of him leading him on. When the human head in the thicket became visible, the farmers who had arrived at the scene rushed forward parting the bushes. What they saw sent some of them reeling back in fright. Those who had just arrived pushed the frightened ones aside. They also came away from the sight that greeted them beating their chests, only the brave ones remaining to stare at the two bodies that lay entangled with each other in the bushes. Both bodies had an intense expression of shock mingled with pain on their faces; they lay sideways their arms locked in a strange dance. Flies hovered over their faces marching in and out of their mouths, noses and ears.

From among the crowd a man emerged pushing everybody aside. "Get back, get back," he said as he moved forward.

He was *Huno* Agboado Dunyo, a man supposed to be well-versed in this sort of affairs. He was rich and had vast farms of shallot. When he reached the thicket and saw the dead men on the ground, he turned his face away muttering, "Ah, ah, ah!..." Those nearer him heard him say under his breath, *"Torhonor* has struck!"

16

Huno Dunyo turned to the crowd and in a loud voice thundered, "For your own safety, everybody should clear away immediately!"

The crowd fell over each other trying to get away, for *Torhonor,* the thunder god of the *Yeve* cult, was a dreadful god, feared by everybody.

"Who are the dead men?" people asked.

Soon the news started filtering through that the dead men were Gbagbladza and Besa Hordzo.

The *Yeve* cult was the most popular local religion in these communities. Its members mingled with the rest of the population in all spheres of human activity but seemed to live a life set apart where religion was concerned. The cult originated from Dahomey, now known as the Republic of Benin, and was most feared because of the ingrained belief that its principal god, the god of thunder, *Torhonor,* otherwise known as *Xebieso,* could strike dead with thunder those he ill-favoured.

The crowd watched from the safety of the street, every tongue wagging, every ear wide open, the gossips stashing away every bit of information for their favourite pastime of story-swapping. For a few moments Sepa achieved stardom. He became the centre of all attention when he was identified as the one who discovered the bodies. He tried to make the best of the moment, babbling and tripping over his words. Tsatsaklitsa was right beside him like a choirmaster conducting an opera. He listened to his friend for enough information and when he realised how colourless his narration was, he took over himself. Tsatsaklitsa now told the story as if he had been an invisible observer of Sepa's experience. He even told of how Sepa had had a bad dream the previous night, and knew right from home that an event of such monstrosity would unfold during the day. He extended the story to a similar occurrence during the Second World War in faraway Burma, when five French soldiers in his battalion were dismembered by thunder with he himself escaping death by a hair's breath.

People who knew of Tsatsaklitsa's fame for telling tall tales turned away from him with a smile; others who did not know him listened for a while longer, then sucked their teeth in disgust and joined other groups. Sepa was dismayed that Tsatsaklitsa had spoiled his party, but despite his valiant efforts to recapture the limelight he became once again an ordinary member of the crowd which had by now grown to sizeable proportions. It stretched along the street but the portion of the street directly above the thicket of ill omen was left bare. Nobody wanted to incur the wrath of *Torhonor*. Despite the proliferation of numberless churches claiming title to the Christian religion, the people of these communities still retained a primeval fear of their local gods. Several vehicles stopped at the scene and the occupants came out briefly to see what was happening before climbing back into their vehicles to carry the story to their various destinations.

None among the crowd wondered why the police had not yet arrived to take charge of the situation, because everybody knew in matters such as this, the police kept a safe distance as if they believed that even their uniform with the formidable power of the state behind it was no armour against the might of the local gods.

When Nani Hordzo and Afiyo Amedzi, the aged parents of Gbagbladza and Besa, heard the news, their mouths just hung open in pain and disbelief. It was Tsatsaklitsa who brought the news, but despite his reputation as the spinner of fantastic tales, the old people believed his story straightaway. Such was his agitation.

Tsatsaklitsa had headed straight for Nani's house when he realised he could no more hold the crowd's attention. He had practically run the distance to Nani's house, praying that no-one would precede him to take the wind out of his sail. When he got to the house the old people were sitting in the compound chatting merrily. Tsatsaklitsa knew at once that they had not yet heard the news and he prepared to make the most of it. Like a plague which needed no invitation, he dashed into the kitchen and brought out a low stool and sat down facing the old people who exchanged amused glances. Both Nani and Afiyo had lost almost all their teeth but they were in good health and had fairly good eyesight. They would tell you they were in their seventies but could not tell exactly when they were born except that their parents told them they were born during the upheavals of the First World War. Nani was once a well-to-do fisherman, but just when old age was creeping on him, he lost his nets at sea. He and his wife had been depending on their sons ever since.

"How are the good people of our home?" Tsatsaklitsa asked, his eyes flashing and darting about, as he rushed through the traditional greeting which he normally relished and embellished.

"They are well," Nani and Afiyo responded.

"Everybody?"

"They are well."

"The children?"

"They are fine."

"Ah..."

"How is our house?"

"It is well."

19

"Our children?"

"They are well."

"Thank you."

"Er, Afiyo," Nani began, and Afiyo prepared to take on the intermediary role that she often played when people visited her husband. Good breeding demands that you formally address other people through a third person, an intermediary, especially in matters of import. The intermediary is called *tsiami*. "Inform our brother that in our home here there is no bad news. Everything is fine through the mercy of God. We got up this morning and after taking some porridge to keep our old bones in place, we sat down here airing our mouths, for it is the mouth that is kept constantly closed that smells." In his youth Nani was a man of few words, but with age he had fallen into the trap of long winding discourses.

"*Efo* Tsatsaklitsa, please have you heard my husband?" Afiyo said, conveying the words of her husband to Tsatsaklitsa.

"Yes, and thank you." Tsatsaklitsa readjusted himself on the stool, his eyes darting about. "My in-law Afiyo, convey it to your husband that I thank God for keeping you in such good spirits. The lives of the two of you are very good examples for the youth. But unfortunately the news that I bring is the one that can knock down the strongest in our land..."

"Hm?" Nani said, his eyebrows rising.

"Have you heard what our visitor said, my husband?" Afiyo said, conveying the message to her husband.

"Yes."

Tsatsaklitsa continued, "What has happened this morning is the sort of thing pregnant women hear of and get miscarriage. In fact, it has never happened in our land

20

before, not in the proportion we saw it today." Tsatsaklitsa paused and looked away theatrically.

"My friend, come straight to the point!" Nani said impatiently. Their visitor's winding narrative was beginning to annoy him.

"The beams that held your roof have been struck down by a single stroke. My brother Nani, *Torhonor* has set fire to your house. Your two sons have been struck down by the mighty hand of *Torhonor...*"

"What is it that you say?" Afiyo asked, her voice rising.

"Your two sons are dead. They were struck down on their farm by thunder during the storm yesterday!"

Afiyo slowly reclined against the wall behind her, her mouth slightly open in shock.

"*Asɔ!*" Nani swore, snapping his fingers.

When Gbagbladza and Besa failed to return home yesterday, the old couple were surprised but not too worried — either son had occasionally stayed away from home for a day or two without notice, but they had never been away together like this before. The food that was left for them the previous night was what the children took this morning before going to school. While their wives, Ablator and Lucy, went about their household chores this morning, they had wondered aloud and indulgently where their husbands had gone. They were traders and were now at Anloga to sell their wares for it was a market day at Anloga. From the tone of their voices before they left for the market they were in no doubt that their husbands had gone to warm someone else's bed in this community where polygamy was a norm.

Nani stood up resolutely. "Look, Tsatsaklitsa," he said, "take me to the farm." He bent down to pick his

21

walking stick and crab-like marched towards the gate. He suffered a dislocated waist during his middle age and as he grew older he walked bent to the right side.

Tsatsaklitsa rushed after the older man leaving Afiyo still reclining against the wall. "We cannot go to the farm now," he said.

"Why not?" Nani asked in annoyance. "Can't I see my dead sons?"

"*Hunɔ* Dunyo has declared the place of death a no-go area."

"Who is *Hunɔ* Dunyo?"

"He is a member of the *Yeve* cult. He says it is the god of *Yeve*, *Torhonor*, which struck your sons dead. He says the cult must be informed first before anything is done to the bodies."

"Ah, ah, ah!" moaned Nani. "So what do I do now?"

"Let's go and see *Hunɔ* Dunyo," Tsatsaklitsa suggested.

At *Hunɔ* Dunyo's house, they were told the man had gone to the cult's shrine. After a little consultation, Nani and Tsatsaklitsa decided to wait while someone was sent to go and bring in Dunyo. The occupants of the house gave them seats then withdrew to a discreet distance, casting them knowing glances. Where they sat was a small porch attached to a rather long building. The porch was raised a couple of feet above the ground and from their vantage point they could see the women of the house and their children going in and out of doors that led off from the side of the building. It was clear the women were Dunyo's wives; each of them carried about her an air that sought to give out proprietary signals.

"So what you told me back at the house is true!" Nani said in a low voice.

"Did you doubt me?"

"I had no reason to doubt you; and the way these people are looking at us confirms what you told me."

Tsatsaklitsa made some sympathetic noises to console the old man, but he revelled more in his new-found importance. He was thrilled he would be an insider to the consultations that were about to begin.

From the distance, the lone cry of a gong could be heard — *tin din cha, tin din cha, tin din din din, tin din cha, tin din cha...* A hush fell over the house and all eyes turned to the main gate of the house. Soon the gate was pushed open and *Hunɔ* Dunyo, bare-chested and clad in a loin cloth entered the house. He was followed immediately by a man in a similar garment wearing sizable strings of beads on his neck and arms. On his forehead he sported a pair of parrot feathers stuck in a band that went round his head. The gong man brought up the rear, also bare-chested and wearing a loin cloth. The men climbed the steps to the porch and, without a word to the men sitting there, went through one of the two doors that opened onto the porch. The gong continued to beat for some time from the room. Then there was silence. The gong man emerged from the room and motioned the two men to enter the room, then he himself sat down on the porch.

It took some time for the eyes of Nani and Tsatsaklitsa to get adjusted to the dimness inside the room. Dunyo and his companion sat on reclining chairs facing the doorway. Across the room away from them was a bench. Dunyo sat forward motioning the two men to sit down.

"You are welcome," he said

"Thank you," the two men replied.

"Gbahode," Dunyo said, addressing his companion,

"this is the father of the deceased men and that is his friend Tsatsaklitsa."

The man replied in a language unintelligible but not unfamiliar to Nani and Tsatsaklitsa. This was the language of the *Yeve* cult.

Dunyo continued, "We know why you are here. Nothing is hidden from us. Things are moving at meteoric speed and consultations and rituals are going on right now, but we have the time to listen to what you have to say."

Nani hated Dunyo for putting himself forward like a judge and he himself a criminal who must submit himself willy-nilly to trial. "Tsatsaklitsa," he began, "convey it to our friends that our hearts are heavy-laden with sorrow but we are on no evil errand. I heard about the deaths of my sons this morning and the only reason why I am here is to find out in what way they are connected to my sons' deaths."

"We are not connected to your sons' deaths,"Dunyo cut in. "They have rather trodden on forbidden ground. They offended *Torhonor* and have received his terrible judgement — death by his gun."

"What offence did they commit?" Nani asked, his voice beginning to rise.

"My very good friend," Dunyo said placatingly, "it is not for us mortals to delve into the deeds of *Torhonor*. Whatever your sons did is between them and the god."

"So what do you intend to do now?" Nani asked, pain, sorrow and anger making his voice almost inaudible.

Tsatsaklitsa sat still, drinking up every detail of the exchanges and already dreaming up his own embellishments for his audiences.

"My elder brother," Dunyo said, "you yourself are no

24

stranger to this land. Members of your family have committed an offence against *Torhonor*. The god must be pacified so that no further punishment befalls your family."

"In what way am I supposed to pacify your god?"

"You will be informed before the day ends. Right now, go home and wait for our emissaries."

"*Yoo*, thank you. I will be expecting them." Nani got up and Tsatsaklitsa followed him out of the room and out of the house. He seemed more bent to the side now and walked with obvious pain. A little way from the house, Tsatsaklitsa cleared his throat and asked permission to leave. Nani thanked him for his companionship and Tsatsaklitsa flew away, pregnant with the news of the latest developments in Nani's predicament.

When Nani got home, his wife was still reclining against the wall, a pained look still in her eyes. Women, he thought as he went towards her to tell her to come indoors so that he could tell her the news. He called her once, then twice, and getting no response he went closer to her and shook her by the shoulder. A shiver ran through him when her body felt cold to his touch. He shook her violently calling out her name. Her body slid off the stool and before she hit the ground he knew she was dead. A shrill cry went forth from his lips. The first neighbour that entered the house found Nani lying face-down by his wife, unconscious.

CHAPTER THREE

Nani regained consciousness the following day at the Keta Government Hospital, feeling weak and nauseated. His nimble mind quickly assessed his surroundings and told him he was at a hospital and which other hospital could it be but Keta Hospital which was the only hospital in the Keta District and three other surrounding districts. A tall metal stand from which hung a transparent plastic bag stood by his bed. His eyes followed the tube that led from the plastic bag. The tube led to his bed and onto his body. He raised his arm to realise the tube was attached to his wrist. From his bed which seemed too soft compared to what he was used to at home, Nani could see wide open windows in the walls facing him and to his side; only the wall behind him had no windows. Through the windows he could see people moving up and down the hospital yard. The ward appeared to him to be over-exposed. There were about eight other beds in the ward with human beings of different shapes and sizes lying in them. He wondered what might have brought them here and his mind automatically switched to his own reason for being here. As the painful memories began to seep back into his mind, he winced and his body shuddered violently. He began to struggle into the sheets trying to hide from the knowledge that from now onwards he was alone. There were his grandchildren but they were too small, and there were his two daughters-in-law but these could never adequately fill the void that he now felt in the pit of his stomach.

Gbagbladza and Besa were very stubborn when they were alive. Their wives seemed to have copied them and were unfriendly, always seeming to be immersed in their own affairs. Nani's own wife was docile, kind and over-generous with her affection and possessions. When his sons were young he had often raved about them being spoiled by his wife.

A nurse walked into the ward, threw rapid glances across the room and quickly came over to his bed when she saw that he was awake.

"How are you old man?" she asked, placing a hand on his chest. Her voice was guttural, masculine, but her touch was soft and gentle, exuding comfort and safety.

"I think I feel better," he said and sat up quite easily to his own surprise. "When can I go home?"

The nurse inclined her head, looking him straight in the eye as if searching from there an answer to his own question. "The doctor will first have to examine you again then a decision will be taken on that."

"Thank you," he said and allowed himself to fall back to the slightly inclined bed.

"You are always welcome. Now try to rest yourself well."

As they talked, Nani's thoughts stumbled over each other, each clamouring for his attention. He was grateful when the nurse left him to attend to another patient. The dull pain in his chest returned as his thoughts went to the sons that he would never see again and the wife whose wrinkled but comforting touch he would never feel again.

From an early age, Nani's life had been governed by an acute knowledge of right and wrong and equal treatment for everybody irrespective of any consideration. That was why in the fishing community at Woe many net-owners did not like him — he was seen as always advocating better terms for their employee-fishermen thus eroding their profits. Nani believed in the rule of law, and this new experience of a section of society dictating to other people how to handle the bodies of their dead relatives weighed on him heavily. And if it was true that it was the god of the cult that struck his sons dead, what right did the cult have to induce its god to do even that when the chiefs' courts and the government's courts were there to settle differences?

As a native, Nani was aware of the *Yeve* cult. He saw the cult just like another segment of the society which must be left in peace to practise their beliefs. He knew the stories about the awesome power of their god. He also knew that anytime his nets caught a dolphin, which the fishermen believed was a mermaid, he must call in the cult to perform purification rites, as mermaids were believed to be reincarnations in the sea of dead members of the cult. But he had always regarded this as part of the routine of being a fisherman. He was an anythingarian belonging to the segment of the society that lay claim to no identifiable set of beliefs. He belonged to no religious group even though as a fisherman he followed the usual practice of occasionally sacrificing animals to idols that every net-owner was expected to possess. Every net-owner of repute, before he ventured into the business of fishing in the sea, must call in experts versed in wooing the goodwill of the gods of the sea. These experts with the help of herbs and other items provided by the prospective fisherman, set up idols and gave out instructions to be observed religiously by the fisherman, his family and employees on pain of poor catches and other tribulations. Nani went through all these but his greatest trust lay in the triumph of right over wrong — nobody got hurt when he did no wrong.

A nurse came to take the drip off Nani and soon after

that a doctor came to examine him. He gave him a prescription and told him he could go home. It was after his discharge that Nani learnt that one of his daughters-in-law, Ablator, Gbagbladza's wife, had all along been waiting outside the ward. She came into the ward, her eyes flashing as usual as if looking for somebody to snap at. She was tall and attractive in a challenging way. She had an angular face and walked straight, her head held high. Nani always thought she should have joined the army or the police.

Ablator was a most reliable partner in adversity, but her loyalty was as stable as a reed in the wind. She would see you through to the end of a calamity but after that the lines must be re-drawn to show whether you were a friend or a foe. In their querulous neighbourhood, nobody dared touch Ablator's children. When crossed, she always had three options to address the situation: fight you, rain insults upon you or give you a scathing look that seemed to smite you across the chest like a hot knife. It was the second option that most people feared, for Ablator could insult you from morning till evening. She would go back and forth, revisiting the subject of her vexation, drenching you in the venom of her tongue. In such moments only her husband could restrain her. She adored him even though she tried not to show it too outwardly. People came to realise that the best insurance against Ablator's tongue was to be in the good books of Gbagbladza.

Ablator had heard many stories about the insolence of nurses. So she came in ready for a fight, but on duty was a nurse who personified friendliness. Ablator's tensed body began to relax as the nurse took her to her father-in-law's bed.

"I'm glad you are now awake," she said. "How do you

29

feel?"

"I am all right. I just feel a little weak. The doctor said I can go home now." Nani was quick to inform Ablator that she did not have to go through the trouble of staying with him at the hospital for a long time.

She avoided his eyes as she asked, "Do we have to buy any medicine?"

She doesn't want me to see the pain in her eyes, the old man thought, then said, "Go and ask the nurse. Then come back so that I can send you to bring some money from home."

"Don't you worry. I have some money with me."

Nani almost whistled. What has come over my favourite daughter-in-law? he asked himself. Ablator had never been known to be liberal with her money. Any money that she spent on anybody who could otherwise fend for himself was accompanied by recrimination and nagging.

Ablator came back with several packets of medicament. She sat on the side of the bed and explained to the old man the dosage of each medicine.

"How much did this cost?" Nani asked her.

"Twelve thousand, six hundred cedis."

"I will pay you when we get home."

"You don't have to pay back. Now that our husbands are no more alive we will take care of you."

Poor child, Nani thought, the icy hand of death has sobered you.

Ablator and Lucy heard of the death of their husbands while in the market. The market had instantly filled up with the howls of the two women. They had swept out of the market in a storm. It was at home that they realised the extent of the tribulation that had befallen them — their mother-in-law too was dead and their father-in-law had been taken to the hospital unconscious. They had rushed to the shallot farms to see the bodies of their husbands, but these had already been covered with palm fronds and none dared go near, not even the tempestuous Ablator.

It was when Ablator started packing up for the journey home that Nani realised the large number of items that she had brought to the hospital to ensure his comfort. There were two thermos flasks, several drinking cups and plates, provisions like sugar, milk, cocoa powder and coffee. There were even some canned foods! Nani suppressed the urge to ask who had brought the items, but could only think if it was Ablator who brought them then a wind of change was really blowing over the remnants of his family. Ablator had always been very careful with her money, in fact very reluctant to part with it. She contributed her quota to the upkeep of the house all right but every expenditure she thought must be borne by her husband, she calculated meticulously and recovered fully from him. But come to think of it now, Nani thought Ablator had not been all nails and spikes all the time. She had had her good and kind moments, like the time Besa's eldest child had a big sore and every morning she dressed the sore and applied medicine till it healed; or the time they heard a little child crying outside the house in the night and she went for the child and kept it for three days until its parents came for it from Anloga. Maybe, because of her fierce outlook on life nobody took the time to look out for the moments of human kindness in her.

"Where is Lucy?" Nani asked her.

"She is at home taking care of the children."

Nani got up from the bed surprisingly with little

pain; to Ablator's eyes his sideways bend at the waist seemed to have improved. She wondered if he had been given some treatment to induce that. As they left the ward, Nani began to consciously push away from his mind the pain of his loss. He knew if there should be any favourable ending in this drama it had to come from him. He had a large extended family but to him it was only a lazy man who expected a stranger to lift up the pot in his room for the mouse in his apartment to be killed.

"Ablator," he said, trying to keep up with the long strides of the tall woman; she seemed to have forgotten that he had just got up from a hospital bed. "When we get home you will have to go and call me Bodza and Nutefe. I want to discuss some issues with them. Tell Adekpitor too to come."

A minibus took them over the six-kilometre journey to Woe. Lucy was washing dishes when she saw them enter the house. She rushed forward shouting, "*Dza, dza dza*...You are welcome." She embraced first the old man, then Ablator who promptly went out to summon the family members Nani had asked her to call in.

Only Nutefe and Bodza answered Nani's summons and they came in great haste. They knew about Nani's predicament for the whole town was already filled with the sad news. After the normal civilities and profuse expression of sympathy for his loss and his health, Nani called out to Ablator to come and act as his *tsiami*.

"Ablator," he said, "let it get to my brothers that I am gratified about the way they have answered my summons with haste. As they are already aware, death has pulled down the fence surrounding my house; it has turned my inside out and wrung me and tossed me aside. My sorrow would not be less if they were ordinary deaths but the circumstances of the deaths have left me at a loss as to what to do. My head has been knocked off my neck; I humbly ask them now to be my head."

"Have you heard what my father said?" Ablator said glaring at the two men. She was always suspicious of family members; when they came to your house it was to borrow some money or some foodstuff like pepper or shallot.

"My daughter," Bodza said, "get it across to our elder brother that we have heard all that he has said, and even more." Bodza was a very thin and tall man, with jutting cheekbones like exposed rocks after the rain had washed away the sand. "You must have a companion when you go out after nightfall to ease yourself. We are his companions, his blood relations and we are prepared to go every inch of the way with him."

The relationship between Bodza and Nani went back several generations. In fact, the father of Bodza's great-grandfather would call the mother of Nani's great-grandmother aunt, but in this part of the world they were supposed to be just cousins, even brothers.

"Our brother has just come back from the hospital, but in his absence we have been monitoring the situation and fishing out information," Bodza continued, looking at Nutefe for confirmation.

Nutefe took up the baton like a relay runner. He had flabby arms and a huge paunch that seemed to roll when he walked. He enjoyed going about the village bare-chested with a huge towel strapped around his waist as a loincloth. People said he did this to show off his broad and hairy chest to attract women, and there seemed to be some truth in this as Nutefe had several wives.

"We have got about every bit of information neces-

33

sary to confront this calamity head-on," Nutefe said. "As my younger brother Bodza just said we are blood brothers (Nutefe's relationship with Nani went even further in the spectrum than that of Bodza). We can do everything on your behalf, but we don't apply medicine to a wound when the wounded man is not there. So we were just waiting and praying for you to come back from the hospital so that we can better see the wound and apply the medicine. We were at the hospital yesternight but you were still sleeping. Now that you are at home let us proceed and purge this abomination from our midst." He sat back, throwing out his huge chest.

Bodza took it up from there. "What we must do now," he said, "is to tackle the riddle of our sons' deaths first before we turn to that of their mother. If you are up to it, if you have recovered enough and feel strong enough to go, let us go and see the *Yeve* lords and negotiate with them. I have heard this sort of thing involves negotiation. If we just sit back for them to come to us with their terms, they will wring the last drop of blood out of us. You may not believe it, but they charge money for this sort of thing, huge sums of money. Let us go and tell them that we don't have a bottomless sack of money."

So it was decided that Bodza and Nutefe would make enquiries about who the lords of the *Yeve* cult were. Then at dawn they would go to them and start the negotiations.

But before the visitors could leave, there was the tell-tale sound of the gong. This time it sounded, *tin gon, tin gon, tin go gon, tin gon...* The three men exchanged apprehensive looks. Without a doubt, they knew where the sound of the gong was heading. Soon the inevitable knocking sounded at the gate, the gong now sounding much louder. Nani motioned Ablator to open the gate.

Three men entered the house, all clad in loin cloths. They were emissaries from the *Yeve* cult. As a rule, members of the cult did not wear top garments when they were performing rites or when they were within the compound of the shrine. Even a non-member who entered the shrine was required to remove his footwear and top garment. The one with the gong continued to beat his gong with strength so that it looked as if a major musical event was about to take place in the house. The emissaries were given seats and it was only then that the gong-man rested his gong. The ears of Nani and his companions rang in the sudden absence of the noise.

The three men were very business-like. After the exchange of greetings, their leader stated the reason for their visit in very unambiguous terms. "The goat-seller does not need to shout out his wares," he said. "The animal itself will do that. We have been sent by *Midawo* Sasu to summon you to his presence. In fact, they are even now assembled in the courtyard waiting for you. Please do not tarry."

"We will be there very soon," Nani replied.

At a sign from their leader, the gong-man resumed his assault on the gong. Then the three men left the house without further ceremony.

Nani and his companions exchanged anxious glances, but Ablator sneered. "*Tsun!*" she said. "We are the bereaved family. The dead men are our own relatives. Why should they come and dictate to us how to bury them?"

"No, Ablator, no," Nani said. "This is not the time for anger or bitter words. We will have to be very calm, very observant and very wise to confront this crisis. Angry words will only compound the problem."

Ablator stood up and walked away from the three men. She entered her room and banged her door shut violently.

"Ei!" Bodza said. "We have a battle on our hands."

"Let's not take her to the shrine. She will only worsen my plight with her vitriolic tongue... I hope you are taking me to the shrine?"

"Of course!" Bodza and Nutefe replied.

"Let's go at once," said Nutefe.

"Give me a minute," said Nani. "I must change this hospital clothes." He hobbled towards his room, his crab-like walk once more very evident.

***   ***   ***

Blemekpinu, or the court of Bleme, was situated at the western end of Woe. Legend had it that long before Woe became half the size of what it is today, a man and his son went fishing in the night. They found an idol in the water and, frightened, they threw it back into the water. They reached for their paddles and started paddling away furiously, but try as much as they could, their boat seemed to remain at the same spot. They paddled and paddled until they fell down in exhaustion. When they woke up in the morning they realised their boat had drifted to the shore and the idol was resting comfortably on one of the seats in the boat. They knew they were stuck with the idol. They brought it out of the boat and headed home but when they reached the spot where Blemekpinu now stood, their feet became rooted to the spot. Father and son spent the whole morning trying to move away but couldn't. They set the idol down at that spot and it was only then that the earth released its hold on their feet. They consulted a soothsayer who told them the god of *Yeve* had chosen them as hosts and they had better comply otherwise there would be no future for their whole family. Bleme, for that was the name of the man, and his son complied and Blemekpinu came into being.

There are many *Yeve* shrines among the Anlos and all of them have various stories to tell about their origins, but they all pay homage to one god, *Yeve*. Blemekpinu was just one shrine among several at Woe. It had a large sandy compound dotted with many idols who were vassals of the god. A big building occupied the northern end of the compound. Half of the building was the living quarters of the Bleme family and other relatives, the other half was the shrine. The front section of the shrine was of a bright pinkish colour and covered with various pictures, the most prominent of which was that of the thunder god, *Torhonor,* riding in a chariot drawn by two fire-breathing rams. There were pictures of snakes, eagles and a lion all in very imposing postures. It was in front of this wall that a small group of men and women had gathered waiting for Nani. As is normal with the *Yeve* cult, both sexes had no top garments even though the women brought up their cloth to cover their bosoms. From the small door that led into the shrine, a woman emerged. Surprisingly, she wore a dress, a gown that reached to her ankles. She swirled into the middle of the gathering. "Today is the big day. We are going to cut off heads," she said, snapping her fingers.

Several of the people assembled dismissed her with a wave of the hand. She belonged to a division of the cult called *avle*. This division was the informal unit of the cult. Members of this unit were always women and got away with things that a normal cult member would not dream of doing. They cracked expensive jokes and dressed in any garment of their choice. During the cult's annual rites when there was a lot of drumming and dancing, the *avle* indulged in many antics, the most popular of which was adorning their loins with wooden penises and running after women to grab them and have mock sex with them.

When Nani, Bodza and Nutefe entered the compound, even the *avle* had to suspend her antics and a solemn air descended over the compound. The visitors were motioned to a bench that faced the gathering. It was not difficult to guess the man who was going to preside over this meeting. He was fat and clad in a white cloth up to his chest; his arms, his chest and neck were smeared with white chalk and he sat on a huge stool that was also smeared with white chalk. The man was *Midawo* Sasu, the head of Blemekpinu.

There was a lot of murmuring and whispering until *Huno* Dunyo called the meeting to order. The *huno* were another unit of the cult. They were non-initiates but performed a lot of functions on behalf of the cult. They were like the link between the cult and the community.

"Our dear *Midawo* and all those gathered here," said *Huno* Dunyo, "I offer you my respect and crave your indulgence. We are gathered here not for a festive occasion but to address a grave issue. Let everybody pay attention. This meeting will not be held twice. It is only held once." He turned to Midawo Sasu. "Our dear *Midawo,* we are all ears."

Midawo Sasu cleared his throat and looked to his right. *"Tsiami,* are you there?" he asked.

"Yes," replied a man who promptly stood up. He was of indeterminable age; his face showed he was advanced in age but his body was that of a growing adolescent.

"Tell our visitors they are welcome."

"Did you hear what *Midawo* said? He said you are welcome," the *tsiami* said.

"Yoo," replied Nani and his friends.

"Tell our visitors we have not summoned them for any evil purpose, neither have we called them for any celebration. Their goat has broken its tether and it is only we who can bring it home to them."

"Did you hear *Midawo?*"

"Tell them the events of these few days are not unique but whenever they occur blood and tears flow. Tell them their family has offended *Xebieso*, they have angered *Torhonor* and yesterday they saw just the tip of *Torhonor's* anger. But our god is a just god. He is also forgiving. He spanks you when you go wrong but calls you back to embrace you when you realise your fault and make amends. Tell our visitors we will not go into the details of what the offence of their sons was. Let it suffice that *Torhonor* is terribly angry as a result of their sons' misdeed. Ask them if they have come prepared to accept their fault and offer the necessary atonement."

"Did you hear what our *Midawo* said?"

Nani and his entourage quickly conferred among themselves and Bodza replied, "Yes, we accept our fault and will make the necessary atonement."

"Please *Midawo,* they say they accept everything."

"Tell them *Torhonor's* gun that killed their sons was fired from our shrine here. They have one option to make amends." *Midawo's* voice was now vibrant and triumphant. "This is what they have to do: they must provide two members of their family to be initiated into our shrine here. They must also pay a fine of one million cedis."

"Did you hear what *Midawo* said?"

"The two members of their family can be of any age or sex. They must be brought here within seven days. And for as long as it takes them to bring them here, the dead bodies of their relatives shall remain where they are now. Nobody can touch them without incurring the wrath of *Torhonor*. They must also provide seven white hens, seven black hens, one jerry can of gin..."

As *Midawo* Sasu recited the terms of the fine, Nani sank deeper and deeper into a trance-like state. When he came to himself he realised Bodza and Nutefe were shaking him violently and there was concern in the eyes of the people around.

"Let's go," Bodza said.

"But, but have we finished?" Nani stammered.

"Yes. Let's go." They helped Nani to his feet, and arm in arm, they walked him out of Blemekpinu.

40

CHAPTER FOUR

Lome is the capital of the Republic of Togo. It lies on the coast on the border between Ghana and Togo. It is a popular tourist destination on the west coast of Africa and one of its distinguishing features is its clean and wide beaches. It is also renowned for the strict discipline enforced by its gendarmes on both citizens and visitors. It is not uncommon for visitors to be physically assaulted by the gendarmes on its border crossings. In spite of this, there is a constant flow of hordes of people criss-crossing the border during the day to do their shopping in Lome. Togo has a free port and therefore imported goods are cheaper there than in Ghana.

One of the suburbs of Lome is Kodzoviakope. It is situated right on the border with Ghana and is the haunt of prostitutes, pickpockets, muggers, black marketeers, smuglers, con men. Kodzoviakope was an outpost for the German colonialists who first colonised Togoland. When the Germans were defeated in the First World War, Togoland was divided between the British and the French. The British incorporated their portion into present-day Ghana and the French called their section Togo.

Kodzoviakope offered many avenues of employment, most of them on the dark side of the law. The most attractive and most lucrative was drug-pushing, and the man who held sway and ruled over the larger part of this trade was François "Boxer" Kwasivi. He was a colourful character who could be mean or very generous as the impulse took him. He had charisma and seemed untouchable by the law; he was known to bark out abusive

41

language at even the much feared gendarmes. There were several theories to explain why François had so much influence over the gendarmes. Some attributed it to spiritual power but the more credible explanation was that many of the gendarmes were on the payroll of François.

François had a big mansion at Kodzoviakope located in an area called Soweto. The mansion ranked among the most beautiful buildings in Togo. It was a two-storey structure with François occupying the top floor to the exclusion of everybody including his three wives. His wives and children and other relatives staying with him shared the ground and first floors. On the ground floor he had a suite where he entertained visitors.

When the division of Togoland took place, it cut right through the Anlo ethnic group. Thus people living around the border between Ghana and Togo have relatives on either side of the border. François was no exception. He came from a big family and had many brothers and sisters some of whom he did not know. His father had been a rich and prominent merchant who followed tradition and married many women. The strange thing was that even though François' father was rich he had very little interest in his children. The children became the burden of their mothers as their father only seemed interested in making as much money as he could and keeping it. The women were never in short supply as the newcomers always came with the illusion of taking a little scoop of the old man's money. They always failed for the man, in spite of his apparent flamboyance, was miserly and found it painful to part with his money. He was called "Boxer" because people said he always had his fists clenched over his money like a boxer.

As François' fame grew as a rich man, he inherited his father's nickname even though by comparison he was a generous man. His only problem was that he had very little interest in his siblings. There was no unifying bond between him and his brothers and sisters as his father, who should have been the catalyst to provide this bond, left each child and its mother to their own fate.

Those who enjoyed the bounty of François were maternal relatives and a lot of these were on the other side of the border in Ghana. Many of them even came to stay in his house. One of these relatives was Johnny Klevor, a cousin. Johnny's parents lived at Woe and the young man of twenty-eight had recently come from there to stay with his cousin. He had been a fisherman back at Woe and had heard many stories about François, some favourable others scathing, but the common theme that ran through all the stories was that François, alias Boxer, was exceedingly rich. One day, on impulse, Johnny had decided to seek financial help from him. He arrived at François' house very nervous and apprehensive of a rebuff. When he came to the presence of François, he was knocked over by the man's affability and generosity. From then he became a regular visitor to the house and then graduated to permanent resident. Occasionally he visited Woe, sometimes staying over for a few days before returning to Kodzoviakope.

François liked Johnny from the start. He found the frank, eager and fearless expression in Johnny's eyes very attractive and as he got to know the young man more he found out he had very steady nerves. François thought a lot about the boy. As a rule he never employed the services of members of his family in his drug trade but these days it was proving difficult to get reliable couriers. He was sure Johnny could be of use to him and in return he could make him financially secure for the rest of his life. François never jumped into an enterprise without first giving it a lot of thought, so it took him a long time to decide finally to take Johnny into his confidence. But the day he decided to have a heart-to-heart talk with Johnny, he was told the boy had left for Woe that very morning. He was exasperated, for once he had decided to do something he loved to do it fast. He had to wait for three days before Johnny returned from Woe.

François called Johnny to his ground floor suite and despite the fact that it was just about six in the morning, he was taking whisky, as usual, straight from the bottle. He was not a habitual drinker but when he drank he liked to drink from the bottle; the rush of the drink as it spurted between his wide-spaced teeth gave him sensuous pleasure.

"Johnny," François said.

"Yes, uncle." Even though they were cousins, Johnny called François uncle.

"I have been watching you." Johnny gave a visible start in the chair where he sat. François continued, "You know some of my business lines, others you do not know. I want to introduce you to one of the business lines you are not aware of. It is a very profitable business but risky. But then every business has its risks."

As François talked Johnny began to relax in his chair. "The human race is very diverse with distinct sections that interrelate, at times attracting, at others opposing. The various sections have their own traits and characteristics. What is the heart's desire for one section, another section may not even like to lay eyes on. The business that I am going to introduce you to is liked by one section of the society even though they are in the minority. The rest of society frowns upon this business and all those who engage in it. But just because the larger society does not approve of it does not mean the minority should not have their kicks. The business is drugs, not the normal drugs you take when you are ill. These drugs are called "knock-outs", others call them "highs" others "cloud seven". More commonly they are known as heroin, cocaine, amphetamine, marijuana. I sell these drugs and I want you to help me in the trade."

Most of these words were strange to Johnny except marijuana which he otherwise knew as wee or Indian hemp. He had known about several people who were arrested for smoking Indian hemp so the import of what his cousin was saying was not lost on him. The question was would he do it? The answer was yes, he would do it. In fact, he would do anything for François. The man was his secret hero. He liked the sharp and no-nonsense manner he went about his affairs. The talk of money also attracted Johnny immensely, for it had always been his aim to be rich, and he was in a big hurry to achieve this.

François continued, "I distribute the drugs not only here in Togo but also overseas. I want you to help in the distribution and sale of the drugs. Will you do it?"

"Yes, uncle, I will do it," Johnny replied eagerly.

"Good. I knew you would not disappoint me." He took a swipe at the bottle and from his movement it was obvious he was beginning to get drunk. "This morning you will make your first delivery," François said and stood up unsteadily. He brought out a package from his pocket. "Take this to Monsieur Agbokli, the man who owns the big store on the border. You know him. He drives a Mercedes car. His house is not far from here. You know the house?"

"Yes uncle," Johnny answered as he took the package. "I know the house, and I will go at once."

"Good. Tell Monsieur Agbokli to give you the money for the stuff."

"Yes uncle."

"Then you bring the money to me."

"Yes uncle." The package was white and a little bigger than a matchbox. Johnny stood up and placed it in his pocket and as he left the room he kept his hand protectively over the pocket.

"Don't do anything that will make you look suspicious. Relax and act normally," François said after him.

"Yes uncle," Johnny said and let himself out.

Monsieur Kodzovi Agbokli was a regular visitor to François' house. He had two gold teeth and was always wearing white flowing gowns. He exuded wealth and was known to be very talkative about his successful business ventures. Johnny had never talked to the man. Today would be the first time he would be in direct contact with the man. He was elated, though a little fearful of falling into the arms of the law.

Exuding an air of confidence, Johnny walked along and occasionally patted the package down to make it less obvious. Out in the street, he tried to look as normal as possible, but anybody with discerning eyes would have easily detected the tension that belied his gait.

Monsieur Agbokli lived in an impressive house though not on as grand a scale as François'. The house was painted in a brilliant white to match the white gowns which were his hallmark. Johnny rang the front bell and nearly jumped back when a voice spoke to him from the pillar in the gate. He smiled when he realised it was an electronic gadget. Very ingenious, he thought.

"Who is it?" the voice from the pillar asked. "Er, I am Johnny. I have a package from Monsieur François for Monsieur Agbokli."

"Merde!" swore the voice in the pillar and then there was silence.

The gate slid open and Johnny stepped inside looking to his sides to see who had opened the gate. He was nonplused when the gate slid shut again on its own accord. Very smart, he thought. Now what happens next? He looked across the compound at the single-storey building that served as the main house. The inside walls of the house were painted the same brilliant white, giving it a sepulchral air. There was an out-house and in front of this were several garden chairs and tables in various postures of disarray. On the tables were several empty bottles. Some of the bottles were scattered on the ground among the legs of the tables and chairs. There must have been a party here the previous night, Johnny thought. As he looked closer he saw through the entangled tables and chairs a man sprawled on a bench ranged against the out-house. He advanced cautiously and as he got closer he could hear the soft sound of snoring coming from the man. The man was in a loose pyjamas, the sides and ends of which hung towards the ground like stalactites. He was barefooted one arm crossed over his chest, the fore-arm of the other lying over an empty beer bottle on the floor.

Johnny he. .ed a sigh of relief, now that he had proof that the house was inhabited by human beings and not just voices that spoke to you from walls. He bent down and shook the man. The man's body was very pliable as if bereft of bone or muscle. If he had not continued to snore, Johnny would have thought him dead. He shook him

47

again, this time vigorously. Then his eyes opened, but for a time, despite his open eyes, the snores continued to come much to the amusement of Johnny.

The snoring stopped finally and the man said in a lazy voice, "What?"

"I am looking for Monsieur Agbokli," Johnny said.

The man swung his fallen arm towards the main building by way of pointing and let it fall again on the beer bottle. Johnny turned to the main house and was surprised to see a man standing in an open door. The man beckoned and Johnny walked towards him.

"Come in," the man said and when Johnny stepped inside the building he softly closed the door.

They stood in a long corridor dimly lit by ornamental lamps on the wall. "Come along," the man said and led the way deeper into the building. He had a bird-like appearance about him; his shoulders were hunched and when Johnny had looked at his face his lower lip appeared to meet the upper lip in mid-air, puffing it upwards. His nose was beaten back giving prominence to the lips and making them look like a beak.

A large living-room opened up in front of them and Johnny's escort motioned him into a chair. "Monsieur Agbokli will be with you soon," he said and disappeared through a door to the right.

Johnny was used to luxurious surroundings having been living at François' house for some time now, but he could not help admiring the lengths Monsieur Agbokli had gone to make his living-room so pleasant. Before he could have sufficiently appraised the objects of art that lined the walls and the soft furnishings, Monsieur Agbokli walked into the room.

"Hello!" he said and walked over to shake Johnny's

hand. He wore a loose T-shirt and boxer's shorts. He looked smaller in stature and Johnny quickly attributed this to the absence of his long flowing white gowns.

"So you have been sent by Boxer," Agbokli said. He had a piercing stare and as he continued to look into Johnny's eyes, the young man began to fidget in his chair.

"Yes," Johnny replied. "My uncle François asked me to give you a parcel."

Johnny began to dip his hand into his pocket to bring out the parcel but Agbokli stopped him with a wave of the hand. "Take your time, young man," he said. "Don't rush. In this business you have to thread very carefully. And you shouldn't have stood at my gate and announced to the whole world that you have a parcel for me!"

"I am sorry, sir," Johnny said, quickly bringing out his hand to rest in his lap.

"Boxer has told me a lot of things about you, most of them nice. Boxer is my friend and anybody that is good for him is good for me too. So you are good for me. Come this way." He stood up and went through a door with a large poster of a scantly dressed female model pasted on it.

Johnny followed him up a short flight of steps into a room that had very little furniture. The floor of the room was covered with a thick woollen carpet and several coffee tables and foot-rests were haphazardly arranged about the room. Monsieur Agbokli knelt onto the carpet and lazily stretched himself out on his side. He motioned John to sit down on the carpet, but John chose a foot-rest and sat down.

"Now bring out the parcel."

Johnny gave him the parcel and as he removed its wrappings, the young man took in the rest of the room.

The walls had huge pictures of females in the nude and the white ceiling had intricate designs.

"Boxer always has the best," Agbokli said and Johnny swung his eyes back to him.

Agbokli pulled one of the coffee tables towards him. On the table were an ashtray, a small saucer and a small wooden spoon that looked like a spatula. He set the open parcel down on the table and Johnny could now see its contents which was a white powdery substance. There was no doubt in Johnny's mind that it was some form of drug but he could not identify its name from those François had mentioned.

"Come over here," Agbokli said waving his hand expansively.

Johnny drew the foot-rest nearer, curiosity written all over his face.

"You know what this is?" the man asked.

"No."

"Cocaine. Cloud seven. We use it to get to cloud seven where you experience the ultimate happiness. You and I are going to be friends, very good friends. Now watch exactly what I am going to do."

With the small wooden spoon, he scooped up a small amount of the white substance and with shaky hands brought it to his left nostril, inhaling deeply.

"Ah..." he exhaled in deep satisfaction. Then he applied the substance to his other nostril. "Now try it," he said to Johnny. "It will do you a lot of good."

Johnny had an abhorrence for anything entering his ear or his nose, but he did not know how to tell this good man who was showing him so much friendliness and openness that he could not partake of his act. He had never heard anything good about anybody who took marijuana, the closest thing that he knew in the realm of illegal drugs. But he was also worried about François, especially if his cousin had sent him here to be introduced to the drug.

I will never disappoint Uncle François, Johnny told himself, then offered a quick silent prayer that François' intentions towards him should be good.

He pulled the coffee table towards himself and took the wooden spoon from Monsieur Agbokli whose eyes were now dilated, a small smile playing at the sides of his mouth. Johnny then took a small quantity of the white substance and lifted it slowly to his nostril. He held his breath for some time before inhaling slowly. The whitish substance disappeared into his left nostril.

"That is good!" said Agbokli. "Now the second one."

Johnny took another quantity and slowly inhaled it through the other nostril. There, he thought, I have done it and I am still alive!

"Good boy, good boy," Agbokli congratulated him and pulled the coffee table back to himself. He sniffed a generous quantity of the stuff again and then sent himself sprawling backwards onto the carpet.

Johnny began to feel like lying down too, but he knew he must get back early to François. All of a sudden he was hungry. His stomach grew warmer and warmer and began to growl. A strong urge to go to the toilet seized him. "Please where is your toilet?" he asked.

"Through there," Agbokli said pointing to a door Johnny had not noticed before; it was also adorned with a huge poster.

The door opened into a big lavatory. John rushed to the water closet and let himself go, unmindful of the gastric din he was creating and which must be reaching

Monsieur Agbokli through the open door. When he was through, he felt a deep sense of well-being that began in waves in the pit of his stomach and exploded in his head. The relief he got from the lavatory after his initial ordeal was like the personal achievement of a great feat. He came out buckling his trousers, free from all inhibitions.

Monsieur Agbokli regarded him from where he lay, an amused look on his face. "Are you all right now?" he asked.

"Yes. I think I must go now."

"Wait." Mr. Agbokli got up and from a corner of the room he picked up a whip. "Do you know what this is?" he asked as he rolled the whip around his wrist.

"No."

"It is a whip. A horse whip."

Through the open door, footsteps began to sound on the stairs leading to the room. The eyes of both men swivelled to the door and they watched until the owner of the footsteps appeared at the door. He was the man Johnny had seen earlier sprawled on the bench outside. He was still in his pyjamas which was very crumpled giving him an untidy look.

"That was a hell of a party last night, wasn't it?" he said in a surprisingly high-pitched voice which was at odds with his huge frame. "I spent the rest of the night in the garden."

Johnny looked at Agbokli expecting him to say something in response, but the latter remained silent.

The intruder saw the whip in Agbokli's hand and said, "Got yourself a new horse rider?"

"Mind your own business!" Agbokli said and closed the door in the man's face. "I have the misfortune of having him as my brother. He is an irresponsible man."

He faced Johnny again in the posture of a judoist, the whip playing around his wrists.

"Sometimes when I feel I have behaved very badly I punish myself," he said. "You know when you are a little child your parents punish you when you misbehave yourself. When you become old you are your own master. You have no-one to punish you when you think you do wrong. I have devised this means to fill the vacuum created by the absence of my parents. Formerly I could whip myself really well but these days I prefer that someone else does it for me. It is more enjoyable that way."

Johnny thought he had not heard the man right — someone whipping himself? It sounded like madness to him. He wanted to tell Agbokli he couldn't bring himself to whip him, but somehow he asked instead, "What did you do this time for which you must be punished?"

Agbokli looked him straight in the eye then said, "Last night I shot somebody dead."

The room suddenly became quiet. Johnny gaped at Agbokli in disbelief. "You what?"

"I killed a man."

"What for?"

"That is not important now."

"And why are you telling me about it?"

"I like you and I trust you."

Johnny suddenly felt tired and afraid. His arms crossed protectively over his chest. He shook his head from side to side. "I can't beat you up," he said. "I don't have the heart to do it."

"Oh, you can," Agbokli said eagerly. "You don't have to whip me very hard, not at first. You start softly, just tapping me with the whip, then making it heavier as you get used to it."

53

"No, I can't do it. Not now, maybe another time. Now I must go. Thank you for everything." He began to move towards the door before he remembered he had forgotten something. "My uncle said you should give me some money."

"Ah, yes."

Agbokli began to walk towards him and Johnny quickly stepped out into the corridor and sped to the living-room. Agbokli went in the other direction and disappeared through a door at the end of the corridor. The only thing Johnny thought of now was to get out of the house as quickly as possible. He could still feel the "high" which seemed to be making it difficult for him to think straight. Agbokli brought him the money in an envelope.

"Take this for yourself," he said and gave him a ten-thousand CFA franc note. "You're a good boy. When can you come back here? We can have lots of fun, even go on trips outside town."

"I don't know. I have to think about it," Johnny said, stumbling over his words.

"You don't have to come only when Boxer sends you. You can come on your own."

"I will come when I get the chance." He began to walk towards the front door and the older man followed him. Johnny couldn't open the door and as Agbokli reached out to open it for him their arms touched. The young man flinched as if he had been touched by a hot object. He went out and walked quickly towards the gate.

"The gate will be opened for you," Agbokli called after him.

Johnny heaved a huge sigh of relief as the gate swished open and he stepped into the open air. He felt very much at peace with himself now and the world looked brighter and cheerful. At the back of his mind he knew that it would be this new-found elation that would drive him back to Monsieur Agbokli. When he reached home he was told François had gone out. He crawled into his bed and promptly fell soundly asleep.

CHAPTER FIVE

In Anloland, the fifth male child in succession is called Anumu. Johnny's father was a fifth male child in succession so he was called Anumu. He was a robust man but owing to an attack of consumption he was now a shadow of his former self. He fought in the Congo during the Second World War but unlike most other war veterans, he rarely talked about his war experiences. The only time that he did so was what had now become monthly bouts of mental disorder, usually when there was a full moon. During these times he would rave against his heartless family that sent him to war and against several men he had killed during the war whose ghosts he claimed were now torturing him.

In the community where Anumu lived, when anyone began to exhibit symptoms of mental disorder, people would quickly cast their minds back to see if there was any history of insanity in the family. As far as anybody could remember there was no history of mental problems within Anumu's family so the family at least escaped the insinuations of being a bunch of crackbrains.

But this "complacency" was given a rude jolt when Johnny was brought back from Lome raving mad. François and his youngest wife, Desirée, brought Johnny to Keta. They came in a taxi because François did not have an international driving licence to enable him cross the border with his own car. When the taxi came to a stop outside Johnny's house, a crowd immediately started gathering. Because of the quietness of this township, any ripple of unusual activity attracted crowds like ants to honey. People would later give the event all shades of

56

narration so that within a few days no narration was anywhere near the true account.

Johnny was sandwiched in the taxi between François and Desirée. François came out first holding firmly onto the young man's wrist. Johnny came out, holding his body very stiff; he straightened himself, very upright surveying the crowd, his head thrown back imperiously. Desirée came out after them, her delicate hands holding onto Johnny's other arm more for support than any motive of restraining him. The crowd opened up to allow the visitors access to the house. Then closed up after them with some intent upon following the visitors right into the house.

Johnny's mother came out to meet them at the gate, barefooted, her hair dishevelled, her voice coming out in gasps asking, "What is it, what is it?"

Johnny and his captors entered the house followed closely by those who considered themselves near enough to the family to be allowed access. But Johnny's mother drove them all out and shut the gate. She did not want anyone to be witness to her shame and later cast insinuations at her. The crowd outside the gate would wait for a long time like newsmen anxiously expecting further developments. They would mark away every detail in their overly retentive memories for their pastime of swapping stories.

From within the house, Johnny's voice rang out in a popular song:

Nuɖe le kɔme lo,
Aziză le kɔme lo.
Nuɖe le kɔme lo,
Aziză le kɔme lo.
Nuɖe le kɔme,

Ne do va mi do go;
Azizā le kɔme,
Ne do va mi do go...

Dwarfs were believed to be spirits inhabiting ant-hills in the countryside; they had only one leg and a very small foot which pointed backwards. When children went out to hunt for snails or little birds, they would deliberately strike their heels into the soft ground and imprint their toe-marks on the depression created by their heels to make it look like the footprints of a dwarf. The children believed anyone passing by would quickly walk away saying to himself, a dwarf just went this way. But most people were aware of the prank and would only smile when they saw the supposed footmarks of the dwarf.

When those outside the gate heard the dwarf song, some concluded that the spirit of the dwarfs was upon the young man; and before the day ended the story was out that before Anumu went to war he consulted the spirit of the dwarfs to protect him from all bullets, but when he came back safe he did not fulfil his part of the bargain to offer sacrifices. That was why he himself at times went mad, and now his son was following his footsteps.

Johnny's mother was in an agitated mood, running around to get the visitors seats and to find a clean cup with which to offer them water to drink. As she moved around she kept wondering aloud, "*Ao*, who am I going to tell this to? What sort of misfortune is this? My dead parents and ancestors, please save me from this calamity..." She was alone in the house — her husband and Johnny's elder brother had gone fishing.

The visitors sat down but Johnny remained standing with François still holding onto his arm. When the old lady brought water Johnny seized the cup and gulped it down; he took the second cupful too before allowing his companions to have their share.

The old lady finally sat down facing her visitors. "*Ao*," she said, "I am just alone in the house. Should I call someone to come and listen to the news with me?"

"No, Granny. We are all from the same family," François said soothingly. The old lady and François' mother were second cousins, so François would call her aunt. But everybody called the old lady Granny. She was kind and readily went to the aid of anyone in trouble.

"What is it? What has happened?" she asked.

Johnny broke into another song:

Miawo mie gbɔna Afegame,
Ƒegametɔwo ne dzra nuawo ɖo.
Miawo mie gbɔna Afegame,
Ƒegametɔwo ne dzra nuawo ɖo.
O, midzra nuawo ɖo.
Alelele, midzra nuawo ɖo.
Miawo mie gbɔna Afegame,
Ƒegametɔwo ne dzra nuawo ɖo...

"Johnny, sit down!" Desirée shouted.

"I won't sit down," Johnny replied, but when François started speaking he lowered his voice and was now only humming his song.

"Desirée," François said, indicating that Desirée was going to be the *tsiami*. "Let it get to Granny that our visit, unfortunately as she herself can see, is not a happy one. As she is aware, Johnny visits us often in Lome but recently he came to stay permanently with us there. He is a good boy and everybody was getting along very well with him, but all of a sudden this problem cropped up. He got up one morning and I was told he had a visitor. He went out with the visitor and came back very late to the surprise of all of us, because he had never been out so late. He went to bed without eating and in the night we heard him shouting in his room. Everybody thought it was high fever and we rushed him to the hospital and he was admitted, but the things he started saying at the hospital made all of us afraid. We were all the more afraid because if the police should hear the things he was saying he could be detained. And you know the Lome police when they detain you, you never know when you may be released." François paused.

"What sort of things was he saying?" Granny asked.

François shook his head sadly and said, "He said he killed someone."

"He did what?" the old lady said, jumping out of her seat and clasping her chest with both hands.

"He said he killed a human being."

"How did he do that?"

"I don't know."

"Whom did he kill?"

"I don't know. He only kept saying he killed somebody and the person's spirit was after him. He complains of stomach-ache. He says it is the dead person attacking his intestines."

Granny turned to Johnny. "Johnny, are you mad?" she said sternly but quietly. She did not want the insult of murderers to be added to the already established one of a family with a history of insanity. "A small child like you, can you kill anybody? Where did you get those things from to say?"

Johnny stopped his humming, regarded his mother for a while and said, "You, you don't know what you are

60

talking about." Then he took up his humming again.

Granny hit her forehead with her open palm, shook her head sharply and said, "Wait, wait, let me think this out properly." This was a well-known habit of hers. When confronted with a difficult problem she would slap her forehead with an open palm and repeat the word "wait" several times; she often came up with brilliant solutions after thinking for a few moments. Her children knew this for her and would intentionally think up difficult questions to see her act out the antic. She caught up quickly with their game and played it along with them.

Desirée and François watched her quizzically as she knitted her brows trying to surmount her confusion and think straight. "Now," she said abruptly, "I must go and call my husband from the beach, then we will address each component of the issue and try to get to the bottom of this problem." She turned to François. "Uncle François," she said, "please watch over your cousin. I am going to call his father and brother. I will be back very soon."

"Woman, where do you think you are going?" Johnny asked her as she dashed into her room to change her top cloth.

She paid him no heed but as she emerged from her room Johnny made a dash for her. "Woman, I asked you a question — Where are you going?" he said, his eyes flashing and rolling in his head.

François pulled Johnny back as the old lady nimbly jumped away. "Look, Johnny," she said, "you must be very, very careful. Whatever is worrying you, you will have to comport yourself otherwise you will end up on the streets."

"Who will end up on the streets?" Johnny retorted. "You and your insane husband will end up on the streets, not me. Didn't you say you were going to bring him? You go and bring him. I will be waiting for you here. Something is going to happen today."

The old lady gave a sad little laugh. "How can you talk about your father like that? Something is really the matter with you. But let me tell you one thing: if you put up any violent act today in this house, then you will have to knock me out senseless to have your way."

She went out but moments later the gate flew open again making François and Desirée wonder if the old lady had come back so soon from the beach. But it was the town's most popular drummer, Zagunor Biekpor, who walked in.

"What is happening in our house here?" Biekpor asked as he shuffled through the loose sand towards the three people in the middle of the house. He was a fat man with big wide feet and people said at his back that he walked like a duck. "You people are welcome," he said in the same breath and sat down on the seat vacated by Granny. He started the lengthy traditional greeting but sensing that François and Desirée were not familiar with the art he cut himself short.

"What is wrong with Johnny?" he asked, looking straight into Johnny's eyes with his palms clasped over his knees. Getting no reply from the young man who had reverted to humming his songs, he turned to François and Desirée. "Who are you people? I think I know you." He pointed a fat finger at François. "Are you not the one who has been coming from Lome?"

"Yes," François answered.

"Oh, you are welcome," he said again, extending a hand towards François but seeing that the man's hands were engaged in restraining Johnny, he let his hand fall back onto his knee. "What is wrong with Johnny?"

"We don't know," François replied. "His mother has gone to bring his father."

"Is he going mad?"

"We don't know. Let's wait for his parents," François said, effectively cutting off further enquiry. They sat in silence with Zagunor Biekpor muttering occasional snorts of exasperation.

***   ***   ***

Granny reached the beach panting. She shuffled across the wide expanse of sand as she asked people where she could locate her husband's fishing company. When she found him, he quickly let go of the net and hurried towards her.

"What is it, Granny?" he asked.

"We are in trouble," she said, out of breath.

"What trouble?"

"François has brought Johnny back from Lome and he seems to be mad."

"Who seems to be mad?"

"Johnny. He is saying terrible things and is shouting at the top of his voice."

"Come on, let's go to the house." The old man broke into a trot as his wife turned to follow him.

"Where is his brother?" Granny called after him.

"They are out at sea."

Anumu was not surprised when he saw the crowd outside his house. He threw the gate open and paused to survey the island of people in the middle of the big compound. Johnny was now sitting down, his head bowed; the other three people had their eyes fixed on him. Anumu

63

closed the gate and walked towards the group. As he got near, Johnny lifted his head and grinned widely at his father.

"Oh, papa," he said rising up, "I have come back to you."

François was still holding onto his wrist, but he now let go of him as the old man came to stand before his son.

"What is the matter, Johnny?"

"Nothing is wrong with me, papa."

The gate flew open again and Granny strode in. "Now ask your son what the problem is with him," she said, almost stumbling down. "Your son says he has killed a human being," she said in a whisper when she reached the group.

"He has done what?" the old man said, turning to her.

"Ask him."

"Johnny, what is the matter?"

Johnny took a step back as if afraid of his father and spoke in a rush. "I didn't mean to kill anybody. I was forced to. I swear I will never do it again. I will never do it again. Tell the ghost of the man I will never do it again. Tell him not to touch my stomach again."

Anumu took a step towards his son and slapped him across the face, cutting out Johnny's tirade of words. The young man gasped and his eyes flashed as he looked from one person to another in confusion. He seemed not to know what had hit him.

Near the group was a small round fence erected with pointed stakes to give protection to a young mango tree. Goats would sometimes break down the fencing and eat away the leaves of the young tree, but the fence was quickly repaired and the brave mango tree would sprout again.

Johnny's movement towards this fence was so swift nobody knew what was happening until he had pulled out one of the sharp stakes and planted it deep into his father's stomach. It was rather the sharp scream of Granny that woke the group into action. Zagunor Biekpor knocked down Johnny with a swipe of his forearm and picked up the old man who had fallen to the ground. François and Desirée also rushed to him while Granny hopped about shouting, "He has killed him; he has killed my husband!"

Zagunor Biekpor turned over the old man whose mouth was wide open in a silent scream, his hands clutched tightly around the stake embedded in his stomach. François unclasped the old man's hands and forced them away from the stick. The old man began to thrash about and Biekpor knelt on his lower body to restrain him.

"Pull out the stake," Biekpor shouted at François.

François strained against the stake with all his might and fell backwards into the sand as the stake came away from Anumu's stomach. Within a few moments the old man's whole dress was wet with blood and Granny's shouts went up.

The crowd outside the house could not control its curiosity any longer; moreover they clearly heard Granny's shout that someone had been killed and it was a communal duty for everyone to go to the aid of any of the community members who was in trouble. The gate first opened a crack, then it flew open and the crowd surged in. In the confusion nobody noticed Johnny slip out of the house.

"Come on, let's take the old man to the hospital," someone shouted.

Eager hands quickly picked up the old man and he was put in François' waiting taxi. Desirée and the old lady squeezed into the front passenger seat and Zagunor Biekpor and François held up Anumu on the back seat. As the taxi pulled away, towards the main road, the old lady looked back with a jerk of her body and asked, "Where is Johnny?"

Nobody knew and none seemed to be too interested in the whereabouts of Johnny now. Their only concern was to take the old man to hospital before it was too late. It was already past six and night was beginning to fall.

"Faster, faster," Biekpor urged the driver. "Let's hope we will meet a doctor at the hospital at this time."

At the hospital the old man was immediately taken to the theatre. There was no doctor at the hospital but a nurse quickly rang up the doctor on call to summon him to the hospital. The doctor came soon afterwards and dashed into the operating theatre. A little while later, he came out with a long look on his face. Everyone knew Anumu was dead.

"Have you made a report to the police yet?" the young doctor asked.

"No," Granny replied, her heart thumping against her chest.

"Do that now. The man is dead."

Granny began to cry.

***   ***   ***

Even in his insane mind, Johnny knew he was in trouble. When the crowd rushed in after he had stabbed his father, he thought they were coming for him to tear him into pieces. Such was the vehemence in their rush.

He was very grateful when he was able to slip past the crowd without anybody paying him any attention. Once out of the house, he began to run. He ran until his path joined the road leading to the big lighthouse on the beach. He ran blindly through a group of several young men who were holding a meeting in the yard surrounding the lighthouse. A few of the young men hurriedly left their seats to give Johnny a chase taking him for a thief. Some of them knew Johnny and when they realised who it was they went back to their seats wondering what had gone into their colleague. Johnny ran through the farms separating the tall light house from the beach. He almost fell into one of the wells in the farms. He turned in a swirl and hit his left knee against the well but he seemed not to feel any pain. He was now out of breath but he continued to run, the air wheezing through his nostrils. He headed for Keta, striking a parallel line to the sea, his feet going in and out of the sand like pistons. On the border between Tegbi and Vui he collapsed into the sand. Alternately, he spread himself out and then curled up again, rolling in the sand and gasping for breath. It was now dark and there was nobody in sight on the beach. After some time he stopped gasping and his breath slowly began to assume a more regular rhythm.

He sat up slowly. He knew he was out of the Woe township but he couldn't tell exactly where he was. He was fully conscious but his mind seemed to be caught up in the region between sleep and wakefulness. The whole world seemed to be one open-ended entity that swirled out of control, making his mind swim. The objects that he could see around him seemed to assume a fluid nature, constantly changing shape and position. He now had a feeling of falling into an abyss if he took a step in any direction, so he sat at the same spot, afraid of moving.

The incident of stabbing his father receded fast from his memory but the picture of the young men rushing on him in the compound of the lighthouse was imprinted on his mind. It was as if the whole world was after him. With his hands, he cautiously felt the ground around where he sat, then he stood up and took a tentative step forward. He continued to walk towards Keta, now without hurry, occasionally rubbing his hands vigorously over his face.

When he reached Keta, there were not a lot of people out on the streets. He located the big market and walked along its walls until he stood on the shore of the big Keta Lagoon.

In days gone by, the Keta Lagoon landing stage used to be very busy especially on market days, with big boats from all over the towns and villages surrounding the lagoon berthing at the stage. The boats still came to Keta, but they were now smaller and fewer. The water in the lagoon had also gone down considerably and during particularly dry seasons almost all the water dried up so that one could walk across the lagoon bed to the towns and villages which hitherto were accessible only by boat.

In the night, the landing site was deserted except for occasional persons who went there to ease themselves on the big rubbish heap at the water's edge. Johnny walked to the edge of the water and looked out over the lagoon as the water lapped his feet. There were very few stars in the sky and the surface of the expanse of water was a dark gloom. Johnny bent down and rolled up his trousers; then he started wading away from the shore.

CHAPTER SIX

Corporal Benjamin Azingo was one of the oldest police-men serving at the Keta Police Station. He was a lanky man with a gaunt face and was a close friend of the bottle. His wife had long left him because of his drinking habit. He had three grown-up children who had stopped school-ing and were living off him without looking for work to do. This irritated Azingo to no end and anytime anyone cared to listen he would moan about the burden of having to take care of three men who were old enough to raise a family of their own. But the fact of the matter was that were it not for his children, he would have long been dead. When he drank he paid little heed to his meals and would often go to bed without eating. On occasions when his children knew he had not eaten the whole day they would practically feed him, forcing his jaws open and putting the food in his mouth. Azingo had been to hospital not once, not twice, but several times because of excessive drinking. The wonder was that despite such blatant disregard for police ethics he was still being kept in the service.

Granny and François met Corporal Azingo at the charge office when they went to report the death of Anumu. Azingo took down their statements without any show of interest and then snapped the Station Diary shut.

"We will take action on it," he said dismissively.

François and Granny were turning away to go when another policeman came into the charge office. He was Inspector Isaac Dongor, the station officer.

"What case is that?" Inspector Dongor asked. He had a fatherly countenance and spoke softly.

"Somebody stabbed someone to death," Azingo said

and climbed down from the high stool he had been sitting on.

Dongor looked at Azingo reproachfully before turning to François and Granny. "Are you the complainants?" he asked.

"Yes," François said.

"Come this way."

He led them to his office. Once inside the office, Granny talked very rapidly. "Mr. Policeman," she said, "we are not actually making a complaint. We are just informing the police about what happened as we were directed to do at the hospital. You see, the issue is a family one and we will settle it at home. We don't want anybody to be arrested."

"Sit down, sit down, old lady," Dongor said, trying to stem the flow of words. "Now tell me what happened." He was a very methodical man, full of zeal and energy for his job.

"Is it really necessary?" Granny asked.

"Yes, it is necessary, old lady; especially if it is a criminal case."

Granny turned to François helplessly. It had been her hope that the matter could be hushed and her husband buried quietly. Now it looked like this policeman was going to cause trouble.

"This is how it happened," François said. "My cousin, that is the old lady's son, is behaving abnormally. He was normal, then all of a sudden he started behaving like someone who was insane. We took him to the hospital when he was staying with me in Lome. Then I brought him to Ghana to his parents. And just as we were all trying to find out what was exactly wrong with him he took a stick and plunged it into his father's stomach. We

70

took the old man to the hospital but unfortunately he died."

"And you want to settle this at home?" Inspector Dongor asked incredulously.

"If it can be done that way we will be grateful," said François.

Dongor shook his head emphatically. "You can't do that. This is a criminal case. It is called murder or at the least manslaughter and it will have to go to court. When was the old man killed?"

"Today. Just this afternoon."

"Where?"

"At Woe."

"And where is the suspect, I mean the man you said killed the old man?"

"He ran away."

"Are you sure you are not hiding him somewhere?"

"No, no, no, we are not hiding him," Granny said. "You see, when he stabbed his father we all rushed to his aid and forgot about Johnny, my son. It was only when we were in the taxi going to the hospital that we realised he was nowhere to be found."

Inspector Dongor sat back in his chair. "Now we will have to look for the suspect, especially when you say he is behaving insanely. He can harm someone else. Give me a description of him."

"He is tall, slim and handsome," Granny said.

Dongor smiled. "Is that all? No distinctive mark like, for example, a tribal mark?"

"No, his face is very smooth."

"What colour is he?"

"He is dark in complexion."

"How does he wear his hair? Long or short?"

"He cuts his hair in the latest style. He cuts it short. And he has two perfect gaps, one in the upper row and the other in the lower row."

"You are very fond of him, aren't you?"

"He is my son."

"Good," Dongor said. "We will be looking for your son. When we get him we will let you know."

"Thank you," Granny said, "but as we indicated we will not like to drag the case."

"We will see what we can do about that. Now we will have to go to the death spot. It is part of the investigations." He went to the door and called out, "Corporal Ahedor!"

"Sir."

"Please come."

Corporal Ahedor came in on the double. He was a very short man, too short for the police service which was noted for advertising for tall men as recruits. Many people often wondered if Corporal Ahedor had had to pay his way through the selection process. But the fact of the matter was that Ahedor was recruited into the service because of his athletic prowess. He was a very fast sprinter in spite of his short legs. When he ran his legs beat a staccato on the ground like pistons doing overtime. He often ran for the police team in competitions.

He came into the room and saluted smartly. Dongor gave an imperceptible nod of approval. "Take the old lady and the man to Woe. There was an incident there this afternoon. A man stabbed his father to death. This is the man's mother. That means the dead man is this woman's husband. Take them to Woe. Have a good look at the incident spot. Take Adzanku with you. He should take some pictures." He turned to the old lady and François.

"Please go with him and give them the necessary assistance. Do you have electric light in your house?"

"Yes, we have," Granny said proudly.

"Good," Dongor said. "Ahedor, bring back with you the murder implement. I hope it will still be in the house. They say it is a stick."

Ahedor quickly located Private Adzanku. There was not much difference between the heights of Ahedor and Adzanku, but because Adzanku was slimmer he looked taller than Ahedor.

Granny and François followed the two men to the police vehicle. Adzanku was loaded with his camera and floodlight and a portable battery.

"We will have to pass through the hospital," François said. "My wife is there with the taxi that we brought."

"What is she doing at the hospital?" asked Ahedor.

"She is with the body of the old man."

Desirée was waiting in the taxi outside the hospital gate when the police Land Rover got to the hospital. She told them the old man's body had been sent to the mortuary and she had already paid for the formalin for embalmment. François got into the taxi with his wife and they followed the police vehicle to Woe.

It was now dark. Solitary electric lights shone from the homes of those who had the means to pay the exorbitant fee for the extension of electric light to their premises. And like vultures who wouldn't let go of a carcass until every little flesh had been picked from the bones, there were still a few people lingering outside Granny's house. She cursed them silently as she led the policemen into the house. A single electric bulb burned in the compound and in one corner of the house three children huddled around a low table. They were the

73

children of Johnny's elder brother. They rose up and came towards the old lady.

"Where is your father?" Granny asked.

"He has gone to the hospital," the eldest child said.

"To the hospital? We didn't meet him."

"He said he was going to the hospital." The children's interest was riveted on the policemen, especially Adzanku with his camera slung over his shoulder and the floodlight and battery in each hand. Ahedor carried a big torchlight.

"Where did the incident take place?" Ahedor asked,

"Here," Granny said and moved to the middle of the house.

Ahedor switched on the torchlight to show dark spots where the old man's blood had flowed into the sand. The fatal wooden spike, its sharp end now smeared dark, lay a little buried in the sand.

Adzanku set down his instruments and quickly connected the floodlight to the battery. He switched it on and held it towards Ahedor. "Please hold it for me."

Ahedor held up the light while Adzanku took several pictures from different angles. The children were very excited and chattered noisily among themselves with some standing at the edge of the incident spot hoping to appear in the photographs. The policemen finished their job and went away, taking with them the wooden spike wrapped in a piece of cloth.

"We will have to go back to Lome this evening," said François

"You can't do that," Granny objected. "It is night and you can't cross the border."

"We can cross it," François said. "We should normally stay with you and comfort you during this unfortunate time. But I have an issue that I have to settle at Lome

74

this night and another early tomorrow morning. We shall come back tomorrow in the afternoon." He thrust a ward of notes into Granny's hands. The old lady rejected the gift initially but then accepted it, thanking him profusely.

"May God reward you plentifully," she said.

***   ***   ***

About two hundred metres from the Keta market, off the lagoon shore, a solitary and dilapidated building stood in the middle of the water. It was built on a raised platform so that even when the lagoon was in flood, it did not go over the platform. The platform was of earth raised to the height of about two and a half metres. The idea of building in the middle of the lagoon had occurred to a man now long dead who had returned home to Keta after a long stay abroad. Mr. Dapilma, for that was the man's name, had sat down and thought about how fanciful it would be to live in the middle of the water and go in and out of his house by boat. His name was an adulteration of the native name "Dafeamekpor".

When the dry season came again, leaving large tracts of the lagoon bed dry, Mr. Dapilma started his project. Money was no problem to him then. He raised walls to the height of two and a half metres to enclose an area of thirty by forty metres on the dry lagoon bed. With cheap labour, he filled the enclosure with soil dug up from other areas of the lagoon. Then he built a house with treated timber. The house had three bedrooms, a living-room, kitchen and store-room and was complete with two bathrooms and a toilet. Steps led from the bed of the lagoon to the house. Mrs. Dapilma, who was not very keen on the idea of living in the middle of the lagoon, reluctantly moved into the house with her three children.

Mr. Dapilma bought a boat complete with an outboard motor and waited for the rains. When the rains came, the lagoon flooded, surrounding the house with its pale green water. Mr. Dapilma's heart knew no bounds for joy. Every day he would roar across the lagoon in his motor boat to the admiration and envy of all.

The high cost of fuel, however, forced Mr. Dapilma to think of other ways to get in and out of his house. In another dry season, when the lagoon had dried away, he built an access way to the house over poles driven into the bed of the lagoon. Now he used the access way more than the motor boat which had become an ornament moored to the side of the islet.

At home, Mr. Dapilma and his family who were used to the temperate weather abroad preferred to move about sparsely dressed. Those who went by the islet would see the family dressed only in swimming wear going about their chores. Soon the islet came to be called Amamakpodzi, or the isle of nakedness.

The Dapilma children attended the local Roman Catholic School and every day walked to and from school over the wooden bridge constructed by their father. In their third year on the islet, when the lagoon was particularly flooded, the youngest Dapilma child fell off the access way and drowned. Mrs. Dapilma was beside herself with grief and rage against her husband. She raved and nagged until the family packed bag and baggage and left Amamakpodzi for the mainland.

They still visited Amamakpodzi occasionally, but when Mr. Dapilma died nobody took much interest in the islet house and it was left to its fate. At one time it became a haven for drug pushers, thieves and other criminals.

Parts of its walls had now caved in and only rodents, crabs, lizards and crawling insects were its inhabitants. The walk-way had also broken down so that the islet was again only accessible by boat. All kinds of legends sprang up about Amamakpodzi and as boat-loads of market women and other travellers went past the islet, these legends were recounted.

The bulk of the people who came to the market to buy and sell came from across the big Keta Lagoon from the villages and towns on the banks of the lagoon. They came in big and small boats that converged on the market town from all directions. The boats from Anyako and Atiavi often passed very close to Amamakpodzi. Today was another market day. The occupants of the boats that passed by Amamakpodzi noticed something different about the islet. The hitherto uninhabited islet now seemed to be inhabited. A man dressed only up to his waist stood in front of the old building and waved at the people in the boats.

"You are all welcome, welcome to Keta," he said over and over again.

And the people in the boat replied, *"Yoo"*, and waved back.

As each boat passed, the man ran from one end of the islet to the other welcoming its passengers. "You are all welcome, welcome to Keta," he said flashing his hands in the air.

At first the people in the boats took the man for a jester, someone who had gone to the islet for a purpose and was trying to be friendly. But the antics that he was displaying began to make some of the passengers wonder if all was well with him, for the man was now imitating the flight of aeroplanes, his arms spread out as he dived

77

across the islet, welcoming the boat people all the while.

"It looks like all is not well with our man," said a man in one of the boats. "I think he is tying up a single tuber of yam."

"You are right," replied a woman sitting across from him. "You don't welcome even your long lost wife like that." Everyone broke into laughter.

The man on the islet was Johnny Klevor. He had been living on Amamakpodzi for five days now. During the night, he would wade ashore and jump over the wall of the market. Then he would steal whatever food items he could lay his hands on from the stalls — fish, fruits, potatoes, plantain and cassava. The second night when he forced the door of a stall open he saw stacks of textile materials piled up high. He pulled out several pieces of the materials to use to cover himself from the cold night air on his one-man island. Just as he was leaving the stall, wads of money fell from the materials he was carrying away. He quickly picked up the notes and threw them back into the stall. The owner of the stall came to the market the following day and detected that some pieces of cloth had been stolen but nobody could tell why the thief stole the cloth but ignored the large sum of money.

At the beginning, Johnny did not know that the market had security men. So on his first foray into the market, he jumped over the wall and landed noisily on the other side. He went from stall to stall opening and banging shut the doors that were not well secured. The market security men heard him, and gave him a chase. Johnny was surprised. He didn't know that people could pass the night in a market. He jumped back over the wall and the security men jumped after him. Johnny sprinted for the water's edge closely followed by the security men but when he entered the water still running and raising huge sprays of water, the security men stopped. Apparently they did not fancy a midnight dip in the lagoon. They consoled themselves with hurling invectives after the fleeing figure.

"*Dzimakpla!*" said the first security man.

"Cat-man!" said the second.

"Lazy and useless man!"

"Come again tomorrow and you will see!"

Johnny went back to the market the following night but this time he was very careful. He pulled himself up the wall by his arms and carefully surveyed the vicinity before scaling the wall. He gathered his loot stealthily and went back quietly to Amamakpodzi. He no more had any trouble with the security men.

He spent the day hiding in the dilapidated building on the islet. He never slept during the day but lay face upwards, his thoughts jumping about like pop corn in a hot pan. His mind was still foggy and he had very little sense of time. During brief moments the fog would lift up from his mind and he would struggle to regain control of his thoughts but he always slipped and was sucked under the quagmire that had taken his brain prisoner.

Johnny suffered severe stomach cramps. The pains came suddenly as if a hand with sharpened overgrown nails had grabbed his intestines. He would cry out sharply and roll over the ground mumbling incomprehensibly and frightening away the crabs and rats that were his companions on the islet.

The crabs and rats and lizards on Amamakpodzi were big. Since he came up to the islet the only logical thought that passed through his mind was when he wondered where these animals got food from on this

79

isolated islet to have grown to such sizes. The crabs came out of their holes during the day and in the night. They had huge claws that they held in front of them as they performed their sideways walk. All day long the lizards caught insects and mated or simply basked in the sun. The rats were mostly nocturnal animals. They would come out in the night and roam over him and nibble at his toes and finger tips. He found this very painful and during the day he would tearfully examine his bleeding toes and fingers.

The first market day that he spent on the island he hid from sight and watched the passenger boats with their huge sails glide past Amamakpodzi. He knew that it must be a market day and in a distant corner of his mind he began to long for human company again. He looked on sadly as the boats went past but he did not have the courage to expose himself. At the end of the day the boats returned with their human cargo and other luggage heading for the towns and villages where they came from.

It was on the second market day, when Johnny could no more suppress his longing for the warm company of human beings, that he came out of his hiding place and in a flourish constituted himself into a welcoming party. It was not long before the news spread in the market and in the town that there was an insane man on Amamakpodzi. Before midday the police knew the whereabouts of Johnny.

***   ***   ***

It was Sergeant Gideon Bansa who broached the idea that the mad man reported to be on Amamakpodzi could be Johnny, the suspect wanted for the murder of his

80

father. Bansa was a stout man, very dark in complexion with a prematurely bald head. The idea quickly caught on at the charge office. The station officer, Inspector Isaac Dongor, was informed and he quickly called the District Commander of Police to seek permission to use the latter's vehicle to go and arrest the suspect. The station's own vehicle had broken down again.

"Good morning, sir," Dongor said into the old weathered telephone receiver.

"Morning," came the guttural response of the District Commander, Assistant Superintendent of Police Mark Adosu. When you had heard his voice and then seen him in person, there was no difference between the two, the man and the voice. Adosu was a burly man, very efficient but overbearing in manner.

"Sir," Dongor said, "we just had information that the insane suspect that we are looking for in the murder case is on Amamakpodzi in the Keta Lagoon. Permission to use your vehicle and go and arrest him, sir."

"Go ahead."

"Thank you, sir."

Inspector Dongor quickly called together a team of four policemen including Sergeant Bansa and they set off at top speed for Keta. They arrived at the water front, their intention obviously to attract maximum attention. The driver came to a screeching halt raising a huge cloud of dust and the policemen jumped out of the vehicle banging the doors shut and fanning out towards the water's edge in battle fashion. Inspector Dongor approached a boat man and asked him to convey them to the islet.

"The journey will cost you five thousand cedis," said the boat man trying to show by his manner that he was unimpressed by the police uniforms.

Dongor turned away from him and approached another boat man. "How much will you charge to take us to Amamakpodzi?" he asked.

"What are you going to do there?" the boat man asked back as he carefully picked his teeth. He had just had a sumptuous meal.

"We are going to arrest a suspect," Bansa replied impatiently.

"A what?"

"A suspect. Someone we think has committed a crime, done a wrong."

"You are talking about the gentleman who has taken up residence there?"

"Yes."

"That will cost a lot of money."

"How much?"

"Eight thousand cedis."

"You can't be serious."

"I am serious. Taking you to Amamakpodzi and back is no problem. But look at it this way: you are going to arrest a mad man. If I take you there and in the process of arresting the man my boat gets damaged, the eight thousand cedis will then be used to repair it."

Dongor saw logic in the man's argument but he still pressed for a reduction. Finally, the man agreed to take four thousand cedis. The five policemen got into the small boat. The boat man pushed the boat into the water and climbed in. He drew a long pole from under the seats of the boat and with this he began to propel the small craft towards Amamakpodzi.

There was a little tide and small waves lashed against the boat spraying the policemen with the salty lagoon water. They kept grimacing and cursing until the boat came alongside Amamakpodzi. Without much difficulty, the policemen climbed onto the islet while the boat man passed a pole through a sling attached to the boat and drove it into the lagoon bed to anchor the boat. Then he also followed the policemen onto the islet. The place was very weedy and lizards and crabs scattered into the bush as the men drew near.

"How can anyone live at a place like this?" Inspector Dongor asked as he looked round. "Where is he anyway?"

They entered what remained of the wooden building and went from room to room but there was no sign of Johnny.

"Damn!" Dongor swore. "The man has run away."

"Maybe he has not run away," said Private Alex Atonsu, the police driver. He was a worm of a man who feared authority and spoke in a small voice, especially when talking to his superiors. "Maybe he has just left the islet temporarily. He does not yet know that we are looking for him. Maybe he will come back."

Inspector Dongor regarded Atonsu thoughtfully then said, "You are right. We will come back another time, soon." They piled back into the boat and were conveyed back to land.

In a corner of the living-room of the building on Amamakpodzi, a wooden board covered with moss like the rest of the floor hid a rectangular cavity in the floor. When Mr. Dapilma and his family occupied the islet they used the cavity as a storage. Johnny discovered the cavity on the second day of his sojourn on the islet. When he saw the small boat loaded with policemen approaching the islet, his first thought was to jump into the lagoon and run away. But he realised he had no chance against people who would be chasing him in a boat, so he sneaked back into the building. He paced the living-room a few times then suddenly his eyes lit up. He rushed to the middle of the room and pulled up the wooden board covering the cavity. He pushed in all his possessions and lowered himself into the hollow and carefully pulled the cover over the cavity again. He had listened to the police as they searched the building, smiling all the while at his own cleverness.

On the way back to the police station, Inspector Dongor kept thinking. "No," he said more to himself than to the people in the vehicle with him. "We can't get this man this way. We can't go back to the station now and keep coming back to see if he's on the islet. We have to keep surveillance over the place." He turned to the other occupants of the vehicle. "When we get to the station, two of us will change into plain clothes and go back to Keta. They will keep the islet under surveillance and when they spot the suspect one person will come back to the station and call for reinforcement. The other person will continue watching to make sure the suspect does not leave the islet." He turned to Private Atonsu. "You will go back to Keta with Sergeant Bansa."

Back on the islet Johnny lifted the cover of the cavity and came out feeling very clever and proud of himself. Without any warning the stomach cramps set upon him again and he tumbled onto the floor. Again, it seemed a giant hand had been shoved into his stomach and was wreaking havoc on his intestines as he rolled on the floor, his eyes tightly closed. In his pain, Johnny forgot about the need to keep his hiding place secret and started yelling.

"Leave me alone! Leave me alone!" he shouted at the

probing hand that would not let go of his stomach. "I didn't mean to kill you. I didn't kill you. Leave me alone!" Then he started calling for help. "Help me-e-e-e... Somebody help me, please..."

The pains subsided just as suddenly as they had started and Johnny slumped to the floor drenched in sweat. He was weary and soon afterwards he fell asleep where he lay. When he woke up, the sun was going down in the early evening sky. He pulled himself up and went out of the building. He was still in a state of timelessness and empty space. At times his mind appeared on the verge of clicking into gear but at the last moment it always slipped. The first boats returning from the market were passing by the islet, loaded with passengers who had finished their business and were returning to their villages and towns.

"Good-bye, good-bye," said Johnny at first silently and sadly. "Good-bye," he said.

Then he became more boisterous, jumping up and down and shouting his farewells at the top of his voice. "Fare you well! May your journey be smooth. Good-bye, loved ones. Greetings to all my friends and relatives. Good-bye..."

Those who had had the opportunity of being welcomed by Johnny earlier in the day eagerly told the newcomers about Johnny's behaviour in the morning. Everybody on the boats waved back at him and even those who did poor business in the market smiled briefly before recoiling into the mental calculation of their losses.

Sweat poured from his body as he jumped from one end of Amamakpodzi to the other. As each boat went past, he followed it along the length of the islet until the passengers were out of earshot, then he would sit down

85

and wait for another boat to come near. Soon a small boat began to approach the islet. It had few passengers, but he was not worried about that. He stood up in preparedness to wish it farewell. There was something curious about the boat, however. Instead of going past Amamakpodzi as the other boats had done, it seemed to be heading straight for the islet. He jumped about half-heartedly, shouting his farewells and wishing the small boat to right its course but the boat kept coming straight for the islet. He came to the realisation that the occupants of the boat could be the very people who had come after him in the morning. They were no more in police uniforms but they could well be the same people. He rushed into the living-room and threw himself into his secret vault and waited for the men to come and conduct their fruitless search and go away.

Inspector Dongor and his party climbed onto the islet and not seeing Johnny in sight outside, they rushed into the building. They went through the living-room, the bedrooms, kitchen, bathrooms and toilet but there was no sign of Johnny. They came out and looked round over the lagoon to see if he had jumped into the lagoon and was wading away but there was no sign of him.

"Is the man a ghost?" Constable Atonsu wondered aloud.

"Shut up!" barked Inspector Dongor. "There are no ghosts." He began to walk round, looking down along the sides of the islet to make sure Johnny was not hiding in its shadow. "No!" he said suddenly. "The man must be hiding somewhere in the house. Let's check again. You, Atonsu, keep a watch outside."

They went back into the building. The building had no ceiling so there was no question of Johnny hiding there. They looked in every nook and cranny but to no avail. Then Dongor began to stamp over the floor of the building, starting from the living room. He smiled broadly when one section of the floor sounded hollow. It did not take any critical look to find out that this section of the floor had a cavity below it. Dongor motioned his men and when the cover over the cavity was pulled up, there was Johnny lying over his few possessions and sweating profusely.

"Come out, you junk!" Dongor said, laughing. "You think you are smart, eh?"

Johnny sat up in the cavity. "Please, leave me alone. I haven't done any wrong. Just leave me alone."

"You have not done any wrong?" Dongor said. "You murderer! Get out of there and get moving!"

Johnny started weeping as he stood up slowly. "I am not a murderer. I didn't mean to kill anybody. I was made to do it. I swear I was deceived into doing it..."

"Liar! Who made you do it?"

Johnny looked blank at the question. For a moment his tears stopped flowing, then he started weeping again, refusing to answer any questions.

CHAPTER SEVEN

The bodies of Gbagbladza and Besa stayed at the spot of death for eight days. A dense stench of putrefying flesh had gradually enveloped the area so that even those who walked along the street above gave it a wide berth. The farming beds in the immediate environ of the bodies had grown weedy because the owners of the beds for fear of their lives would not go near. The police also notoriously pretended not to know about the dead men and took no action. All of a sudden the Local Government Environmental Health Officers began doing their rounds at the other end of town.

On the eighth day, the people woke up to the sustained and boisterous music of the *Yeve* cult members. Their gongs, drums and other musical instruments seemed to sound louder than before and the cult members danced and moved about in a frenzy. They made several rounds of the town and finally congregated at the courtyard of the cult at Blemekpinu. Nobody addressed the gathering neither were any announcements made; there were only furtive movements in and out of the shrine and people talking in whispers to each other.

To the eastern end of the courtyard was a small enclosure up to waist level. In it was an assortment of objects that represented charms of the cult. A small group of people started moving towards this enclosure, giving rise to a suppressed but intense excitement that swept through the gathering. This group was made up of non-initiates, the men among whom were called the *huno* and their female counterparts the *dasi*. They were allowed to perform tasks that were considered to be taboo for the initiates. Even though they were not initiates, they were very powerful and sat on the disciplinary committee of the cult. When the disciplinary committee pronounced punishment on culprits, especially whipping, it was the *huno* who carried out the whipping. They were a feared group.

When the *huno* and *dasi* reached the enclosure at the end of the compound, one of them entered and the others surrounded it so that the crowd could not see what was being done inside. The small group stayed at the enclosure for several minutes while the crowd held its breath in anticipation. The group finally concluded their business at the enclosure but instead of moving back into the shrine, they formed a bee-line and started moving out of the courtyard. Then the rest of the cult members broke into song and drumming. They would sing and drum and dance until the select group returned from their mission.

The *huno* and *dasi* picked their way in silence along the sandy paths of the town. Crowds of people, men, women and children, began to follow the group and before long it looked as if the whole township had turned out to watch the procession. The crowd seemed to know where the *huno* and *dasi* were heading. The procession hit the main road and turned in the direction of the spot where the decomposing bodies of Gbagbladza and Besa lay. The story surrounding the death of the two men had been on the lips of everybody since the incident happened. But now it was rejuvenated by the crowd which churned it up, spewed it out and drank it in as if they were hearing the story anew; it was given new colour, new texture, new dimension and updated.

The family of Gbagbladza and Besa had not been able to pay the heavy fine imposed by the cult. Neither could they offer any member of the family to be initiated into the cult in atonement because no mother was ready to part with her child to become a *Yeve* initiate, not even when the cult later agreed to take only one male member of the family. The penalty of the family for not paying the fine was that the dead bodies would be disgracefully treated and taken out of town and left at the mercy of the elements. But that was not the end of the story — the family would continue to suffer calamities until the fine was made good.

Torn between the funeral arrangements for his dead wife and the fine that must be paid, Nani resigned himself to his fate. In his private moments he felt guilty for being selfish, for one of his reasons for deciding to let matters take their own course was that he was advanced in years and would be dying soon anyway.

Nani was now a very sad man. His family seemed to have deserted him in his greatest time of need. He was beginning to see a regular pattern in the behaviour of his relatives; when they chanced upon him, their first reaction was to attempt avoiding meeting him. When this failed, they were always in a hurry to part company with him. He knew the underlying cause of their behaviour — they feared that he might ask them for help. In this community where cost of living was high and meaningful employment not readily available, everyone was wary of parting with their money.

At family meetings to deliberate on the funeral of Nani's wife, the funeral arrangements were discussed at length, but whenever there was the hint of the fine of the Yeve cult creeping into the discussions, the meeting quickly came to a close. The only issue the family was concerned with was the repercussion on the family if the fine was not paid, but not how to pay it. Nani's favourite adage, "An untried friend is a death trap", was beginning to have more meaning for him.

The crowd surged after the *huno* and *dasi*, threatening to engulf them. Almost anybody that met the crowd joined it when they heard about the destination of the group. The procession took the last bend in the road and ahead of them, above the spot where Gbagbladza and his brother lay, an even larger crowd waited. The excitement in the air was so thick that some people seemed to be possessed. The two crowds finally merged, one side eager to tell the other what had been happening at the spot of death and the other anxious to narrate the stages the procession had gone through. The *huno* and *dasi* descended the steep incline leading to where the dead bodies lay. The stench from the bodies rose anew and many in the crowd held their hands to their noses.

The lead *huno* collected two chicken from a member of the group and raised it to the four cardinal points of the earth. Then he threw the chicken onto the mound of leaves and twigs. The chicken escaped over the shallot beds flapping their wings. They were to lure away the angry spirits; they were also used to test if there was any remnant electrical force that could be harmful. The lead *huno* took a small pot from another member of the group. Into this he dipped a small whisk and sprinkled its contents over the surrounding area. He mumbled a long incantation to which his followers responded in deep tones, stretching their arms towards the spot of death. The gestures were meant as admonition to the dead bodies, a sign that they would receive their due punishment, for their offences had not been atoned for by their family.

From the folds of his loin cloth one of the *huno*

91

produced a coil of twine which he handed over to the leader. The leader's mouth indicated that he was uttering more incantations. Then with a loud voice he raised his arms and showed the twine first to the four cardinal points of the earth, starting from the east to the west. The sun wanes and sets in the west, so this was a sign that the dead men were ill-favoured by *Torhonor*. The leader then took the hands of each of the *huno* in his palm and fortified them with more incantations. Then they all set to work.

They removed the branches and twigs from the dead bodies. The stench of decaying human flesh was now so strong that even some of the *huno* could not help but put their hands to their noses. The dead bodies were first straightened out and laid side by side on palm fronds face upwards. Then each of the bodies' feet were tied up with the palm fronds with a separate twines. Two teams of three men each stood by the bodies while the rest of the group drew back and then burst into a song. It was a melancholic song, pledging their allegiance to *Torhonor* and vowing to do his will even at the peril of their own lives. As if by design, the team that stood by Gbagbladza was made up of three hefty men; in death Gbagbladza's body looked even bigger than it was in life. Each of the teams took up the end of a twine and slung it over their shoulders. The song of the *huno* rose up in crescendo as the two teams began to pull the dead bodies slowly out of the thicket then up the steep incline that led to the street above.

The crowd on the street fell back in a hurry, covering their mouths in horror. Many in the crowd began to weep uncontrollably when the *huno* reached the street with their cargo. They paused as if contemplating which way to go, then the haulers turned towards the western end of the town, dragging their human loads along the tarred road. The bloated bodies of the dead men inched along the road making whooshing sounds which were drowned by the song of the *huno* and the shouts from the crowd. After a distance of about two hundred metres two fresh teams replaced the haulers. And thus, with fresh limbs replacing weary ones, the dead bodies were dragged along the street for about one kilometre. By this time practically the whole town had turned out to watch the spectacle!

The *huno* turned off the street and began to move down the incline at the side of the street towards the lagoon. They went through several farms, trampling under their feet crops of cassava and maize. The lead *huno* turned on the crowd and motioned them not to follow. The crowd obeyed instantly, those who had already entered the cassava and maize farms climbing back to the safety of the street to watch from there. By this time the dresses in which the two men had died was torn into shreds. Their heels were bare of flesh and bits of their skin lined the streets of Woe.

A little distance to the edge of the lagoon, the group came to a stop near two low rectangular sheds constructed from trimmed tree branches lashed together with twines. The sheds had been made during the night by the *huno*. By the sides of the sheds were several straw mats. Each body was laid on a shed and the straw mats were used to cover them. The little pot was given to the leader again and with his whisk, he sprayed the contents of the pot over the straw mats. At a word from the leader, the group turned its back on the sheds and walked away without a single glance backwards. Halfway to the street, and at a word from the leader, the team broke into a trot. They ran all the way to the street where the crowd broke away in all directions. The *huno* entered the town still running and those who knew the history of events of this nature shook their heads sadly for they knew where the *huno* were going. As they ran through town, those *huno* who were not used to this sort of exercise began to fall back, but they did not seem worried for they were aware of the destination of the group and knew they would get there eventually.

The target of the *huno* was Nani's house, precisely Gbagbladza and Besa's apartments. The cleansing that the *huno* were engaged in would only be complete after every trace of the two men had been obliterated. Nani and his two daughters-in-law were in the house and expecting the marauding group. The children had been sent to relatives to prevent them from witnessing what was about to happen to their fathers' apartments. The *huno* stormed into the house with little ceremony. They quickly split themselves into two groups. One group broke into the apartment of Gbagbladza and the other into that of Besa. They brought out everything they could lay their hands on — bags of clothing, little pieces of furniture, old foot wear. The humane element in the exercise was that Nani and his daughters-in-law had been forewarned by the *huno* the previous night about the exercise. This was to enable them remove from the house items that did not belong to the two men. But everyone knew this would be extended to mean any useful item whether it belonged to the two men or not, so that all that the *huno* brought out were old clothes and old bags and other odds and ends, some not even belonging to the two men but only added to give bulk.

Like mad men moving house, the *huno* took up their

loot and rushed out of the house. They marched through the town like conquering soldiers and headed back for the spot where they had laid out the bodies of Gbagbladza and Besa. By the sheds on which the two men lay, the looted items were strewn about. From this day onwards no-one was allowed to go near the spot. Anyone who trespassed would be dealt with by *Torhonor*. The bodies and their belongings would be left there at the mercy of the elements until the family paid the fine imposed by the shrine. It was only then that they could be buried.

The *huno* trooped back to the town, weary and looking like people who had woken up from a trance. They arrived back at the courtyard where the drumming and dancing were still going on. They would have to undergo cleansing ceremonies before going home to their families.

If Nani had any illusions about the might and the seriousness of the *Yeve* cult, the events of the day thoroughly cured him of these. He had to admit to himself he was now frightened. He had always had a lingering hope that the state's law enforcement agents would not stand aside and allow the cult members to do as they pleased with the bodies of his two sons. But when the bodies were left at the death spot for many days without the police taking any action he began to lose hope. The thought of reporting the issue to the police crossed his mind not once but many times, but he was terrorised into silence by the fear of what the cult and its god might do to him in return.

Like a mother hen, he called together his two daughters-in-law. Ablator had a haggard look on her face and from her blood-shot eyes it was evident that she had been crying. Lucy also came in, her head turned to one side and a lost look in her eyes. The women sat down facing the old man. It took the old man a long time before he started talking. It was about eleven o'clock in the morning and on a normal day he would have been on the beach lending his little strength to the fishing companies in return for a small share of the catch. Then he would send his catch home for the evening meal.

"My daughters," Nani said in a weary voice, "I have called you together again not for any reason but for the single reason of the blaze that is roaring through our house. Who would have thought that the sons of me, Nani Hordzo, Kortogo, the one the big snakes grabbed but could not pull down, would be so disgraced even in their death, treated like mad dogs that the children have stoned to death? Eh, who would have thought that?" Tears choked his voice. He used the end of the cloth that he was wearing to clean his face.

The two women also started weeping. They wept not only for their dead husbands but also for the hapless old man before them.

Nani found his voice again and said, "I have decided to join the cult."

"No, grandpa," Ablator said, her hands flashing out in total rejection of the idea. "You cannot do that! Let those goats do whatever they like with our husbands. Even if they want to tear them into pieces and scatter them all over town let them do it. As for them they are already dead. What do they care about? Their souls are already departed and whatever they do to their empty bodies is of no consequence."

Despite her brave words, Ablator knew dead bodies were not merely discarded empty vessels. Even mad people were buried when they died.

"Grandpa," said Lucy, "do not do this to yourself. You

96

don't believe in the *Yeve* cult so why join it? I for one will never join it, neither will my children. I know my husband would never have agreed for any of us to join that cult."

"Ablator and Lucy," Nani said, "how long can you and your children continue to go about this town, walking along the street, knowing that your dead husbands are lying on sheds drying out in the sun forever and ever? Do you trust yourselves to continue to keep a straight face, pretending that you don't care? No, my daughters, let us not deceive ourselves. We will have to do something to get your husbands and my sons removed from the sun and given a decent burial. No, we will have to do something!"

The women broke into fresh weeping.

"My daughters, do not cry. Crying does not solve problems. Look at me. How long have I got to live? Two years, five, ten? Allow me to join the cult to remove this stain from our family. After the bodies are buried we will remember this time only as a bad dream. But there will not be any bodies drying out in the sun to constantly remind us of our shame. And when I am dead and gone the whole incident will be forgotten in a short time. No, I am sorry to tell you that no matter what you say I will join the cult. The only thing I am asking from you is your support. You will have to give me moral support. But if you are going to withhold this from me in protest, then go ahead but it will not change my decision."

"Grandpa, if that is the way you are going to put it, then go ahead and join the cult," Ablator said. "We won't stand in your way. What do you think, Lucy?"

"If grandpa wants to join the cult, we can't stand in his way. Let him do what he thinks is best for the family. He is our father. We will forever remain indebted to him for sacrificing himself this way. We will never forsake him, we will be with him every inch of the way."

"Thank you my daughters," said the old man. "Let's hope they don't use age to disqualify me. They themselves said the age of the person we offer does not matter. We will inform the cult about our decision tomorrow."

He rose up and walked to his apartment, the eyes of his daughters-in-law trailing his weary steps. He sat down heavily on his straw bed and covered his face with his palms, his elbows resting on his thighs. Now that the difficult decision had been spoken out he was assailed by doubts. Had he taken the right decision? How will he find life as a *Yeve* initiate? How long will the initiation be? Will it involve a lot of expenditure? Tears welled in his eyes. He wiped them away and got up. He had never been a friend of the bottle but since his troubles began, they had struck quite an acquaintance. He pulled out an empty bottle under his bed and placed it carefully within the folds of his cloth.

Ablator and Lucy exchanged knowing glances when Nani went out of the house without saying a word to them. They knew he had started drinking, but poor man, what did they expect him to do? You can't beat up a child and forbid it to cry.

In the evening, Nani called at *Huno* Dunyo's house accompanied by Ablator. They told *Huno* Dunyo about the decision of the old man. Dunyo looked surprised.

"Can you dance?" he asked, appraising the frail body of the old man. "As for us it is only dancing that we do."

"Oh, yes, I can dance," Nani replied. "I am stronger than I look. The only thing is that I will have to bury my wife before I get initiated."

"No problem," Dunyo said with a wave of his hand. "We can wait. We are not in a hurry."

"The burial is next weekend. You will hear from us after that."

"That is okay," Dunyo replied. As the old man and Ablator rose up to go, he asked, watching the woman appreciatively, "Is this your daughter?"

"No, my daughter-in-law. Gbagladza's wife."

"How unfortunate! She is a beautiful woman."

Ablator looked at Dunyo from the corner of her eye and sucked her teeth silently. The he-goat, she thought.

CHAPTER EIGHT

The True Open Bible Church, TOBC for short, had no permanent structure of its own. It held its sessions under a shed in a large compound house at Dzelukope. The head pastor, the Reverend Prophet Elijah Patu, lived in an apartment rented in the same house and paid for by the church.

The basic doctrine of the True Open Bible Church was that the Bible, the source of all life, should never be kept closed. Where circumstances did not permit its being kept open, for example, when one was walking to church, a marker must be placed between the pages. This way, the divine power of the Holy Spirit was kept in constant flow to clean a sinful world. So every member of TOBC, whether at home or at work, kept the Bible open at a page; it did not matter which page. At church, everybody kept their Bibles open whether they were being read or not. One thing that this practice did was that it kept TOBC members in close contact with their Bibles. Many of them could not say two sentences without quoting some part of the Bible.

The Reverend Prophet Elijah Patu, the leader of TOBC, was a charismatic and pragmatic character. TOBC was his own brain child. Unlike other churches in the town, TOBC had no mother church anywhere. His favourite subject for a sermon was that God did not intend anyone to be poor. Anybody who was poor consciously or unconsciously made the decision to be poor himself. All TOBC members therefore had the firm belief that they would be rich one day, even if it was for a single day before their death. Prophet Patu was a shining example for them; he had two saloon cars, a Mercedes and a BMW, all gleaming white, and you did not need to take a second look at the man to know that he was rich. But unlike other church leaders who dipped their hands into the church's kitty, Prophet Patu rather pumped his own money into the church. He was a businessman. He did his business far away in the nation's capital city, Accra.

Prophet Patu did not bear the name "prophet" in vain. He sometimes prophesied. One of his prophesies that came to pass to the amazement of the church was that a day would come when some members of the church would rise against his leadership and break away from the church. On the day Prophet Patu proclaimed this prophesy, the whole church was filled with consternation. Like the day Jesus Christ told his disciples that one of them would betray him, TOBC members turned on their benches to look suspiciously at those sitting beside them.

The prophesy came to pass and in trickles some members of the church began to break away. They did not form another church of their own as sometimes happened in these cases. They just joined other churches. Curiously, most of those who broke away were married men whose wives were also members of TOBC. When they left they took their wives with them. There were two cases where two women refused to leave the church when their husbands did. The two cases resulted in divorce. A few young men also left the church taking away their fiancees. Gradually, the rumour began to gain ground that Prophet Patu had been seeking intimate favours from the female members of the church. Within three months of the first member breaking away, total member-ship of the TOBC nose-dived from over a hundred to less than forty. Those left behind were unfailingly devoted to the prophet. One of these faithfuls was Constable Alex Atonsu, the policeman driver.

It was at this critical time in the history of TOBC that Prophet Patu began his attempts to perform miracle healing in his church. A dog-eared book on hypnotism given him by a friend aided him greatly in this. Every other Sunday now the church had healing sessions and the prophet would prance about talking in tongues and screaming, "Your faith would save you... Your faith will deliver you..." A few times the prophet tried his hands at hypnotising members of the church but he had not yet had any spectacular success.

***   ***   ***

The handling of Johnny's case was left to Sergeant Gideon Bansa. It looked like an open and close case that needed no detective work. The three detectives in the district were already over-burdened anyway. Moreover there were witnesses to the crime including the suspect's own relatives. What would happen was that at court the judge would order a psychiatric examination of the suspect and base his judgement on the results of the examination.

On the day of his arrest, Johnny refused to talk. He was put in a cell and spent the night there. His mother and brother heard of his arrest the next day and came to the police station bringing him food. When the old lady saw her son she began to cry. He was very dirty and looked like an animal. After they had left, Johnny was handcuffed and led to the interrogation room. There were two other men with Bansa; one of them Johnny recognised as the driver of the previous day. The other policeman was Corporal Ahedor who was to take down the interrogation.

Johnny stood in the middle of the room, his mind scarcely registering what was going on around him. During the night he had woken up to the realisation that he was in police cells but try as he could, he could not remember the reason for his arrest. Everything was so foggy. He wished he had someone to help him.

"Where are my mother and brother?" he asked.

"They have gone home," Bansa said. "What do you want them to do for you?"

"And where is my father?"

"Your father?" Bansa couldn't believe his ears. "The one you killed? You must be joking!"

Johnny's head jerked back. "Me, killed my father?"

"Do not annoy us," Bansa said, trying to retain his cool. "No amount of denial will save you. It is even not necessary to interrogate you in the face of the amount of evidence against you. What we are going to do now is just a formality. Now, let's begin. What is your name?"

"My name?"

"Yes, your name."

"My name is Johnny Klevor."

"How old are you."

"Twenty-eight years."

"Your hometown?"

"Woe."

"The names of your parents?"

"Anumu Klevor and Amiyo Agbeme."

"Is there any quarrel or misunderstanding between you and your parents?"

"No."

"No quarrel between you and your mother?"

"No."

"What about your father?"

"No."

"Where is your father?"

"At this time he will be at the beach."

"You mean in the other life."

"What other life?"

Bansa stood up. "Look young man, stop wasting everybody's time. Now answer this question: Did you kill your father."

"I did not kill my father! How can I do that?"

"So you mean your mother, your brother and everybody else who saw you commit the crime is a liar?"

"My mother and my brother say I killed my father?" Johnny asked incredulously.

"Yes!"

"It is not true!"

"Don't waste our time," Bansa said. "You will be taken to court tomorrow. Later evidence will be produced to show that you killed your father. The spike you used to commit the crime has the blood of your father and your finger prints on it. Your mother and other family members will testify against you."

"I am telling you it was not my father that I killed."

"Then whom did you kill?"

"I don't know him."

"Ha, ha, ha..." The policemen broke into noisy laughter. "You don't know your own father. Were you blindfolded when you committed the crime?"

Johnny began to cry.

"Take him away," Bansa told Atonsu. Then he went and briefed Inspector Dongor on the results of the interrogation.

It was a quiet session when Johnny's case was called at court. His mother and brother sat with gloomy faces on the front bench. There wasn't any "interesting" case on that day so the townspeople did not flock to the court premises to witness the drama. Inspector Dongor was going to prosecute Johnny. When the case was called and Johnny was brought to the dock, he stated the case very simply — Johnny was misbehaving in the house. When his father told him to desist he refused. So his father slapped him. Johnny took offence and stabbed his father in the stomach with a wooden spike. The old man died at the hospital on the same day.

"Your honour," Dongor said, "the blood-stained wooden spike with the fingerprints of the accused have been sent to our laboratory and will be produced in evidence after the necessary tests. Witnesses who were present when the accused committed the crime will also be called to testify."

"Has the accused got a lawyer to represent him?" the judge asked. When Inspector Dongor looked blankly at him, he turned to Johnny. "Do you have a lawyer?"

Johnny began to cry again. "Judge, I swear I didn't kill my father. These people are trying to make me admit things I didn't do."

"Which people?"

"The police."

"So you deny you killed your father?"

"It wasn't him. It wasn't my father."

"You mean you killed somebody else?"

For some time Johnny could only cry. Then he said, "I am willing to say everything just to be free. But as for my father if he is dead, I did not kill him."

"What is everything that you are willing to talk about?" the judge asked.

"Not here. I can't say it here."

"Why can't you say it here? This is the court where you say everything."

"I can't say it here."

"Then where?"

"Somewhere private."

The judge motioned Inspector Dongor over to him and whispered, "Why didn't you tell me the man is a nut case?"

"I am sorry, your worship," Dongor said contritely.

The judge banged his mallet on the table and announced, "The case is adjourned to the 7th of July. Meanwhile, the police should send the accused to a qualified psychiatrist to ascertain his level of sanity. The result should be available to the court before the 7th of July."

"Yes, your honour," Inspector Dongor said and sat down. Then he said to Bansa who sat near him, "Let me see the suspect when we get back to the station."

The next case the judge called was Stephen Atsu versus Daniel Agortui. Stephen Atsu, a member of the True Open Bible Church, owed Daniel Agortui a large sum of money. All attempts by Daniel to make Stephen pay proved fruitless. TOBC, on behalf of Stephen, undertook to pay the debt but had been very slow in doing this. Daniel had no other option than to resort to the law to redeem the debt from Stephen.

Present in the courtroom was the Reverend Prophet Elijah Patu. He had come to plead with the judge to have the case settled out of court. If the judge refused, he came prepared to pay the debt there and then. Prophet Patu had been very intrigued by the preceding case, The Republic versus Johnny Klevor. He made a mental note to make enquiries about the young man after the court session.

The judge turned down the prophet's plea to have the case settled out of court. So the prophet paid the principal money owed and other costs. Then he hurried to the police station which was not far from the courthouse to look for Constable Atonsu. He found him after a quick enquiry.

"How are you, my brother?" he asked the policeman who felt very honoured to have been looked up by the prophet.

"I am fine, prophet," he replied as he bowed his head low respectfully.

"How is your work, and your family?"

"Everything is fine, thank you. Can I be of any assistance to you, prophet?"

The prophet cleared his throat. "Er, yes and no," he said. "One of the flock had a problem and was brought to court. You know Stephen Atsu? Aha!... It is his case. The man brought him to court today. Anyway, I have paid the debt from my own pocket and he has been released."

"That is good. You have done very well."

The prophet paused then said, "Er, there is this other issue. A young man was brought to the court today charged with killing his father. The young man denied the charge."

"He denied, but tell you what, I think he did it."

"What is the story behind his case?"

Atonsu told him.

"Oh I see," the prophet said. "I think he has a little mental problem. There is more to this case than meets the eye. I can help the police unravel this case."

"In what way?" Atonsu asked.

"If I can have the young man to myself, I can make him tell everything that he knows, including things that he himself wants to keep a secret."

Atonsu smiled complacently. "How are you going to do that?"

"That is my secret. The Lord our God moves in mysterious ways. Let me have access to the young man and I will prove it to you."

"Er," Atonsu said pensively, "I don't know how that can be arranged. In fact I doubt very much if the man can be put at your disposal."

"Can't we arrange something just between the two of us?"

"What?"

"If through your own arrangement you can let me see the man without the official knowledge of the police, I will be immensely indebted to you."

Atonsu shifted uneasily from one foot to the other. "That will be difficult. It will be against regulation."

"It will be in the interest of the church, in the service of the work in the Lord's vineyard. It will form part of a programme I am designing for the little flock. Remember, whatever you do for these little ones you will have done it for me."

"Er, prophet, I don't know if this can be done. But I will think about it."

"That alone is enough. I thank you in the name of the Lord."

Atonsu led the prophet to the main gate where he hailed a taxi for him. The prophet shook his hand, thanked him again and left in the taxi. The policeman watched the taxi until it disappeared in a bend in the road. Then he walked back to the station slowly, deep in thought.

Just after the court session, Bansa sent Johnny to Inspector Dongor.

"Leave the suspect here and go," Dongor said.

"Yes, sir," Bansa said and left the room.

Inspector Dongor continued to tap his pen on the table for a while after Sergeant Bansa had left the room. Then he looked up slowly in the direction of Johnny who stood to one side in the office, his hands held behind him by the handcuffs.

"What is your name?" the inspector asked.

"Johnny," Johnny replied wondering how many times he would have to recite his name to the police.

"Johnny what?"

"Klevor."

"Johnny Klevor," Dongor repeated slowly. "Do you know why you are here?"

"In this office?" Johnny asked.

"No, I mean the police station."

"They say I killed my father."

"And you don't think you killed him?"

"No, I didn't do it."

"Everybody including your relatives are saying you killed him."

Johnny shook his head in confusion. "I didn't do it. I don't remember anything of the sort." Tears began to creep into his voice again. "Why is everybody doing this to me? If I should be called a murderer it will not be for my father."

"Then for whom will it be?"

"I have been saying this over and over again but nobody wants to believe me. I took part in killing some people but not my father. The ghost of one of these people has been tormenting me in the stomach. When the pains come I don't remember anything. I think that is what is wrong with me. That is why people think I am mad."

"How many people did you kill?"

"I think four."

"You think?"

"We threw one into the sea. I don't know if she died or not."

"What are the names of the people you killed?"

"I don't know their names."

"You don't know their names?"

"No, I don't."

Dongor took a deep breath. "Do you realise the import of what you are saying, young man?"

"Yes, I want to confess so that I can be free."

"Where are the bodies of the people you killed?"

"I can't show you now, but later on I will be able to show you the spots where we buried them."

"Are you prepared to repeat all that you have said in court?"

"Yes."

"And if I bring somebody in now you will repeat exactly what you have told me?"

"Yes."

"Who were your accomplices?"

"Two of them are dead. They were struck down by thunder."

"Where?"

"At Woe."

"You mean the two men who died recently?"

"Yes."

Dongor whistled. He rang the buzzer on his desk and

his messenger entered almost immediately.

"Call me Detective Sergeant Amlima."

Sergeant Hilarious Amlima was one of the three detectives at the station and Dongor had decided to assign him to this case. It was always difficult placing two policemen of the same rank on a case, especially if one of them was to play the leadership role. But if Dongor knew Amlima, he was sure the detective would not have any trouble getting the over-zealous Bansa to submit to his authority. If Bansa proved uncontrollable he would simply remove him from the case. He had a hunch this was going to be an important case; he would not entrust it to anybody but the man he considered his best detective.

CHAPTER NINE

Three days after Ablator and her father-in-law had gone to *Hunɔ* Dunyo to announce Nani's decision to offer himself for initiation, Ablator received her first love emissary from *Hunɔ* Dunyo. The emissary who bore a panful of fresh fish told Ablator, "*Hunɔ* Dunyo sends you this fish to enrich your soup tonight, even though he will not be there to enjoy it with you." He was a little man of indeterminable age with receding hair which had been dyed to conceal the greys. Seen from afar, he looked like a teenager. He was called Atuklui, a nickname that depicted his small stature.

Ablator's first thought was to return the fish to Dunyo but on second thought she accepted it. "Tell *Hunɔ* Dunyo I am grateful," she told the emissary.

She poured the fish into a basket and gave the pan to the messenger who asked, with a twinkle in his eyes, "Do you wish me to tell *Hunɔ* Dunyo anything else?"

"What more do I have to tell him?" Ablator snapped. "Just send him my thanks."

"That is okay, that is okay," said Atuklui. At the gate he looked back and winked at Ablator before going out of the house.

Ablator pretended not to see the wink. "The big-headed he-goat!" she said not referring to the emissary but to *Hunɔ* Dunyo. She was half-annoyed, half-amused. Since the day Dunyo complemented her on her beauty, she had thought about the man a few times, wondering if he was entertaining any thoughts of adding her to his many wives. The panful of fish confirmed her suspicions. This man has no shame, she thought. I have just been

112

widowed and already he has amorous intentions towards me!

That evening when they sat down to eat, Nani asked his daughters-in-law, "Did any of you go to the beach today?"

"Yes," Ablator replied quickly.

Lucy looked at her in surprise but said nothing. Ablator had told her the source of the fish and after the meal, she took her aside and asked, "Why did you tell the old man a lie?"

"He will not be happy if I tell him the fish is from Hunɔ Dunyo. In the present circumstances I think he will be upset."

Lucy's stare lingered on Ablator for a while. "I hope you know what you are doing," she said.

Ablator patted her on the shoulder. "There is no cause for alarm."

Life in Nani's household was becoming more and more difficult since the demise of the principal breadwinners of the family. The petty trading that Ablator and Lucy did brought in little income. Ablator had two children and Lucy had three. Four of these children went to school and soon it would be time again to pay their terminal school fees.

There was also the forthcoming funeral of Granny to think about. Even though Nani had provided some money for the initial preparations, Ablator and Lucy knew more money would be required. The little trading capital the two women had was fast dwindling into the effort of sustaining the besieged household.

Hunɔ Dunyo's emissary brought another panful of fish the following day. "Please give me a seat to sit down for a while," Atuklui told Ablator after he had given her

113

the fish. "I am so tired."

Ablator looked at him suspiciously but gave him the seat. The man also asked for a cup of water. Ablator set down the pan of fish and went to get the water. Lucy watched from a distance, the whole scenario appearing to her like a well-rehearsed drama. It was so plain that Atuklui was going to act as the matchmaker. Lucy hoped it was obvious to Ablator herself.

As she came back with the water, Atuklui said, "You are a lucky woman."

"What do you mean by that?" Ablator asked.

The messenger collected the water and drank it with relish before replying, "*Hunɔ* Dunyo does not easily give out gifts. He must think very highly of you. He is a very rich man, in fact, richer than most people in this town I know. But when it comes to giving out gifts he is as dry as a patch of desert land. However, once he opens his heart and gives somebody a gift then that person must have left a very good impression on him. And the person must count herself lucky because the first gift is the beginning of greater things to come. That is why I said you are a lucky woman."

"I see," Ablator said, looking pensively at the little man.

"Let's hope," Atuklui said, "that *Hunɔ* Dunyo's gifts increase in worth. After all what will anyone do with pans of fish? Anybody can go to the beach and get fish. Let us hope he gives you more substantial gifts. Sometimes when you are unlucky *Hunɔ* Dunyo's gifts stop at just these — panfuls of fish. But I think your case is different. From the way his eyes twinkle when he is sending me to you, I know surely that there is more to it. So you keep your fingers crossed. Life is so hard these days and

114

anybody who offers to help anyone should be seen as an angel."

Ablator stared blankly at the little man, refusing to speak.

Atuklui stood up with a flourish. "Well, I must be going," he said.

"Good-bye," Ablator said simply.

He looked at her inquiringly. "No messages?"

"No, no messages."

He began to walk towards the gate, then he came to a stop and went back to Ablator. Whispering conspiratorially, he said, "Show some interest, woman, show some interest. I know what I am talking about. *Huno* Dunyo has been known to make gifts of as much as five hundred thousand cedis!"

"What has that got to do with me?" Ablator asked.

"It could be you! You could be the lucky recipient of such an amount!" The little man inched closer to Ablator. "What should I tell *Huno* Dunyo when I go back? You have to say something. That will urge him on."

"Tell him I am grateful for his kindness."

"Good. That is enough, for now. You will see what I am talking about."

Ablator looked in the direction of Lucy to see if she was watching. Lucy who was looking on from her door quickly entered her apartment and closed the door.

"Good-bye, *Davi* Ablator," Atuklui said and hurried out of the house.

Atuklui had already made several love matches for *Huno* Dunyo. Apart from one instance when one woman literally threw him out of her house, he always succeeded in bringing the women to his master's bed. He was sure Ablator would also succumb. If he could trust his sixth sense, then he could say with certainty that the woman was in financial difficulties. He would have to impress this on Dunyo so that the man would delve deeper into his pocket. When Dunyo gave him money for his women, Atuklui always delivered less than the amounts to the women. He called the shortfalls his commission. Dunyo pretended not to be aware of this underhand dealing; once he got his women he was satisfied.

When he visited Ablator again, this time with sachets of rice and sugar, she told him, "Please don't come here anymore. My mother-in-law's funeral is starting tomorrow. When the funeral starts I will not give thought to anything else."

"That is all right," Atuklui said. "I understand your point. Does *Huno* Dunyo know about the funeral arrangements?"

"I don't think so."

"Oh, I will tell him!"

"You don't have to. He doesn't need to know. After all, what part has he got to play in my mother-in-law's funeral?"

"You don't know what you are talking about," Atuklui said, feigning incredulity. "*Huno* Dunyo will never forgive me if I don't tell him about the funeral. You may not know, but he now considers everything that concerns you as his business. I will go right now and tell him. And please, please, don't hesitate to let him know through me if you face any difficulty."

"Okay," Ablator said lamely. As she watched Atuklui walk away, the thought began to form on her mind — is it possible to escape the sentence of the *Yeve* cult through the influence of Dunyo?

116

*** *** ***

The funeral for Ablator's mother-in-law was without pomp and pageantry. She belonged to the Baté clan. When her body was collected from the mortuary, selected members of the Baté clan bathed her with soap and sponge. The soap and sponge together with the towel used in wiping her dry would be buried with her to signal a final parting between her and the clan.

Not many people attended Afiyo's funeral. However, there were many unusual sympathizers; some of them had come out of curiosity to witness the burial of the woman whose sons had been killed by thunder. Others came for other reasons. One of the latter was Hunɔ Dunyo. He sat among the elders of the family and was very eager to offer help. Not many took notice of Dunyo's solicitousness; those who did, took it to be out of sympathy for the plight of the family. Only Ablator and Lucy and Dunyo himself knew the reason for his zeal to be of assistance.

An all-night wake was kept and the following day after mourners had filed past Afiyo's body to pay their last respects, members of the Baté clan put the body into the coffin. They placed in the coffin the sponge, soap and towel used in her last bath, and some money tied in a piece of cloth for her to use to pay the fare when Kutsiami ferried her across the river on her journey to the abode of departed souls. A length of rafia palm was tied around her forehead with the shreds covering her face. Members of the clan also wore these rafia fronds around their foreheads to accompany the body to the cemetery.

After the burial, Atuklui took Ablator aside. Once again, he expressed his condolences, then looking around to make sure nobody was watching them, he dipped his

117

hand in the folds of his cloth and brought out a parcel wrapped up in old newsprint. "This is eighty thousand cedis," he said. "It is from my boss. He says it is just to meet your immediate expenses. He expects you to give him a final account of all your expenses so that he can reimburse you."

Ablator took the parcel immediately, more out of her anxiety not to let people see what was going on than her readiness to accept the gift. "What is wrong with you people?" she asked with annoyance. "Can't you see I am bereaved on all sides? Go and tell your master Dunyo that he should at least allow me to go through my widowhood rites before he starts including me in his plans!"

Atuklui watched her walk away, a smile on his face. Poor woman, he thought.

***   ***   ***

In the evening, after the burial of Afiyo, Nani was summoned to a meeting by three elders of his family. Adekpitor, one of the elders, was a wealthy transport owner. He acted as the head of Nani's large family, but the trademark of his leadership was that when it came to money he distanced himself from the affairs of the family; otherwise he was very prominent at family meetings and always wanted his voice to carry the day. When anyone called him a miser to the face he replied he was not appointed the head of the family to spend his money on them.

The other elders at the meeting were Adzibolo and Bodza. Nani went to the meeting with Ablator who was now effectively his aide-de-camp. The meeting was held in Adzibolo's house. Even though Adekpitor had a big spacious house he never allowed family meetings to be held there. Some said it was because he feared he might be called upon as host to provide refreshment for the meetings.

After the exchange of greetings Adekpitor turned to Bodza, the youngest among the men present, and said, "My brother Bodza, tell our brother Nani and his daughter-in-law that they are welcome. We have not called them for evil but for the good of the family. Before the funeral of our Sister Afiyo who was our brother Nani's wife, some news came to the ears of us the elders of the family. This news left us greatly surprised and confused. We heard that our brother Nani here had gone to the Yeʋe cult and offered himself to be initiated to atone for the death of his sons. Now, we the elders think such an issue was a very weighty one and if our brother had come to such a decision he should have informed the elders of the family so that together we could see what best could be done. The conduct of our brother constitutes disrespect for the family and a declaration that he does not need the support of the family. But just as you don't slice away the skin of your thigh when your child defecates on it, we have called our brother this evening to hear what he has to say."

Adekpitor sat back and readjusted his big cloth. Bodza cleared his throat and said, "Our brother Nani, I hope you heard our elder brother. He has expressed the sentiments of the family and says if you have anything to say let's hear it."

"Tell him I have heard everything," Nani said, his voice a little agitated. "I thank him for the concern he has expressed for my welfare. But I also want to tell him that one knows one's true friends and well-wishers best in one's time of difficulty. Friendship and family ties are for

119

both sunny and rainy days. When you are attacked by a rat and your companion runs away from you, when next time you come across a lion you don't even bother to let him know about it."

Nani paused and pulled himself forward on his chair to get closer to Adekpitor. "The experiences I went through when my two sons suddenly died showed me that I have a fair-weather family. Let me ask you this: since my sons died how many of you have been to my house to sympathise with me? How many of you? And those of you who did were there only once. You have amply demonstrated to me that our family abhors trouble and when any of its members is in trouble the others leave him to his fate. There are some of you who take different routes when they come across me just to avoid meeting me! This is not the type of family that I should take my troubles to! Tell our brother Adekpitor that!"

For a brief moment there was silence. Bodza cleared his throat again and said, "My brothers, you have heard Nani. He says our behaviour has made him feel he is not part of the family."

Adekpitor was immediately conciliatory. "Tell our brother Nani that we have heard all that he said. Let him not turn his grievances into salt that will hurt his heart. The way he put it I think we the family are in the wrong. I, for example, think when his children died I went to his house only once even though during his wife's funeral I had been there numerous times. He shouldn't take the family's attitude to mean disinterest in his welfare. We cannot see him going down in quicksand and turn our backs on him. We will throw him ropes, wooden boards, anything, and if possible follow him into the quicksand to pull him out. In short, I want our brother Nani to forget all his grudge against the family. In the name of the family, I apologise for any behaviour from any family member that seemed to show disinterest in his affairs. What I want us to do now is to address what happens from now on. Tell him that."

"I have heard him," Nani replied after Bodza had conveyed Adekpitor's message to him. "Tell our elder brother that a grudge harboured for long is a slow poison that eats away the heart. Whatever assistance the family is ready to offer me will not be turned down. I am ready to forget about everything not because of your offer of assistance but because you have been brave enough to accept your fault and apologise."

Adekpitor heaved a sigh of relief. "We thank you for your words," he said. "Does anybody have anything else to say?"

Adzibolo was a stammerer. "I-I-I am al-al-also gra-gra-gratefu-ful for the amicable way we have resolved the issue," he said. "Le-Le-Let Nani tell us now what he intends to do, then we can pool our resources together to help him."

There was the sharp scream of a child from outside cutting Adzibolo's jerky speech short.

"What is that?" Ablator asked, her motherly instincts aroused.

"Do-Do-Don't mind those children," Adzibolo said. "Sometimes they can make your heart drop into your stomach in fright from the way they shout when they play."

"My brother Bodza," said Nani, "tell our elders that I am grateful for their offer of help. As our elder brother Adekpitor stated from the beginning of this meeting, I have offered myself to be initiated into the *Yeve* cult.

Then there are the items I must provide for the initiation."

"What are they?"

"They said I have to provide one jerrycan of akpeteshie, corn flour, seven white hens, seven black hens, white cloth and one million cedis cash."

Adekpitor whistled. "That is a lot of money," he said. "And what did you tell them?"

"I told them I could provide the items but the money will be a problem for me. They told me I can start with the initiation; the money can be paid in instalments whilst I am undergoing initiation."

"Didn't they object to your advanced age?"

"No, no mention was made of that."

"The-the pa-pa-payment by insta-ta-talments is acceptable," Adzibolo said, "but how fast we can pay is the problem. I know of people who have been in initiation for several years now not because they are dumb but because they can't find money to complete the instalment payments."

Adekpitor patted Adzibolo reassuringly on the shoulder. "A journey of a thousand miles begins with a step. Let us start the initiation and we will see where things move on from there."

Bodza eyed Adekpitor inquiringly and said, "Let us get everything straight. Will all of us gathered here now be ready to make contributions in cash towards Nani's initiation?"

"Yes, of course," Adekpitor replied.

The others looked at each other, their surprise at Adekpitor's unexpected offer of financial assistance ill-concealed. The reason for Adekpitor's sudden generosity was Ablator. He had realised with a jolt during Afiyo's

122

funeral that Ablator was a very attractive woman. At the meeting he kept taking furtive glances at her and part of his mind was working feverishly on a scheme to woo her. His first shot was his offer of financial assistance to the woman's father-in-law. Though she was younger than some of his own children, Adekpitor believed that the younger a person's spouse was, the longer one lived. He had other wives but polygamy was a norm in the community.

"When are you going to start the initiation?" Bodza asked, not quite having overcome his surprise at Adekpitor's generosity.

"On Friday, at midnight," Nani replied.

"Is it not too soon?"

"No, I am ready for it."

"Have you got all the items ready?" Adekpitor asked and everybody looked at him again in renewed surprise.

"With the exception of the white cloth, everything is ready. I will buy the white cloth on market day."

"Please keep us informed," said Adekpitor. "You don't just walk into a *Yeve* shrine to get initiated. Your family must hand you over to the shrine."

On their way home, Ablator asked Nani, "Do you think Adekpitor's offer to help is genuine?"

"I have my doubts too," Nani said, "but I am tempted to believe him. Since I have known him he has never so readily offered financial assistance."

***   ***   ***

Though Nani kept an outward appearance of calm, his heart knew no peace. He was filled with disquiet about the prospect of his initiation. Friday arrived faster than he would have wished. Much to his displeasure, the moon was high up and very bright in the night when he was to be taken to the shrine. He had hoped he could be sneaked into the *Yeve* shrine without anybody seeing him. But he consoled himself that no-one was likely to be about at midnight when he would be taken to the shrine. Adekpitor and Bodza had offered to take him to the shrine. They came to his house just before midnight. The fourteen fowls were already in a raffia cage. Ablator set this on her head while the feathered inmates of the cage cackled uneasily in their sleep. Bodza carried the jerry-can of local gin and Adekpitor picked up the bundle containing corn flour and the white cloth.

"Let's go," Nani said bravely, the magnitude of his decision threatening to weigh him down. Tears were not far from his eyes. He hated with his whole heart the loss of personal freedom that he was about to suffer.

They went out of the house quietly, careful not to wake the children who had long gone to bed. Lucy who was also up, but had been told to stay behind to keep watch over the house, embraced her father-in-law quickly and went back to her apartment crying.

To Nani's relief, the party met no-one on the way. When they reached the shrine the whole courtyard was deserted. There was no light in the courtyard but the moon illuminated the place in a soft light giving the gaudy pictures on the walls of the compound an eerie life-like appearance. They walked to the door of the shrine, each of the men afraid that the others might hear the heavy beat of his heart and term him a coward.

Adekpitor knocked on the shrine door and it was immediately opened by a man clad in a loin cloth. He must have been waiting behind the door. The man checked to see that none of them were wearing either footwear or top garments. He motioned them into the shrine and closed the door. He led them into a room and again with motions that told them to sit down. A small hurricane lamp burned in the room. He went out and when he came back he was accompanied by a frail old man.

"You are welcome," the old man said, and without any formalities continued, "Now that you have brought the subject here, you don't need to tarry anymore. Your task is done. You can leave. We will see to everything." He went out as silently as he had come.

The other man motioned the party to their feet. Nani remained seated and as his family left the room, he felt like the gates of hell were closing on him. At the shrine door, the man tapped Ablator on the shoulder and said, "You will have to be bringing him food every day. We don't feed people here." It was then that she recognised the man. He was *Katidao*, one of the feared men of the cult.

Ablator shuddered as she replied, "Yes, please." They went away with heavy hearts; even Adekpitor sighed from time to time.

The men took Ablator to her house before leaving for their separate homes.

Lucy was at her door waiting for Ablator. "How did it go?" she asked.

"They have taken him," Ablator said.

Lucy followed Ablator to her apartment and together they wept silently till day broke.

***   ***   ***

Nani's initiation started that very night. As soon as his family left, he was led to a small inner compound in the shrine where four men including the frail old man

125

were seated, all wearing loin cloths. The fowls, the corn floor and akpeteshie were brought to the small compound and the initiation rites began.

There are three arms to the *Yeve* cult — the *Avleketi,* the *Vodu Da* and the *So.* The arm of the cult which you join is determined by the circumstances through which you are initiated. The *Avleketi* perpetuate their membership through reincarnation. When a child is born and an oracle is consulted and it says the child is the reincarnation of an *Avleketi* the child is initiated into the cult to become an *Avleketi.* If the parents of the child refuse to give up their child to the cult, the child will be continuously tormented by illness and other misfortunes.

The *Dashi,* the initiates of *Vodu Da,* usually enter the cult through illness. If an oracle is consulted to find out the reason for the illness of an individual who is continuously ill, and the oracle says it is the *Yeve* cult courting the individual, the individual is initiated to become a *Dashi.* The chronic illness will go away after the initiation.

The *Soshi* belong to the arm of *So.* This arm of the cult draws its membership from the exploits of the thunder god, *Torhonor,* otherwise known as *Xebieso.* They are the most feared arm of the cult. One can be initiated to become a *Soshi* if one is struck down by thunder but not killed. Like Nani, one can also be initiated to become a *Soshi* to atone for the wrong done by a member of one's family who has earlier offended the thunder god and is struck dead by thunder.

When people are initiated they take cult names and are no longer known by their former names. Anyone who calls them by their former names commits an offence against the cult. In that case the initiate becomes possessed and would flee into the bush and roam about covered with leaves. It will now be the duty of the offender to bring in the possessed initiate through paying a fine and buying several items for cleansing rites. The names of the initiates depend on which arm of the cult they belong to.

Unknown to Nani, a new name had already been chosen for him — he would be called Hutorwohoe. Katidao was among the four men waiting for Nani. They were seated under a mango tree whose shadow and the shadows of the surrounding walls blocked out much of the light of the moon from the small compound. The men around Nani spoke in a language not alien to Nani but he could not understand them. This was the language of the *Yeve* cult known only to the members.

"*Wotemehe*," said Katidao, motioning Nani to come forward. He was by his title the disciplinarian of the cult. When a member of the cult misbehaved and was found guilty by a panel of cult members, it was the Katidao who inflicts the punishment, usually by caning or tying up the offender and leaving him in the sun for a length of time.

"*Zhɔkli*," Katidao said again, gesturing to Nani to go on his knees. Nani knelt down. One of the other men stepped forward with a razor in his hand and proceeded to shave his head clean.

Then a gong began to sound, *tin gón...tin gon... tin gon...* It was accompanied by the sound of a drum, the *wudi*. When the barber finished shaving Nani, he set aside the razor and then opened the cage where the hens and cocks were nestling. He brought out two fowls, one black, the other white. Another man brought out a coalpot and set a fire. The necks of the two fowls were slit open and it was only then that Nani saw the idols at the foot of the young mango tree. He could count about five of them. The blood from the slaughtered fowls was allowed to flow into a basin.

The old frail man stood up from his stool. "*Tukpayidakpa,*" he said, invoking the spirits, "*ewude kpɔtɔ de, anyrakɔtowotɔ...*" He dipped his hand into the fresh blood several times, touching the mouth of each idol with the blood.

To Nani's consternation, the men set upon the dead fowls and without dipping the fowls in hot water, plucked the two birds clean. The fire in the coalpot was already burning bright red. The two fowls were held over the fire and the rest of their feathers were singed. Two big bowls were brought out and one fowl placed in each of them. Then some corn floor was poured into the bowls. With their bare hands, two men started mashing the fowls and the corn floor together. Into one bowl was poured some red oil but no oil was added to the other. The two bowls were placed before Katidao who mashed the contents again, then took the bowls to the idols. He took some amount of mixture from each bowl, counted one up to seven, then touched the mixtures to the lip of each idol. He turned next to Nani who was still on his knees, eyes shining bright in the soft moonlight. The Katidao counted one up to seven again and touched the mixtures, to the lips of Nani. This was the ceremony of *vevenyanya*. A cock's crow sounded from somewhere in town, breaking the silence of the night.

"From this time onward," the Katidao said, "you will no more eat the fish barracuda or the mud fish. They are taboo to you. When you eat them you will have offended Hebieso and the punishment will be severe."

Nani nodded in silence. He didn't know if he was

128

supposed to speak. The two bowls were placed aside and two more fowls, one black and one white, were brought out of the cage. To Nani's alarm, the first fowl was held over his head and its throat slit. Blood sputtered onto his shaven head and dribbled over his face and chest. He closed his mouth and eyes tight to keep out the fresh blood. The second fowl was also slaughtered over his head. Nani had never felt so helpless in his life. One of the men, the old frail man, helped Nani to his feet. He led him into an enclosure where there were several pots containing water and various herbs.

"*Esru, hade ni azu zangɔ,*" the old men said, gesturing that Nani should take off his loin cloth.

Nani obeyed the instructions without objection and stood before the man in only his underpants. With the help of the herbs, the old man bathed him from head to toe with the cold water from the pots. Nani started shivering. The man towelled him dry and led him outside. To Nani's surprise the other men were nowhere to be found. He looked into the shadows expecting them to be there but there was no sign of them. The old man took him to a room where there was a single spring bed with a thin mattress.

"This will be your room during your initiation," he said. "The first part of your initiation will be for ten days. During this time we will teach you the cult language, our dances and songs, our signs and the do's and don'ts of the cult. You must be very attentive and learn quickly otherwise you will spend a lot of time here. From now onwards everybody will speak to you only in the cult language. This is to help you learn fast. For these ten days you are not to come out of this room during the day. You can only come out during the night." Without waiting for a response from Nani, the old man went out of the room and silently closed the door.

Dawn was breaking fast and already Nani could hear the movement of people in the compound outside. He sat on the bed, not quite certain whether he should lie down and get some sleep. He had not slept a wink the whole night and his head felt heavy. He looked up when the door opened and a woman entered the room. A cult song was on her lips.

"Gɔni," she said as she paused in her song. She drew out the single stool in the room and sat down. Then she broke into song again.

> Daŋgoe lee, enu ya newɔa,
> Enua menyo o.
> Menye woŋtɔe tso vodu Xebieso
> De fefe me aheviwo nɔa kokom o ha?
> Daŋgoe fe kuyie ɖo vɔ.
> Guda, atsiawo blee,
> Be aho dzɔ lo!
> Amla mee ye wole,
> Daŋgoe va dzo...

Line by line, the woman started teaching Nani his first cult song.

When the sun finally rose from the eastern horizon, bathing the land in its brilliant light, the bodies of Gbagbladza and Besa were no longer on the shed near the lagoon. They had been buried in the night by people from the shrine and their belongings carted to no-one-knows-where.

CHAPTER TEN

Between threats, some rough handling and empty promises of non-prosecution, Johnny finally agreed to show the police where he and his cronies had buried the victims of their ritual murders. That night a police vehicle left the police station and sped towards Abutiakope. In it were three policemen — Sergeants Amlima and Bansa and Corporal Ahedor with Constable Atonsu at the steering wheel Johnny who was in handcuffs was also in the vehicle. The vehicle picked up three workers of the Environmental Health Office, then took one of the side roads leading to the beach. It was about 11.00 p.m. and pitch dark and as the headlights of the police vehicle swung over the houses and trees lining the road, many people could still be seen moving about town. It was a Friday night, the night wake was kept for dead bodies which were to be buried the following day, Saturday. The people of this locality buried their dead on Saturdays mostly and on the preceding Friday night wake was kept for each dead person with drumming and dancing, and if the person was a Christian, with church services.

Sergeant Hilarious Amlima was a native of this area and if anyone should be known by the name Hilarious, it shouldn't be him. He always wore a serious countenance and rarely showed his teeth in a smile. The most that he did in his moments of pleasure or mirth was a slight lift of the right side of his lips. He was called "Stone Face" to his back. He was knock-kneed but was endowed with impressive agility. He was a karate expert and held a brown belt.

When he was first posted to Keta, the District

Commander of Police looked through his personal details and told him, "You will be organising karate lessons for all staff from sergeant downwards. Fix your own time and schedule and report to me."

"Yes, sir," Amlima had responded in silent pleasure. But the lukewarm response of the policemen disappointed him and three months later the idea of karate lessons was buried.

Amlima had wide nostrils but otherwise his face was pleasant. When Inspector Dongor had called him in to listen to Johnny's story, he had listened with horror as the young man told of the gruesome murders he said he had taken part in. When Johnny had finished speaking, Inspector Dongor said, "Sergeant Amlima, you are now in charge of this case. Take over from Sergeant Bansa but involve him in the investigation."

They were now heading for the beach to investigate one of the spots where Johnny said the dead people had been buried. The Keta Police had requested national headquarters to send a pathologist to be present at the exhumation, but no pathologist was readily available. To prevent anybody from tampering with the burial spots, the Police had been instructed to exhume the bodies and keep them at the mortuary until a pathologist arrived.

Private Atonsu under the direction of Johnny brought the vehicle to a halt on the edge of the sandy beach at Abutiakope. He engaged auxiliary gear and the sound of the vehicle went up as it started ploughing through the sand.

Sergeant Amlima, who was in the front passenger seat, turned to the back of the vehicle and asked, "Where is the place?"

"Let's go right," Johnny replied in a small voice from

132

the back of the vehicle. He was sandwiched between Sergeant Bansa and Corporal Ahedor.

The vehicle inched along, its headlights sweeping the beach and blinding the nocturnal crabs until Johnny said, "Let's stop here."

Sergeant Bansa jumped down and pulled Johnny after him. The other policemen and the Environmental workers also came down, bringing out with them two shovels and a cutlass. The policemen had their pistols drawn.

"Right, show the spot," Sergeant Amlima said, switching on a powerful torchlight.

With Bansa's hand clutching his arm, Johnny led the team to a mashy area on the beach. The place was overgrown with reeds. The men made their way through the tall reeds until Johnny said, "Here."

Sergeant Amlima moved forward and flashed the torchlight over the spot Johnny was pointing at. The reeds covering this spot were lying on their side and were withered. The young grass growing to replace the dead reeds were not yet up to knee level.

"Our friends from the Environmental Office," Amlima said, "let's get to work." Two of the Environmental workers started to dig with the shovels. The ground was soft and required little effort to turn it up. The men dug carefully, shovelling out the soft soil. It didn't take long when they struck a solid material in the sand.

"We have hit something," one of the Environmental men said.

"Bring it up," said Amlima.

The two diggers carefully eased their shovels beneath a big dark object and heaved it up. It was a bulging fibre sack. A putrid scent instantly flooded the area and the diggers and the policemen turned away from the hole, holding their noses. Amlima removed a handkerchief from his pocket and covered his nose. They lifted the sack and put it at the side of the hole. Then they undid the mouth of the sack and when Amlima shone his torchlight inside, all the men except Johnny craned their necks forward to see what was inside. What they saw made them back away, muttering, "Oh, oh, oh..." Crumpled in the sack with the hair still intact on its head was the body of a dead man.

"How many people are in the sack?" Amlima asked, turning to Johnny.

"Only one," Johnny replied, backing away.

"Jesus! You know the spots where the others too were buried?"

"Yes."

"The jobs that we have to do!" Bansa said.

"You don't have to complain," said Amlima.

The dead body was deposited at the Keta Hospital Mortuary that night, then the policemen took the Environmental Health workers home and returned to their barracks.

***   ***   ***

Many fishermen along the Keta-Anloga littoral had their houses fronting the sea. Mostly, these houses were built with make-shift materials and the fishermen, after the main fishing season, retired to their permanent homes in town. However, as the years went by some of these fishermen turned their temporary homes into permanent ones and built them with longer lasting building materials. One of these houses belonged to Komi

Tsormanya. It was a sprawling house, the biggest along the beach. It was built of bricks and terrazoed, with asbestos roofing.

Komi Tsormanya lived at Woe and was reputed to be the richest man in the town. He had several apartments in the house which he shared among his numerous wives and their children. There was no knowing the exact number of his wives because the women came and went at his pleasure. Those who had attained some permanency in the house were his favourites or the stubborn types who would not go easily when the man of the house had grown tired of them and no longer enjoyed their company; they were the types who would not leave the house even if Tsormanya were to employ bulldozers to pull them out.

Tsormanya had so many children that he had even lost count of them. Some he did not even know, especially those whose mothers left with them in their infancy and he had not seen since. His prayer was that he wouldn't in his numerous travels cohabit with any of them unknowingly. Many of Tsormanya's children did not go to school, the boys took to sea and the girls took up the trade of their mothers — smoking the catch and selling it in the market.

Tsormanya had several houses in the town and others in faraway places like Ho, Accra and Takoradi. He even had houses in the Republic of Togo and Nigeria which he rented out to tenants. It was rumoured he was so rich that he did not even bother to collect the rent from his tenants. As was usual with successful individuals, Tsormanya had his detractors some of whom claimed the source of his wealth was linked to supernatural powers. It was true Tsormanya had a few idols, some housed on the beach, but every fisherman worth his salt had idols. Still the rumours persisted, some saying Tsormanyo made annual sacrifices of human beings to his idols.

Tsormanya was a very skilful fisherman. He knew the sea intimately and could read the currents and the movement of fish like a soothsayer. Unlike most net-owners who stayed on land while their employee-fishermen went to sea, Tsormanya preferred to be out at sea when the nets were cast. Thus on days when other fishermen had very little catch, Tsormanya's nets could be bursting at the seams with fish, further fuelling the rumour that he had supernatural powers.

Tsormanya ran his fishing company like a private army. Before one joined his company one must attend an interview and satisfy certain criteria. His men were loyal to him because he took an interest in their welfare. He gave out soft loans in cash and in kind which they paid back from their earnings. He divided his workforce into gangs with leaders whom he held responsible for any shortfall in the gang. He paid the leaders higher wages and held regular meetings with them. It was just after one of such meetings late in the evening that Tsormanya received some unusual visitors.

"Tell them to wait," he told the child who came to tell him some people were looking for him.

When his men had gone, he came to the door and saw four men sitting on a bench in the compound. Most visitors invariably came to ask for loans and he was sure this was just another bunch.

"Please, come in," he called to the men and went back to the room.

The men followed him to the room and he offered them seats. "You are welcome," he told them.

"Thank you," the men said.

Unknown to Tsormanya, they were plain-clothes policemen from the Keta Police Station. The man leading them was Detective Sergeant Amlima. During interrogation, Johnny had mentioned several people as being involved in the killings he had confessed to. Tsormanya was one of them. Another one was Kofi Legede, a lad who also lived at Woe.

However, the plain-clothes policemen did not deceive Leve Akpai, Tsormanya's boatswain, called simply *Bozua* by the fishermen. Leve was a member of the inner core team who had just dispersed from a meeting with Tsormanya. As he and his colleagues walked away, he came to a sudden stop, taking hold of the two men nearest him by the shoulders.

"Wait a minute," he said. "Are those not policemen? I think I recognise one of them... I smell trouble. Let's wait and see what they want with our boss. He may need our help."

Leve Akpai was a short stocky fellow with a short fuse to his temper. He had been with Tsormanya's company for as long as the company existed. He was very loyal to Tsormanya and the latter had complete trust in him. The workers feared Leve. He could behave very brutally when he chose to and when he was in a rage it was only Tsormanya who could restrain him.

Leve and four of his men went and sat down on the bench just vacated by Sergeant Amlima and his team. His ears were primed for the least sound from Tsormanya's room even though he could not hear anything. His sixth sense told him the visit of the policemen portended trouble. Policemen did not normally visit the house of Tsormanya. Those that visited him went to his nets on the beach from where they normally came away with gifts of fish.

Unmindful of the drama unfolding around them, Tsormanya's household went about their evening chores with gusto. Mothers called to their children to hurry up with the preparations for the evening meal. Babies wailed and the smaller children performed the last stages of their daily games. From the midst of this commotion came the deep sound of a heavy hand landing on a bare back. Even the men on the bench winced as they looked in the direction of the woman who had just hit her child as if the child knew no pain. The child fled away screaming, her shoulders bent back and her hands fluttering like the wings of a small bird.

"If my wife hit my child like that I would kill her!" Leve said not too quietly.

The others murmured their assent and continued to watch the door of Tsormanya's room with unconcealed anxiety. When the shuffling of feet sounded in the room, Leve and his men stood up. They watched as Tsormanya came out first followed closely by the policemen. Fear showed clearly in Tsormanya's eyes and he seemed a little relieved when he saw his men outside.

Leve picked up an old paddle lying in the sand and moved forward with his men towards the policemen. In the fishing community incidents of brutality against the police were not uncommon. There was menace in Leve's voice as he said, "Boss, what is the matter?"

"Er-er, no-nothing exactly," stammered Tsormanya who had never been known to hesitate in whatever he wanted to say. "These are policemen. They say I am wanted at the police station at Keta to answer a few questions."

"What questions?"

Tsormanya looked helplessly at the policemen whose faces remained expressionless. "They said they will tell me when we get to the police station."

"They can't do that," Leve growled, raising the paddle. "They first have to tell us why they are taking you away."

In a single motion, the hands of the policemen flew into their pockets to clutch the pistols that nestled there.

"It is okay," said Tsormanya. "Hold your temper. Let me go with them and hear whatever they have to say. If I am not back in time, come to the police station and check up."

"We will go with you," said Leve.

Sergeant Amlima spoke, his voice portraying a calmness that he did not feel. "The vehicle we brought is not big enough to take you."

"We will come to the station on our own," Leve said.

"That is fine with us," Amlima replied. "You can come to the station. We will overlook the fact that you threatened peace officers with an offensive weapon."

The police began to move, shepherding Tsormanya towards the gate. "Tell Dodziada," the fisherman said, "that I am gone to the police station and that I will be back soon." Dodziada, or Dodzi's mother, was Tsormanya's eldest wife. She was one of the few people that could stand up to him and over the years he had come to respect her for that.

Leve and his colleagues watched in helpless rage as their master was led out of the house and into the police vehicle. By now most of Tsormanya's big family in the house had noticed that something was amiss. They crowded around Leve and his men inquiring about what was happening.

"Master has gone to the police station," Leve told them. "The police want to ask him some questions."

"About what?" Dodziada asked, pushing her way to the fore of the crowd.

"I don't know," Leve replied. "He said I should tell you he would be back soon."

"Come on! What are you waiting for?" Dodziada asked. "Let's follow him to the police station."

"No," Leve said. "He said we should wait for some time and if he is not coming back then we can follow him to the station. We don't know why he said that, so let's wait."

Dodziada looked angrily at Leve. Between her and Leve was an unspoken rivalry for the attention of Tsormanya. She hated him for not limiting himself to the fishing company but also poking his nose into the family's affairs. She turned away and returned to her cooking.

Leve and his men left the house and with telepathic agreement they moved to a drinking bar nearby. They scarcely spoke, each of them silently analysing the possible reasons why their boss would be wanted by the police. When it was eight o'clock and Tsormanya had still not returned, Leve and his men set off for the police station. They went in Tsormanya's rickety pick-up vehicle. Leve marched to the charge office expecting to be accorded the same reverence he got from his men.

"Good evening," he said as the men who followed him lined up along the counter on either side of him.

"Good evening," replied the policeman on duty.

"Is Mr. Komi Tsormanya still here?" he asked.

"Who is Komi Tsormanya?"

"You don't know Tsormanya? Are you new in this town?"

"I have been at this station for nine good years," said the policeman, "and I know all the important men in this area, but not Tsormanya." This cop knew Tsormanya all right and was aware of his arrest, but Leve's air of self-importance irritated him.

"Then you are still a stranger," said Leve, turning to his men for confirmation. "Everybody in this area knows Komi Tsormanya."

"Well, I don't know him," the policeman said.

"Will you please find out if he is still here at the police station?"

"Er, let me see..." The policeman leafed through the station diary, his fingers going down the list of reported cases on that day. His finger stopped in the middle of the last page and he looked up. "Yes, Mr. Tsormanya is here. He has been detained."

"Detained? For what?" Leve was incredulous.

"I am not in a position to tell you. Maybe when you come back tomorrow you will hear something."

"No, this can't be," Leve said, turning to his men.

"No, it can't be," his men said in a chorus.

Leve turned back to the policeman. "I want to bail him."

"Sorry, you can't bail him. He is under detention."

Another policeman wandered into the charge office. "What do these people want?" he asked.

"They are Tsormanya's men."

"What do they want?"

"They say they want to bail him."

"Bail him? Maybe we should detain all of them."

"I think so too."

Leve's men drew away from the counter in a wave. Obviously they did not like the trend the policemen's thoughts were taking. From the corner of his eyes, Leve saw his men waver. He also took a step back and said, "Let's go. We'll be back tomorrow to bail him."

"Stop, don't go," said the second policeman. "We'll detain you too!"

Leve and his men left the charge office in indecent haste and the policemen broke into merry laughter. The fishermen piled into the pick-up and drove away.

*** *** ***

There was an old woman in the town of Woe who was often called a witch to her face. She was very advanced in years and had wrinkled skin. She walked with the help of a stick and never answered back her accusers who called her a witch. Fortunately for her, in this community witches were not burnt at the stake, neither were they sent to the forest to lead secluded lives.

Mama Kokui, for that was the old lady's name, lived with the son of her only daughter. Her grandson was called Kofi Legede, the second name not being a surname but an appellation testifying to Kofi's renown as the most dishonest character in the township. Kofi Legede was such a habitual liar he now lived in a state of permanent confusion, he himself not knowing when he was lying or telling the truth. Kofi was also a kleptomaniac. He did not break down doors or force windows open, but he readily helped himself to anything left unguarded. Once when Kofi was sent to the police station for stealing and was left on his own for a few minutes behind the counter, he stole a policeman's cap, his baton and a pair of handcuffs and vanished from the police station. He was eventually re-arrested and his mother had to come down from Accra to settle the fine imposed by the judge who tried him.

Kofi's mother sent him from Accra to come and live with his grandmother because he refused to continue schooling and was always getting into trouble. At first the old lady was at her wit's end how to contain Kofi's stealing habit. Eventually she hit upon a strategy — she converted most of her belongings into cash and never bought anything unless it was very necessary; she kept her money always on her body and when she went to bed at night, she tied up the money in a scarf and strapped it to her upper arm with the money resting in her armpit. Fortunately for her, she was a light sleeper and Kofi dared not touch her in her sleep, for at the least touch she would jump up from the bed and scratch him in the face. The simple explanation people had for Kofi's acute dishonesty was that the grandmother exchanged his good qualities for witchcraft.

Mama Kokui always went to bed early but her itinerant grandchild most often came in late. Tonight Kofi came home drunk and went to bed early. When the old lady was ready to go to bed too, she swung the main door shut and turned the key. But just as she was about to enter her bedroom, several knocks sounded on the door.

"Who is it?" she asked.

"Please open the door. We want to discuss something with you."

The old lady opened the door and held up her kerosene lantern to see who had business with her that night. The nocturnal callers were Sergeants Amlima and Bansa. Corporal Ahedor and Private Atonsu who were not in sight waited behind the house beneath the windows. They had just deposited Komi Tsormanya at the police station and were making their last foray into the town before retiring for the night.

"Can we come in, old lady?" Amlima asked.

"Er, well yes," the old lady said hesitantly.

She gave them low kitchen stools to sit on but remained standing herself. "What can I do for you?" she asked.

"We are looking for Kofi, Kofi Legede," Bansa replied.

"Kofi!" the old lady said, turning to the door behind which the young man slept. "Kofiii! Some people are looking for you."

There was the sound of grunts from Kofi's room, then his voice came, slurred, "Which people?"

"Come and see them."

The door opened and Kofi appeared in the doorway in his underpants. He was of medium build. His yes were drowsy and he hung to the doorpost as if for support. The eyes of the policemen swept to a large plaster on his forehead.

"What do you want?" he said. "Can I help you?"

"Yes," said Amlima. "We want to ask you a few questions."

"Then excuse me," Kofi said. "Let me put on something decent." He went back to the room and everybody waited. After about two minutes when he was still not coming out, Bansa asked "Has he gone back to bed?"

"Kofiii!" the old woman called. There was silence. Amlima and Bansa exchanged quick glances and stood up.

"Kofi," Amlima said as he entered the room followed closely by Bansa. The room was dark. Bansa removed a torchlight from his pocket and flashed it round the room.

The room was empty. He looked under the bed and behind the boxes stacked high against one wall but there was no sign of Kofi.

"Damn!" he swore.

"Ahedor, Atonsu!" shouted Amlima.

"Yes, sir," came the response from behind the windows.

"Did the suspect jump through the window?"

"No, sir."

"Are you sure?"

"Yes, sir."

"But he couldn't have vanished," Bansa said. He lifted the torchlight up and both men said in unison, "Ahaa...!"

There was no ceiling to the roof and it was obvious Kofi had made his escape through the roof.

"Could he be still up there?" Amlima asked.

"Wait here," Bansa said. He went outside and started going round the building, the torchlight and his eyes trained on the ground. Soon he came upon two deep footmarks in the wet sand. Other footmarks in the sand led away from the deep ones.

"The bastard jumped out here!" he said. He went back to the door. "Sergeant Amlima," he said, "it's no use. He has escaped through the roof. Let's go."

Amlima came out and they were joined by Ahedor and Atonsu. The old lady came to the door, her lantern in her hand.

"Old lady, we are sorry to have disturbed you," Amlima said. "Your son is wanted at the police station in connection with a case. He has escaped but we'll keep looking for him."

"When you find him," the old lady said, "don't let him

come back here." That morning Kofi had stolen and sold some cooking utensils and the last table in the house.

The policemen piled into their vehicle and drove off.

"You know what we are going to do now?" Amlima said, turning back in his seat to talk to the men at the back. "It is not yet late. Let's now go to the house where Johnny said thunder killed two of his accomplices. Let's question the relatives now instead of tomorrow. This is a good time to get them at home."

The rest of the men groaned. It was past eight o'clock and they were tired. They started making enquiries about the house where the two men were struck dead by thunder. It did not take them long to locate the house. Ablator, Lucy and their children had just had their evening meal when the policemen arrived at the house. The women offered the men a bench to sit on while they quickly washed their hands. Anlo women who were traders often prepared the evening meal late. These women brought back with them the ingredients for the evening meal when they returned from the market at dusk. It was only then that the children would be told to make the fire and preparations for the evening meal would begin. It was not unusual to find the families of these women having supper as late as 9.00 p.m.

While they waited, Amlima took out of his pocket a slip of paper on which he had written the names of the two men killed by lightning as told them by Johnny. By the light of Bansa's torchlight he recalled the names to memory.

Ablator and Lucy picked up the low stools on which they had sat for supper and came and sat down facing the policemen. "You are welcome," they said.

"Thank you," the cops replied.

"Let us greet you," Bansa said, looking at Amlima for silent permission to start proceedings. Amlima nodded and Bansa continued, "Ah, evening."

Bansa came from the middle part of the Volta Region where the forms of greeting were not as long as those of the Anlo people. But one thing he had learnt during his duty post among the Anlos was that they loved their forms of greeting, especially the elderly people. You were more likely to get what you wanted if you took the trouble to go through the long traditional greeting. It showed that you were mature. Elderly Anlos consider short greetings like "Good morning" or "Good evening" a sign of laziness or lack of maturity, or even disrespect.

"Evening," Ablator and Lucy replied. "The people of your house?"

"They are well," replied the policemen in unison.

"The children?"

"They are fine."

Pause.

"Ah, your family?"

"They are fine."

"The children?"

"They are all fine."

"Lucy," Ablator said; she had more or less become the head of the house. "Tell our visitors that they are welcome. In our house there is some heat as all is not well with us, but there is peace. If they please, let us hear the object of their visit."

"Have you heard what my sister said?" Lucy said, assuming the role of *tsiami* for the exchanges.

Bansa looked at Amlima again, and seeing in his face a benevolent expression, he answered for the group. "Er, my sister," he said, "convey it to your sister that we are on a hot mission but we bring no evil intentions. We have heard about your troubles and we offer you our heart-felt condolences. We have a few questions to ask you, so let me hand over to our leader to continue."

Amlima sat up straight. "First let me introduce ourselves," he said and placed his right hand on Bansa's shoulder. "On my right here is Sergeant Bansa. This man is Corporal Ahedor and this is Constable Atonsu."

Ablator and Lucy exchanged anxious glances. What business have the police in their house? they asked each other silently.

Amlima continued, "May I now ask you to introduce yourselves?"

"I am Ablator Dzumave, wife of Gbagbladza Hordzo, and this is Lucy Kporsu, wife of Besa Hordzo."

"Are you the only elders in the house or there are some other people?"

"We are the only ones."

"Then let's begin. We have heard that your husbands, er Gbagbladza and Besa, were killed by thunder recently. We also heard that their mother died on hearing the news. We are investigating a case right now and we would have wished your husbands were alive. As it is we should address our questions to you... What work did your husbands do?"

"They were fishermen, but also did some farming."

"Did they have their own nets or they worked for someone else?"

"Initially they worked with their father's nets but before their death they were working for someone else."

"Whom were they working for?"

"Tsormanya, Komi Tsormanya."

"Were they close to this man?"

"I don't understand," Ablator replied, suddenly on the defensive. She had heard some of the unpleasant rumours about Tsormanya.

Amlima was patient. "When you work with someone you will either be close to him or do just your job and nothing else. Also depending upon how close you are to your employer, he may take you into his confidence. That is what I am asking."

"No, they were not close to Tsormanya at all. They just did the fishing and nothing else."

"You are sure of that?"

"Very sure."

"What about you?" Amlima turned to Lucy. "Are you also sure your husbands were not close to Tsormanya?"

"I am also very sure," Lucy replied.

Amlima yawned. "We have information, evidence that certain people go about killing other people for ritual purposes. We have in our custody one of such killers. He said he was working for Tsormanya, the fisherman and that your husbands were among his accomplices."

"Ei!" both women exclaimed.

"Yes, that is the information we have. Unfortunately, your husbands are dead. If there is any information that you can give us that will help us make a case against this bad fisherman that made your husbands do evil things, we will be very grateful. From the way I see it, if it is true that this fisherman has been making people commit ritual murders on his behalf then you owe it as a duty to the memory of your dead husbands to help punish him. Do you remember anything no matter how trivial that your husbands said or did that linked them suspiciously to the fisherman?"

The women thought for a while, their minds in a

turmoil. "No, I don't," Ablator said.

"I don't either," said Lucy.

"We will leave you now," said Amlima. "But keep thinking. If you remember anything that may be helpful to us, let us know immediately. We are at the Keta Police Station. And if anybody tries to contact you on behalf of the fisherman I talked about let us know immediately. When you come to the police station ask of Sergeant Amlima. I am the one."

"Sergeant Amlima," Ablator repeated.

The policemen stood up. "Is there anybody else that you think we might talk to?" Bansa asked. Amlima wondered how Bansa knew the question that he had strategically intended for the last.

The women looked at each other, then Ablator said, "There is our father-in-law."

"Where is he?" Amlima asked.

"He is not here."

"Where is he?" Amlima repeated.

The women exchanged glances in silent consultation. "He is at the Blemekpinu shrine."

"What is that?"

"It is a *Yeve* shrine."

"A *Yeve* shrine?"

"Yes."

"What is he doing there?"

Between themselves, the women told the police the story of Nani Hordzo's initiation into the *Yeve* cult.

***   ***   ***

Sergeant Amlima left Ablator and Lucy with a tall order — to arrange an interview with Nani in the *Yeve*

150

shrine through *Huno* Dunyo who the women told the policemen, was well known to them. Ablator was not going to agree to the arrangement at first but Amlima's argument that it would serve her husband's memory well forced her to agree to the arrangement. But even after the departure of the policemen she still continued to waver.

"This is going to put me in *Huno* Dunyo's debt," she told Lucy.

"You are already in his debt and this request will not make much difference," Lucy said.

Ablator had told Lucy about the money Dunyo had sent her. Her intention was clear — if there should be any rumour in town linking her to Dunyo, she wanted an ally who could testify that at least she had not gone to bed with the man. So she told Lucy everything.

"What do you think his wives would think of me when they see me in their house?" Ablator asked.

"You don't have to go there. Meet him somewhere else," Lucy said.

"Where?"

"Anywhere apart from his house."

"Look," Ablator said, "both of us will meet him, here. I will send for his aide-de-camp Atuklui to bring him here."

"Good. Can we do it tonight? It is not too late."

"Yes, let's do it now," Ablator said eagerly. "Yao," she called her elder child.

"Yes, mother," the child responded.

"Come with Mawusi."

Mawusi was Lucy's eldest child. She was a year younger than Yao but had grown so plumpy she looked older than the skinny Yao. When the two children presented themselves before their parents, Ablator told

151

them, "Take one of the lanterns and go to Atuklui's house. You know the man? The one who has been bringing fish here... Good. Tell him that I wish to see him urgently now. Come back quickly. Don't play on the way."

The youngest child of Lucy drew near. "I will also go," she said.

The child broke into tears, but on this occasion Lucy ignored her tears which were a major weapon of hers to get what she wanted.

"What are you going to tell Atuklui when he comes?" Lucy asked.

"I will just tell him to go and bring Dunyo."

"He will most probably rejoice that you are finally giving in to his master."

"Let them think what they like. I know what I want."

Lucy rose to start packing up her cooking utensils for the night. Soon Yao and Mawusi came back accompanied by Atuklui.

"Lucy, our man has come, " Ablator called. "Please sit down," she told Atuklui, indicating the bench.

Atuklui sat down and greeted Ablator. "Good evening."

"Good evening. Please wait till Lucy comes."

Atuklui was surprised. "Does what you wish to tell me involve her?" he asked.

"Yes," Ablator replied simply.

Lucy joined them and sat down.

"Efo Atuklui," Ablator began, "I am sorry to have bothered you at this time of the night but I need to see *Huno* Dunyo urgently tonight."

"That is no problem," Atuklui said. "*Huno* Dunyo will heed your call no matter what time of the day or night. I will go and bring him straightaway." He was elated. He hoped this was a process leading finally to Ablator's capitulation to his master's proposal. He was in a hurry to get Ablator for Dunyo, for he needed money badly and knew that once Dunyo had Ablator, he would almost certainly give him the money.

Atuklui hurried into the darkness and Ablator and Lucy started putting their children to bed. They had their bath and sat outside waiting for Dunyo. They waited for a long time and at a point they thought Dunyo would not come. When he finally came accompanied by Atuklui, it was a little to ten o'clock. He was all apologies.

"I am sorry to have kept you waiting," he said. "I had some people with me when Atuklui came."

"Sit down," Ablator said. "Can Efo Atuklui excuse us for a while?"

"Of course," Atuklui said and moved to a distance.

"Er, Atuklui," Dunyo said, "I won't keep you up much longer. You can go home now."

"Thank you, *Huno*," Atuklui said. "Have a good night's rest."

By now most people had retired to bed. The night was very still and windless. The weather was hot and the ever present mosquitoes harassed those who were not well protected against their bites. From the distance a cock gave a throaty crow.

"Whatever is happening to our cocks these days?" *Huno* Dunyo said in mock annoyance. "They now crow anytime of the day or night. If it were in the former days, that cock would be slaughtered immediately. A cock which does not crow at the normal time portends evil."

"A lot of things have changed since the days of our forefathers," Lucy said in sympathy.

"*Huno* Dunyo," said Ablator, "we are sorry to have disturbed you so late at night."

"Don't worry about that," said Dunyo, cutting off her apologies. "You can call me any time and I will not fail you."

"Our problem is that the police are investigating a case involving our late husbands. As they are no more alive to answer the policemen's questions, they have expressed the desire to talk to their father instead. Can you arrange so that the police talk to the old man?"

"Ha, ha, ha," Dunyo laughed. "Is that all? Is that all the favour you want to ask me? I thought it was something more weighty. I can get the police to talk to your old man without any sweat."

"Oh, thank you very much," both women said.

Dunyo lifted up his forefinger and said, "But I will do this for you on one condition."

"What condition?" Ablator asked with apprehension.

"That you find time to socialize with me."

"Socialize with you?"

"Yes."

"In what way?"

"Oh, I buy you a drink or two. We sit down and chat, that's all."

"Er, that shouldn't be a problem. My only fear is what people may think seeing me out with you so soon after my husband's death. You know I have not performed the widowhood rites yet."

"I am aware of that. That is why I don't in anyway intend to put pressure on you. I wish you and I could be saying these things in private, but I am not ashamed to admit before your sister that I am very interested in you. It is not as if I am happy that your husband is dead so that I can have you. And I hope you don't intend to stay single because of your husband's death. If you should decide to marry I want to be the one that you marry."

"You don't need to say all that now," Ablator said embarrassed. "I am not in the mood to consider love proposals now. Let's see to the matter at hand first. When can the police have access to my father-in-law?"

"Anytime they want. I've told you it's no problem. And when can we have our drink together?"

"After you have arranged the interview."

"When do the police want to see him?"

"Tomorrow."

"Er, I can't promise tomorrow. But anytime I get the clearance I will let you know."

"Thank you very much. We are grateful."

"Thank you," Lucy also said.

"You don't need to thank me," Dunyo said, rising. "Whatever I can do to ease your pain I will be glad to do it. I must go now. It is late."

The two women also rose. "Good night," they said.

"Good night."

Dunyo left into the night and the two women locked the gate.

"I think we had a good bargain," Lucy said. "When the man started talking about a condition, I was afraid he was going to ask for the ultimate."

"Maybe he wants one thing to lead to another," said Ablator, "but he is going to be disappointed."

The cock that they had heard earlier that night crowed again. The two women looked at each other. They laughed uneasily and separated, each retiring to her room.

CHAPTER ELEVEN

Johnny could not sleep. All his nights in the police cell had been like this. He sat in a corner of the cell, then he stood up, threw his legs into the air for exercise and did some press-ups. He hated the cramped cell and he felt so helpless at times he would just sit and cry for long periods. The police brought him out every day to wash himself, but apart from that he spent every minute of the day and night in the cell. When he had confessed everything about his activities in the service of Komi Tsormanya, he had hoped the police would deal with him leniently from that point onwards, but his treatment only seemed to have grown worse. The police barked at him and shoved him, at times giving him subtle blows.

He still could not remember harming his father even though the police insisted he killed him. How could he kill his own father? He tried very hard to remember every wrong that he had done in his whole life, but the period that he was said to have killed his father was a blank. It was as if nothing at all had happened during that time, as if he had lost consciousness of himself.

He remembered the morning Kofi Legede came to visit him in Lome. He was not happy about Kofi's visit because wherever Kofi went he was followed by trouble. It was just after François had taken Johnny into his confidence and Johnny was eager to please his cousin. He did not want Kofi to come and spoil his party. His mind had worked furiously about how to tell Kofi in an inoffensive way not to visit him in Lome.

Johnny remembered he told Kofi to go back to Woe. When his friend left, Johnny quickly dressed up and took a taxi to the home of Monsieur Agbokli. He was now regularly sniffing cocaine with Monsieur Agbokli. On the day that Kofi visited him from Woe, he sniffed more cocaine than he had ever done before. He managed to reach home but after that he could not remember what happened. All that he could manage now was a faint recollection of being brought to Woe. After that everything was blank until the police grabbed him on Amamakpodzi. He killed his father? No, that was not possible! There had been times when he had flown into a rage against his father. But to kill him? No and no! The police and his family had got it all wrong. He had been a man and confessed to his wrongdoing. But the lack of sympathy from the police afterwards was making him regret his confession.

Tsormanya? All that he felt for the man now was a cold rage. How could he have been so naive? He had got to know Tsormanya from going to the beach during school holidays to help haul in the nets so that he would be given a share of the catch. Part of this he took home and the remainder he sold. Then he started going to the beach even during hours that he was supposed to be at school. He was finding it difficult to cope with the lessons. After he had played truant on the beach for a whole term, his father accepted that his son would never grow into the scholar he had dreamed of. He took Johnny to Komi Tsormanya and after an interview Johnny became a member of Tsormanya's fishing company.

Kordra Dornyo, a short and robust fellow, was a member of Tsormanya's fishing company. Despite the strict discipline in the company, Dornyo seemed to do what he liked. Johnny admired Dornyo especially his huge muscles. He wished he could behave like Dornyo —

do as he liked. Johnny wanted, like anything, to be friends with the man. His joy knew no bounds when out of the blue, Dornyo called him one day and told him he liked him. The young man and Dornyo seemed inseparable after that.

One day, Dornyo made a proposal that stunned Johnny. He told the young man that if he could get a quantity of human blood and present it to Tsormanya, the net-owner, the latter was ready to put up a house for him.

"Where can I get human blood?" Johnny asked in disbelief.

"You can get it, quite easily," Dornyo said.

"From where?"

"I can help you get it."

"By killing somebody?"

"No, no. It's not like that. We will just get hold of maybe a mad man, make him bleed a little and then let him go."

"Won't he die?"

"No, he will not die."

"But he will be left with a wound."

"Oh, it will be a little wound. It will heal in no time."

Johnny fell into thought. Then he said, "Won't the man report us to he police?"

Dornyo laughed. "He won't know us, especially if he is a mad man. Look, do you know how many houses I have?"

"Er, one."

"You are mistaken. There are two others and I got all of them from this business."

"You don't mean it!"

"It is true. I am offering you the chance of a lifetime."

Three days later, Dornyo asked Johnny to meet him

at the outskirts of town in the night. There were three other men with Dornyo when Johnny met him at the appointed hour. One of the men was Kofi Legede whom Johnny knew slightly. The other men whom he did not know then were Gbagbladza and Besa.

They waylaid a lonely man on the street and tricked him through the shallot farms at the side of the street to the edge of the lagoon. True enough, the man was a mad man. All that they needed to tell him was that he should follow them for some money. But to Johnny's horror, while the rest of the men held onto the man, Dornyo slit his throat. Johnny cried silently as he held onto the man's leg while his blood oozed into a plastic container. They buried the man in an abandoned portion of the farms.

The following day, Johnny cornered Dornyo and asked, "Didn't you say the person needed not to be killed?"

"Sometimes such things happen. Look, these things are not discussed this way," Dornyo said and moved away.

From that day Dornyo was aloof towards Johnny. Johnny was hurt and thought the man had just used him. Soon afterwards, Dornyo vanished from town. Nobody knew where he had gone. He just stopped coming to the beach and was not seen in town anymore.

Johnny began to see Gbagbladza and Besa at the beach. He assumed they had also joined the company, but he never spoke to them. One day Gbagbladza approached Johnny and through threats and more promises, Johnny was involved in another murder.

In the corner of the cell where he sat, Johnny shivered, then he launched into one of his now habitual long bouts of weeping. The other detainee in the room, a man of middle age, watched the young man as he wept. He also wiped a few tears from his eyes.

Constable Atonsu normally parked the police vehicle in front of the charge office. But on days when he wanted to visit his girlfriend in style or go on some unofficial errand for a senior officer, he parked the vehicle at the barracks. Tonight after they had come back from the failed mission to arrest Kofi Legede, he parked the vehicle at the barracks again. After that he went home and changed into civilian clothes. He waited till it was past midnight, then he took a stroll to the charge office. As he had expected the policeman on duty at the charge office was sleeping on a bench behind the counter. Atonsu tiptoed into the charge office. He stopped in his tracks when the man on the bench slapped a mosquito hovering around his ears and turned on the bench. Atonsu waited a few moments for the man's soft snoring to resume then tiptoed to the key rack. He took the bunch of cell keys and a pair of handcuffs that also hung on the key rack and went to the back of the office where the cells were located.

There were two cells, one for the men detainees, the other for the women. Atonsu opened the men's cell. He flashed the torchlight into the room. The light picked up first Johnny's cell-mate, the middle-aged man, then Johnny. Both of them were awake.

"Suspect Johnny Klevor," Atonsu said.

"Hm?" responded Johnny.

"Come with me."

"At this time?" Johnny asked.

"Come and stop asking questions."

Johnny got up, his whole body aching. "Where are you taking me?" he asked.

"Just follow me," Atonsu said and slipped the

handcuffs over his wrists. "Let's go." He pushed him out and locked the cell. "Come on, hurry up."

He took Johnny to the back of the barracks where he had stationed the vehicle, hoping they would not come across anybody. He opened the front passenger door and pushed Johnny inside. He closed the door quietly and ran to the other side of the car, jumped behind the wheel and drove out of the police yard.

"Where are you taking me at this hour of the night?" Johnny asked again.

"You will know when we get there. We are continuing the investigation."

Atonsu drove to Dzelukope, along the main road and stopped by a house with a huge gate fronting the street. He got out of the car and pushed against the gate which swung open with a whine as if in protest against this late intrusion. Atonsu went to the car and brought out Johnny and together they entered the house. A fluorescent light shining from the wall of the main building illuminated the house. A huge shed stood to the right of the intruders. This was where members of the True Open Bible Church worshipped. Several goats lay on the ground in the compound, some still chewing the cud at this hour. Parked side by side in the midst of the goats was Prophet Patu's two cars, the Mercedes Benz and the BMW saloon cars.

Atonsu took Johnny to the main building where Prophet Patu lived and knocked on the door. Footsteps sounded in the apartment and stopped behind the door.

"Who is it?" the prophet called through the door. He lived alone; his wife and two children who stayed in Accra only visited him occasionally.

"Prophet, it's me Atonsu."

The prophet opened the door and when he saw

Johnny his face cracked into a smile, the sleep in his eyes disappearing into the cracks. He wore a long morning coat. "Please come in," he said making way for them. He flicked on a switch and fluorescent lights in the sitting-room, blinked several times before coming on. The room was divided to carve off a waiting area from the living-room.

"Please sit down," the prophet said waving his visitors into chairs in the waiting-room. The room was lavishly furnished with its own T.V. set and video deck player. It had stuffed chairs that sunk deep. A huge room divider stood on the border between the waiting area and the living-room.

"Excuse me," the prophet said and disappeared behind the room divider. He came back after a few minutes, changed into pyjamas. "You are welcome again," he said, sitting down.

"Thank you," Atonsu said. "Can I see you aside for a minute, prophet?"

"Er, brother Atonsu," the prophet said, "let's not do it that way. Our brother here may think we are hiding something from him. Let's say everything in the open. But first of all, let's pray. Please close your eyes... Oh, merciful Lord, we thank you again for the day just gone. We are grateful to you for keeping watch over us during the night till this hour. We trust that your guardian angels will be with us until we see the next day. And when day breaks, fill us with your Spirit. Let everything that we do be to the glory of your name and in the service of mankind. Father, we are about to set off on an enterprise. Let us see our way clear in whatever we do. Let your Spirit descend upon this gathering here this night. Let the Holy Ghost so fill me that I will be the one to save this brother of ours who seems to be tormented by demons. Father, when I speak, let all evil spirits in this room quake. Cast them into the lake of fire from where they shall never come back to torment our brother... *Raba, raba, raba matu! Matu zu to manya. Re do do do ma na he. Raba toro mani koho. Re vitoto mato bin...He ra ra, he ra ra, ra ra mani, he ra re...* Amen."

"Amen," Atonsu and Johnny replied and opened their eyes.

Tongue-speaking was one of the strong points of Prophet Patu. He encouraged every member of his flock to develop this talent. He rubbed his hands together then stood up and flexed his muscles. "What is our brother's name again?" he asked.

"Johnny Klevor," Atonsu said.

"Brother Johnny,"

"Sir," responded Johnny.

"You can call me prophet, brother Johnny. Brother Johnny, I saw you in court the other day when you were being tried. I am a spiritual man and what I saw about you disturbed me a lot so I sent for you. You are not aware of the full extent of the trouble that lies over your head. It is only those of us endowed with spiritual powers who know. There is a lot of darkness hanging over you and those around you. It is not all of this darkness that is due to natural forces, some of it, in fact the larger part of it, is due to the forces of the evil one, Satan. Without spiritual assistance you can't escape from this darkness and save your soul. Your soul is the most important thing. As for your body it will perish into the soil. Unfortunately, Satan has imprisoned your soul. But don't worry, I am going to help you liberate your soul from the bondage of the evil one.

"What I am going to do is that I will take you through some processes. Through these processes you will rise from the darkness that presently engulfs you. You will rise and rise and in the process gain cleansing which will reunite you with your maker Jehovah, the Almighty God... Brother Atonsu, please remove the handcuffs."

"That is not safe," Atonsu said.

The prophet smiled complacently. "Don't worry. Nothing will happen. You are in the house of God where you don't need physical things to restrain human beings or the devil. It is the Word that is working. Our brother cannot take a step from that chair if I tell him not to!"

A shiver ran over Johnny. He raised his hands as Atonsu stood over him to remove the cuffs. The cuffs were removed and he rubbed his wrists to take the stiffness out of them.

"Brother Atonsu, please wait in the other room," Prophet Patu said, pointing the policeman to the living-room.

Atonsu hesitated. "What is going to happen?" he asked.

"Nothing that you should be worried about," said the man of God. "Just go. Nothing will happen. Everything is under the control of the Word."

Private Atonsu went and sat in the living-room. He was not happy about the trend events were taking. He primed his ears for the least sound.

In the waiting-room, the prophet stood over Johnny and placed his hand on his shoulder. "Look at me, Johnny," he said. "Look me straight in the eyes. Tell yourself strongly that you trust me absolutely and that I cannot do any harm to you. Now, give me your hand. I am going to lead you on a spiritual journey that will be of immense benefit to you..."

Johnny placed his hand in that of the prophet. He listened to the prophet and allowed his mind to flow with his instructions. Then he found himself slipping as if he was going to fall into unconsciousness. He jerked himself awake. The prophet stood over him, tall and huge with a benevolent smile on his face. He began to slip again, but this time he did not struggle, he let himself go.

The prophet watched Johnny, speaking softly and trying to make him relax completely. He saw the young man's eyes dilate and acquire an empty look. He waved his hand over Johnny's eyes but they did not blink.

"Thank you, Lord," the prophet said and clenched his fists in triumph. Then he continued, "Johnny, we are now going to lift the darkness from your body and your spirit."

Suddenly, there was the screeching of tires over asphalt followed by a loud bang. The noise came from outside. Atonsu jumped from his seat and rushed to the waiting-room. "What was that?" he asked.

"I don't know!" the prophet said.

"Let's find out," said Atonsu. He quickly slapped the handcuffs over Johnny's wrists.

"Oh, no," the prophet groaned as Johnny's eyes started to regain focus and he slowly sat up.

"I think that is an accident," Atonsu said. "Let's find out." He opened the door and rushed outside. When he got to the main road, he saw two people bent over a body in the road. He ran to them and asked, "Is he dead?"

"I think so," one of the men said, rising up. "He ran across the road all of a sudden. I couldn't avoid him."

"Take him to the Keta Hospital and report yourself to the police. What is your vehicle number?"

"Are you a policeman?"

"Yes, that is my car parked over there."

The men gave the registration number of their vehicle. Atonsu went nearer to the car which stood some distance away to verify. "Take the body to the hospital and report yourselves at the police station," Atonsu said again and re-entered the prophet's house.

The prophet was standing on the steps leading to his apartment.

"Prophet, we'll have to go," Atonsu said.

"Well," the prophet said helplessly. "Was it an accident?"

"Yes. A car knocked down somebody!" He walked past the prophet and beckoned to Johnny. "Let's go." Johnny came to the door.

"Can you come over again tomorrow?" the prophet asked.

"I can't promise. It will depend on a lot of things. I will see you in the morning for further discussions." He grabbed Johnny by the wrists and pulled him along. "See you tomorrow, prophet."

"Good night," Prophet Patu replied. He entered his apartment and closed the door and as he listened to the engine of the vehicle fading away into the distance, he raised his hands into the air and told himself, "I am getting somewhere."

CHAPTER TWELVE

Tsormanya was interrogated the following day in the District Commander's office. Present at the interrogation were the District Commander himself, ASP Mark Adosu, the Station Officer Inspector Dongor, Detective Sergeant Amlima, Sergeant Bansa and Corporal Ahedor who was acting as recorder. There were three straight-back chairs in front of the District Commander's desk. Tsormanya sat in the middle one and on either side of him sat the two sergeants. Inspector Dongor and Corporal Ahedor sat in the armchairs ranged against the wall. In front of Ahedor was a coffee table which he intended to use as something to write on.

"Good morning, gentlemen," ASP Adosu said, "let's begin the interview. We normally do these interviews to help suspects organise their thoughts. If they wish to make any confessions, they make it. And if there are any steps the police can advise them to take, we advise them. Mr. Tsormanya, your statement has already been taken, but we will question you afresh. Let me tell you, however, that you have every right to refuse to speak except in the presence of your counsel, your lawyer. Okay, let's begin. Sergeant Amlima, your questions."

Tsormanya's face was grim. He looked pale and seemed to have lost weight overnight. He had listened in silence as Adosu spoke.

Sergeant Amlima turned his chair to face the suspect. "What is your name?" he asked.

"Komi Tsormanya."

"Where do you stay?"

"Woe."

"What is your profession?"

"I am a fisherman."

"Do you know Johnny Klevor?"

Tsormanya hesitated before saying, "Yes."

"How do you know him?"

"He once worked for me. I think he no more comes to my net, I can't be very sure. I have many employees."

"What is the relationship between you and Johnny?"

"He worked for me as a fisherman. He helped in bringing in the net."

"Did he do any other work for you?"

"No, no other work."

"What if Johnny says he had been doing other work for you?"

"He will be telling lies."

"You have never engaged him to do work other than fishing for you?"

"Never."

"Have you ever engaged in ritual murder?"

"Me? Never!" Tsormanya's denial was emphatic.

"Have you ever engaged other people to kill people for ritual purposes?"

"Never!"

"What if we produce witnesses to say you engaged them to commit murder for ritual purposes?"

"They will be telling lies."

"Even if they show us the spot where you have buried some of your victims?"

"I have never buried anybody anywhere!"

"Maybe not you yourself. You get other people to do that for you. They kill the people and bury them. Then they bring you the blood."

"That is not true."

"Mr. Tsormanya, you say you are a fisherman. Do you perform rites to make you catch a lot of fish?"

"No!"

"Not even prayers to the gods?"

"As for that one I do it."

"That is also a rite, isn't it?"

"Well, yes."

"Do you make sacrifices?"

"Of what?"

"Of anything. It could be of animals."

"Of animals, yes."

"What about human beings?"

"No! Never!"

Amlima turned to Adosu. "I think that will be all for now, sir."

ASP Adosu emitted a deep breath. "Mr. Tsormanya," he said, "we will take you to court tomorrow. In your own interest, find yourself a lawyer. You will need one."

"Can I be bailed so that I look for a lawyer?"

"No, no bail for you. Your family can look for the lawyer for you. Sergeant Amlima, take him away and formally charge him."

Tsormanya stood up and Amlima followed him out of the room.

"Inspector Dongor," ASP Adosu said, "have you posted men to look for the young man who escaped?"

"Kofi Legede?"

"Yes."

"Yes, sir. There is a twenty-four hour watch for him. As soon as he resurfaces he will be arrested."

"Good," Adosu said. "Tonight we will go to the two other burial grounds the first suspect mentioned. We will dig up everything and keep it at the mortuary for the pathologists. We can disperse for now. Thank you."

The men stood up and shuffled towards the door.

"Just a minute, Inspector," ASP Adosu said. "Have we already sent the first suspect, Johnny, for the psychiatric test?"

"No, sir."

"When are we sending him?"

"Day after tomorrow, sir."

"Who is taking him?"

"Sergeant Amlima, sir."

"That will be all right."

***　　***　　***

Lawyer Henry Sekle was about the only lawyer resident at Keta. He was always present at the Keta Circuit Court on court days. Sometimes he went to the court to defend his clients, at other times he went there to look for clients. When a suspect went into the dock and it became clear that he was not using the services of a lawyer, Mr. Sekle would offer his services voluntarily. Later he would come to an agreement with the suspect about his fees. Through this method, Lawyer Sekle was never short of clients.

Nobody in the Keta area knew that Mr. Sekle's licence had long been withdrawn by the Ghana Bar Association for abuse of ethics. His faults ranged from double-dealing to outright fraud. Mr. Sekle started his practice in the capital city, Accra. He had been practising for about six years when he fell out with the Bar Association. Sekle made little noise when the Bar Association pulled the rug from under his feet. He came home to Keta quietly. He did not have a house of his own and he had no wish to live in the family house, so he rented an apartment and settled down to pick up his law practice from where he had left off. He had his office in his apartment. When his cases are referred to higher courts outside Keta he never followed them; he always advised his clients to look for another lawyer.

Sekle had charm and he used this well to his advantage in court. He had a winning smile that he employed at the least opportunity; he was a delight to watch when he tried to convince judges about the innocence of his clients.

When Tsormanya asked Leve to look for a good lawyer, it was to Lawyer Sekle that he was directed. Sekle could hardly believe his luck. He knew Tsormanya very well and was aware of his immense wealth, and to think that he was to defend this man in a case of murder was like manna sent from heaven.

He declined to name his fee for taking up the case. "When I tackle a case," he told Leve, "I am not interested in the financial gain. I put my whole self into the case and it is only when I am almost through with the case that I start talking about a fee. So you relax. You will only be paying my expenses as we go along."

Leve was very pleased. This must be a very good lawyer, he told himself.

Sekle, his impressive portfolio firmly in his grip, went straight to the police station after Leve had gone. He marched to the charge office and greeted the officer on duty.

"I have a client here," he told the officer.

"Who is your client, sir?" All the policemen knew Sekle and accorded him much respect.

"He is by name Komi Tsormanya."

"Oh, just a minute, sir. I will bring him out. Come this way. You can sit in this office while I bring him out."

Sekle sat down in the familiar office where lawyers met clients who were under detention or remand. As he often did, he thought about how easy it would be to run away with a client once he was brought to this office. Apart from the handcuffs restraining detainees, there was no other provision. The door was left unlocked with only the policeman on duty outside at the counter. Sekle often fantasized about sneaking behind the officer at the counter and knocking him out; then he would put the suspect in his car and drive off.

The policeman came back with Tsormanya and ushered him into the office where Sekle waited. Then he closed the door and went back to his counter.

Tsormanya greeted Sekle and sat down, his head bowed.

"Mr. Tsormanya, I am your lawyer," Sekle said.

"Is that so?" Tsormanya said and lifted his head.

"Yes. Lift up your spirits, Mr. Tsormanya. Don't look so downcast. We don't fight a case like that. You must have a positive outlook even when you are guilty. You must believe you will win the case. This is very important. Now, you have to be very frank with me. You must tell me all that you know. It is then that I will be in a position to defend you effectively."

Tsormanya looked up and studied the countenance of the man before him. Should he lay all his cards on the table before this man? "All that the police are saying about me are false," he said.

"What are they saying about you?"

"They say I have been killing human beings to catch more fish in the sea."

"Is it true?"

"It is not true!"

Lawyer Sekle could see at once that his client was not telling the truth; he was hiding something. But he was not the man to start pushing issues at this stage. "Mr. Tsormanya," he said, "we are going to court tomorrow. You must give me all your cooperation. I can assure you that once you have come to me you have won half the case. I know what I must do to get you freed. Don't entertain any fear at all. We will meet tomorrow in court. But if you wish to tell me anything before then just send for me. All the policemen know me." He lowered his voice and added, "And they fear me!"

Tsormanya's eyes brightened but he said nothing.

The lawyer stood up. "I will see you tomorrow in court," he said. "I will go home now and prepare the case and tomorrow I will face our accusers squarely in court."

"Thank you, lawyer," Tsormanya said.

"Don't worry. You will be smiling. See you tomorrow."

"Good-bye."

Sekle opened the door. "Officer, I am finished," he called.

"Okay, sir," the policeman said and came and led Tsormanya back to his cell.

***   ***   ***

In the night Johnny was again taken out of his cell and put in the police vehicle. He was going to show the police two other spots where they had buried their ritual victims. Armed with pistols and digging tools, Sergeants Amlima and Bansa and Corporal Ahedor went and picked

173

the three Environmental Health workers who had helped them dig up the body on the beach the previous day. They drove through Dzelukope, Vui, Tegbi and Woe. All these towns were quiet as most people had retired indoors. On the border between Woe and Anloga, Johnny told the driver to stop. Atonsu parked the vehicle on the shoulder of the road and everybody got down. Johnny led the policemen through the shallot fields towards the lagoon. Some of the policemen fell on their hands as they walked through the narrow furrows between the shallot beds.

When they were out of the shallot fields, Johnny said, "Please shine the torchlight over the area."

Sergeant Amlima flicked on the powerful torchlight and Johnny started searching for the exact spot where they had buried the victim of the first ritual murder he had been involved in. After searching for about ten minutes he could still not identify the spot. Just then, Atonsu stepped on a spot and his foot sunk into the soil.

"Sergeant, sir," he said, "please bring the torchlight here."

The torchlight was shone over the spot indicated by Atonsu. It was covered by broken twigs and freshly uprooted grass. Bansa kicked aside some of the twigs and grass. The top soil here was lighter in colour than the surrounding area and it looked wet. Bansa bent down and began to remove the rest of the twigs and dead grass.

"Stop that!" Amlima said. He turned to Johnny. "Johnny, how long ago is it since you buried the body here?"

"A little less than a year," Johnny replied.

Amlima took Bansa by the shoulder. "Do you know what I think? We have been beaten to it. Some people have already been here to dig up and carry away what we are looking for. Look at the uprooted green grass. Let us not touch the spot. We will get forensic experts from Accra to come and examine this. And please, keep this a secret. I don't want any of you to breathe a word about this to anybody. Is that clear?"

The others nodded in the darkness.

"That goes for you, too, Johnny. Do you understand?"

"Yes, sir," Johnny said.

"Now lead us to the other spot."

They went back to the vehicle and drove on. At the fork in the road at Savietula, a suburb of Srogboe, they took the right turn, the Dabala road. This section of the road, a "Y" junction, was the site of numerous accidents. Most people who passed here wondered what sort of professional designed the road. The road was designed to curve sharply to the right before forking off to the left towards Anyanui. Right in the curve was a small storey building that gave name to this area, Savietula, the builder of the little storey building. This storey building hid the curve from any driver approaching from the direction of Keta and a misjudgement of the sharp angle of the curve often resulted in an accident. Any time there was an accident here, everybody cursed the contractor for a few days then they let off.

Under the direction of Johnny, Amlima and his team left the main road and took the dusty road leading to Fiahor, the hometown of one of the famous military coup makers of this country, Emmanuel Kwasi Kotoka. About five kilometres from the main road, Johnny asked Atonsu to stop.

"I will not be surprised if this place too has already been dug up," Amlima said as they all got down.

The land here was salty and had little vegetation.

175

Every wet season the lagoon flooded it. In the dry season, the lagoon dries off leaving behind patches of white crystals of salt which was scraped off by the local women and sold in the market.

Amlima and his men had to search for a long time before finding the spot where Johnny and his gang had buried another of their victims. But for the fact that this spot had also been recently dug up they wouldn't have been able to find it at all. Those who had dug up the spot had gone to great lengths to hide traces of the digging but any careful search would reveal it.

"Just as I thought," Amlima said. "We will leave this place too untouched for the forensic experts from Accra. Let's go. And not a word about this to anybody, except Inspector Dongor and the District Commander. When I hear anything about this anywhere I will know that it is one of you who leaked it." They turned back and walked towards the road.

"How did you feel when you were murdering all these people?" Bansa asked Johnny.

Amlima cut Bansa short. "Don't worry Johnny. He is only a child. He didn't know what he was doing," Amlima made a mental note to tell Bansa that you don't antagonise a suspect who is willing to co-operate with investigations.

When they got back to the station Johnny was put back in his cell. In two days he would be sent to the Accra Psychiatric Hospital for examination. Atonsu was aware of this and was determined to send Johnny once more to Prophet Patu before he was sent to Accra. He hung around the charge office, bidding his time but even though it was getting to midnight, the policeman on duty refused to doze off to give him the chance to get Johnny.

The duty policeman just sat at the counter and gazed into space. Once in a while he would put his head on the counter and just when Atonsu was sure he had dozed off he would lift up his head again and continue staring into space. There were supposed to be two policemen on duty, the duty officer and the police orderly. But the common practice was that one of the two would go home to sleep for a while then come back so that the other one too could go and have his turn. Atonsu could no more bear the wakefulness of the duty officer, so he entered the charge office. The duty officer was also a constable and a pal of Atonsu.

"George," Atonsu said addressing the duty officer," I need to take one suspect out on an investigation."

"Is that why you've been hanging around and keeping me awake?" George asked with a yawn.

Atonsu laughed. "I didn't know you were feeling sleepy. Can I take the suspect so that you can enjoy your sleep?"

"Who is it?"

"Johnny."

"That is a tricky one. This is not official, is it?"

"Er, not exactly. I've got an angle to this case that I want to explore. I want to spring a pleasant surprise on Sergeant Amlima."

"And earn a stripe on your shoulder, huh?"

"You can put it like that."

"Okay, get Johnny. But please, be careful. You are aware of the weight of his case."

Atonsu took the keys of the cells, singing. He was very happy to have got his way. George Aboagye was a good cop, he was easygoing and a friend to everybody.

Atonsu came back with Johnny in handcuffs.

"Sign this for me," George said indicating a slip of paper on the counter. Atonsu took the paper. What was on it read, "I, Private Alex Atonsu, have taken out suspect Johnny Klevor on official investigation on the night of 23/06/1998 — at 11.36 p.m."

"I will still get a rap in case anything happens but I will risk that for you, pal," George said.

"Thank you," Atonsu said and signed the paper. He took Johnny to the police vehicle and set off for Prophet Patu's house. The prophet opened the door at the first knock. Atonsu had told him during the day that he would be bringing Johnny during the night and he had lain awake waiting for them.

"Please sit down," the prophet said. "We will begin at once, so brother Atonsu you can sit over there at your usual place. Johnny and I will be here." Atonsu went to the sitting-room and sat down. The prophet first said a short prayer. "Now Johnny," he said, "we will start from where we left off the other day. You will be carried to the same heights as yesterday. Let your body relax, sit comfortably, let every muscle and organ in your body relax. Now, let your mind follow me, put yourself completely in my control. Trust that while you are in my control you are safe. Now come with me, you are very safe..."

Again Johnny's eyes seemed to dilate and acquire an empty look. The prophet waved his hands over his eyes, but the young man did not blink.

"Thank you, Almighty God," the prophet said, clenching his fists, his face lifted to heaven. Then he turned back to Johnny. "Now let your whole self be filled with the spirit. Remove the blanket of darkness that envelopes your mind, refusing to let you see your actions in retrospect. It is there in your mind, let your mind's eye see. Open your eyes very wide, look carefully and observe where I am going to lead you.

"Now you are in Lome. It is the day you are finally coming to Ghana, the day you are being brought to Woe by your cousin François. You are in a car coming to Woe. Open your eyes and observe the road. What do you see, Johnny? Tell me what you see. Open your mouth and express what you see."

Johnny's lips parted but no words came out of his mouth. His stared past the prophet unblinkingly.

"Johnny, speak. What do you see? Set the muscles in your mouth free. Tell me what you see along the road. Come on, you can do it."

Johnny began to murmur inaudibly.

"Come on. Johnny, your voice is not clear. Clear it, go on, clear it."

Johnny stuttered at first, then his words flowed more easily. "I see-see a-a-a lo-lo-lot of people wa-walking along the road. Some are going to Lome... Now there are very few people..."

"Yes, what else do you see?"

"We-we are overtaking other vehicles. This driver is driving too fast. I am afraid we are going to have an accident!" Johnny cringed into the seat. "This driver is going to kill us all. Please, tell him to slow down. Please, please..."

"He won't kill you. What do you see?"

Johnny let his body relax in the seat again. "...The car has stopped outside my house. We are getting out. People are looking at us curiously. They think I am mad, but I am in pain, a lot of pain. Somebody is trying to murder me. He is tearing my intestines into pieces... Aiiii..." Johnny wailed so loudly Prophet Patu had to cover his mouth with his hand.

Atonsu came in from the sitting-room with alarm written on his face. "That is okay for tonight, Prophet. I will bring him another time."

The prophet was disappointed. "We are getting along very fine. Give me some few more minutes then I will wrap it up."

"We will have to go. If he wakes up the neighbourhood and word gets to the station, I will be in trouble."

"Just a few moments, just a few more minutes."

Atonsu wavered. But when the prophet turned to Johnny, the young man was already coming out of his hypnotic trance. His eyes were beginning to focus as he looked from one man to the other. The prophet knew at once the situation was hopeless. "All right, let's meet again tomorrow night," he said.

"That may not be possible. Johnny is going to Accra for a test. You can see him after that."

"Oh, that's unfortunate. Well, there is nothing we can do about it. Or can you delay his going to Accra for a day or two?"

"No, that is beyond my power."

"When is he coming back?"

"I don't know. Maybe after a day or two."

"Well, you bring him when he comes back. I thank you very much for your co-operation. The Church is grateful and we will reward you at the opportune time. Good night."

Atonsu led his charge away and a few minutes later Johnny was back in his cell.

***   ***   ***

The news of Tsormanya's arrest spread along the

Vodza-Anloga littoral and beyond like wild fire in the dry season. The arrest confirmed the widespread suspicion that the man's riches were not "clean". Everybody waited for Tuesday with bated breath, for Tuesday was the day set for Tsormanya's first appearance in court.

Early in the morning of Tuesday, the small courthouse behind the District Assembly hall was already full and a large crowd was rapidly engulfing the whole courthouse. When court officials arrived for work at 8.00 a.m. they had to literally fight their way through the crowd to get to their offices.

It was not only at the courthouse that the crowd had gathered. The whole of the street in front of the police station was inundated with people and vehicles were finding it difficult to pass this stretch of the road. Those among the crowd whose relatives had gone missing or had died in suspicious circumstances, vowed revenge for they believed they at last knew the murderer of their relatives.

Inside the police station, ASP Adosu held council with his men. He could gauge the mood in the crowd and he knew that if they were not careful Tsormanya could be lynched before their very eyes. They decided that Tsormanya would be taken over the short distance to the court premises in a police van. Policemen would surround the vehicle as it moved slowly to the court. The policemen would be armed with batons and a few of them with rifles loaded with blank shots. Deep in his heart Adosu did not want anybody to get hurt for the sake of a man he believed had callously murdered other people. If he had his way, he would release Tsormanya to face the wrath of the crowd. First, Adosu caused anybody who was not a policeman to be moved away from the police premises. Then two police vehicles reversed to the front of the charge office.

The crowd could clearly see everything from the street over the short wall surrounding the police station. When Tsormanya was led out of the charge office onto the verandah, a tremendous boo arose from the crowd: "*Hooooo... Hooooo...*" Tsormanya was led into the second vehicle and the policemen quickly took their positions around the vehicle. As the vehicles moved towards the gate the boos from the crowd went up in crescendo. The two vehicles inched into the crowd with the police fighting off people who wanted to swarm the vehicle in which Tsormanya was riding. They hit a few people with their batons and this held the crowd at bay. But it took over thirty minutes to cover the short distance to the circuit court. The police had a more hectic time getting Tsormanya out of the vehicle into the courtroom. Everybody wanted to get their hands at him. It took a couple of warning shots from the police rifles to make room for Tsormanya to be led into the court premises. He was led to his seat surrounded by several policemen armed with batons and rifles.

The crowd which had besieged the police station found out they could not gain access to the court premises for the place was already choked, but very few people left for their homes. The great majority waited patiently for news from the courtroom and this was not in short supply. Reports on every minute in the courthouse came in waves from the direction of the court, from details of Tsormanya's facial expressions to the hurried preparations being made by the court officials to start proceedings. The old stories surrounding the wealthy fisherman were resurrected and dissected and re-analysed.

The judge's official vehicle finally made it through

the crowds and arrived at the court at 10.00 a.m. Everybody rose when he entered the courtroom. He quickly conferred with the registrar and decided that Tsormanya's case should be called first to clear the crowds from the premises.

The court clerk stood up and announced the first case: "The Republic of Ghana versus Komi Tsormanya." The fisherman was called to the dock and as he walked there, the crowd booed him. Of Tsormanya's numerous wives only Dodziada had defied the wrath of the crowds to be present in the courtroom. She sat in the front row, her palm supporting her chin. Though Tsormanya could not see her, he knew she would be somewhere among the crowd.

The judge called out, "Is there anybody to defend the accused?"

The ubiquitous Lawyer Henry Sekle stood up. He was greeted with a boo from the crowd as if the offence of his client had rubbed off on him. Then a hush fell over the crowd as the prosecutor stood up to present the facts of the case against Tsormanya. He described Johnny's revelations as a tip-off that the police had. He went over the initial investigations that the police had done and their discoveries. He then appealed to the judge to remand the accused in prison custody for the police to complete their investigations.

"What plea do you enter for the accused?" the judge asked the fisherman's counsel.

"Not guilty, my lord," said Sekle, and the boos went up again.

"We will leave it at that," said the judge. "The case is adjourned to the 7th of July. The accused is remanded in prison custody."

Lawyer Sekle protested vehemently against the judge's refusal of bail but the judge stood by his word. "In view of the magnitude of the charges against the accused," he said, "and the high possibility that the accused could jump bail, added to the fear of crowd violence, he is remanded in custody."

The police quickly surrounded Tsormanya again and he was led amid renewed boos from the crowd. They followed the police vehicles every inch of the way back to the police station. They remained a long time outside the police station even after Tsormanya had been put back in his cell. Late in the afternoon, pockets of people could still be seen in the vicinity of the police station discussing the case and waiting for something to happen.

CHAPTER THIRTEEN

It took *Huno* Dunyo about a week to finally arrange an interview for the police with Nani Hordzo at the *Yeve* shrine. It was on a Wednesday and at the appointed time, Sergeants Amlima and Bansa were taken to the shrine by *Huno* Dunyo.

"Every town has its own way of cutting up the chicken," Dunyo told the cops on the way to the shrine. "Here, we have our own rules. If you want to play with us you must obey our rules. That is all."

"What are your rules?" Amlima asked.

"First, the man you are looking for is no more an ordinary man; he can't come out of the shrine to talk to you. You will have to go inside and meet him, but before that you must do certain things. You must remove your shirts and your footwear. And your caps too."

Sergeant Amlima was in plain clothes but Bansa was dressed in uniform.

"We have no choice in the matter," Amlima said. "Is there anywhere that we can have the privacy to remove our clothes?"

"I will show you."

When they reached the shrine, Dunyo led them to an antechamber. "You can remove your things here," he said and went out. The policemen looked at each other and laughed; then they started removing the undesired clothes.

"The things that we have to do in the line of duty!" Bansa said.

"You don't have to complain. You joined the service voluntarily."

185

When they came out, Dunyo was waiting for them outside the door. "Rule number two," he said. "The man you are going to meet now does not bear his former name any longer. If you address him by his former name, serious repercussions will befall you. You may not even be able to come out of the shrine. Just call him *kporkpor.*"

"Did you hear that, Bansa? *Kporkpor.* Keep that firmly in mind."

"Come."

They followed the *Huno* bare-footed and bare-chested through the main entrance of the shrine. He led them into a compound and gave them seats. Then he disappeared through a door in the opposite wall. When he re-appeared he was accompanied by Nani. The old man had lost some weight but his skin sparkled in the early morning sun and he looked younger. His head was clean-shaven and smeared with sheer butter as was the rest of his body. He wore a white cloth from his chest down to below his knees. He kept his head bowed and looked at the cops from under his brows. Dunyo came to sit by the cops while Nani remained standing.

"Now," Dunyo said, "this is the man you want. He can't speak our language any more. He speaks the special language of the cult. You can speak to him in our language but he will reply in the cult language which I will translate for you. I am going to be your interpreter. You can begin."

"Er, *kporkpor,* " Amlima began, looking at Bansa sternly as if to remind him to keep the name in mind. "We offer you our condolences on the death of your sons. As you may already have been told we are policemen. We are investigating a case and we need to ask you a few questions. Please be frank with us and answer our

186

questions truthfully."

Nani nodded, his eyes still focused on the ground. As a rule people undergoing the *Yeve* initiation always keep their heads bowed. Bansa brought out a pad from his pocket ready to take notes.

"What work did your sons do?"

Nani answered in the cult language and Dunyo translated. "He says they were both fishermen and farmers."

"Did they have their own farms and nets or they worked for other people?"

Nani spoke and Dunyo translated. For a fresh initiate, Nani spoke the cult language fairly well even though he had to struggle for some of the words.

"We have our own farms but they did the fishing with other people's nets."

"When they fished did they work for one particular person?"

"They belonged to Komi Tsormanya's company."

"How close was the relationship between your sons and Tsormanya?"

"*Tsoe na lo doe nya ngor.*"

"*Kporkpor* does not understand the angle of the question," Dunyo translated.

"I mean how close were his sons with their employer? Did they have a close relationship with Tsormanya, or it was just a normal employee-employer relationship?"

"Tsormanya sometimes called on them in our house and at times sent for them. So it must be a close relationship. They were hardworking men."

"Do you know the nature of the relationship your sons had with Tsormanya?"

"*Kporkpor* does not understand the angle of the

question."

"Was his sons' relationship with Tsormanya only for fishing purposes or did they do other jobs for him apart from fishing?"

"I am not aware of any other relationship. I know that they only fished for Tsormanya."

"Had Tsormanya ever visited your sons at hours that you considered odd?"

"Tsormanya is not a regular visitor to our home. He came to our house a few times but not at odd hours."

Amlima turned to Bansa. "Do you have any questions to ask?"

Bansa cleared his throat. "Was Tsormanya very generous to your sons? I mean did he give them money and other things freely?"

"On some occasions, yes, but it was because my sons were very hardworking."

"Are you aware of any specific amount of money Tsormanya gave them?"

"No."

"What other gifts did he give them?"

"I don't know but he gave them a lot of fish."

"Does Tsormanya treat all his employees like that or your sons' treatment was different?"

"I may say he extended extra favour to my sons even though a few other members of the company also enjoyed such treatment."

"Did you yourself enjoy such special treatment?"

"No, I am just an old man. They don't make me do a lot of work."

"Were your sons going out at odd hours, for example, deep in the night?"

"Not exactly. They sometimes attended wakekeepings, but apart from that they just went about their normal duties."

"Thank you."

"Thank you very much, *kporkpor,* " Amlima also said. "But one last question — do you think your sons were capable of extreme cruelty?"

"Tsoe na lo doe nya ngor."

"Do you think they could seriously harm other people, even kill them?"

"They had bad tempers and when in a rage, they easily used their hands on people but I don't think they were capable of killing anybody."

"You are sure of that?"

"Yes, very sure."

"Thank you very much for your co-operation."

Nani lifted his head slightly and spoke rapidly to Dunyo. Dunyo translated. "*Kporkpor* wants to know why you are asking him these strange questions. Did his children do some wrong?"

Amlima answered the question. "We are only investigating a case. Unfortunately we can't disclose the details now. But we will keep in touch with him. When we need to talk to him again we will contact him. We are grateful to the two of you."

"Can he go now?" Dunyo asked indicating Nani.

"Yes, and we will also be going now."

The two cops stood up as Dunyo led Nani back to his room. He came back to take them out of the shrine.

"Are there no other people in the shrine?" Bansa asked.

"Yes, there are other people, a lot. It is a big shrine. But they did not want to be witnesses to what just happened. We don't normally grant such favours to people. That is why you didn't see anybody outside."

Amlima and Bansa quickly put on their clothes and bid good-bye to Dunyo.

"The jobs that we have to do!" Bansa said.

"It is all in the line of duty!" said Amlima.

***   ***   ***

Hunɔ Dunyo went for his pound of flesh that night. Just after his visit to the shrine with the policemen, he sent his match-maker, Atuklui, to inform Ablator that he had delivered on his promise and that he expected Ablator to keep her part of the bargain.

That night, Dunyo wore a dress he had made for himself the previous week. It was a pair of loose pants that reached below his knees and a loose shirt of the same material. He reeked of an excess dose of perfume. He reached Ablator's house at about eight o'clock expecting her to have finished her evening chores. But Ablator was then washing her plates and pans. She wiped her hands in her cloth and gave Dunyo a seat.

"I will be with you soon," she said.

Dunyo sat down with a sigh. He saw Lucy emerge from her room and called out to her amiably. "Good evening, my sister."

"Good evening," Lucy replied.

While Ablator washed her dishes, Lucy quickly had her bath and retired indoors with her children. She bid good-night to Ablator and Dunyo and closed her door. Dunyo smacked his lips in delight — things were going just the way he had hoped. Ablator finished her dishes and sent her children to bed. She picked a low stool and came and sat down adjacent to Dunyo.

190

"I don't want to keep you waiting too long so I won't have my bath now," she said.

"Oh, please go and have your bath. I can wait," Dunyo said. "After the long day's work you need to freshen up yourself."

"You are sure you don't mind waiting?"

"Not at all?"

Ablator quickly had her bath and came and sat down again. "Now, what?" she said, laughter in her voice.

"An appointed date usually arrives faster than we expect," Dunyo said. "I have kept my part of our little bargain and you are now keeping yours. That is very fine. Now what do we do?"

Dunyo set his finger on his lips and looked up, as if in deep thought. Then he said, "Let's get some drinks and just sit here."

"That is fine by me," Ablator said.

"Who will go for the drinks, you or me?"

"Since you are my guest I guess I have to go. But you will have to buy."

"No problem. Come for the money." Dunyo dipped his hand in his pocket and brought out some money.

"Let me get something to put the drinks in," Ablator said and went for a basket. When she came back Dunyo gave her the money then patted her on the buttock as he said, "Ei, my beautiful lady!"

Ablator stepped quickly back. "Let's get one thing straight," she said. "If your hand touches any part of my body again, I will throw you out of this house!"

"Oh, don't get angry with me, I am only being playful," Dunyo apologised. "Buy me two bottles of beer and anything for yourself."

Ablator went out for the drinks leaving Dunyo to

ponder over the difficult task ahead of him for it was his aim to get Ablator into bed that night. She came back within a short time and set the drinks on a low table in front of Dunyo. She had bought two bottles of minerals for herself. She brought out drinking glasses and opened all four bottles. Dunyo tried valiantly to get the conversation going again but the atmosphere was strained; Ablator only answered him with monosyllables.

"*Davi* Ablator, cheer up. This is not the type of evening I was looking forward to."

Ablator flared up. "What type of evening were you expecting? To carry me into bed and make love to me?"

Dunyo was shocked at the woman's bluntness. "No, no, no, that is not what I have in mind. As I told you before, my aim is just to socialise with you. I have made it known to you that I desire you, but I am a very patient man. I can wait for as long as it takes you to be in the right frame of mind before I propose anything to you."

"Propose to me? Ha, ha, ha... You don't need to since my answer will be a firm No! Look, it's even late. I had a difficult day. Please hurry up so that we can all go to bed."

"Ei, my iron woman! Beer is not drunk in a hurry so please give me a little time otherwise I will get a bloated stomach."

"Just go as fast as you can." She threw her head back and upturned one of the minerals into her mouth and gulped it all down. "Excuse me." She got up to send some few items to her room.

This was the chance Dunyo had been waiting for. He had begun to despair if he would ever get the opportunity. Quickly his hands dashed into his pocket and brought out a small roll of paper which he spread out. The slip of paper contained a powdery substance. He took a pinch between his thumb and forefinger and dropped it into Ablator's untouched bottle of mineral. He added two more pinches and replaced the paper in his pocket. He now relaxed and waited with a sense of accomplishment and anticipation.

Ablator came back to the table and without sitting down, upturned her second bottle into her mouth and almost drank it all off. "How are you getting on? Have you finished?" she asked.

"I am going as fast as I can. Please be a little patient with me," Dunyo pleaded with a secret smile.

She sat down and finished the rest of her drink.

"Are you going to the market tomorrow?" Dunyo asked, still trying to make some conversation.

"Yes, I go every day." She yawned wide, covering her mouth with the back of her hand. "Please hurry up; I am now really sleepy."

"Okay, okay. Show me somewhere to pass water so that I can come back and finish the rest of the drink."

"Just go over there and do it against the wall."

"Very well." He took as much time as he could and when he came back the woman was resting her head on the small table. He sat down quietly and regarded the woman. It was obvious she was dozing. He continued sipping his drink for some minutes before tapping Ablator on the shoulder. He shook her a little but the woman had fallen asleep. Her arm slid down from the table and fell lifeless beside her. A wide smile of satisfaction broke over Dunyo's face. He tossed off the rest of his drink and stood up. He tiptoed to Ablator's room and pushed open the door which was ajar. By the light of a kerosene lamp that burned in the room he could see two children sleeping on mats and snoring softly. Ahead of him was another door;

193

he removed his sandals and tiptoed to the door and as he expected, it was Ablator's bedroom. The white sheet on the well-laid bed glittered in the semi darkness.

Dunyo went back to where Ablator lay sleeping. The small table had tilted to one side and the woman was almost lying in the sand. Dunyo shook her once more and satisfied that she was deep in sleep he pulled her up and, throwing her lifeless arm over his shoulder, he carried her into the room. The woman's head hung over her chest like a drunk man's. While he carried her through the ante-room, his foot kicked against a pan on the floor and he stopped dead. The two children turned in their sleep, their snoring ceasing for a moment. Dunyo waited until their soft snores started again before he moved on with his load into the bedroom. He set her on the bed and let out a deep breath. The woman was heavier than he had thought. Quietly he began to remove her clothes — first her loin cloth under which she wore a pair of tight shorts.

This must have been to protect herself against me, Dunyo thought with mirth.

He removed the shorts with difficulty; underneath the woman wore nothing. He patted her between the thighs and then removed her blouse. She wore no brassieres and for a woman of her age her breasts were still quite firm. Dunyo spread-eagled her limbs on the bed, then went to peep into the children's room. They were still fast asleep. He quickly removed his clothes, dropping them on the floor. Then he crept beside the helpless woman. He spat into his palm and spreading the woman's legs further wetted her between the thighs. Supporting himself on his knees and elbows he entered her, not too gently.

This was Dunyo's stock-in-trade. He had tricked

several women into this position to satisfy his sexual urges. Two women he treated this way were now his wives. The ignorant women thought they might have fallen asleep and unwittingly allowed the brute to have his way, so they followed the obvious course and married him. On one occasion, however, one of his victims saw through his act when she woke up and found herself wet with semen. She reported him to the elders of the town and Dunyo was made to pay a very heavy fine. Dunyo learnt a lesson from this woman.

So after satisfying himself he searched through his clothes and brought out a small cotton towel. Carefully, he wiped Ablator of all traces of semen and covered her naked body with a piece of cloth that hung from the bedpost. He slid back into his clothes and making sure that he had left no object behind that could be identified with him, he slipped out of the apartment and pulled the door shut. He looked round to make sure there was nobody about in the compound and then let himself out through the gate.

Dunyo was very satisfied with himself and his steps felt light in the crisp sand. As he turned the first corner he almost bumped into a man coming from the opposite direction. Both men stepped back and looked at each other. The other man was Kobla Adekpitor. He was on his way ostensibly to see if Nani's family was safe, but secretly to grab a late evening chat with Ablator. Who knows? Anything could happen at that time of night. Since the funeral of Ablator's mother-in-law, Adekpitor had started regarding Dunyo with suspicion. Thieves easily recognised each other. Adekpitor had seen the way Dunyo was making all efforts to ingratiate himself with the family, and he did not like it. He suspected rightly that Dunyo had just come out of Ablator's house.

"Where are you coming from, you treacherous man?" Adekpitor asked, hooking his hand into Dunyo's shirt with lightning speed.

Dunyo was surprised. "Where I am coming from, old man, is no concern of yours," he said.

A man loomed out of the darkness and stopped beside the two men. "What is the matter with you two?" he asked when he recognised the two men. He was Gbekle, the popular drunkard town-crier.

"This man is a nuisance," Adekpitor said, letting go of Dunyo's shirt. "He is a leech and we don't want him in our family." He spat into the sand and walked away.

Dunyo and Gbekle watched until Adekpitor opened Ablator's gate and entered the house.

"That man is mad," Dunyo said.

"When a mad man takes hold of your pants and runs away with it," Gbekle said, "you don't run after him; otherwise the two of you will be put into the same category. Good night, my brother."

"Good night."

The two men parted and Dunyo walked home, his satisfaction with the night a little tainted by Adekpitor's impetuous behaviour.

When Adekpitor entered Ablator's house, he was surprised that everything was so quiet. He was sure Dunyo had just left the house and that meant someone in the house had just met him. He listened at Lucy's door. He tried the handle but found the door to be locked. He tried Ablator's door too and it opened wide at the first push. He peeped into the room and saw the children sleeping.

"Why haven't these people locked the door?" he asked

himself. He entered the room and peeped into the chamber, He saw Ablator's form on the bed and stepped back. He made to turn away and leave the room, then he stopped. He entered the room again and approached the bed.

"Ablator," he called softly, bending down to touch the woman. "Ablator."

He shook the woman a little, his hand dropping to her navel but the woman showed no sign of waking up. More confident now, he began to explore the woman's body through the thin cloth. Then he gently lifted the cloth aside and to his extreme delight he saw that she wore no clothes beneath the cloth. With his heart now thundering against his chest in excitement, he went and peeped into the children's room; the little kids continued to sleep peacefully. Then he threw off his huge cloth and stepped out of his loose shorts. He crept onto the woman and, spreading her legs apart, he slid inside her.

These women! he thought, his pleasure knowing no bounds. I am sure she is awake but is pretending to be asleep. I knew she also wanted me all along!

***   ***   ***

Lucy noticed a sudden change in Ablator the following day. When she was ready to go to the market to sell her wares and Ablator had still not shown any indication that she was also going to the market, she asked if she was all right.

"I am not feeling well," Ablator replied.

"What is it?"

"I am just feeling weak." Her eyes were blood-shot and she wore a mournful look.

197

"You look as if you have been crying. What happened last night?"

"Nothing. I will keep the house. You go to the market."

Lucy stared long at Ablator. She sighed and left for the market.

Ablator had woken up in the morning and found herself and her bed wet with semen. She had let out a long silent scream and wept silently and bitterly. "This man has raped me, the he-goat has raped me!" she repeated several times as she wept.

She was engulfed by shame. What will people think of me? she asked herself. She had remained a long time in her bed, her mind working furiously. As she cleaned away the stains on her body, she decided she would not tell Lucy about her humiliating experience.

Now, left alone in the house, she wandered aimlessly from one end of the house to the other, tears streaming down her face. She went to her room and lay down on the sheetless bed. She felt tired and sleepy but sleep eluded her. She got up and had a thorough bath, the second one that morning. She was hungry but had no appetite. She powdered her face to hide the strain marks around her eyes and then went out of the house.

***   ***   ***

When night fell, clouds hid the light of the moon from the earth. It was very dark and not a single star could be seen in the sky. At the town's durbar ground, the night was blackest. Here the shady mango and nim trees that formed a perimeter around the grounds threw woolly shadows that made the darkness under them almost

198

impenetrable to the eye. These trees were the haunt of big owls whose eerie cries in the night kept people away from the square out of fear. This night the hoots of the owls seemed to be at their loudest.

From the direction of the marketplace which lay about a hundred metres from the square the lonely figure of a man approached the square. He moved furtively even though the darkness provided enough cover to hide him from any prying eyes, not that anybody would be brave enough to be at the square at this time of the night, anyway.

The owls set off a cacophony of hoots and the man shuddered. Tales of witches perching on the durbar ground's shady trees to devour their human victims flashed through his mind, but he resolutely pushed them away. He began to sing a war song to bolster up his faltering courage:

Amewo tso tu
Tso tu yi aʋa wɔge;
Amewo tso yi,
Tso yi yi aʋa wɔge.
Aʋawɔŋutsuvi ya mesia ku o ɖe
Eso ɖe gbe mie wɔge,
Ame wo be adzido adzido.
Eso ɖe gbe mie wɔge...

Mega yi bo o,
Amekuku ta egla mele nu o he.
Ðe me be mayi boo,
Ðe me be mayi boo,
Xedewo tsi amlima he...

The adrenalin began to pump up in his blood and he took a few steps of the war dance. He reached the trees, no more afraid, and leaning against an electric pole that rose through the foliage of the trees, he began to wait. Soon after another figure loomed out of the darkness. It wore dark clothes — a pair of trousers and a long-sleeved shirt and a cap popularly called *coolie high* to match.

The man disengaged himself from the electric pole. "You are very much on time," he said as the figure came to stand before him.

"So are you."

The man stretched forth his arms and the two people fell into an embrace. "Ah..." the man sighed.

"Did you tell anybody you were coming here?" the figure in dark clothes asked.

"Not at all," the man said. "I am not a woman."

The arms of the figure had been thrown around the man's neck in the embrace. Now one arm disengaged itself and from the pocket of its trousers the figure pulled out a long knife. The arm drew back and in swift movements drove the knife repeatedly into the man's stomach.

"*Adzei!*" the man shouted, his arms flying off from the embrace to clutch at his stomach. The figure watched as the man tottered back and fell on the ground with a thud. Carefully, it cleaned the knife in the man's clothes. Then it turned and left the scene as silently as it had come.

CHAPTER FOURTEEN

Two dead bodies were discovered at Woe in the morning. Shock waves ran through the town as multitudes of people trooped to the two death spots to view the horrifying spectacle. Some people shuttled between the two spots while others stuck to one, absorbing the scene and the commentary that was in no short supply.

The first dead body was discovered at the durbar ground below the shady trees. It was quickly identified as that of *Hunɔ* Dunyo. Ants crawled all over the body, going in and out of his ears, nose and mouth. His face, even in death, was a picture of profound shock and the front part of his shirt was still wet with blood. Dunyo's wives and children rushed to the durbar ground wailing and flailing their arms in anguish. People gave them way and two of his children fell on the dead body weeping.

Woe was a murky area so far as police administration was concerned. There are 110 political districts in Ghana. For their administration, the police have more than 110 districts, so that in one political district there can be several police districts. The police districts are zoned into divisions headed by divisional commanders. The Volta Region has three divisions — the Keta, Ho and Hohoe divisions. The political district of Keta has three police districts, namely, the Keta, Anloga and Abor police districts. Woe was caught right in the middle between Keta and Anloga police districts. So criminal reports from Woe were sometimes tossed about for some time before they were allowed to land in one of the two police districts. But when ASP Mark Adosu, the Keta District Police Commander, assumed office things changed for the better; he was always ready to take up any case that happened between Tegbi and Anloga.

Dunyo's murder was reported to the Keta Police at 9.00 a.m. and his body was conveyed to the Keta Hospital mortuary. ASP Adosu went mad with rage when he heard the news. He quickly summoned Inspector Dongor to his office.

"Have you heard the latest?" he asked before the inspector could sit down.

"Sadly, yes," Dongor replied.

"Do people kill as a pastime? How can people be so wicked?"

"It beats my mind," Dongor said.

Adosu grunted. "Who are we going to put on this one?"

"Er, Sergeant Amlima's hands are full at the moment. Let's put Corporal Richard Bena on it. He is a good detective."

"We will have to have some quick results on this one, otherwise at the rate at which these things are happening we will all be buried under murder cases. Let's bring in Corporal Bena."

ASP Adosu rang the powerful electric bell on his desk. The bell was so loud that when it rang it could be heard as far as across the street. A police messenger came in and Adosu asked him to bring in Corporal Bena. The two officers knew Bena leaned too hard on the bottle. Each of them had at different times talked to the corporal about his drinking habit, but the man continued to drink, sometimes even before coming to the office. There was very little they could do other than recommend that Bena be dismissed from the service. But most senior officers were very hesitant when it came to recommending punitive measures against their subordinates, especially offences that were likely to attract dismissal as punishment. Nobody wanted to carry the blame for somebody being thrown out of work.

Bena came in on the double, a ready smile on his lips. He had not taken any liquor that morning and he was anxious that his senior men should know about it. He went as near as he could dare to Adosu's desk before saluting smartly. "Good morning, sirs."

"Good morning. How are you?"

"I am fine, thank you, sir."

"Sit down."

"Thank you, sir." Bena was tall and spare of flesh. He was an intelligent officer but was otherwise lazy and put very little hours into his work. He preferred getting tipsy on liquor and sleeping it off in bed. But when a case hooked his interest he never rested until he cracked it. He had big eyes that were all the more noticeable because of his lean face.

"Have you heard of the murder case this morning?" ASP Adosu asked, looking at Bena intently.

"I just heard it, sir."

"What are you working on now?"

"A theft case, sir."

"What does it involve?"

"Some wooden boards. One inch by twelve inches by sixteen feet odum boards. Twenty of them stolen."

"How are you getting on?"

"The suspect is on bail. His case is for court next week."

"We want you to take up this murder case also. You must work very quickly. I want the case solved as soon as possible."

"Yes, sir."

"Whatever help you need let me know."

"Yes, sir. Please, is there anything that you would like to tell me about the case?"

"There is nothing that we know that you don't know."

"Thank you, sir." Bena saluted and left the office. Sergeant Amlima was waiting at the door when Bena came out. The two men exchanged nods. Bena stood aside for his senior officer to enter the room before he walked out.

"Good morning, sirs," Amlima said.

"Good morning. How are you?" One good thing about ASP Adosu was that he always inquired about the health of his staff. His subordinates liked this; he was not like other senior officers who just nodded at your greetings.

"Fine, thank you, sir."

"Yes, what can I do for you?"

Amlima extended an envelope he was holding towards the officer. "The psychiatric report on the suspect Johnny Klevor is ready, sir. This is a copy for you."

"Oh, when did you come back?"

"Last night, sir."

"Have you brought the suspect back?"

"Yes, sir."

"Why are you bringing me the report instead of sending it to the court registrar?"

"This is only a copy for you, sir. I have already sent the original to the court registrar. The doctor said there is some important information in the envelop for you, sir."

"What does the report say on Johnny?"

"It says he is sane, at least now. Read it for yourself, sir."

Adosu opened the envelop and two folded slips of

204

paper fell out. One was the psychiatric report on Johnny Klevor. It was written and signed by Dr. K. C. Amissah, Senior Medical Officer, Accra Psychiatric Hospital. Adosu read through quickly and then looked up.

"It says the suspect is sane, now."

"Yes, sir."

"It also says he appeared to have suffered a brief period of insanity of which he has now completely lost memory."

"Yes, sir."

"Does that help our case?"

"In a way, no sir. I think his brief insanity and loss of memory cast some doubts on his evidence against Tsormanya."

"What about the body we exhumed and the empty graves at the two other sites? Are those not evidence enough?"

"Those are strong points in our favour."

"Did you send the soil we collected from the graves to the lab?"

"Yes, sir."

Accra had directed that a bucketful of soil be collected from each grave and sent to the police laboratory in Accra for analysis. Amlima had been asked to take the sand to Accra along with Johnny.

"When can we have the report on the sand?"

"They said next week, sir. I hope they will finish their work early so that we can present the evidence in court."

"When next is Tsormanya going to court?"

"On the 7th of July, sir."

Adosu opened the other folded slip of paper and began to read. As he read, the two other men could see on his face at first amusement, then surprise and then outright excitement. He finished reading and tossed the slip of paper to Inspector Dongor. "Well, read that!" he said.

The first part of the letter was effusive salutation followed by a statement on the good health of the writer and his family. Then it launched into a lengthy tirade against the wickedness of man:

...What is wrong with people? Whoever said that human blood or human body parts possess any magic?... When is man going to abandon the wicked mentality of profiting at the expense of his brother, not caring if his brother loses even his life?...

One other thing that I discovered in my investigations on the suspect is that apart from the intense guilt that must have contributed to his temporary insanity, drugs also may have played a part. The suspect confessed to using narcotic drugs. He also engaged in distribution of the drugs in Lome, Togo. He mentioned a cousin of his as the one who introduced him to the drugs. If you think this aspect of my investigation will help your case in court then let me know quickly so that I can incorporate it in my final report. On the other hand if you think it will harm your case as I suspect, then forget about it. But if you can, investigate the drug trafficking the suspect talked about. Please destroy this letter after reading it.

Yours in the fight against evil,

K.C. AMMISAH
SNR. MED. OFFICER.

206

Dongor looked up from the letter, his face wearing an expression of amusement.

"Well, what do you think?" Adosu asked. "Give it to Amlima also to read."

Dongor shook his head as he gave the letter to Amlima. "I have heard it said that some of these guys who examine other people's heads sometimes get touched in the head too."

"So you think he imagined all that?" Adosu asked.

"No, not that. I am only amused by his keen interest in the case."

"He is only doing his duty as a concerned citizen."

"That is true, sir. Shall we take it up? I mean the drug case."

"Of course we will! Let Amlima take it up in addition."

Sergeant Amlima groaned inwardly. "Yes, sir," he said.

"I want a report on my desk by this time next week."

"Yes, sir," Dongor said and led Amlima out of the ASP's office.

At times like this Dongor wished he were a station officer in a little village somewhere in the district. Even though he was the station officer at Keta, he had little independence. The district commander kept getting in the way.

As they walked towards the station office, Dongor asked Amlima, "Have you heard about the latest murder?"

"No!"

"A man was knifed at Woe. His body was sent to the morgue this morning."

"Wow! When was he killed?" Amlima asked his

mouth hanging open.

"How do I know when the postmortem report is not ready? But I think he was killed last night."

"Who has been put on this case?"

"Detective Corporal Bena."

"Well, he is good when he chooses to work."

***   ***   ***

A second dead body was discovered that morning on the beach at Woe, caught in the net of some fishermen. It was the body of a man and there was very little else in the net. These days fishermen had very little catch and even though this area lies between two water bodies, the sea and the lagoon, the cost of fish was becoming very dear. Some attribute the poor catches to over-fishing while others thought it was due to the sins of the people, especially the moral decadence among the youth who indulged in all sorts of immoral acts on the beach during festive occasions like Christmas and the *Hogbetsotso* festival.

When the fishermen landed the dead body, everyone fled in panic. People from other nets saw the consternation from afar and rushed to the scene. One by one the bravest among the crowd approached the net and spread it out. The body was brought out of the net by its limbs and a shout went out from the crowd.

"What wickedness!" people said. "Who could have done this? When are people going to stop doing this sort of thing?"

Ritual murder had so much taken up their pysche that it did not cross anyone's mind that the man could have drowned on his own without anyone's involvement.

The dead body was laid out in the sand and the crowd surged forward to have a closer look.

The net owner who was among the first people to approach the body now elbowed his way out of the crowd and called to one of his men. "Run and inform the police," he said. He was already thinking about the expensive rituals he must now perform to cleanse his net. He was very angry, not at the loss of life that had occurred but at the toll that the cleansing rites would take on his already lean finances. A sudden surge of agitation among the crowd made the net owner walk back to the crowd.

"It is Kofi Legede!" the crowd said excitedly.

Indeed it was the body of Kofi Legede. He was in a blue T-shirt and long knickers. His skin was pale and patches of it had been eaten away by the fish. His stomach bulged out horribly as if it was on the verge of bursting open. Thin trickles of water escaped from his ears, nostrils and mouth.

While some remained to see things for themselves to the end, others quickly left the beach to spread the news in town of the murder of Kofi Legede. The conclusion everyone on the beach had arrived at was that the boy had been murdered.

The officer at the counter at the Keta Police Station who received the report of the dead body at the beach did not at first believe the two fishermen who came to make the report.

"Are the inhabitants of this area at war with each other?" he asked no-one in particular. He took down the case, then he called ASP Adosu to report the latest death. Even the two fishermen who stood some distance away from the counter could clearly hear the voice of the district commander as he exploded into expletives over the phone. Three men were sent to the beach and Kofi's body was also conveyed to the mortuary. The police went and brought Mama Kokui, Kofi's grandmother, from Woe to come and positively identify the body.

She was led through the crowd at the mortuary and when she stood over the body, she wailed loudly, "Oh, Kofi!" she said. "Is this your end? What will your poor mother say, you being her only child? This is what you wanted to happen to you. This is the fate you have been chasing all your life!..."

The police took Mama Kokui back to Woe and the mortuary-men put Kofi's body in the morgue without embalming it. Dead bodies brought to the morgue from outside the hospital were embalmed only after postmortem.

*** *** ***

Sergeant Amlima woke up from a long sleep still feeling tired. He looked at his watch. It was almost 7.00 p.m. He was tempted to continue sleeping but he pulled himself up from the bed, not without effort. He had promised himself that he would talk to Johnny before the day was out. His wife, a nurse, was on afternoon duty and had not yet returned from work. She would close at eight o'clock and get home at about nine. His two children were not in the house. No doubt they were out playing.

Amlima washed his face and wiped it dry. He threw on a shirt and went to the charge office to collect the key to Johnny's cell. The officer at the counter looked up from the ledger in which he was making an entry. "You went after a suspect who escaped through the rafters the other time, didn't you?" the officer asked.

"Yes," Amlima replied.

"What was his name?"

"Kofi ...Kofi something."

"Kofi Legede."

"Yes, that is his name."

"He is dead."

"What?" Amlima left the key on its hook and came to stand at the counter beside the officer. "What did you say?"

"He is dead, my brother. He was fished out of the sea this afternoon."

"My God! When is this going to end?"

"I don't know. Some of us will soon leave town with our tails between our legs."

Amlima went back to the rack and picked the key. He was in a furious mood. He could swear on his uniform that Kofi did not die a natural death — he had been killed to keep his mouth shut. He unlocked Johnny's cell, handcuffed him and took him to the interrogation room. "Sit down," he told the boy.

Johnny sat down. He also appeared tired from the long journey to Accra.

"My friend, the sergeant began, you are in danger, very serious danger. Do you know that your friend Kofi Legede has been killed? He has been killed so that he will not corroborate your revelations. What does that tell you, eh?"

Johnny sat up at the vehemence in the detective's voice, but he said nothing.

"What does that tell you, Johnny? It tells you that you can also be killed. Yes, if whoever killed Kofi gets you, he will finish you off, pam! like that. So you'd better tell me every little wrong that you have ever done in

211

collaboration with other people. We will arrest all of them so that whoever amongst them wants you dead cannot harm you. They will safely be behind prison bars. Understand?"

Johnny nodded and said weakly, "Yes."

"Good. Now I want you to tell me everything about yourself, right from infancy up to this time. Your life history."

"My life history? What has that got to do with my case?"

"You never know. Just tell me everything."

Johnny sighed. He felt very tired and wished he would be left in peace. "Can you take my handcuffs off?" he asked extending his hands to Amlima.

"Will that help you talk better?"

"My wrists are sore. "

Amlima looked at Johnny long and hard. "Okay, I'll take them off but you'd better behave yourself." He unlocked the handcuffs and placed them noisily between him and Johnny. "Now talk."

"Where do I start from?" Johnny asked flexing his wrists.

"From the beginning. Your life history."

Johnny hesitated. "Er, I was born on 21st May, 1969... Er, er, I can't remember anything!"

"You can't remember anything?"

"Yes those times are too far back. I can't remember them."

The detective reclined in his chair and waved his hand. "Calm down, Johnny, calm down. I am not asking you to tell me every detail about yourself right from birth. I want you to tell me only those details that you can remember. Relax. Just take it easy and tell me anything that comes to your mind about yourself."

Johnny sighed. "Well, that makes it easier," he said, then fell into thought. "I remember I played with my brothers when we were small. I-I went to school at Salvation Army Primary School..."

"Where was that?"

"At Woe. Then I continued at Bensah Memorial Middle School also at Woe but I couldn't complete. So I took after my dead father and started fishing."

"You now accept that your father is dead?"

"Since you all say so," Johnny said, spreading out his hands helplessly.

"Go on."

Johnny talked about his recruitment into Tsormanya's fishing company and again about the ritual murders he participated in. When he got to his departure for Lome, Togo, the detective's questions became more insistent.

"Why exactly did you go to Lome?" Amlima asked.

"I just went there to seek the benevolence of my cousin François."

"His benevolence?"

"Yes."

"Is he a very rich man?"

"Hm, quite rich, very rich."

"What work does he do?"

"He is a businessman."

"What business does he do?"

"Er, he owns stores."

"What else?"

"Er, nothing."

Amlima sat back making a show of being exasperated. "Johnny," he said, "you and I agreed from the beginning that we were not going to hide anything from

213

each other."

"Yes."

"Then what about the other activities of your cousin? What about the drugs?"

It was Johnny's turn to sit back in his chair. "The doctor in Accra talked to you about his conversation with me, eh?" he asked.

Amlima waved the question away. "That is not important now. What we are saying now is between you and me."

"That was what the doctor in Accra said."

"Never mind that. Now tell me exactly what you were doing in Lome and the activities of your cousin, François."

Johnny sighed again. "Well," he said, "I told the doctor I sometimes used drugs."

"How often?"

"Oh, once in a while."

"Did you use it with your cousin?"

"No, not with my cousin."

"Then with whom?"

"I did it on my own, sometimes with a certain man."

"Who is this man?"

"Monsieur Agbokli. He is a friend of my cousin François."

"What sort of drugs were you using?"

"Cocaine, only cocaine."

"How did you feel when you first used the cocaine?"

"Um, I just felt different, like I could do anything. I felt free and powerful."

"After that what happened?"

"Nothing."

"You were helping your cousin to distribute the

drugs, weren't you?"

"Okay, yes, I was doing that. The doctor in Accra told you that too, didn't he? He told me whatever I discussed with him would be between him and me, but he has told you everything."

Amlima reached over the narrow table between them and took Johnny gently by the shoulders. "What we are doing, Johnny, is partly for your own good, your own safety. I've told you what has happened to your friend Kofi. The same thing can happen to you. If we are aware of all the angles of your case then we can provide you with better security here."

"I understand," Johnny said.

"Good. Now tell me the modus operandi of your cousin's drug trade."

"The what?"

"I mean the way your cousin carries out his drug business."

"No way! I am not here because of that. I am here because of another case."

"That is true," the detective said, barely able to control his impatience. He decided to change his line of approach. "Johnny, do you know the punishment for the murders you have committed?"

"What is it?"

"Death, by hanging maybe, but certainly death."

There were cracks in Johnny's voice as he said, "If that is my fate, so be it. I've been bad so I am ready for my punishment."

"Your situation is not helpless, Johnny," the detective said. "If you agree to tell me everything we can arrange so that you will not be put to death."

"That is a trick. I won't fall for that. If I am going to

215

be punished, let me be punished. I won't put anybody else in trouble."

"You don't understand, Johnny. In law if anyone kills another person, he could be charged for either murder or manslaughter. If you are convicted of murder you will almost certainly be put to death. If you get a conviction for manslaughter you get only a prison sentence."

"Are you saying you can manage to get a conviction for manslaughter for me?"

"Exactly, and in exchange you tell me everything about the drug business of your cousin." Amlima said a little mental prayer to God to forgive him this false promise.

"That sounds appealing," Johnny said. "For, to tell you the truth, I am terrified of being put to death."

Amlima heaved a sigh of relief. "Good," he said. "Now go ahead and tell me everything and you can rest assured that you will not be put to death."

Johnny took his face between his palms and rubbed it hard, his hands coming to rest in front of his face with his thumbs supporting his chin. "It is not as easy as that," he said. "You don't so easily betray a brother who has been very good to you."

"Good to you?" the detective snorted. "Your cousin was ruining your life. Narcotic drugs don't do you any good. Their possession and use are injurious to society. They are against the law."

"You don't understand. My cousin was very kind to me."

Amlima made an exasperated sound. "You were being poisoned slowly and if it were not because of the mess you have fallen into, you would have sooner or later gone completely mad or been apprehended by the law."

216

Johnny breathed noisily. "Okay, okay. My cousin sold his drugs in Togo and in Ghana."

"In Ghana too?"

"Yes."

"How does he bring it into Ghana?"

"Some people take it across the border."

"Which people?"

"I don't know them. I only know that some people bring it for him."

"Where does your cousin stay in Lome?"

"He stays at Kodzoviakope on the border."

Johnny and Sergeant Amlima talked for a long time. He gave the policeman the direction to, and a description of François' house in Lome. Afterwards, the policeman took him back to his cell and locked him up.

Amlima took the keys back to the rack and went down the steps of the charge office in a pensive mood.

"Good night, sir," the counter NCO called after him.

Amlima turned back and walked slowly to the officer. "Please keep an eye on the suspect I just talked to, and tell the man who takes over from you for the night to do the same."

"You are afraid he might run away?"

"I have my reasons."

Arrogant fool, the officer thought as he watched Amlima walk away.

***   ***   ***

That night Private Alex Atonsu again took Johnny to see Prophet Patu. As on the first occasion he had to steal the cell keys. The officer on duty was sound asleep on the bench behind the counter and it was the easiest

217

thing for Atonsu to remove the keys from the rack.

On the way to Patu's house, Johnny asked Atonsu, "These nocturnal outings are not official, are they?"

Atonsu was taken aback by the question. Johnny had usually remained in sullen silence but this night his voice sounded light and care-free.

"You could say they are sort of semi-official," Atonsu replied, "because on the one hand these visits will help our investigations and on the other hand they will help you spiritually; some sort of spiritual upliftment."

"I see," Johnny said and lapsed into silence. Then he started humming a song.

Atonsu threw him a quizzical glance. "You seem to be quite happy."

"Not exactly happy, just resigned to my fate."

Atonsu became uneasy. Johnny's change in attitude made him wonder if the suspect was about to pull any tricks on him. When they reached the prophet's house, Atonsu jumped down before the vehicle came to a complete standstill. He ran round to Johnny's side and opened the door for him.

"You are extra smart this night, aren't you?" Johnny said as he got down from the vehicle.

In irritation, Atonsu grabbed him by the handcuffs and almost pulled him along.

"Tell you what," Johnny said, "I will not come on these nocturnal outings any more."

Atonsu recovered quickly from his surprise. Calmly he said, "You don't have to. You'll soon be shot dead."

Johnny started. "Who told you that?"

"Shut up!"

The prophet came to the door at the first knock. He wore a sleeveless shirt and a big towel wrapped around

218

his waist. My own guinea pig, he thought when he saw Johnny.

"Please come in, and do sit down," he said. He lifted his eyes to the clock on the wall. "I didn't realise it was so late. I am busily preparing some material for our revival meeting tomorrow night. You are coming, aren't you? I wish our friend Johnny could come too. How are you Johnny?"

"Fine, thank you, prophet."

"You are in a better mood today. You see what the Spirit can do for you? Brother Atonsu, let me see you for a minute."

Atonsu stood up and with a hand on his shoulder, the prophet propelled him towards the door and took him outside. After a few minutes, the prophet came back to the room to fetch a bunch of keys. When he re-entered the room he was alone.

"Our friend is in my car relaxing," he told Johnny. "He is listening to good music. I don't want him to distract you. You remember the way he kept interrupting us the other days? Good, now let's take off these handcuffs... Fine. Now, just sit back and let yourself relax."

Johnny wondered if the prophet had his own key with which he unlocked the handcuffs but when the prophet placed the keys and the handcuffs on the table he realised they were the same keys the police had been using. He wriggled his wrists and sat back waiting for the prophet to put him to sleep again, for that was how he termed what the man had been doing to him. When his eyes met those of the prophet's, he found himself beginning to float again.

The prophet's voice came to him from afar. Johnny, now you are free of your physical body. You can go

219

anywhere, into the past or into the future. Now we are going into the past. Let's go to Lome. You are in Lome. What do you see? What are you doing?"

Johnny began to speak in a monotone. "We are in Monsieur Agbokli's house. We are sniffing cocaine."

"What?"

The vehemence in the prophet's voice jolted Johnny and his eyes began to regain focus. But the prophet's soothing voice urged him back into the hypnotic state.

"What are you doing now, Johnny?"

"We are sniffing cocaine." Johnny's voice was now firm and he spoke clearly. "We are sniffing cocaine, Monsieur Agbokli and I. Monsieur Agbokli's brother has come in to disturb us, but Monsieur Agbokli told him to go away... Oh, it's so delicious! What a feeling! I have never enjoyed anything like this..."

The prophet watched the ecstasy in the boy's eyes as they seemed to roll in their sockets. "Who has given you the cocaine?" he asked.

"Monseiur Agbokli," Johnny replied. "He is a very good man. He gives me money too."

"Where does Monsieur Agbokli get the drugs from?"

"My cousin gives them to him. My cousin is the supplier. He is a very rich man."

"What is your cousin's name?"

"François, alias Boxer. He is not a boxer. But they call him boxer..."

"Have you been telling a lot of people about your brother?"

"No, no, it's a secret, a big secret."

"You have not told anybody?"

"No, but I am going to tell the police."

"Why?"

"If I tell them, then they will not kill me for my murders."

"I see. You worm!" The prophet thought for a while, then he said, "Now Johnny, you are going to be very quiet, very, very still. Do not move an inch. Hold the sides of the chair firmly while I am away. Good. I will be back with you very soon."

He went out and closed the door behind him. He went down the flight of steps quickly to where he had parked his Mercedes Benz car. He knocked on the rolled-up glass before opening the door on the driver's side. Atonsu who was lying on the reclined driver's seat sat up. A popular highlife tune was sounding a little too loudly from the car's powerful speakers.

"Have you finished?" Atonsu asked.

"Not yet. A problem has cropped up."

Atonsu got out from the car. "What problem?"

Patu took in a deep breath. "I am afraid Johnny cannot go back to the station with you."

"What?"

"Relax. Don't get excited. Did anyone see you when you were bringing the suspect here?"

"No."

"Wasn't anyone on duty?"

"Yes, but, er, the officer on duty was dozing so he did not see me."

"Good. That means when you go back to the station without the suspect no-one will be none the wiser. Nobody will know his whereabouts. After a few days when he reappears no-one will know what exactly happened."

"What are you talking about? You want to ruin my career?"

"My brother Atonsu," the prophet said sternly, "don't

221

be a man of this world. Which is more important — your career or the work of the Holy Spirit, the work of God?... Hein?"

Atonsu looked away and said miserably, "The work of the Holy Spirit."

"Good! The problem is that with the state the suspect is in now it will be more dangerous to take him to the station. Better leave him here so that when he gets better you can come here secretly and take him back to the station."

"What state is he in?"

"Come with me." He took Atonsu by the hand and led him into the room. He spread his hands towards Johnny. "Do you want to take the young man back in this state?"

Atonsu's mouth fell open. Johnny sat very straight in the chair, his eyes focussed on empty space. His hands which gripped the sides of the chair had become drained of blood and looked very pale.

The prophet began to pray. "...Lord of miracles, manifest yourself. Do not let anyone hinder your work. Soften all hardened hearts to work towards the realisation of your ultimate goal for mankind. Touch our hearts right at this moment and make them instruments in your vineyard. Show us miracles, Lord. Manifest the work of the Spirit. *Hey ba, ba, ba, azematu dogo va tu go di. Hey azematu ba ba ba no no. Ke le de mi azematu bababa. Are matu gede me...*"

Atonsu reluctantly closed his eyes to join the prophet in prayer, reluctantly uttering punctuations of "Amen" and "Hallelujah."

"Sorry about that," the prophet said after the final amen. "Sometimes the Spirit just touches you and you can't do anything about it."

"That is okay, prophet."

"Now the Spirit has spoken," said the prophet. "If you still want to take Johnny away, I challenge you in the name of the Holy Spirit to unclasp his hands from that chair."

Atonsu looked at the pale hands of Johnny gripping the chair and said hurriedly, "Prophet, I am not challenging the Holy Spirit. I just want to do what is right."

"What is right is for you to leave the suspect here for a day or two. Come back for him quietly and I assure you nobody will lift an eyebrow."

"Are you sure, prophet?"

"Do you doubt my word? I who have been anointed to do the work of the Holy Spirit?"

"No, prophet, I don't doubt you."

"So what are you going to do?"

"I will leave the suspect here."

"Good."

Atonsu was almost heartbroken. "What about the handcuffs?" he asked. "Should I take them away?"

"Let's see," Patu said. "Was the suspect in handcuffs in his cell?"

"No, I put them on when we were coming here."

"Then take them away and put them exactly where you took them."

"Yes, prophet."

"Good night.

"Good night, prophet."

Atonsu drove furiously back to the station. He parked the vehicle at the barracks and surreptitiously went to the vicinity of the charge office. The officer on duty was now awake and was standing at the counter leafing through a ledger. Atonsu sighed. Wearily, he went back to the barracks and climbed the stairs to his room, the handcuffs making metallic sounds in his pocket. He threw the handcuffs under his bed, removed his clothes and crept into bed. He went over in his mind in what ways Johnny's disappearance could be linked to him. He could not see any. If questioned about his use of the vehicle in the night he could come up with any excuse. Everyone knew he used the vehicle at odd times. He sat up with a jerk when he remembered the night Constable George Aboagye made him sign a note before taking Johnny out. He muttered a foul four-letter word. How was he going to explain that one if George should talk?

"Damn it!" he said and fell back onto the bed.

CHAPTER FIFTEEN

Nani had now been at the Blemekpinu shrine for ten days. At times when he woke up from sleep he would wish fervently that it were all a dream. He could still not reconcile himself to the idea that he would have to live the rest of his life as a *Yeve* initiate. The thought of getting up one day and walking away from it all was never far from his mind. What still kept him at the shrine was the fear of the unknown, the fear of the repercussions that might befall his relatives should he abandon the initiation mid-stream. He could now speak the cult language quite well, though haltingly. He had learnt most of the dances of the cult and several songs. In spite of himself he liked some of the dances and songs.

Another source of mental agony for Nani was the news that his sons had been involved in ritual murders before their death. He kept pondering over the question — could his sons have been murderers? No! But in the deep recesses of his mind a cold unease kept reminding him about the bad temper of his sons, their introvert character and unwillingness to mix freely with other people. But could they have been murderers? As the days went by and Nani thought about the character of his sons he became more and more afraid to answer this question.

During the initial stages of his initiation, Nani had often been told that he would have to have his identity as a *Yeve* initiate tattooed on his body. This was in the form of short dashes stretching from each shoulder across his back to the small of his back. The two lines of dashes cut across each other in-between his shoulder blades. The marks were called *dakpla*. He would also have marks tatooed on his face. The tattoos were made with a sharp knife with herbs smeared into the wounds to stop the bleeding and speed up healing.

On the morning of his tenth day at the shrine, Nani was told to prepare for his *dakpla*. A cold sweat broke on him suddenly. He had seen the *dakpla* on the backs of many initiates. The thought of having to endure the pain of so many cuts sent shivers all over his body.

After he had eaten his breakfast, Nani changed his white loin cloth for a dark one and was taken to the enclosure where he had had his first herbal bath at the shrine. He was given a stool to sit on so that his back was turned on the entrance. One of the *somlatɔ,* the magician of the cult, came into the enclosure with an assistant and started talking to him.

"*Kporkpor,* how are you this morning?" he asked.

"I am fine," Nani replied in the cult language.

"The days fly very fast. So soon you have already spent ten days here. It is as if you came here only yesterday. Look at your hair, all grown back already..."

Nani realised the man was just talking to take his mind off the pain that he was about to inflict on him, a sort of anaesthesia.

"...Sadly I have to take off your hair again," the *somlatɔ* continued. "But don't worry. You have very good hair that grows back in no time..."

Nani felt cold water on his head and he knew his hair was being lathered again before being shaved off. The *somlatɔ* applied soap to Nani's head and then expertly began shaving the head clean. Nani's head itched all over and he began to enjoy the scrape of the knife against his pate, willing the knife to go the spots that itched him most. In a short while, the shaving was over and Nani's head was bereft of every particle of hair. The magician handed the knife to his assistant and wiped Nani's head clean with a wet towel. He gave the towel to an assistant who handed him another knife.

"Now," he said, "this aspect is going to hurt a little but be a man and endure it. Let's see if we can go through without a sound from you."

Nani knew the man was going to cut him up and he felt faint all of a sudden. With one hand, the magician pushed Nani's head forward until he was bent double on the low stool. He started the incisions from the small of the initiate's back. He grabbed Nani's skin in a small fold between his left forefinger and thumb and with his right hand he deftly made the first cut. Nani jumped when he felt the hot searing pain.

"Easy, easy," the magician said as he pushed him back to the crouching position on the stool. He took a pinch of black powdered herbs called *etsi* from a plate his assistant held and smeared it into the bleeding cut. And between the cuts of the magician and the starts from Nani, the initiate received his *dakpla*. Blood dripped from his back in rivulets which the *somlatɔ* was patiently trying to stop with his herbs.

"Now your face," the magician said and helped Nani to turn round on the seat.

Nani was so eaten up with pain that he did not mind a few more incisions. Expertly, the *somlatɔ* cut three incisions each on his cheeks and forehead. He applied the black powdery substance and patted Nani on the neck. "There, you look beautiful now," he said. "You are a real initiate now."

Nani was so angered by this remark he slipped into his own language and asked, "Does blood make people

227

beautiful?"

"Do not lose your temper," the *somlatɔ* said patiently. "You could be punished, you know. Our *katidao* is a very harsh man. But we will forget about this. You can come out now."

Led by the *somlatɔ* and his assistant, Nani came out of the enclosure, his face and back dripping blood. "How am I going to sleep now?" he asked.

"On your stomach for the first few days," the magician replied. "Then you can sleep normally. Forget about the cuts. That way they heal faster. Tomorrow is your big day. I wish you all the best." Then he was gone with his assistant, leaving Nani alone in the small compound.

Nani had been told his naming ceremony would take place the next day. He would be outdoored for the first time amid drumming and dancing. He would be given a cult name and from that day, woe betide anyone who referred to him with any name other than his cult name. The naming ceremony would be the first in a series of outdoorings until Nani became a full initiate. Tomorrow's outdooring would last for three days. Ablator and Lucy had already bought Nani a new white cloth for the ceremony.

*** *** ***

The day after his foray into Ablator's bed, Adekpitor travelled out of town very early in the morning. Before he left, he told one of his children to tell Ablator that he would be out of town for a few days and would see her as soon as he returned. He returned from his journey on the third day and made a bee-line for Ablator's house as soon

228

as he got down from the omnibus. He had bought two large loaves of bread for his sweet heart. He found Lucy alone in the house. She told him Ablator had taken food to the shrine for Nani. He left the loaves with Lucy with a message for Ablator that he would be back in the evening and would be glad if Ablator prepared a meal for him. Lucy smiled secretly, thinking what a fool Adekpitor was if he thought Ablator would fall for an old man like him.

When Adekpitor reached home his children told him a man who was looking for him had just left the house.

"Quick," he said, "run after him and tell him I am back."

The other children clamoured around him inquiring about what he had brought them from the journey. He gave them a packet of sweets and told them to send his bag to his room. His elder wife gave him water and then exchanged greetings with him.

"How is everybody?" he inquired.

"We are all fine," the woman replied.

"No trouble when I was away?"

"Nothing. Everything went on well."

The gate flew open and the child who had gone out shouted, "The man is coming," and in the same breath asked, "Where is my share of the sweets?"

"See your brothers and sisters," Adekpitor said, his eyes on the gate to see who his visitor was. The gate swung open again and a man stepped into the house. Adekpitor's eyes narrowed; he did not know the man. He was always wary of strangers. "You are welcome," he said.

"Thank you," the man replied.

Adekpitor's wife stood up and gave her seat to the stranger. She excused herself and left the two men alone.

After greetings, the stranger introduced himself. "I am Detective Corporal Richard Bena from the Keta Police," he said. "If you will grant me some minutes I will ask you a few questions."

The last time a policeman called at Adekpitor's house was about a year ago. It was about a stealing case involving one of his children. So Adekpitor was not amused by Bena's visit. "How do I know you are a policeman?" he asked. "You are not wearing uniform. And you know the bad people who have been going about impersonating the police and causing trouble."

Bena took out his ID card. Adekpitor could not read but he took the card and peered closely at the photograph on it, then he gave it back. "All right, let's hear your questions."

Bena cleared his throat. "Two days ago, the dead body of a man was found at the durbar ground. He had been stabbed to death."

"I have heard about the story," Adekpitor cut in.

"Who told you?"

"I was not in town when it happened. I travelled. I heard it on my journey back. You know news travels fast."

"Where exactly did you travel to?"

"I went to Half Assini. But let me ask you something — why are you asking me these questions?"

"I will tell you," Bena said and re-adjusted himself on the seat. "I am investigating the death of the man who was killed on the durbar ground, *Huno* Dunyo. During my investigations I have found out that you and Dunyo share bad blood. You are not on good terms. In fact, just before his death you engaged in a scuffle with him. My aim is to ascertain that you did not have a hand in Dunyo's death because of the bad relationship between you."

230

Adekpitor whistled. "But who told you there is any bad relationship between me and Dunyo?"

"That is not important now. But if you deny it witnesses will be produced to show exactly that."

Adekpitor bit his lip. "I am not denying it. Dunyo and I were not on good terms because of his underhand dealings. He was always poking his nose where he had no business."

"What sort of underhand dealings?"

Adekpitor hesitated. He felt cornered. "Do your questions have to be so intimate?"

"I am afraid so. I have to establish that whatever hatred was between you and Dunyo was not so strong as to make you wish his death."

Adekpitor coughed and spat into the sand. "When my brother's wife died, this man Dunyo was all over the place. He was poking his nose into everything and telling people what to do. He practically took over the funeral, he a stranger to our family!"

"Was that what caused the scuffle between you and him the night before he was killed?"

Damn that meddling town-crier! Adekpitor swore silently. "Yes. I had just seen him coming out of my brother's house."

"What time was that?"

"I can't tell but it was very late."

"Why were you up so late? Where were you going and where were you coming from?"

Adekpitor smiled wryly. "Young man," he said, "your questions are very weighty, but I will tell you everything. You can't hide your hernia from the water-pot in the bathroom. I was coming home, here, from my second wife's house."

231

"Who is your second wife?"

"Lebene."

"I see." Bena fell into thought for a few moments before asking his next question. "Where you had the scuffle with Dunyo, is it on the direct route between your house here and Lebene's house?"

"Er, not exactly."

"That means you were going somewhere else before coming home here?"

'Er, yes."

"Where?"

"My brother Nani is not at home. He is undergoing initiation rites at the *Yeve* shrine. So I passed by his house to make sure his family was fine."

"At that time of the night?"

"What is wrong with that? I go to that house any time I like."

"Did you meet anybody in the house?"

"Yes, I met them."

Adekpitor's wife approached the two men from the direction of the kitchen. "*Efo*, excuse me," she said, "what food will you take?"

Adekpitor answered with irritation. "Anything." When the woman had turned away he said, "They are always thinking about food, women."

Bena laughed. "Food is necessary," he said. "It is the fuel on which our body thrives."

"Does it have to be so often? *Kpoea*, let's forget about them and continue our conversation. Where were we?"

"I just have one or two more questions for you. Where were you on the night of the twenty-sixth of June, that is two days ago, on Thursday?"

"I travelled very early in the morning on Thursday.

I told you I went to Half Assini."

"What did you go to do at Half Assini?"

"I went to see my daughter. She is staying with her husband there. They are having problems. In fact, the man keeps beating her. So I went there to see exactly what the problem was."

"Did you meet your daughter and her husband?"

"Yes."

"And everything is now fine between them?"

"Let's hope so. I did my best and talked to them."

"Where does your daughter stay at Half Assini?"

"She stays at Amevikope, a fishing village. Her husband is with Kodzo Akplor's net. He is a fisherman."

"What is her name?"

"Akuwor."

"Akuwor Adekpitor?"

"Yes."

"And her husband's name?"

"Koku Naza. He is the son of my uncle Gbede Naza."

"Thank you very much. We will leave it at this. When I need your help again I will call upon you."

"You can come any time you want. I am not a murderer. I don't have the heart to take another person's life."

Bena stood up. "The object of my investigation is to separate the innocent from the guilty. So don't worry. If you are clean, you don't have anything to fear."

"Farewell." Adekpitor watched until Bena left the house, then he said, "Farewell, Dunyo. It served you right."

Detective Sergeant Amlima got up early in the morning. He had lain awake most of the night thinking about his next line of action in the light of Johnny's revelations about his cousin's drug trade. From experience, he knew that enlisting the help of the Togo gendarmes in investigations had not always been fruitful. The Togo gendarmes had a keen sense of kinship with their countrymen and did not easily give them up. Taking Johnny to Lome to identify his cousin and his accomplices was out of the question. The risks were too many. On the other hand, he could take Johnny to Aflao and keep vigilance on the border-crossing to see if he could identify anybody linked to his cousin. But how many days would he have to spend at Aflao to get Johnny to do the identification?

Amlima planned to devote the next few days to investigate Johnny's drug revelations. The ritual murder investigations were more or less on hold waiting for the reports of the pathologists and forensic experts from Accra. He quickly had his bath. Breakfast was not ready when he left the house so he passed by the store in the big kiosk at the roadside to buy a packet of biscuits. The proprietress of the store was extra slow this morning in serving him. Amlima remembered the beginnings of this woman very well. She started by selling little mounds of sweets on a table in front of her house. Gradually the range and quantity of her wares increased. She made a small kiosk and then changed it to the present big one. She was now quite well-to-do. But she was no more the affable customer-loving trader she once was. She and her children who also sold in the store, now had an arrogant

234

air about them and moved with preponderance.

That is what is wrong with us Ghanaians, Amlima thought sadly. Little successes are enough for us. They get to our heads making them bloated and instead of reaching out for more success, we rest on our oars, savouring our new sense of importance.

He hurried to the charge office. He wanted a word with Johnny once more before laying out his plans before ASP Adosu.

"Good morning," he said to the officer at the counter. "Did you have a busy night?"

"Only with the mosquitoes," the officer laughed.

"Take some chloroquine." Amlima took the cell keys and a pair of handcuffs from the rack and went to get Johnny. He came back to the charge office after a minute, a frown on his face. "Has anyone come for Johnny?" he asked.

"Your suspect? No, he is in there, in the cells."

"He is not there."

"What?"

"He is not there!"

"You don't mean it!" The officer rushed past Amlima to the cells. There were two cells but the door of one had been broken down a few days back by a suspect who was in detention. So only one cell was in use. This was used for the men. If there were any female detainees these were kept behind the counter handcuffed to the counter. The previous night only Johnny had been in the cell. An empty room greeted the duty officer when he entered the cell. His breathing stopped and he became short of breath. He came out of the cell holding onto the walls for support.

Amlima met him at the door. "Well?" he said.

"He-he-he is not the-ther-there."

"Then where is he?"

"I-I don't know. He-he should be here. Oh God, I am dead!"

"Where is the counter NCO?"

"He-he has gone home to pick an item."

"To pick an item or to sleep?"

"To pick an item."

"What is his name?"

"Corporal Francis Dekornu."

"Wait at the counter." Amlima re-locked the cell then he headed for Corporal Dekornu's house. Dekornu's wife and children were about the house doing their morning duties.

"Where is your husband?" Amlima asked the woman.

"He is in the room."

"Please call him for me."

It took several minutes for Dekornu to come out and when he did, still buckling his belt, it was obvious he had dressed up in a great hurry. His eyes were sleep-weary and his hair not well combed.

"Meet me at the charge office immediately," Amlima said and left the house. It was still early in the morning, not yet eight o'clock, so Amlima went to Inspector Dongor's house to report the disappearance of Johnny from his cell. Inspector Dongor was in the bathroom when Amlima got to his house. When the inspector came out some minutes later, he looked very fresh and prim in his uniform.

"Good morning, Sergeant Amlima," he said.

Amlima stood up and saluted. "Good morning, sir."

"How are you?"

"Fine, thank you. There is trouble, sir."

"What trouble?"

"Johnny, the suspect, has disappeared from his cell."

"You don't mean it!"

"It is true, sir."

"Disappeared? How?"

"I don't know, sir. The locks to the cell were intact. There was no break-in."

"My God!" Dongor sat down. "And what are the duty officers saying?"

"One was on duty behind the counter, the other one was at home sleeping."

"My God! What has become of the Police Service?"

Amlima couldn't answer that one so he remained silent.

"Go back to the station and wait for me," the inspector told the detective. "Keep an eye on the two duty officers. Don't let them out of your sight. I will call the District Commander immediately."

Word was already spreading through the barracks about the disappearance of Johnny. On his way to the station, several policemen accosted Amlima to ask "Is it true?" And he gave them the same answer: "We are yet to find out what happened."

***   ***   ***

Private George Aboagye was having breakfast when he heard the news of Johnny's disappearance. He left the meal unfinished and rushed to Private Atonsu's house. Atonsu met him at the door, his eyes bloodshot from lack of sleep.

"Good morning," George said.

"Good morning. What can I do for you?" Atonsu's attitude was dismissive.

"Can I sit down?" George said patiently.

Atonsu's heart pace accelerated as he went back to the room followed by Aboagye. The room which served as the sitting-room was very small, typical of junior barracks all over the country. There were just a few furniture items in the room but even that left very little space to move about in. George manouvered himself into a chair and Atonsu sat opposite him.

"There is a big problem at the station," George said.

"What problem?" Atonsu could hardly keep his voice steady.

"The suspect has disappeared. Johnny has disappeared."

"How can he disappear?" Even before the words were out of his mouth, Atonsu knew that George knew he was lying.

George gave him a hard stare. "Let's not go into his mode of disappearance," he said. "What is important to me is the other night when you came to the charge office while I was on duty. What are we going to do about that? Everybody is going to be questioned, you know."

Atonsu did not speak for some time. Mentally, he battled with himself whether he should tell George everything. When he spoke his voice was choked with emotion. "Aboagye," he said. "I am in trouble. My career is over!"

George was annoyed with himself and Atonsu, himself for his laxity, and Atonsu for presenting the opportunity for him to behave stupidly. "This is how small things can balloon into big problems," he said, throwing his hands into the air. "What game are you playing at, hm? What game are you playing?... Won't you talk?"

Atonsu stood up. "Aboagye, I am going to ask you a

favour."

"What favour?"

"Don't say anything about what happened between us the other time."

"That I allowed you to take out the suspect unauthorised?"

"Yes. Please don't say anything about that. Give me three days. Within three days at the most the suspect will be back."

"Three days? Where are you hiding him?"

"Let's not go into that. Please give me three days and everything will be solved."

"And what happens when you are exposed before then? Do you know what I will be charged with? I will tell you; first I will be charged with stupidity, then the other charges will follow."

"Please, Aboagye."

Aboagye wriggled in his chair. "Sit down," he told the miserable man before him. "This is my answer to your request: Do not, I repeat, do not under any circumstances mention anywhere that I allowed you to take the suspect out and I will also keep my mouth shut. Even if you are exposed through some other means, promise me you will never bring my name in."

"I promise."

"In other words, from this time onwards you and I will forget about that night."

"Yes."

George stood up. "Even when you say it anywhere I will deny it with all my body and with all my soul. So help me God. Bye-bye."

When George opened the door to let himself out he nearly collapsed from shock. Standing at the door was Sergeant Amlima.

Detective Corporal Bena was back at Adekpitor's house in the afternoon. Adekpitor had just woken up from a restful sleep. If there was anything on his mind it wasn't the earlier visit of the police or the possibility that they might visit him again. What was on his mind was Ablator.

Adekpitor reacted with irritation when one of his children came to tell him that the man who came to see him in the morning had come again.

"Tell him to wait!" he told the child. He continued to lie in bed for more than five minutes before coming out. He saw Bena seated under the shady mango tree in his compound. He yawned audibly and stretched himself.

"Bring me a seat," he shouted into the air. One of his children appeared with a seat. "Put it under the tree and bring me some water."

When the child brought the water, he washed his face and rinsed his mouth. He went back to the room to get his towel. He wiped his face dry and with the towel slung over his shoulder, he joined Bena under the tree. "You are back again so soon," he said.

"Yes," Bena said. "I am sorry to bother you, but that is the nature of our work. We were three coming here but my friends have gone to see their relatives nearby."

"I see. So what can I do for you this time?"

"I told you in the morning that my aim is to clear suspicion from any innocent person who may be linked to Dunyo's death."

"But I am not linked to his death!"

Bena raised a restraining hand. "You wait and hear me out."

240

"All right, go on."

"Since I left this house this morning I have been working on the case from your angle. What I want you to do now is to tell me all that you did, the places you visited from the 25th of June, that is last Wednesday up till this time today."

"This is a big bother, my friend."

"Please oblige me," Bena pleaded. "It is in your interest and in mine too. We don't want any innocent person to stand accused."

Adekpitor shook his head in exasperation. "Let's see," he said. "Tuesday... Tuesday. Tuesday, I went to the farm. Yes, I have just bought some new shallot beds. Some boys sowed the beds for me on Tuesday, in the morning. After that I went to my mechanic. One of my buses is broken down. I spent a lot of time with the mechanic. I came back home late in the afternoon. Let's see... I took my bath here but had supper at my second wife's house. I stayed there for some time. It was when I was coming home that I met Dunyo. It is true I held him by his shirt but apart from that I did not do anything to him. Gbekle, the town-crier is my witness. I left the two of them and went to my brother Nani's house."

"Did you meet anybody in the house?"

"Yes, I met Ablator."

"Was she the only one you met in the house?"

"Yes."

"And you spoke with her?"

"Why, yes."

"Did she tell you Dunyo had been there earlier?"

"Er, yes."

"Continue."

"The following day Wednesday at dawn, I left for

241

Half Assini through Accra. I spent the night at Half Assini and came back to Accra yesterday evening. Today at dawn I left Accra and arrived in town this morning. That was when you came here."

"Who did you spend the night with in Accra?"

"With a nephew of mine. Ben Dordzo. He is a contractor."

"Well," Bena bent himself forward towards Adekpitor. "Mr., er, Adekpitor, I have checked out your story and I have found out you told me a lot of untruths. It is true you saw Dunyo outside Ablator's house on Tuesday but the rest of your story is full of untruths. Number one: Ablator says you never came to their house in the night that day. Yet you claim you saw her and even spoke with her."

"These women! She told you that?" Adekpitor laughed.

"Yes. You wait till I finish. Number two: you told me you left this town for Half Assini on Thursday but my inquiries have shown that you were in fact in this town on Thursday and only left town on Friday at dawn, that is yesterday."

"But-but how-how can you prove that?" Adekpitor stammered.

"Let us not drag that. You know it is true. I can bring in witnesses, including the driver whose bus you took to Accra yesterday. Let me go on. It means that on the night Dunyo was killed you were in fact in town."

"*Ao!*" moaned Adekpitor, his mouth suddenly dry.

"Lie number three: you said you have a daughter in Half Assini. That is true. But when you said you visited her on Thursday you were telling lies."

"What do you mean? Who told you I didn't go to Half Assini?"

"It was very easy to find out. I telephoned the police

at Half Assini. They looked for your daughter and located her. She told them she had not seen you the whole of this year."

Sweat began to break all over Adekpitor's brow. He used his large towel to wipe away the sweat, momentarily hiding his face.

"Lie number four," Bena continued relentlessly. "You did not come back from Accra this morning as you claim. You came back last night."

"Who told you that?"

"The other passengers in the bus that brought you from Accra last night."

"It is not true."

"You deny all that I have said?"

"Yes, I deny them. They are not true."

Bena sat up. "In the circumstances I have no option but to arrest you on suspicion of the murder of *Hunɔ Dunyo.*"

"Arrest me? You can't be serious!"

"I am serious. Unless you can explain satisfactorily the distortions you have given to your movements and activities since Wednesday to date, you will have to come with me to the police station." Bena sneezed loudly, not very gentleman-like.

Shortly, the main gate to the house opened in answer to Bena's sneeze and two policemen in uniform walked in.

"Mr. Adekpitor," Bena said, "shall we go quietly to the station or you will put up resistance?"

Adekpitor decided quickly. "Let's go to the station. I will tell you everything there. You will see that I have done no wrong."

CHAPTER SIXTEEN

Soon after the discovery of the disappearance of Johnny from his cell, Constable Atonsu took Sergeant Amlima to Aflao. Sergeant Amlima was going to enlist the assistance of the Ghana Customs and Preventive Service, CEPS, to locate Johnny's cousin's house in Lome and mount surveillance on him. ASP Adosu had accepted the idea about not involving the Togo gendamerie. He knew the Togolese authorities would raise hell if the operation was discovered and heads might roll including his own, but it was a scheme he was willing to stick his neck out for. Amlima was asked to talk to the Customs Commander at Aflao to find out the feasibility of the idea. So he had gone out to look for Private Atonsu to drive him there, and that was when he met Constable Aboagye coming out of Atonsu's room.

They took the shorter route to Aflao, the road that had been washed away by the ravages of sea erosion. The four-wheel vehicle shuffled over stretches of sand that had once been solid asphalt or the floor of warm homes.

"What were you and George Aboagye doing when I came to your house?" Amlima asked suddenly. "The two of you looked like little kids who had been caught stealing from the soup pot."

They had been going in silence and Amlima's sudden question startled Atonsu. He had been driving uneasily, his mind racked by worries of what part Amlima might have heard of his conversation with Aboagye.

"We-We were doing nothing, sir," he managed to say.

"Nothing?"

"We were only conversing."

Nothing more was said until they reached Aflao. At the border post, Amlima showed Atonsu where to park the vehicle, then he went looking for the CEPS Commander. He was taken to an office to wait for the commander who he was told had gone out on his morning rounds. The customs officer who took Amlima there introduced him to the commander's secretary as a police detective on assignment from Keta.

"Please sit down," the secretary said and Amlima took a seat among several people who had also come to see the head of customs.

The commander came in some minutes later and, after a hasty greeting to the people in the room, entered his office. The secretary followed him and then came out and beckoned to Amlima. Amlima stood up quickly and slipped past the secretary into the rather small office. A massive building had been put up for the customs post at Aflao but since the building was not yet completed, customs officials continued to operate from their small wooden offices. The first thing Amlima noticed was that the commander's desk was huge and occupied almost all the space in the room. The desk dwarfed the smallish commander who appeared perched like a bird on the edge of the desk.

"Please sit down," the commander said. "I am Ben Larsen, Commander of the Ghana Customs Post at Aflao." He could have added that he was a conscientious man who struck terror into the hearts of those of his subordinates who were crooked. Already, during his short stay at Aflao, about twelve customs officers had either been dismissed outright or suspended for colluding with smugglers. He could not be called exactly affable but he was patient and had time for everybody, especially those who called on him to make enquiries.

The detective sat down. "I am Detective Sergeant Amlima from the Keta District Police. I am here with the authorization of my District Commander to seek your assistance in a case we are investigating."

"Fine," Larsen said rubbing his hands together. "Of what assistance can I be to you?"

"It looks like there is a gang of drug smugglers operating across this border, to and from Togo. We want to smash this gang and lay hands on the members."

"Mhm?" the Customs Commander said, his eyebrows rising.

"Normally," Amlima said, "we should contact Interpol in this case but that takes a lot of time. And you know our brothers across the border; they tend to protect their own even if they are in the wrong. Now this is what we want to do: the man who appears to be the kingpin of the traffickers lives in Lome, Kodzoviakope. Our investigations have revealed that we can easily locate him. We want to discreetly observe him and those that are connected with him. We will trace his couriers and find out who are their contacts in Ghana. Then we will swoop down on the couriers when they enter Ghana and arrest their contacts in Ghana too."

Larsen nodded his head. "Not bad. Looks like a good plan. But the Togolese will not take kindly to it if they find out what you are up to."

"That is a risk we are ready to take. Of course, we shall be very careful."

"And where do I come in?"

"Being the commander here we need to inform you about what we are doing so that if the need arises you will come to our aid. We will be grateful if you will tell the immigration people to grant us unimpeded passage."

"Why don't you tell them yourself just as you have come to me?"

"Er, we don't want to expose ourselves too much. You can just tell them it is a security operation and you don't know much about it."

"Well, I think that can be managed."

"Thank you very much. Can I wait here while you talk to the immigration people?"

Larsen permitted himself a little smile. "You are in a hurry aren't you?"

"I'm afraid so."

"Okay, wait here." He stood up and took himself around the desk, then like someone who had just remembered something, he said, "Ah, anything to identify you? I forgot to ask for that."

Amlima brought out his I.D. card. "I was becoming more and more surprised when you were not asking for it."

Larsen took the card and examined it, turning it over. "That satisfies me. Just a minute." Before he went out, he whispered to his secretary, "Do not let that man get out under any circumstances until I am back."

His secretary's eyebrows shot up as she said, "Yes, sir."

Amlima was leafing through a magazine on the huge desk when Larsen came back. He put the magazine away as Larsen went round to his chair.

"You have the all-clear," the CEPS Commander said. "But on one condition — if anything goes wrong, none of us here know you or anybody from Keta and I have never had any discussion with you on any subject. That means you are on your own. If that is understood and accepted

247

then you have the green light."

Amlima slapped his thighs. "Well, I think that is fair," he said. "From this time until when I come to break news of success to you, we don't know each other."

"Very well."

The detective stood up and extended his hand. "Thank you, commander."

Larsen stood up and shook the extended hand. "It's been a pleasure. I wish you all the best."

"Thank you."

When Amlima came out into the outer office, the secretary ran in to the commander and asked, "Should I let him go now?"

"Yes, yes," Larsen said. "Let him go. Everything ended well."

Aflao lies on the southern-most tip of the east of Ghana. It is the busiest crossing point along the long border between Ghana and Togo. It is a huge commercial town, a melting pot in which every ethnic group in the West African subregion and beyond finds representation. Thousands and thousands of people cross the border from Ghana into Togo and back every day. The Republic of Togo uses the CFA currency which is anchored by the French franc. As a result their currency is more stable than the free-floating Ghanaian cedi, and inflation is lower there. Many Ghanaians therefore find it cheaper to shop in Togo. No wonder the largest part of the daily commuters to Togo are Ghanaians.

Aflao is also a haven for smugglers. Fortunes can be made and lost on the same day and one can never be too careful with possessions. One of the commonest sources of employment for both the old and the young at Aflao is acting as couriers for smuggled goods. At times these

248

smuggled goods are carted across the authorised crossing point in small quantities so as not to arouse the suspicion of the customs officials. When the goods are taken at once in large quantities they are taken through unauthorised routes known popularly as "beats" which were numerically labelled. Beat Nine was the most popular among the unauthorised routes.

When Amlima came back from Commander Larsen, he found Atonsu sleeping in the vehicle, his head resting on the steering wheel. He felt like Jesus who said to Peter at Gethsemane, "So could you not watch with me one hour?" Atonsu woke up as Amlima opened the door and pulled himself into the passenger seat.

"I am crossing over to Lome to do an investigation," Amlima said. "I will have liked you to accompany me, but since you are in uniform, you will have to wait for me here. I don't hope to be long. Do not stray too far away from the car."

"Yes, sir," said Atonsu, trying unsuccessfully to suppress a yawn.

"See you," Amlima said and went out.

"See you, sir."

As soon as Amlima left, Atonsu rolled up the glasses and then wandered off to explore the vicinity.

*** *** ***

While Amlima was away at Aflao, a swift investigation was set in motion to determine the circumstances under which Johnny vanished from his cell. The investigations were headed by ASP Adosu himself. At his orders the two police officers who were on duty the previous night were locked up while preparations were made to interrogate them.

The phrase *Johnny has done a Houdini* was fast gaining currency at the police barracks. When Dongor had gone to report Johnny's disappearance to the District Commander, the first thing he said was, "Sir, Johnny has done a 'Houdini'." After making Dongor explain the term, Adosu took proprietorship of the phrase and could not make mention of the incident without remarking "How could Johnny do a Houdini under our very noses?"

At ten o'clock Corporal Francis Dekornu and Private Atiku, the two officers on duty when Johnny "vanished", were brought before the District Commander for interrogation. They came in looking sheepish and very frightened. They who had often led or pushed along suspects and convicts now found themselves at the receiving end.

"Stand over there!" ASP Adosu barked at them, pointing to the wall.

Also in the room were Inspector Dongor and Sergeant Bansa and another officer with pen and paper to take notes.

"Now, tell me in your own words," said Adosu, "what your problem is!"

The two cops jerked to attention. They glanced at each other then continued to stare at the floor.

"Won't you talk?"

"Yes, sir," said Corporal Dekornu.

"Yes, sir," whispered Private Atiku.

"Then talk!"

Private Atiku gave Corporal Dekornu a sharp glance as if to say, "You are the senior, you do the talking."

Corporal Dekornu took the hint and stuttered, "We-we-we don-don't have a problem, sir."

Adosu jumped up. "You don't have a problem? Then

250

who has the problem? Me? Or Inspector Dongor here? You people are playing with fire! You don't know the trouble you have landed yourselves in. Better tell me something sensible!" He banged his hand on the desk. "I want to hear you talking. Now! And you'd better tell the truth. Start from when you first came on duty yesterday, step by step."

Corporal Dekornu stepped forward a little and cleared his throat. The look of fear was still in his eyes but the sheepish look was now replaced by a resolve to behave like a man and face the music.

"Sir," he said, "yesterday I reported for duty at 7.50 p.m. Private Atiku came five minutes later. We took over from Corporals Frimpong and Atandosu..."

"Did you take inventory of everything?"

"Yes, sir." Dekornu cleared his throat again. A lump of mucus was creeping into his voice.

"Was the suspect, Johnny, in his cell?"

"Yes, sir."

"Did you do the hourly checks on the cells?"

"Not all the hours, sir." More mucus.

"Go on."

Dekornu coughed to clear the mucus away. He swallowed, then continued, "There were a few other officers around. Some of them stayed in the office for some time but by ten-thirty they had all gone away. The two of us continued to be on duty. At eleven-fifty a complainant came to lodge a complaint."

"What is the complainant's name?"

"I have forgotten, sir."

Adosu pursed his lips tightly and blew them scornfully. "Some policeman!"

"What was the complaint about?" Dongor asked.

"The woman, the complainant, said her husband had

251

assaulted her."

"Go on."

"I, we took down the statement from the woman and told her to report again in the morning. Er, nothing else happened till this morning when we discovered the disappearance of the suspect."

Adosu was fuming with anger. He wriggled forward in his chair, in the process pushing forward the table whose legs made a screeching noise on the floor. "The two of you are joking!" he shouted. "You and who discovered the disappearance of the suspect? Were you there when the discovery was made?"

"No, no sir." Dekornu was beginning to look sheepish again.

"Then why did you say 'we discovered the disappearance'? Where were you when you were supposed to be at post?"

"I we-we-went to ease myself, sir."

"Where?"

"In-in the house."

"Isn't a toilet at the station?"

"Yes, sir."

"Then why did you go to your house?"

"No, sir."

Adosu's anger was now choking him. He turned away, breathing noisily.

Dongor took over the interrogation, his voice surprisingly soft. He might have realised anger and fire and brimstone would not make any difference to the investigation. "Mr. Dekornu," he said, "are you sure you are telling the truth?"

"Yes, sir."

Dongor shook his head. "The officer who came to look

252

for you in the house said your eyes looked so sleepy and your hair uncombed and you were still dressing up when you came out, meaning you had just been woken up from sleep."

"It is not true, sir. I was coming from the toilet."

"You still stand by that?"

"Yes, sir."

"Look Dekornu, this is the time for you to speak the truth and ask for forgiveness."

"I am speaking the truth, sir."

"Very well." Dongor turned to Constable Atiku, his voice hardening a little. "Mr. Atiku, draw forward! Tell us your version of the case."

Atiku shuffled forward and repeated what Dekornu had said.

ASP Adosu suddenly bounced back to life. "Take them away! Take the imbeciles away," he said. "You people think we do not know what you have been doing. The way you go home to sleep when you are on duty. You have ten days to produce the suspect, otherwise trouble for you."

Bansah stood up to lead the two men out of the room while Constable Atiku began to plead for forgiveness. "Please, sir," he said, "forgive us. We are innocent. We did not do anything wrong. I think it was juju. The suspect used juju to escape; I swear by it..."

"Juju?" Adosu snorted. "Why haven't other people done it before? Who are you kidding? Take them away!"

Bansa led them out with Atiku whining in a monotone, "It was juju, I swear it was juju. . ."

The officer who was taking notes stood up. "Can I go sir?" he asked.

"Yes," Adosu said.

"Thank you, sir."

Adosu turned in his chair to face Inspector Dongor, his face flushed, and his hair standing on end. They looked at each other in silence until Dongor looked away. "Are we relaxing in our supervision?" the ASP asked.

The question stung Dongor. "No, sir," he said. "We are still supervising."

Adosu grunted. "But if one of them was on duty while the other went to sleep, then the other should know what took place. Unless he was also sleeping. Jesus, what a mess!"

"I also think the one who was left on duty also fell asleep. That was when the suspect escaped. With outside help. The outside help simply took the key from the rack, opened the cell and let the suspect out."

"It was that simple?"

"Yes, sir."

"And you say we are not lax in our supervision?"

Dongor felt like saying, I am not supposed to be on duty twenty-four hours a day. But instead he said, "We do our best under the circumstances, sir."

"Your best? Your best obviously is not enough. Inspector Dongor, do not think you are blameless in this incident."

"Yes, sir," Dongor said, thinking, neither are you. You virtually run the station over my head.

"You can go."

"Thank you, sir."

***   ***   ***

When Corporal Bena brought Adekpitor to the police station he needed to do very little prompting to get the old man to talk.

"Look, my son," Adekpitor told Corporal Bena, "murder is not a matter to be joked with. If by any mistake or unintentional act on my part suspicion now lies on me, I will tell you the truth, the whole truth and nothing but the truth to clear my name."

They were alone in the interrogation room, the old man and Corporal Bena. Bena was inclined to believe the old man's words but he was wary. Such sweet words often preceded hardened lies. He told the old man, "I am glad that you have decided to tell me the whole truth as you put it. It will save us all a lot of trouble. Now, we start from the beginning again, your activities from Wednesday till today Sunday. But hold on. I am going to write down what you say as your statement."

"No, no, no!" protested Adekpitor. "There is absolutely no need for that. Just let me tell you the truth, then you let me go. There shouldn't be any records. I don't want any shame to come out of this. What I will tell you should be between just you and me."

"The police don't work like that," Bena said patiently. "I promise I will not divulge what you tell me to anybody unless it becomes absolutely necessary. But there needs to be a record as witness to what you say. We detectives are trained to work in confidentiality. So have no fears about any little secret of yours leaking out."

"Okay, okay," Adekpitor said. Then he began to talk. "I told you that on Wednesday I went to the farm, then to my mechanic's shop. That is true. I also told you that I took supper at my second wife's house, that is also true. The reason why I appeared to be off my normal route when returning to my house was that I went to see another woman. But I want this to be a secret between us. The reason is that the woman is a married woman."

255

"What is her name?" Bena asked.

"Do I need to tell you her name?"

"Yes, you need to, so that we can check if you are telling the truth."

Adekpitor told the woman's name then continued. "I met Dunyo that night and after that little altercation between us, I entered my brother Nani's house. Gbekle, the town-crier, will attest to this. He and Dunyo saw me enter the house. I actually saw Ablator. I don't know why she is saying she did not see me that night. Maybe, it is because of what took place between us."

"What took place between you?"

"I slept with her."

"You mean you knew her sexually?"

"Yes," Adekpitor answered, not without a trace of pride in his voice.

"Wait, wait a minute," Bena said holding up his hand. "You mean you actually had sexual intercourse with Ablator?"

"Of course I did!"

"Then why is she denying that she did not see you that night?"

"Maybe she wants to keep it a secret. You know women. That night she pretended to be asleep but what woman can sleep through all that activity? Unless she is drunk or drugged."

"That means she did not actually, er, take part in the act? You just climbed on her, did your thing and then climbed off?"

"Well, yes. But she knew. She was just pretending to be asleep."

"I went home after that and at dawn the following I left home telling my family that I was travelling. But

256

in actual fact, I went to the married woman I have just told you about. Her husband had travelled the previous day. But I never went out throughout my stay with her because I didn't want my family to know that I was still in town. I stayed with the woman till the following day when I left for Accra. It is true I didn't go to Half Assini. I came back to Woe in the night that same day. I spent the night with the woman again and then went home this morning. That is the truth, the absolute truth. And if I am lying may Torgbi Nyigbla strike me dead this very minute. I have no hand in the murder of Dunyo."

"Hmn," sighed Bena. He knew that Torgbi Nyigbla was the most revered god of the Anlos. Even though the youth these days did not put much stock by the traditional gods, for an old man to swear by the revered god meant something to Bena.

"So your main purpose," Bena said, "in leaving home on Wednesday was to have some private time with this married woman?"

"Yes, we can say that, even though I had to buy some floats and fishing net from Accra. I only told my wives I was going to Half Assini so that I could go to this woman."

"But are you not afraid that your daughter can tell your wives that you never visited her?"

"No. She is not the daughter of either of my present wives, and she is not on good terms with them. So she can't tell them. Even if she tells them what can they do? If every woman was so jealous *they* themselves wouldn't have had me."

"I see." Bena fell into thought for a while then said, "But I am afraid you will have to stay here overnight."

"Why?" Adekpitor almost screamed. "Haven't I told you everything?"

257

"Well, we can say you have, but I need to check out the veracity of your story."

"Abomination!" the old man swore. "Me, Adekpitor, to spend the night in police cells? What!"

Bena stood up. "I am afraid that is what is going to happen. There is nothing we can do about it. As you yourself said murder is not something to be joked with. Tomorrow I will check out your story then we'll see what happens after that."

The old man was beside himself with rage. "I can't believe this is happening to me, Adekpitor! What will my family say?"

Bena motioned him to stand up. "I've been informed they are waiting for you at the counter. Come on. We will not put you in a cell. We will keep you behind the counter."

He led the old man to the charge office where members of his family were waiting. He made a sign to the officer on duty at the counter then left the office quickly in order not to witness the protests of Adekpitor when they handcuffed him to the counter.

Bena felt very tired but he knew he must give himself the maximum chance to solve this case. He must see Ablator and the married woman before Adekpitor could get word to them. He went home and quickly wolfed down a lump of bread with the soup prepared by his girlfriend the previous day. Then he took a taxi to Woe and after some enquiries located the house of the woman who had been committing adultery with Adekpitor. The woman was very frightened when the detective told her the purpose of his visit. She drove her kids away from within earshot. Her husband who had travelled out of town had not yet come back.

Just like Adekpitor, the woman promised to tell "the whole truth" and begged Bena not to make the affair public. "Otherwise my husband will kill me!"

You should have thought of that before going wayward, Bena felt like saying, but he kept his tongue. He did not feel like a moralist just now.

The woman's story corraborated that of Adekpitor, but Bena was still wary. All this could be a carefully cooked plot to offer Adekpitor an alibi.

"How long have you been seeing Adekpitor?" he asked the woman.

"About three months. In fact, this is my first time of doing this sort of thing."

Many thieves have said that before you, Bena thought. "At what time did Adekpitor leave you on Wednesday night?"

"I can't say, but it was very late."

"Did your children see him that day?"

"Yes, but they went to bed before he left."

"What about the following day? Did they see him when he came here at dawn and spent the day and night with you?"

"No. They have their own room and throughout Adekpitor's stay I didn't allow them to enter my room."

"Did anybody else see Adekpitor during the time he was with you?"

"No."

Bena stood up. "Thank you. When I need your help I will call on you again."

The woman began to weep. "Please do not come to me in the house. My husband will kill me if he knows the reason for your visit. Please show me somewhere that I can meet you."

259

"You should have thought about your husband when you started it."

"Please," the woman sobbed, "I won't do it again. But don't come to me in the house. My husband will be back anytime now. Let me meet you anywhere other than the house here."

"Do you know the Keta Police Station?" Bena asked.

"Yes, I know there."

"Come there tomorrow morning."

"What time?"

"Eight o'clock."

"Thank you. I will be there."

From there, Bena went to see Gbekle again, armed with a bottle of *akpeteshi*. Gbekle was not more than fifty but he had aged prematurely due to excessive intake of alcohol. This fact was not lost on Bena. He saw in the older man a picture of what he himself would be if he did not stop his drinking habit.

"This is just a social visit," Bena said, exposing the drink he was carrying.

"Ho, ho, ho," laughed Gbekle, pointing to the bottle, "and you come with the right accompaniment."

The two men talked for a long time. When Bena finally left Gbekle, he felt very tired. He was also a little tipsy. It was now a little past eight and his limbs cried for a rest. The temptation to close the investigation for the day was very great, but resolutely, he made his way to Ablator's house.

Lucy was not at home when Bena called. Ablator was in the kitchen cooking, surrounded by all the children. She was reluctant to leave her cooking but Bena persuaded her out of the kitchen to see to him first before continuing her cooking. Ablator issued instructions to

260

Mawusi, Lucy's eldest child and came out of the kitchen. The soft light thrown by the lantern in the kitchen revealed beads of sweat all over her face and neck. She wiped her face with the tail of her cloth and led Bena to a seat. Even in the dim light of the lantern outside, her attractiveness tinged by a hint of masculinity was not lost on Bena.

"Good evening," Bena said. Judging by Ablator's mood, this was no time to launch into the lengthy traditional greeting.

"Good evening."

"This is already the second time today that I have come to you. I am sorry to bother you. I need to ask you some further questions. During my investigations I have talked to Adekpitor as you know. Parts of his story touched on you that is why I came to you earlier today. What is apparent now is that what he told me is different from what you told me. I just want to quickly clear those aspects then I will be gone."

"I am listening," Ablator said.

"You told me Dunyo came to this house on Wednesday night. Adekpitor also told me the same thing. You said Dunyo was here because of a favour he had done you in arranging an interview with your father-in-law. You also told me you never saw Adekpitor that night, but the man is insisting that he saw you that very night."

"He is lying!"

"What time did Dunyo leave you that night?"

"About nine-thirty."

"You told me you took some drinks with Dunyo. What type of drink exactly did you take?"

"I took minerals and he took beer."

"How many bottles did each of you take?"

261

"I took two bottles minerals and he two bottles beer."

"You yourself did not take beer or any other alcoholic drink?"

"No."

"Did you buy the drinks?"

"No."

"Who bought them?"

"He gave me money to go and bring the drinks."

"Where did you buy them?"

"Kpormor Na Yehowa Store."

"Where is that?"

"It is at the roadside, as you leave here towards Keta."

"Good. Were you alone when Dunyo left you?"

"Yes. Everybody else had gone to bed."

"I see. Davi Ablator, when Dunyo left this house on Wednesday night a few people saw him coming out of the house. Adekpitor also saw him. Incidentally, Adekpitor is interested in you just as Dunyo was, isn't it?"

"What am I going to do with such an old man?"

Bena sighed. He seemed lost for more questions. He inclined his body backwards and kicked his shoes through the sand while Ablator watched him impatiently. "Davi Ablator," he said, "excuse me my question, but if you were asleep and somebody started making love to you, you would know, won't you?"

Ablator nearly fell off the bench. Her hands gripped the edges of the bench firmly to steady herself. "Wh-Wh-what do you mean?" she asked.

"I mean," Bena said unruffled, "if you were asleep and someone came in quietly and started having sexual intercourse with you do you think you would wake up?"

"Yes, of course I will wake up."

"I see," Bena said and started swinging his legs again. "I am going to ask you another silly question, but forgive me... When you woke up on Thursday morning, that is the day after Dunyo visited you in the night and Adekpitor also claimed he visited you, did you see semen in your private parts?"

Ablator stood up sharply but fell back on the seat. For sometime she could not speak.

"Davi Ablator, I asked you a question," Bena said. "Did you see semen in your private parts when you woke up on Thursday morning?"

"Wh-why-why do-do you ask such a question?"

"I have my reasons, but just tell me truthfully. Did you see any semen?"

"No."

"You are positive?"

"Yes."

"Davi Ablator, I have some news for you. It is unpleasant, but that is life. You will have to take it as it is. You have been very unfairly treated. Two wicked men have taken advantage of you. One drugged you into unconsciousness, then the two of them knew you sexually one after the other. This is what happened to you: when you were drinking with *Huno* Dunyo on Wednesday night, he secretly put some sleep-inducing drug in your drink. You fell asleep. Then he carried you to your bed and assaulted you sexually. He left the house quietly and on his way met Adekpitor who was also coming here. After a hot exchange between the two men, Adekpitor came in and found you helplessly in a deep sleep, naked. The bastard also jumped on you and after knowing you sexually, he also left. When you woke up in the morning, you found semen in your private part. Since it was Dunyo

263

who was with you before you fell unconscious, you concluded that it was he who assaulted you. But unknown to you, it was the two of them. That is why you did not know that Adekpitor also came to this house Wednesday night. These two men have wronged you terribly and we the police are going to take action against them, I mean against Adekpitor. As for Dunyo he is already dead..."

As Bena talked, Ablator was filled with a cold rage that had her heart beating violently as if the organ wanted to wrench itself free of her body. It was a rage that ate away at her stomach, leaving her feeling numb. Her hands which had been gripping the bench on which they sat now came up to support her head which seemed to weigh a ton.

The gate swung open and Lucy came in. She was surprised to see Bena. She greeted him and entered her room. Then Bena stood up. "Thank you, Davi Ablator," he said. "I will go now. When I need your help again I will call on you."

Ablator remained fixed to the seat after the detective had gone. With much effort, she lifted her head and called to Lucy. When Lucy came, she told her, "I am going to start my widowhood rites tomorrow."

Lucy was surprised. "Why so suddenly?"

"I just want to get it over with."

"Well, that is fine," Lucy said and went back to her room.

CHAPTER SEVENTEEN

In Anloland, when one's spouse dies, one has to perform widowhood rites to avoid being trailed for life by the ghost of the deceased. The ghost can torment the living spouse in her sleep or in anything else that she does. This may even extend to any relationship with another man.

There are special people who perform the widowhood rites for people who lose their spouses. They are called *ahoga*. These people should of necessity have undergone widowhood rites themselves. They are themselves widows. They should also have assisted others in the performance of the rites before they graduate to be called *ahoga*.

Wofemda Dzanyiekpor was an *ahoga*. She was widowed twice and had had to undergo the widowhood rites twice. She was distantly related to Ablator on the paternal side so Ablator called her aunt. Both Ablator and Wofemda assumed that it would be the latter who would perform the widowhood rites for Ablator. In fact, they had talked about the rites often, the procedures and what items Ablator had to provide. Wofemda was, however, taken aback when early Monday morning, Ablator came to tell her she wanted to start the widowhood rites immediately.

"How immediate is your immediately?" the old lady asked her.

"I mean today, this evening," Ablator said with determination.

"What is the reason for this sudden rush?" the old woman asked, her eyes popping out in her wrinkled face.

Ablator looked away before answering, "I just want

265

to get it over with."

"Well, if that is what you want, so be it. Fortunately for you today is a market day. I am sure you have already thought of that." Market days were thought to be lucky days for the performance of widowhood rites. "I have already told you the items you have to provide, so if you are ready we can go and see the medium this evening."

Before she could perform the rites, Ablator would have to first consult a medium who would summon the spirit of her dead husband. She would have the opportunity to talk with the ghost about the rites and any other issues. The ghost would tell her the items to provide for the rites and how many days she should stay in confinement, otherwise called "indooring". The consultations had to be made on a market day because market days were favourable days for ghosts and they were benevolent on such days. The ghost would be summoned in the evening but the medium must be given advance notice.

"I have already told you the items we must take to the medium to do the summoning," Wofemda said. She was advanced in age, but she had very good eyesight and bright eyeballs. She stared straight into her niece's eyes, trying to discern the reason behind Ablator's sudden haste.

"What are the items, aunt?" Ablator had listened with divided attention when she and the old lady earlier discussed the items. Then, she had been in no hurry to perform the rites soon.

"First, we must send some money in the morning to give the medium advance notice; about two hundred cedis will be okay," said the old lady. "Then when we are going in the evening for the summoning of the spirit, we must

266

take along a quantity of dry corn, some *liha,* a bottle of gin and some money to pay for the services of the medium. Two thousand cedis will do. If you are really serious about starting the rites today, then we must send the two hundred cedis to the medium this morning."

"I am serious about it."

"Then go and start looking for the items. And while you are about it, I will go and inform the medium about our coming."

"Thank you, aunt. Here you are with the two hundred cedis."

"Be ready at five-thirty this evening," the old lady said as she took the money.

The items needed for the notice-giving were readily available on sale. Ablator quickly bought them and took them to Aunt Wofemda's house. Then she went home.

Lucy had still not got over her surprise at Ablator's sudden rush. "You really are determined, aren't you?" she said.

"Why wait?" Ablator asked. "You will accompany me to the medium, won't you?"

"Of course, I will go with you. I can't let you go alone." Lucy turned to walk away but Ablator had more surprises up her sleeve.

"Lucy," she said, "I am going to be indoored this night."

"You don't mean it!" Lucy exclaimed, her mouth hanging open.

"It is true. Aunt Wofemda has agreed to start it for me tonight."

"What has come over you? Are you afraid the world is about to end and you may not have the chance to perform the rites?"

"Nothing of the sort. I told you, I just want to get it over with."

Indooring is part of the widowhood rites. The widow must be kept indoors for a number of days. She can only come out during the night to wash herself or to attend to nature's call. If it is absolutely necessary for her to come out during the day, she must first cover her face.

Ablator had begged and pleaded with Wofemda to allow her to start her indooring that very night. The old lady's objections gave way in the face of her persistence. Normally people allowed a few days to elapse between consulting the medium and the indooring. When the old lady finally said yes, Ablator quickly put together the items needed for the indooring: clothes to wear, a sponge and a towel, *godidzi*, lime fruit, a clay pot, a calabash, a small mat and one bottle of gin. The clothes, sponge and towel needed not be new things because they would be disposed of after the rites. Ablator sent the items to Wofemda, then came back home to wait for the evening.

** *** ***

Crossing the Ghana-Togo border in either direction can be quite hazardous. You practically run the gauntlet between immigration and customs officials on both sides of the border. Under the protocol of the Economic Commission for West African States (ECOWAS), nationals of the West African subregion are allowed to enter any West African country without a visa. This is known to most West Africans who have some formal education, and they voice this out at the least sign of impedance. What is not clear is whether one needed a form of identification or even a passport to cross the borders. So those who carry

268

no form of identification suffer all kinds of harassment. Especially on the Togo side of the border, you can be heckled, whipped, slapped or in extreme cases shot as happened to several Ghanaians during political upheavals in Togo. If you do not have a passport you have to pay your way across the border. The Ghanaian side is more genial about this — they ask for the payment gently but firmly and you pay at only one point. But the Togolese are real Shylocks: you can pay at as many points as four. The Togolese gendarmes fix the amount that travellers have to pay. These payments are illegal and go into the pockets of the border officials. The language that you speak and your mode of dressing decide how much pressure is brought upon you to pay. The border officials believe that your mode of dressing shows the ethnic group you belong to. Some tribes are made to pay higher than others.

Those who carry passports are not free either. Especially on the Togolese side, you must pay before your passport is stamped. And dare you challenge the gendarmes about your ECOWAS rights with your big mouth. If you have quick wits, you will quickly apologise for your rashness, otherwise you will be given a few slaps and may be detained for as long as the gendarmes please. What people say at the border is that Ghanaians were the first to start the illegal fees at the border but the Togolese have simply surpassed them. By an unwritten and unspoken rule, most women were at first not forced to pay the illegal fees, but even they are feeling the heat these days.

Sergeant Amlima knew all this so on the first day he crossed the border into Lome, he paid the levies willingly in order not to attract undue attention. Today, he had come with Sergeant Bansa so they had to pay double. They had come in a taxi which they left at the Ghana side of the border with the driver waiting.

"These people must be making millions a day," Bansa said aloud as they crossed the border. "Look at all these travellers!"

"Shh," said Amlima. "These gendarmes are lords unto themselves. We shouldn't attract their attention with our utterances."

The two officers were in Togo to continue the work Amlima started the day before — mount surveillance on François, Johnny's cousin. What Amlima did during his first visit was that he kept watch in the vicinity of François' house. He had tried to capture in his mind the faces of those who entered or came out of the house. François himself came out of the house only once and was pointed out to Amlima by a man with whom he had fallen into conversation at a nearby drinking bar from where he had kept watch. Locating François' house had not been difficult. The man was one of the wealthiest men in Lome, definitely the wealthiest in this suburb of Kodzoviakope. The first person he asked took him straight to François' house.

The game plan of Amlima and Bansa was simple. Amlima had already noted some of the visitors to François' house as suspicious. If any of these suspicious faces was seen coming out of the house, either of them would trail them. If they remained in Togo, the trail would be called off; if they crossed into Ghana they would be followed as far as their destination. Their point of contact would then be investigated.

Amlima and Bansa walked to within sight of François' house. "That is the house," Amlima said without pointing to the obvious. "And that is the drinking bar from where I kept watch yesterday." Then they parted company.

Amlima entered the drinking bar and Bansa walked straight towards the sprawling house. He turned right in front of the house and walked the wide lanes between the houses. Compared with the lanes at Keta and its environs, these lanes were highways. Lanes between houses at Keta are so narrow, what with everybody not willing to leave the mandatory footage before putting up their houses.

Bansa skirted François' house until he came to the front again. From the corner of his eyes he saw Amlima seated in the drinking bar. He widened his circle around the house to familiarise himself with the surrounding area, then he walked back to the bar. He sat as far away from Amlima as possible. He bought "pom-pom", a popular soft drink, his eyes all the while casually fixed on the gate to François' house. He was amused to see that Amlima had ordered the same drink. He glanced at his watch. It was just fourteen after eight.

There were just two other people in the bar, a man and a woman. Bansa was uneasy about what people might think of them seeing them at a drinking spot so early in the morning. The bar itself had not yet recovered from the hilarities of the previous day. The furniture was in disarray. There were spills of drink in various stages of drying on the tables and on the floor. Bottle tops and the bottles themselves and glasses littered the tables and floor. The boy who had served Bansa with his drink was obviously there not to serve customers but to clean the place as shown by the frown on his face when Bansa called for the drink; so deep was the frown on his face.

The gate of François' house belched open and a group of little children broke forth, carrying school bags on their little backs. Almost simultaneously, a taxi swung into the space in front of the house and braked sharply, raising little clouds of dust. With a whoop, the children charged on the taxi, flung the doors open and scrambled inside.

"That cabbie should be charging double," Bansa thought when he saw that the cab driver did not in the least protest at the violence with which the school children had charged into the vehicle. He simply waited until the kids had shut themselves in, then he drove off. "Or maybe the taxi belongs to François and the driver does not care a hoot if his kids tore it apart." Bansa thought this the more probable explanation.

Soon afterwards the gate opened again and a man came out. He wore blue jeans and a sleeveless shirt neatly tucked into the jeans. His haircut was so ludicrous Bansa was alarmed the gendarmes might break into the area any time. The sides of the man's head were clean-shaven; the high rise of hair on top of the head was done in waves, the waves ending at the back of the head where a long tuft of hair was brushed to be parallel with the neck.

Bansa saw Amlima's head jerk up in interest. He wondered if he was about to follow the man, but Amlima turned back to his drink and resumed his hen-like sipping. Two men went past the man with waves for hair and almost imperceptibly nodded to him. The two men entered François' house first casting quick glances around to see if they were being watched. Bansa almost stood to go after the wavy-haired man, but he restrained himself. The voices of the other occupants of the bar, the man and the woman, began to rise in a monotone.

"Cinq mille francs."
"Merde! Un mille cinq cent."
"Quatre mille."

272

"Deux."

"Non, trois mille cinq cent. Final!"

"Deux mille cinq cent, non plus."

"Maintenant, trois mille. Final, final!"

"Non, deux mille cinq cent. Final!"

"Bon. Allons."

The two people stood up and left the bar.

Bansa needed not to be a French scholar to know that the man and woman were bargaining over a price. "Prostitute!" he said under his breath as he watched the level of his drink which was dwindling fast. He wondered if he would have to order another bottle.

Just then one of the two men who had entered the house came out and Bansa casually stood up. He stretched himself and made a show of tucking in his shirt before stepping out of the bar. The man wore a big pair of shorts and loose shirt all made from wax print. This was a popular form of dress for the Togolese. The man walked quickly, not looking over his shoulder, unaware that he was being followed. Bansa was overjoyed at this as it made his job easier. Amlima had told him to be careful in choosing his quarry. If the quarry did not cross into Ghana, it would be difficult to return to the vicinity of François' house to continue the watch. People could begin to notice them.

Bansa's heartbeat began to accelerate as he realised that his quarry was moving in the direction of the border. When the man reached the border he bought a pack of cigarettes. Then he turned towards the beach where the taxi rank was located and Bansa's heart sank — the taxis over here do not cross the border, they ply between Kodzoviakope and the heart of Lome. The man got into one of the taxis and the taxi drove away deeper into Lome.

Bansa stood for a moment undecided what to do. He began to wander around. It would be unwise to return to the vicinity of François' house immediately. He watched the brisk business going on at the border. He watched traders arrive at the border in taxis loaded with large quantities of merchandise bought at the huge market in the centre of Lome. These merchandise were distributed to carriers, mostly middle-aged women, who smuggled them across the border in small quantities. Bansa was no stranger to Lome and he wondered, not for the first time, why customs officials had not yet been able to develop a strategy to beat the smugglers.

Bansa turned back in the direction of François' house. I will just walk past, he told himself. He walked as close to the drinking bar as possible. With a jerk he noticed that Amlima was no more there. He must have also gone off after a quarry. Bansa walked past François' house and widened the perimeter he had earlier drawn around the house. When he came to the front of the house again, he heard the house gate creak open. He glanced back to see the companion of the man he had just followed leaving the house. The man clutched a briefcase in his right hand. Bansa did not remember him holding anything when he entered the house. The man paused on the threshold to talk with someone who was inside the house. Then the gate closed and the man began to hurry away. The man wore the same style of dress as the first man though of a different colour. Bansa reluctantly followed him, certain that this chase would also end with the man heading for the centre of Lome.

After the first block, the man turned sharply to the right and began to walk quickly. This one is not even going for a taxi, he lives in the vicinity, Bansa thought sadly. But he continued the chase. Like the first man, this man too did not once glance back, rather his pace quickened with every step. Bansa was beginning to find it difficult to maintain his casual stride without making his interest in the man obvious. His spirits began to lift when he realised that the man was moving in the direction of the border after all. But instead of using the approved crossing point he was heading for one of the "beats", the paths that cut across the border and were used illegally as crossing points. Border security men from both Ghana and Togo patrolled the "beats" but all that you needed to do was pay moderate fees and you would be allowed to cross. The fees went up higher if you were found to be carrying smuggled goods.

Bansa and the man reached the crossing point. There were houses all over the place and you needed to be told that this was actually a border crossing. There was only one gendarme on the Togo side. As Bansa's quarry reached him, the gendarme held out his hand. Bansa did not hear him say, "cross my palm with silver", but the man he pursued pushed a thousand-franc note into the outstretched hand and hurried past. Bansa felt the few hundred-franc coins in his pocket. He prayed that the gendarme's appetite would not have been whetted by his quarry's one-thousand-franc note.

Bansa took out two hundred-franc coins and trans-ferred them to the gendarme in a handshake saying, "Bonjour."

"Bonjour, frère," said the gendarme and Bansa walked on.

He hurried after his prey who was already with the Ghana Customs officials and going through the ritual of greasing palms. Bansa paid his fee, this time in cedis and said gleefully to himself, "Now we are in my territory!"

The quarry led the policeman behind the sprawling uncompleted customs and immigration offices. They went past the foreign exchange bureaux beside which was a restaurant. The man went straight into the restaurant as if this had been his destination all along. Bansah hesitated for a minute, then he also entered the restaurant. He was beginning to feel hungry and the opportunity came in handy. Panic gripped him for a moment when he could not see the man in the restaurant. Had he been given the slip? A few eyes in the restaurant watched him quizzically when he began to whirl about, searching for his quarry.

This is where the pursued man steps out of a corner and bashes his pursuer on the head, Bansa thought uneasily. But the sizeable number of people in the restaurant reassured him that that was a remote possibility. Then he saw the man. He was sitting behind a huge water pot that served as a source of drinking water for diners. He had also noticed Bansa's antics and their eyes met. The policeman tried to look his most innocent, and after satisfying himself that no other door led out of the restaurant, he took a seat with his back emphatically turned to his quarry. To his right was the corner from which the food was being dished out to diners. Huge pots and pans with steaming food formed a semi-circle in which sat a woman like a master drummer behind her drums.

Bansa ordered yam slices and vegetable and egg stew. He ate quickly, from time to time taking gulps of water to push down the food. He went and washed his hands, pouring water over his hands from a cup into a big basin that served as the washing stand. From the corner of his eyes he saw that his quarry was about half-way through his food. The policeman wiped his hands on a towel hanging from a pole beside the washing basin and went out. He moved quickly to a nearby foreign exchange bureau as if he was going to change some money. He stopped on the corridor and after waiting for a couple of minutes, he took off his shirt. Underneath this he had another shirt, different in colour.

The man in the restaurant did not come out for a long time. When he did at long last there was no more haste in his gait. He set off towards the main lorry park at Aflao and Bansa went after him at a leisurely pace.

The taxi Bansa and Amlima hired to Aflao had been parked opposite the lorry park with the driver given strict orders not to move from the vehicle. Of course, this made the fee higher but it was an investment ASP Adosu was willing to make. Bansa could not see the taxi from the distance as he approached the station. He began to crane his neck, at the same time careful not to lose sight of his prey. He was caught off balance when what he suspected from the distance was confirmed; the vehicle was no more at the spot where the driver had earlier parked it. But the absence of the vehicle needed not have upset him. The arrangement he had with Sergeant Amlima was that any one of them who came back to Aflao first in pursuit of a suspicious character could make use of the vehicle if the need arose. Each of the two policemen had enough money in his pocket to hire the services of another vehicle.

Bansa pushed his momentary unease out of his mind and concentrated on the man just ahead of him. They entered the lorry park and wove their way through waiting passengers and driver's mates shouting the various destinations of their vehicles at the top of their voices. The man walked past the vehicles going to Accra to the surprise of Bansa. If the man was a drug trafficker, Bansa had thought, then he should be heading for Accra. In the newspapers, stories of drug abuse or drug trafficking came from Accra or Kumasi, the second largest city of Ghana.

Two groups of vehicles plied between Aflao and Keta. One group went through Abor, Akatsi, Dabala, Anloga then to Keta. The other group of vehicles went through Blekusu to Kedzi. It was at Kedzi that the road had been totally washed away by the sea and lagoon. Vehicles discharged their passengers at Kedzi and the passengers then completed the journey to Keta by boat.

Bansa's quarry seemed to know exactly where he was going. Without hesitation, he stopped beside a mini-bus, opened the front passenger door and sat down. The driver's mate who was standing in front of the vehicle was shouting, "Kedzi, Vodza, Keta... Kedzi, Vodza, Keta..." Bansa was now sure he had picked up the wrong trail. There are no drug traffickers at Keta, he told himself. Drug smugglers do not head for small towns, they go for the big towns. It was more the thought that he would be getting nearer home if he continued the chase that made him enter the vehicle. There were two long seats on either side of the vehicle. Bansa chose the seat on the left side and sat at the farthest end, near the driver's cabin, from where he could easily see his quarry through the glass partition. Little by little, passenger by passenger, the vehicle got full. The mate appeared at the back door and started counting the passengers, his lips moving but making no sounds.

"One, two, three... six, seven." Then he went to the other side, "One, two... five, six. One more passenger here!" he shouted. "Kedzi, Vodza, Keta, one... Kedzi, Vodza, Keta, one..."

A man appeared out of nowhere, running.

"Get inside," said the mate. But there was very little space left at the end of the long seat for the man to sit. The mate went to the side of the vehicle and started banging on the vehicle.

"Shift, shift, shift a little," he urged the passengers on that side of the vehicle. "Shift a little; we are getting late."

Bansa who sat at the extreme end of the seat found himself being squeezed into the corner. What the hell, he thought. Are we tinned fish?

The latest passenger managed to squeeze himself onto the seat and the vehicle began to move out of the station. The mate went and paid the station levy at the booth at the "OUT" gate of the station and then swung himself into the moving vehicle.

"Where is he going to sit?" Bansa asked himself, seeing that there was no space left on either seat. But he needed not have worried. The mate pushed aside the legs of the man sitting near the door.

"Excuse me," he said. He groped under the seat and brought out a small stool. He set it in the middle of the vehicle, between the knees of the row of passengers on either side and sat down, regally resting his arms on the knees of those nearest him as if he was sitting in an armchair. Bansa looked away, a wry smile on his face.

The vehicle was fairly decent, judging by the appearance of the new paint on it. But the first pothole it fell into set off howls in its joints. It groaned and creaked before stabilizing again. It was going to be a slow and joint-wracking journey over the pothole-infested road to Kedzi.

At the Aflao police station, the cops had set up a barrier. The driver apparently knew the policemen at the barrier. He hailed them and one of them drew away from the others and approached the vehicle.

"Where are you going?" the policeman asked, peering into the vehicle.

"Keta," the mate replied.

The policeman went to the side of the driver and Bansa did not have to watch to know that some money had changed hands. The car moved on, slowly. Some of the passengers began to fidget in their seats, dissatisfaction showing in their faces.

"It's going to be a long way to Kedzi," one passenger said and the others laughed.

The mate glared at the outspoken passenger.

The short journey to Kedzi took more than half an hour to complete. The vehicle came to a halt at the exact spot where the sea had cut away the road. Here, the road ended abruptly. Between themselves, the sea and the lagoon had washed away the sand from the sides of the remaining portion of the road, leaving its end jutting into the sandy beach. The roar of the sea, whose edge was just a few metres away to the left, filled the air. The lagoon, calmer, stretched away to the right. It was here that you either walked the five or so kilometres to Keta or went by boat over the lagoon.

The passengers got down from the vehicle, stretching away the cramps in their body and looking for their luggage. Bansa, sitting furthest from the door, was almost the last man out. He got down from the vehicle and began to look for his quarry. He espied him already at the edge of the lagoon. Several boats, some using sails and others outboard motors, were at the landing stage, pulled up on the sand a little to hold them at anchor. Bansa's quarry was talking to one of the boat boys. It was obvious he was bargaining over chartering a boat. That meant he was in a hurry. Bansa walked quickly through the women selling several food items at the water's edge. He reached the line of boats and to his consternation he realised that the boy his quarry was talking to was the owner of the only boat with an outboard motor at the water's edge. If he chartered another boat that would have to be a sail boat and sail boats took more than double the time to reach Keta. Bansa began to panic as he watched the man, the bargain apparently completed, begin to roll up his trousers in preparation to enter the boat. He bit his lips furiously. Then very resolutely, he walked to the man.

"Can I join you so that we share the fare?" he asked.

"Why not?" the man said, scarcely looking in Bansa's direction. He was short and had a swarthy complexion.

Several slabs of wood nailed across the mouth of the boat served as seats. The man sat on the second slab from the bow and Bansa walked past him, stepping over the slabs towards the stern. He looked for a dry slab in vain as all of them were wet. He chose a seat that appeared the least wet and sat down. Strung along the length of the boat was a long strip of plastic sheeting. It lay on the seats from stern to bow. Bansa knew what this was used for — as the boat rode towards Keta against the tide, the salty lagoon water splashed into the boat, wetting passengers. The plastic sheeting was to protect passengers from getting wet.

Another boy joined the boat boy and they pushed the boat into the water and climbed aboard. With a long pole, one of the boys pushed the boat further away from the shore while the other boy fidgeted with the outboard motor. The motor sputtered, coughed, then jumped to life. The boy revved it long and hard, then slowly, the boat began to pick up speed, cutting its way through the tide. The salty lagoon water began to splash over the boat.

"Cover yourselves!" one of the boat boys shouted over the noise of the motor.

Bansa pulled the plastic sheeting up his right side and over his head. Ahead of him, he saw the man doing likewise. Bansa would have liked to keep his head above the sheeting to be able to see the shore-line as it slid past, but such was the violence of the water against the boat that he kept his head completely covered.

The whole journey was a boring monotonous roar of the outboard motor. At long last there was a reduction in the high pitch of the motor. The boat's speed slackened, the splash of the water against the boat lessened and Bansa knew they were near their destination. He pulled the plastic sheeting away from his head as the boat turned towards the shore. The motor was turned off and the bow of the boat glided ashore, making a swishing sound against the sand.

"How much do I pay?" Bansa said as he extracted himself from the long plastic sheeting.

"Forget about it," the man said without looking back. He spoke the English language with an accent foreign to these parts of Ghana. He did not have the authentic Anlo accent. He jumped ashore and handed a wad of notes to one of the boat boys who had already waded ashore. The man waited until the boy had counted the money, then he strode forward towards the market. At the side of the market, two taxis waited for passengers. The man entered one of the taxis and Bansa knew the taxi was not going to wait for other passengers — the man would charter it.

He walked quickly towards the other taxi and got in.

"Quick! Let's go," he told the driver as the other taxi began to pull away. "Follow that taxi, the one ahead of you, but don't be too close. I don't want them to know we are following them."

"Okay," the cab driver said as he turned to have a better look at Bansa. "C.I.A., is it?"

"The C.I.A. does not have a branch in Ghana," Bansa said curtly, cutting off the conversation.

The two taxis went through Kedzikope and Abutiakope. As they went past the Keta Police Station, Bansa looked round quickly to see if he could spot Sergeant Amlima. The detective was nowhere in sight even though he saw other familiar faces moving about. The first taxi reduced speed as it reached Dzelukope.

It came to a stop opposite the building that once housed the Premier Rural Bank.

"Slow down and drive past," Bansa told his cab driver. They drove past the first taxi and without seeking the permission of the cabbie, Bansa re-adjusted the driving mirror and from it saw his quarry get down.

"Stop and park," Bansa told his driver.

The taxi stopped and Bansa continued to watch his quarry from the driving mirror. The man bent down to the level of the passenger door window and paid the taxi driver. The taxi moved away as the man crossed the street and entered a house by the side of the road.

"Quick!" Bansa said turning to the cab driver. "Go to the police station and ask of Sergeant Amlima. You know me?"

"I've been seeing you," said the cabbie, the look on his face saying, what the hell is going on?

"Good. I am a policeman. I am following somebody

and I need assistance. Go to the station and ask of Sergeant Amlima. If you find him tell him to come here quick, on the double. If you don't see him, ask of ASP Adosu. Tell him I am here, near the Rural Bank. He should send me reinforcement!"

The cab driver's eyes brightened up. "Some C.I.A. work, surely, *heh*?"

Bansa did not bother to remind him that the C.I.A. did not have a branch in Ghana. "Yes. Look for Sergeant Amlima or ASP Adosu. Tell them to come quickly!"

"Sergeant Amlima, ASP Adosu," the cabbie repeated, committing the names to memory. "And my fare?"

"Don't worry about the money; I will pay you amply." Bansa got down from the vehicle and closed the door.

"Right on." The cabbie said. He made a "U" turn and began to speed towards the police station. Bansa sat down on the steps of the Rural Bank and began to watch the house his quarry had entered. For all I know, he thought, I am making all this fuss over nothing.

Unknown to him, the house his quarry had entered was where a renowned church leader resided. This was where Prophet Elijah Patu lived.

CHAPTER EIGHTEEN

When the cab driver arrived at the Keta Police Station charge office, several policemen were huddled at the counter talking in low voices. No-one paid him the least attention when he entered the room. He cleared his throat to attract some attention but the cops continued to whisper among themselves. The excitement in their voices was easily discernible.

"Excuse me," the cabbie said.

Reluctantly, a few of the policemen turned to look in his direction.

"Please, I am looking for ASP Adosu," the cabbie said.

"He is at a meeting. You can't see him," the counter orderly said.

"Oh," said the cabbie. "What about Corporal Amlima?"

The counter orderly whose name was Constable Bright Agbolosu glared at the taxi driver. "Mr. Amlima is not a corporal! He is a sergeant."

"Sorry, sir," the cabbie said, clicking his heels in mock salute. "If I can't see ASP Adosu then let me see Sergeant Amlima. I have an important message for them."

"What message?"

The cab driver leaned his weight on his right arm on the counter, a swagger creeping into his voice to emphasise the importance of the information he was about to divulge. "You see, I am a taxi driver. I picked a man doing some C.I.A. work today. He is following a dangerous criminal. The criminal has entered a house opposite the Rural Bank at Dzelukope, obviously for some nefarious

285

activities. The policeman, I mean the one doing the C.I.A work, is now keeping a hawk's eye on the house the criminal entered. He said he should be sent reinforcement otherwise he will be outnumbered and God alone knows what will happen then."

Constable Agbolosu eyed the cabbie with suspicious eyes. Other policemen who had overheard the cabbie also drew nearer. "What is the name of the policeman you picked in your taxi?" one of them asked.

The cabbie looked momentarily confused. "I-I- don't know his name but I have been seeing him at the police station here."

"Where did you pick him?" the policeman who asked the first question said as he stepped belligerently towards the cabbie.

The cabbie stretched forward both hands to restrain him. "Take it easy, man," the cabbie said. "If this is the way you behave, next time I won't bring you any message even if it concerns the survival of your wife."

The bellicose policeman stopped in his tracks. "Nobody is threatening you. We are only asking questions. Where did you say you picked up this policeman of yours?"

"At Keta. At the landing stage of boats from Kedzi. I think he and the man he was following were coming from Aflao."

"Wait a minute," the counter orderly said. "Was the policeman stout, almost totally bald?"

"Yes!" the cabbie said emphatically. "That is your man!"

"That is Sergeant Bansa," the counter orderly said. "Let me report this to ASP Adosu at once. Excuse me."

Constable Agbolosu went out of the office and walked quickly towards the new administration building. He entered the building and knocked on ASP Adosu's door.

"Who is it?" the District Commander bellowed from inside.

"Constable Bright Agbolosu, sir. An important message for you, sir."

"Come in."

Agbolosu entered the office and saluted. For a moment he hesitated to talk as his eyes went round the room. Seated around the District Commander's desk with grim faces were Inspector Dongor and Sergeant Constant Elebu, an officer on posting who had not yet seen three months at Keta. Corporal Francis Dekornu and Private John Atiku, the two officers who were on night duty when Johnny vanished from his cell, stood to the left of the door and in the furthest corner stood Constable Alex Atonsu in civvies and looking very contrite.

"What is it?" ASP Adosu asked, the look on his face telling Agbolosu that his message had better be as important as he said, otherwise...

The tension in the room was highly infectious and Constable Agbolosu found himself stumbling over his words. "The-The-There is-is a certain taxi driver at the counter. He said he took Sergeant Bansa from Keta in his cab. Sergeant Bansa was following a certain man from Aflao. The man has entered a house near the Rural Bank. Sergeant Bansa is keeping surveillance and wants reinforcement, sir."

The men in the room exchanged quick glances.

"You can go," said ASP Adosu. "And tell the taxi driver to wait.

Agbolosu saluted and gratefully left the tension-filled room. "Phew!" he whistled when he was safely out in the corridor. He rejoined his colleagues at the charge

287

office. They huddled around him, probing for news from the District Commander's office.

"What is happening inside? What is the latest?" they asked.

"It's dreadful," Agbolosu said, shaking his head.

The cabbie coughed loudly and asked, "Can I go?"

"No," Agbolosu said over the cacophony of voices around him. "ASP said you should wait."

"Me?" the taxi driver asked, hitting his chest with his index finger. But he received no more attention from the policemen who now fell silent as Agbolosu began to give them an account of what he saw inside the District Commander's office.

The cab driver wandered out of the office. Just at that moment a group of policemen came out of the new administration building. There was urgency in their steps as they moved in the cab driver's direction.

"What the hell is about to happen?" the cabbie asked himself. "Are these policemen going to arrest me?" He thought of bolting to his cab and driving away but the group of policemen were already near where he had parked the cab. One policeman detached himself from the group as the rest of the group crowded around one of the police Land Rovers and began to get inside.

The policeman who had detached himself from the group was Corporal Francis Dekornu. He ran towards the charge office and jumped over the steps to stand beside the cabbie. The cab driver was so frightened he began to shake.

"Are you the taxi driver?" Dekornu asked.

"Ye–Yes."

"Let's go," Corporal Dekornu said and jumped back over the steps.

"To-to where?" the cabbie asked.

Dekornu stopped and impatiently waved to him to get moving. "Just follow me. And be quick!"

The cab driver went down the steps. To his surprise, Dekornu stopped beside his taxi and opened the passenger door, all the while waving to him to hurry up. The taxi driver began to double his steps. Before he could get to the taxi, the police Land Rover turned round and drove through the gate, stopping at the main road with screeching tyres. The cabbie stopped to see the vehicle swing into the main road, the engine's voice rising and falling in quick succession between gears as the police sped towards Dzelukope.

"Come on, damn you!" Dekornu shouted from the taxi.

The driver ran to the taxi and threw himself behind the wheel. He reversed quickly and went through the gate, scarcely stopping at the main road to watch out for traffic. He went through the gears quickly and from the corner of his eye he saw the policemen at the charge office crowding out onto the veranda to watch the spectacle. He waved to them, a warm feeling washing over him at the thought that now he had their undivided attention.

He drove fast and managed to shorten the distance between him and the police vehicle. The Land Rover stopped a few metres away from the Rural Bank. To the taxi driver's disappointment, the policemen did not jump out and spread out, ready for action. He came to a stop behind the police vehicle. One policeman casually got out and began to walk towards the Rural Bank.

"Wait here," Dekornu told the taxi driver and got out.

What an anti-climax! The cabbie thought as he watched Dekornu walk without a hurry towards the

289

police vehicle. He stopped beside it and began to talk with those in the vehicle.

The policeman who had got down reached Bansa at the Rural Bank. The two exchanged a few words, then they began to walk back to the Land Rover. Bansa came over to him. "You will have to wait a while for your money," he said. "Don't worry, you will be paid."

Bansa turned his back to the cab driver. He looked left, then right. He looked left again before crossing the street to the other side. The other policemen in the Land Rover got down and followed him across the street.

ASP Adosu did not normally follow his men when they arrested suspects. But today he insisted upon going along. "This case is all interesting and trickish," he had said at the station before leading out his men. Now as they moved across the street, he gave them quick, crisp instructions. Accompanying him were Inspector Dongor, Sergeant Elebu, Corporal Dekornu, Private Atiku who were all in uniform, and Private Atonsu who was in civilian clothes. Atonsu had been resting at home when he was summoned to ASP Adosu's office. The policemen made a bee-line for the house accommodating the True Open Bible Church, where Prophet Patu also resided.

"Inspector," said Adosu, "please wait at the gate here with Mr. Atonsu, out of sight. I will go in with Sergeant Bansa to see the prophet. Sergeant Elebu and Corporal Dekornu, you go round the building and be on the look-out. Anybody who gets out of this house in a hurry or through an unapproved route, a window, for example, arrest him."

"Yes, sir," Elebu and Dekornu said in unison.

Inspector Dongor was not very happy about being left at the gate, out of the action. His displeasure showed clearly on his face and was apparent to ASP Adosu.

"Inspector, we will be needing you inside," the District Commander said placatingly. "And when we do, we will call you by the whistle or Sergeant Bansa will come and call you in."

"Yes, sir," Dongor said and took Atonsu's hand. He leaned against the wall of the house and Atonsu leaned beside him.

ASP Adosu gave Bansa a sharp sideways glance, then indicated with a sharp jerk of his chin that he move forward. It was now about one o'clock. The sun was high in the sky and its sharp rays beat mercilessly upon the earth. The policemen entered the house, their eyes switching from side to side and looking over the house. Prophet Patu's two gleaming white cars were parked to the left, side by side. To the right, a few people waited under the shed that served as the chapel for the TOBC, obviously for a church ceremony.

Behind the two cars was a small shed where a woman and a group of children were going about their household chores, pots and pans clanging against each other as one of the children did the dishes. ASP Adosu veered in their direction and Bansa followed him.

"Let's ask of the prophet from those people," Adosu said.

"Prophet?" Bansa said, his eyebrows rising.

Adosu shot him a choleric glance. "Whom did you think we were coming here to see?"

Bansa bit his reply back as they were already near the woman and her children.

"Good afternoon, madam," ASP Adosu said.

"Good afternoon," the woman said, re-adjusting her

cloth which had slipped down to reveal generous portions of her bosom. "You are welcome."

"Thank you, madam. We are looking for the prophet, Prophet Pati."

"Not Pati," the woman said, a smile lighting up her face and revealing very white teeth with a gap between the upper row. "Patu, Prophet Elijah Patu. But then almost everybody mispronounces his name."

"Oh, is that so?"

"Yes. That is his door." The woman pointed at the prophet's front door.

"Thank you." Adosu began to move towards the prophet's door, but Bansa hesitated, his desire to ask the woman more questions obvious. "Come along, Mr. Bansa," the ASP said.

Bansa caught up with him quickly. "Sir," he said, "we are looking for a man who just entered this house. Let's ask the woman about him. She would have seen him entering the house."

"And who told you we will not find him at the prophet's apartment, my dear Bansa?"

"Yes, sir," Bansa said. "I just wanted to cover all possible areas."

"Don't worry, Bansa. Tag along."

They climbed over the steps and Adosu knocked on the prophet's door. He knocked again but there was still no response from within. He set an ear against the keyhole. He straightened up and jabbed the air with his forefinger indicating that there were people within.

"Ring the bell, sir," Bansa said.

Adosu had not seen the newly installed bell knob. He pressed his finger on it and kept it there for a while.

"Who is it?" came a voice from inside the apartment.

"Please open the door. You have some visitors," Adosu said.

There was the shuffle of feet from within. The key turned twice and the door was slowly opened to reveal Prophet Patu. ASP Adosu's uniform momentarily threw him off guard. He quickly regained control of himself and said very smoothly, "Are you not knocking at the wrong door?" He parted his lips in a smile that did not quite reach his eyes.

"Are we?" Adosu said, chuckling. "Well, I don't think so. We are looking for Prophet Patu."

"In that case," the prophet said, "you have knocked at the right door. I am Prophet Elijah Patu. Can I be of help to you?"

"Yes, I think so," said Adosu. "Can we come in?"

"Er, no. You see I am very busy at the moment, so let's just sit under the shed."

"Prophet, I am sorry to object to that," Adosu said. "We are on a very important mission. And look at all those people sitting under the shed. We can't sit among them and start talking!"

"Oh, don't mind them. They are my church members. I will just tell them to move to one side so that we can have privacy." The prophet came out of the door and was about to pull it shut, but ASP Adosu gently leaned his right hand against it.

"Prophet," he said, "it is in your own interest that we talk inside. If you don't mind, I insist that we go inside."

"Wow!" the prophet exclaimed. "In my own house you are telling me where to receive visitors? Incredible!"

"I am sorry it looks like that," the ASP said. "But let's leave it at that now. Please, let's go inside."

Prophet Patu gave in and said graciously, "In that

293

case, do please come inside."

"Thank you very much," Adosu said and waved Bansa to enter first.

Bansa stood as if rooted to the spot. He was in complete disagreement with the way ASP Adosu was comporting himself. What if they went in and the man they were trailing was not in the prophet's apartment? Wouldn't they look like fools?

"Mr. Bansa, please go in."

Bansa took a deep breath and preceded his District Commander into the apartment.

Like all first-time visitors, the two policemen were hit by the excessive luxury the apartment exuded. The outward appearance of the house which looked dilapidated and neglected was in sharp contrast to the luxurious furnishing in the prophet's apartment. The prophet allowed the policemen enough time to recover from their astonishment, a little smile playing at the corners of his mouth. You thought I was some small fry, didn't you?

"Please, sit down," he said expansively. "Will you like something to drink?"

"No, no thank you," Adosu said. He tapped Bansa on his back and the two of them sat down in the waiting area.

The prophet also sat down. "Now let's hear of your mission."

"Good afternoon, prophet," Adosu said.

"Good afternoon."

"Prophet, we will not waste time over this since you are occupied with other matters. As you can see we are police officers. I am ASP Adosu, the District Commander, and this is Sergeant Bansa. That is by way of introduction. Now, this is the object of our intrusion into your home. Two days ago a suspect who was in detention in one

294

of our cells at the police station vanished during the night..."

Bansa was disgusted with the line ASP Adosu's presentation was taking. Why didn't he just go to the point?

"...Our investigations have shown that the suspect, Johnny Klevor, was brought to you in this apartment on that night two days ago and you detained him. Our mission here is first to take the suspect, Johnny Klevor, back to the police station, and second, you will have to explain why you shouldn't be charged for unlawful detention."

The prophet was suddenly thrown into discomfort in his chair. He wriggled in his chair, stood up half-way and sat down again. "Inspector," he said, "let me get this right."

"I am not an inspector," Adosu interjected. "I am an Assistant Superintendent of Police."

"Sorry," Patu said. "What I am asking is this: Are you saying I came to the police station, broke down your cell and took away a suspect?"

"Prophet," Adosu said patiently. "Let's not distort the issue. You know very well that was not what I said. Maybe you are saying that to give yourself time to think. What I said was somebody brought the suspect here, Private Alex Atonsu to be exact. He is a member of your church, isn't he?" Adosu waited for a reply from the prophet but none was forthcoming. "Isn't he, prophet? Isn't Private Atonsu a member of your church?"

"Ye-Yes, I think so," Patu said.

"You don't think so. He is a member. Prophet, let's not waste time over this. Give the suspect back, now, peacefully, otherwise you will be compounding your own problems."

Bansa's mouth was now wide open in wonder. He looked from his superior officer to the prophet, his confusion deepening by the second. *If this is some kind of bluff, my dear ASP, then your methods are outlandish,* he thought. *But if all that you are saying is true, then a lot has happened in my absence from the station.*

"Inspector, sorry, er, er..." the prophet floundered.

"ASP, ASP Adosu."

"Thank you, ASP Adosu. I don't have an inkling of what you are talking about. I know Atonsu as a member of my church, but he has never come to my place here in the night, alone or accompanied by somebody."

"Prophet, you are lying," Adosu said, momentarily forgetting etiquette. *You don't call a prophet a liar to his face.*

Predictably, Prophet Patu's face flushed dark at the insult. "ASP," he said, "I am a man of God and I object to your language!"

"Sorry," Adosu said in mock apology. "Since you are insisting that Private Atonsu never brought the suspect to you, I am going to bring him in so that you can confront each other. Private Atonsu is right at your gate at this moment. Mr. Bansa, please bring in Mr. Atonsu and Inspector Dongor."

"But-but-but..."

"No buts. Bansa bring them."

Bansa left the room, leaving the two men, the prophet and the ASP, alone. The latter sat stonily in his chair, watching the former as he fidgeted in his chair as if looking for a way of escape. Soon, footsteps sounded on the stairs outside. The prophet's eyes turned sharply to the door then looked away. The door opened and Bansa entered first, followed by Private Atonsu. Inspector Dongor brought up the rear.

"Please sit down, gentlemen," Adosu said, suddenly playing host.

The men sat down and Adosu continued, "Prophet, Mr. Atonsu you know. This other gentleman is Inspector Dongor, the station officer at Keta." Prophet Patu remained silent. Adosu turned to Atonsu. "Mr. Atonsu, you told us at the station that you brought Johnny Klevor, the suspect, here to Prophet Patu who said he was going to exorcise some evil spirits from the suspect. Is that true?"

"It is true, sir."

"The prophet says it is not true."

"He is lying, sir."

Prophet Patu jumped up, his hands flying up. "You also call me a liar? Me, a man of God? Do not bring abomination upon your soul, young man! Do not do it!"

Atonsu's eyes went down in the face of the Prophet's agitation.

"Hey, Atonsu," ASP Adosu said sharply. "Do not let this man frighten you. The word of God dwells on truth. If it is the truth that you are telling, you shouldn't fear him. Stand your ground. The Lord God abhors evil and deceit. If what you are saying is true, you don't have anything to fear from this man. He can't touch you, spiritually or physically!"

The prophet sat down abruptly as if singed by Adosu's words. ASP Adosu was a regular church-goer and when the occasion demanded it he could quote the Bible extensively.

Atonsu looked up, a glare creeping into his eyes. "I am surprised that the prophet is denying I brought the suspect to him," he said. "I brought the suspect here, not once or twice, but three times." He pointed at the chair Dongor and Bansa sat in. "That was where the suspect usually sat while the prophet performed his things. Prophet Patu, are you saying I am telling lies?"

"But-but, yes, you are telling lies. You never brought the suspect into my home."

Atonsu turned to ASP Adosu. "Sir," he said, "he is denying it but it is true. On the last day that I brought the suspect here, he said the suspect would have to stay with him."

"Don't worry, Atonsu," Adosu said. "We have several options open to us. First we will search his apartment."

The prophet was incredulous. "Search my apartment?"

"Yes."

"You can't do that?"

"Why not?"

"You will need a search warrant to do that."

"No problem about that. It is here." Adosu reached into his breast pocket and brought out a folded sheet of paper. He spread it out and extended it to the prophet.

The prophet did not take the paper. "When did you get that?" he asked.

"About an hour ago," Adosu said as if engaged in a normal conversation. "We realised we might need it so we got the judge to sign one for us. Do you still have any objection to us searching this place?"

The prophet suddenly looked like a very tired man. "But-but, you can't do this. I am a man of God."

"We have already talked about that." ASP Adosu stood up. "Come on, men. No time to waste. Let's do this quickly. Inspector Dongor, please stay with the prophet and Atonsu. Use every means at your disposal to restrain them from moving an inch."

A small sound escaped from Prophet Patu's throat as Inspector Dongor brought out his service revolver.

"Come on, Bansa," Adosu said. "Let's pull this place apart. Not literally, though. Prophet, do you have any doors locked in here?"

"No, no, all the doors are open."

"Thank you."

Adosu and Bansa stepped round the room divider into the living-room. This area was more luxuriously furnished than the waiting-room. The policemen stepped gingerly on the soft woolen carpet. They looked under the huge stuffed chairs, behind the book-shelf and under the tables but did not find anything. A door stood to their right. Bansa pushed it open. It was the kitchen. He looked under the sink and the kitchen table but did not find anything. He opened the tall refrigerator and saliva instantly flooded his mouth at the sight of the assortment of food and drinks in the fridge.

"Anything there?" Adosu asked when Bansa came out of the kitchen.

"Nothing, sir."

"Let's go in there," Adosu said, indicating two doors in the wall opposite the kitchen. "You search that room and I will search this one."

They moved over to the two rooms on the other side of the living-room. Adosu entered the room on the left and Bansa entered the other one. Bansa's room was the master bedroom. He marvelled at the wide bed that stretched across the breadth of the room. My children can play football on that, he thought. The first place to look was obviously under the bed. The room was dim, with very little light coming in through the heavy curtains framing the windows. Bansa looked for the switch and put on the light. He went down on all fours and peered into the darkness beneath the bed. At first he could not see anything. Then as his eyes got adjusted to the darkness, a long dark form began to take shape beneath the bed. Bansa crept closer, almost getting himself under the bed. He wished he had a torchlight. Slowly, his eyes began to see quite clearly under the bed. His heart started beating faster and his breath came quickly as the identity of the object under the bed manifested itself. It was a human form.

Bansa straightened up quickly and went to the door. "ASP, sir," he called, his voice loaded with excitement.

"Hm?" Adosu answered from the other room. "Have you found anything?"

"Please, come quickly!" Bansa went back to the room and started looking for something to prod the body under the bed.

Adosu joined him. "What is it?" he asked.

"There is somebody under the bed," Bansa whispered.

The District Commander bent down. At first he could also not see anything. Then his vision cleared and he straightened up, saying, "Of course, there is somebody under the bed. Go and bring the prophet or whoever he is."

Bansa came out to the living-room and called, "Prophet, please come."

The prophet joined them in the room almost immediately. The calm that was in his face confused Adosu. He had expected him to be extremely alarmed. Could it be he was unaware that somebody was hiding under his bed?

Adosu beckoned to him to come closer. "Prophet," he

said, "who is hiding under your bed?"

Prophet Patu shook his head wearily. "It must be my friend."

"Your friend?"

"Yes. I don't know why he has done this, but he must have been very frightened by your visit."

"Very interesting. Can you tell him to come out?"

"Yes." Patu bent down and called, "Boat?"

"Mhm?" came from under the bed.

"Come out. You needn't have done this. There is no danger."

There was some shuffling noise from under the bed, then the head of a man emerged, covered with cobwebs and dust. The man extricated the rest of his body from under the bed and stood up. His whole body was covered with cobwebs and dust. But in spite of his poor state Bansa recognised him as the man he had trailed from Lome.

"ASP, sir," Bansa said excitedly, "this is the man I followed from Lome!"

"I know," said ASP Adosu.

Bansa's excitement was deflated. What airs? He thought. As if he was with me in Lome!

The man from Lome started brushing the dirt off himself. The prophet helped him. "You shouldn't have done this, Boat," the prophet said. "Only the evil-minded fear the police. Come, let's get out of here."

Adosu restrained the prophet. "Just one moment," he said. "Bansa, search him."

The prophet was now angry. "My friend, Mr. Policeman, you are going too far. Have you come here intentionally to humiliate me. What will you be looking for in his pockets? Your suspect?"

"Leave that to me. Bansa, search him."

Bansa quickly frisked the man, going through the pockets of his dress. "Nothing, sir."

"Okay," Adosu said. He moved to the foot of the bed. "Help me with this. We are going to lift it aside. It is possible our friend forgot something under the bed."

"Inspector!" Patu almost screamed.

"ASP, not inspector."

"ASP, this is going too far!"

"Not far enough. Come on, Bansa."

Bansa took hold of the head of the bed and together they pulled the heavy bed away from the wall. All four men craned their necks to see what was on the other side of the bed. Lying against the exposed wall was a black executive briefcase, the one Bansa had seen the man carrying from Lome.

"That is his briefcase!" Bansa said.

"I know," said Adosu. He stepped around the bed and picked up the briefcase. "Do you want to take a bet on what is inside?"

Bansa shook his head.

"You need not." The District Commander set the briefcase on the bed. He flicked it open and carefully started lifting its contents onto the bed. At the bottom was revealed two black rubber sachets the size of half-kilo polythene bags, the type market women use to bag sugar and rice.

Adosu poked the black bags with his finger. He looked up at Bansa. "Want to take a guess what these contain?"

Bansa shook his head. "No, sir."

"Of course, we will not play any guessing games now," Adosu said. He turned to the two men, the prophet and the man from Lome. Beads of sweat had broken on

302

the brows of each man. "Do you have anything to say for yourselves?"

"Er-er-er," stammered the prophet. "I di-didn't know he was carrying that in his bag."

"What is it he is carrying in his bag?"

"I- I- I don't know."

Adosu allowed himself a little smile. "Then how come you seem to think it is something bad?"

"I am not saying it is bad."

"Let's get out of here. It is becoming hot," Adosu said. He replaced the contents in the briefcase and closed it. He picked it up and they trooped to the waiting area where Inspector Dongor had his service revolver dutifully trained on Atonsu. Bansa kept glancing at ASP Adosu in admiration. But instead of the look of triumph he expected to see on the ASP's face, the man seemed to be in deep thought, his brows screwed in concentration.

"Inspector," Adosu told Dongor, "please put handcuffs on these two men. We are taking them to the police station. They have here in this briefcase suspicious substances."

Dongor replaced his revolver in his pocket. He took out two pairs of handcuffs and handed one to Bansa. "Help me," he said.

Bansa handcuffed the prophet and Dongor did the same for Boat, the man from Lome. The two policemen now turned to look quizzically at their superior who was unmistakably very ill at ease. ASP Adosu kept turning at the same spot, his eyes very perturbed.

"What is it, boss?" Dongor asked.

"Nothing, nothing." Adosu replied.

Dongor exchanged glances with Bansa. "Can we go now?" he asked.

"No, just a minute," the District Commander said. "Please hold this for me." He gave the briefcase to Dongor and went back to the living-room. He entered the room he had been searching earlier on. After a couple of minutes he came out. "Prophet," he said, "why are you keeping the deepfreezer in your bedroom?"

"Tha-That is where I have been keeping it since I bought it."

"Can I have the key?"

"It-It is not locked."

"It is locked."

"It is not."

"Please come over, everybody."

Dongor shepherded the rest of the men through the living-room into the bedroom.

"Inspector Dongor," Adosu said. "Please open the freezer."

Dongor set down the briefcase and tried lifting up the door of the freezer. "It is locked," he said.

"You try, Bansa," Adosu said.

"It is locked, sir," Bansa also said after trying.

ASP Adosu turned to Patu. "Will you like to try too, prophet."

"I think it is locked," the prophet said in a dry voice.

"Where is the key?"

"I have misplaced it."

"Since when?"

"I can't remember."

"Then the freezer must be bursting with ice by now."

"It is frost-free."

"Thank you for reminding me. It is even written on the side here." Adosu caressed the section of the freezer where the label said FROST FREE. "It is a beautiful

304

freezer," he said. "I will hate for us to damage it. But if you insist you can't find the key we will have to break it open."

"You can't do that!" said Patu with vehemence. "This is my private property!"

"I thought we had gone over all that. We have a search warrant. Now, the key or we break it open."

Patu looked away. "Give me some time to look for the key."

"Too late now," Adosu said. "You are not coming back to this apartment for a long time. The key or we break it open."

Prophet Elijah Patu kept quiet.

"Bansa," said Adosu. "Go to the kitchen and bring anything that can force this open. It doesn't look like it has a strong lock."

Bansa went to the kitchen and came back with a machete.

"Good," said Adosu. "Give it to me."

With the strong blade of the machete it did not take long for the door of the freezer to fly open. A wave of ice-cold mist rose from the freezer making Adosu back away momentarily. When the wave of mist subsided, he stepped back to the freezer and peered inside. A blue plastic sheet was spread over the contents of the freezer. Adosu lifted up one end of the sheet but it was stuck to what lay underneath. With a sudden force he wrenched away the sheet. What he saw underneath made his whole body shudder.

"My God!" he said, turning away. "Oh, my God!"

The others, with the exception of the prophet, crowded round the freezer and peered inside. There was a sharp collective intake of breath as of a flock of birds

305

suddenly taking to flight — trussed like a chicken with scarcely any ice on him was Johnny Klevor, the suspect who had vanished from his cell two days earlier. He lay in the freezer his face upwards, like a big foetus whose birth had been overly delayed. The dark pigments in his skin seemed to be fading so that he looked blackish white. His mouth was a little open, the surprise on his face unobliterated by his cold surroundings.

The man from Lome was the first to back away from the freezer. He sought ASP Adosu and it took him some time to locate him. He was standing facing the door, his back turned on the group.

"I know nothing about the dead body," the man from Lome said. "As for the cocaine, yes! I am in it. But the dead body, I know nothing about it!"

"Are you ready to sign a statement to that effect?" Adosu asked, his face struggling to recover from the shock he had had from the freezer.

"Yes, yes!"

Adosu turned away from him. "We know everything already. But you are going to have a hard time proving that you had no hand in that death, especially if the prophet wants to implicate you. He looks like the sort... Come on, everybody." He clapped his hands. "We will take the body to the mortuary, then we will go back to the station and try and sort this out."

"Officer," the prophet said and Adosu whirled around. "What is it?" he asked.

The prophet's voice was surprisingly calm. "Your suspect's death was an accident," he said. "He hit his head against the furniture. Nobody touched him."

"Oh yeah?" Adosu sneered. "What was he doing when he had the accident? Dancing?"

306

"He was under hypnotism. I was trying to drive away from him an evil spirit."

"Oh yeah?" Adosu sneered again.

"Some of these things are not easily understood by us mortals," the prophet continued in the same calm voice that was infuriating Adosu so much. "They are the ways of God."

"Tell that to a judge," Adosu said and turned his back on the prophet. "Yes, come on," he urged his men.

Johnny's body was lifted from the freezer and wrapped in a blanket wrenched from the prophet's bed. ASP Adosu was the last person that went out of the apartment. He locked the doors and pocketed the key. Sergeant Bansa and Private Atonsu carried Johnny's stiff body. Atonsu was all the while crying, not for the loss of life that had occurred but for his complicity in it.

Sergeant Elebu and Corporal Dekornu met the group at the gate. With them was Sergeant Amlima.

"How did you get here?" the ASP asked Amlima.

"I came back from Lome and heard you were here, so I rushed over," Amlima replied.

Adosu turned his gaze to Bansa who was standing still, Johnny's body held between him and Atonsu. "Were the two of you not supposed to be together?" he asked.

"Yes," Bansa replied. "But we split up."

"Come on," Adosu said. "Put the body in the vehicle and let's get to the mortuary. We will talk about all that at the station." He marched to the front of the vehicle and sat down as the policemen arranged Johnny's body on the back seat. The prophet and his friend from Lome were pushed into the vehicle and the policemen crammed in after them.

A crowd had started to gather. The people talked

307

excitedly among themselves, but try as they did they could not fathom what was the trouble at the prophet's house. Some among the crowd quickly started moving towards the police station to fish for news from there. So it was that later, after the police had deposited Johnny's body at the mortuary and headed for the station, a fairly large crowd was already there to receive them. Prophet Patu and the man from Lome were allocated places in the cell. Then ASP Adosu called a meeting at his office. Present were Inspector Dongor, Sergeants Amlima, Bansa and Elebu.

Before the meeting could begin, the door opened and Deputy Superintendent of Police Donald Aboagye, the Divisional Commander, walked in without knocking. That was an odd habit he had. He never knocked before entering any office.

Adosu detested Aboagye with his whole heart. Here we go again, he thought, as they all stood up in respect to the Deputy Superintendent.

Adosu was about to give up his seat to Aboagye, but the latter waved the offer aside and selected a seat a little way away from the group. "Don't mind me," he said. "Continue with your meeting. I just came to listen in."

"Thank you, sir," Adosu said. He sat down and motioned the others to do likewise. "We will go straight to the point. We will fill each other in on what we have been doing so far, then we will see where we go on from there... You the group from Lome, Sergeants Amlima and Bansa, tell us about your day."

Amlima caught Bansa's eye and urged him to talk first. He was burning with curiosity to know what had been going on since the two of them split up. Bansa narrated his story in short crisp sentences. When he got to the point where he sent the taxi driver to the station to summon help, ASP Adosu lifted his hand and stopped him.

"Let Sergeant Amlima take it up from there," he said.

"I don't have a story as exciting as that of Sergeant Bansa," Amlima said.

"Tell it and stop wasting time!" Adosu said impatiently.

Amlima talked rapidly. "After Mr. Bansa had gone after his first man and left me alone at the drinking bar in Lome, another man came out of the house we were watching. He headed for the border and I followed him. We crossed the border. He boarded a passenger bus and I followed the vehicle in the taxi we had chartered. The chase led me to Akatsi. My man joined another vehicle and got down at a farming village along the Ho-Akatsi road. My investigations revealed that the farm belonged to him. I marked the area for further investigation and came straight back to Keta, knowing that by that time Mr. Bansa will be difficult to locate elsewhere. When I got back to the station, I was told Mr. Bansa was near the Rural Bank and had sent for reinforcement. I had scarcely arrived there when you emerged from that house with the rest of the group."

"Good," Adosu said. "I will fill you in on what has been happening in your absence. Corporal Dekornu and Private Atiku were on duty when the suspect, Johnny, vanished from his cell. As you are aware, they were tasked to find the suspect. They started their own investigations. They looked for and interrogated suspects who had been in detention during Johnny's time. Their investigations led to the revelation that Private Alex

309

Atonsu had on two previous occasions taken the suspect out in the night. They reported the matter to me. I called Mr. Atonsu and questioned him. Initially he denied everything but later he confessed and told us he had sent the suspect to a prophet's house. It was unbelievable! Quickly, I arranged for an emergency search warrant from the judge. We were just on the verge of leaving for the so-called prophet's house when we received Bansa's call for reinforcement.

"The rest, as they say, is history. We met Bansa outside the prophet's house. When we confronted the prophet he denied everything. Then we began searching the house. First, we discovered the man Bansa had followed from Lome hiding under one of the prophet's beds, together with a portfolio containing two sachets of a powdery substance I suspect to be cocaine. Johnny, the suspect, we later found in the prophet's deep-freezer, dead as a log. The prophet told us he didn't intentionally kill Johnny. He said it was an accident; he hit his head against a piece of furniture during hypnotism."

"Who was hypnotising who?" Deputy Superintendent Donald Aboagye asked.

"The prophet said he was hypnotising Johnny to exorcise from him an evil spirit," Adosu said.

Aboagye let out a deep sigh. "What is this world coming to?" he said. "A prophet, a murderer?"

"Sir," Adosu said, "we have not established that yet."

"But why would the prophet want to kill Johnny?"

"There is no clear answer to that yet, sir. My own theory is that either Johnny died through an accident as the prophet is saying or maybe the prophet gave something to Johnny to drink that turned out to be poisonous. Then there is this other angle: if the prophet is involved in this drug connection, then it is possible he and Johnny knew each other through Johnny's cousin in Lome. Or, er, let's say they did not know each other, then through this hypnotism of his the prophet discovered that Johnny knew something about their drug connection. The prophet already knew that Johnny is in the hands of the police. It is possible that the prophet got frightened and killed Johnny to prevent him from saying anything to the police."

"That is a likely theory," Aboagye said, nodding his head.

"And that will make it murder class one," Adosu said.

"Keep me informed of developments," the Divisional Commander said and stood up. The rest of the men also stood up. "And take their statements now while they are still hot, before they concoct more lies. As for the men who were sleeping on duty when the suspect was taken away, and the man who took the suspect to the prophet, let's write a report to headquarters for advice." Then he went out as informally as he had come in.

"Wow!" Adosu exhaled, almost giving words to his distaste of his superior officer. He sat down. "We will not waste more time here. Sergeants Amlima and Bansa!"

"Yes, sir," the two officers responded and stood up.

"Take statements from the suspects. Then we will see where we move on from there."

"Yes, sir."

ASP Adosu sat back wearily as his subordinates filed out of the office.

CHAPTER NINETEEN

Even though Aunt Wofemda was childless, it was not as if she had never been pregnant. She took seed soon after she married her first husband but in the fifth month of the pregnancy she miscarried. Try as they could, she could not conceive again until her husband died. She got pregnant again a few months after she re-married. This time when her time was due she had a macerated still birth. She never got pregnant again. Then her second husband also died and tongues began to wag in the town — could she be a witch? Could she be killing her own husbands and the babies in her womb? Wofemda became afraid to marry again for, she reasoned, should the improbable happen and her third husband also die before her, this would seem to confirm her neighbours' suspicions that she was a witch.

Wofemda was a simple woman and this was what endeared her to Ablator who herself abhorred ostentatiousness. The matter of the death of Ablator's husband drew them even closer to each other. Once Wofemda decided to go along with Ablator's rush with the widowhood rites, she threw herself into it.

At five o'clock in the evening she was at Ablator's house to enquire if she was ready for the consultation at the medium's shrine. Ablator was not ready; neither was Lucy who was going to accompany them to the shrine. The latter was indoors when Wofemda entered the house.

"Luc-y-y-y-y-y-y!" Ablator shouted. "Aunt Wofemda is here already. Hurry up!"

"*Yoo!*" Lucy responded from inside.

The two women had already taken their bath so it

took them very little time to get ready. Aunt Wofemda had brought along the items Ablator had deposited with her in the morning — the dry corn, the bottle of gin, *liha* and the cash of two thousand cedis. Now, she made Ablator bring a little amount of corn powder from her kitchen.

"We have to pour libation before we set off," she said. She put the corn powder in a calabash full of water and stirred the mixture. While still stirring, she began to call the ancestors. She called people who had long been dead, both from the paternal and maternal families of Ablator. She also called the ancestors from the family of Ablator's husband. She implored them to accompany them through the widowhood rites they were about to begin. She asked them to give Ablator the strength and patience to go through the rites successfully.

Then Ablator set the basket containing the gin, *liha* and dry corn on her head and together the three women set off for the medium's shrine.

Mediums in the local dialect are called *amegashi*. They are spiritually very powerful people. Since they are in constant communication with the spirits of the dead, people fear to fall foul of them as they can direct the wrath of the dead against you.

Amegashi Abley was by far the most popular medium at Woe. Members of her family had been mediums as long as anyone could remember. Her great, great grandmother was a medium, so was her great grandmother, her grandmother and mother. It was only a matter of course that Abley also became a medium. The strange thing about her line of family was that the women never gave birth to more than one female child. They could have as many children as they wished, but only one

313

of them would be a female. So Abley's great, great grandmother right down to herself were only female children. Abley now had two children, all male, but even though she was close to forty she was not worried about having a female child. She knew she would have one before she reached her menopause.

Amegashi Abley's house was situated on the outskirts of Woe, close to the boundary with Anloga. Her house was a three-room brick building with a rusted corrugated iron sheet enclosure for a kitchen. And for one who was in constant contact with the spirits of the dead, this was not surprising. She must have been convinced about the flighty nature of this life and the futility of amassing material things on this earth. She was preparing for the longer-lasting, eternal resting place.

One of the rooms in the brick building was occupied by Abley's children. The other two rooms, a chamber and an ante-chamber, were where Abley herself lived. The chamber doubled as her shrine and on the days that she performed rites, visitors stayed in the antechamber while she performed the rites in the chamber. None of her children were allowed in the shrine; it was only a female child who could enter the shrine. Once every month, Abley said prayers and cleaned the shrine.

It was for Abley's shrine that Aunt Wofemda and her entourage were headed. They arrived at the shrine a little to six o'clock. Abley, in full regalia of her office, was ready and waiting for them. She wore a very white cloth, a wrap, that was tucked in above her bosom and reached to her ankles, and a huge white headgear sat on her head. She wore necklaces, bangles, anklets and armlets all made from beads and cowrie shells. White chalk was smeared on almost all the exposed parts of her body. She wore no footwear. This was in reverence to the spirits of the dead that she could sense milling about in the house. Her children, boys aged eleven and fourteen, sat on stools in front of the kitchen. They wore shorts and were bare-chested and like their mother their feet were bare.

"You are welcome," the medium said.

"Thank you," replied the visitors.

"I know of your mission," said the medium. "You have a long conversation ahead of you with those that you seek to speak to. Let us therefore waste no time. Please come inside."

She led the visitors into the ante-chamber. The room contained very little else apart from two low stools and a bench. A large cane basket with a wide range of cooking utensils piled high in it sat on a table in one corner. In another corner was an earthenware drinking pot the mouth of which was covered by an enamel plate containing a plastic cup turned upside down.

"Please sit down," said the medium. "*Mama* Wofemda, you are not a stranger to the rites, but our daughters are. You will sit here with your back to the wall." She indicated a stool near the door of the chamber. "Our daughters will sit there." She pointed to the bench ranged against the opposite wall. "I will be inside with our spirit visitors." She waited until Aunt Wofemda, Ablator and Lucy were seated, then she knocked on the door of the chamber and entered, leaving the door ajar.

Though Ablator and Lucy would not confess it to each other, they were scared. At the beginning, Ablator had been skeptical of the whole procedure. But now when she found herself removed from her own home, on the outskirts of the town, she had to admit that she was scared, even if only a little. She remembered belatedly

315

that she had forgotten to ask her aunt if Gbagbladza, her husband, was going to manifest himself in flesh. Too late now, she thought, afraid to speak as her heart gave out prolonged weighted beats which she was sure was audible to her companions.

After *Amegashi* Abley had entered her shrine, there was a pregnant silence of about two minutes with no sound coming from the chamber. Then, barely audible at first, a sound as of groaning and a light struggle began to come from the chamber. Ablator and Lucy looked at each other, not in merriment as they would normally have done, but with a mixture of fear and alarm. Lucy thought, why didn't we think of bringing along a man to take charge if things get messy? And Ablator's thought was, will I be able to maintain my tough devil-may-care attitude if anything emerges from that door?

The groans stopped and the medium sounded a metal rattle a few times. Then her voice came forth calling, "*Fielevi, Fielevi... Fielevi.*"

There was silence; the medium called again, "*Fielevi, Fielevi...*"

Then there was a response, dull and weary, "Mhm?" as of somebody coming unwillingly awake when shaken. The medium called again, "*Fielevi.*"

"Mhm?" This time the voice was clearer. "What is it?" It was the guttural masculine voice of a man.

"*Fielevi?*"

"Yes? What can I do for you?"

Fielevi was the medium's spiritual messenger to the spirit world. Anytime people came to the medium to consult the departed souls of their kindred, it was *Fielevi* that the medium sent to the spirit world to summon the spirits of the dead people being sought. The suspicion that

Ablator had entertained all along began to rear its head again; could the medium have hidden somebody in the chamber before their arrival?

"Some people wish to send you to the beyond," the medium told *Fielevi*.

"Aah," *Fielevi* moaned. "Me that I am so tired? Where do they wish to send me?"

"Go to the Bate clan, to the family of Hordzo, Nani's grandfather; tell Nani's father, Azilevu, that their daughter-in-law Ablator wishes to consult them. They should bring along their son Sagada, also called Gbagbladza. Then go to the To clan, tell Dzumave Avuemewor that his grand-daughter Ablator wishes to talk to him. He should bring along Ablator's father Dordzavudzi. His daughter wishes to talk to him. Hurry up. The people are waiting."

"Aah," *Fielevi* moaned again. "When am I going to be free?"

"Nobody is free!" the medium admonished. "Not here or even over there. Now get moving."

"*Yoo*," *Fielevi* said.

In the ante-chamber where the visitors waited with abated breath, a cold wind blew through as if originating from the inner chamber. The wind rushed outside, rustling the leaves of the few coconut trees that stood in the compound. Goose pimples suddenly appeared on the skin of Ablator and Lucy. Their eyes focussed on Aunt Wofemda, looking for some assurance that nothing unpleasant was about to happen. But Wofemda had a vacant look on her face. She appeared to be no longer aware of the presence of the two women. The medium resumed sounding her metal rattle again, solemn and sonorous.

This time of the year the days were long and the

nights shorter, so that even though it was some minutes past six when Ablator and the others entered the ante-chamber, the day was still clear. But now darkness seemed to fall all of a sudden, not pitch darkness, but darkness enough to give fuzzy outlines to the figures of the visitors in the ante-chamber. The evening temperature seemed to drop substantially below the normal and Ablator and Lucy found themselves shivering. The look on their faces was now open terror. The two of them kept glancing at the door leading outside to make sure it was still open in case there was need for a quick getaway.

When the wind blew first, it was as if it was emanating from the inner chamber. It blew again, this time emanating from outside and rushing into the room. It was colder, loaded with urgency and a rustling sound as of the shuffle of footsteps. Ablator and Lucy simultaneously grabbed each other's arm, trembling. Were these the ghosts that had been summoned entering the room? They could now only see the dark silhouette of Aunt Wofemda as she leaned against the wall, so they couldn't tell how she was taking all this. The wind died down as suddenly as it had begun and the two women relaxed their grip on each other.

From inside the inner chamber, there was the sound of the release of a deep breath, almost a sigh, then the medium said, "Ah, you are back, *Fielevi.*"

"Yes, I am back. Can I go now?" said *Fielevi.*

"No," replied the medium. "You will have to take all these people back."

Fielevi did not sound happy when he said, "*Eyo-o.*"

Another voice, different from that of Fielevi and the medium said, "*Ago-o-o.*"

"*Ame-e-e,*" replied the medium.

"Evening to you, *Efiashi*," said the voice.

"Who is it that is speaking?" asked the medium.

This was the custom with the medium. When she summoned ghosts, she did not start talking with them until they had disclosed their identity, otherwise she could be talking to a malevolent spirit. The ghosts called her *efiashi*, the wife of the chief.

"I am Azilevu," replied the voice of the ghost.

In the ante-chamber Ablator listened to the conversation intently. She barely knew Azilevu, Gbagbladza's grandfather, before he died and she couldn't be sure if it was the old man's voice she was hearing or a fake. As for Lucy, she did not know the old man at all. He died before she married Besa.

"Oh," the medium said and began the exchange of greetings. "Evening to you. How is your home?"

"Fine," said a host of voices in addition to that of Azilevu.

"The children?" said the medium.

"They are fine," replied the host of voices.

"Everybody?"

"They are all fine."

"Ah..."

"How are yours?"

"They are well."

"The children?"

"They are all well."

After the greetings, Azilevu said, "Can we sit down?"

"Of course," said the medium. "Please sit down."

There was the sound of stools being pulled about.

"Thank you... thank you," said several voices.

Ablator and Lucy were now trembling on their seats. Unless there were a lot of people hidden in the medium's

319

shrine before their arrival, then what they were witnessing could not be a fake. No matter how good a mimic the medium was, she could not mimic several voices at the same time. The blanket of night had now completely shrouded the evening. The medium's children had lit a small kerosene lamp and set it outside the door, but this did little to light up the room.

Someone cleared his throat in the inner chamber, then the voice of Azilevu said, "*Efiashi*, not all of us have been able to come. Some are engaged. But why is it that you have called us?"

"Some people wish to speak to you," said the medium.

"Oh?" said Azilevu.

"*Ahoga*, are you there?" the medium said.

"Yes," replied Wofemda from the ante-chamber. Her voice was surprisingly clear. From the stillness of her body, Ablator and Lucy had thought she had fallen into a doze. In the semi-darkness, they saw her sit forward and cock her ears towards the chamber.

"Your people have arrived."

"Tell them they are welcome," said Wofemda.

The medium told the ghosts, "Those who seek you say you are welcome."

"*Yo-o-o*," came the voices of the ghosts. Then Azilevu said, "Evening to you of the outside world."

"Who are you speaking?" said Wofemda. The *ahoga* also had to ask of the identity of the ghost.

"I am Azilevu, the father of Nani."

"Oh," said Wofemda. "Evening to you from beyond. How is the beyond?

"Fine," said the host of voices. "How is the outer world?"

"Very well."

"Have our sympathy," said the ghosts.

"Have our sympathy, too," said Wofemda.

Ghosts believe they are better off where they are than the living in this world. So when they are summoned they offer their condolences to those still living for their suffering in this world. But the living, for fear of being spirited away into the beyond by the ghosts, try to assure the latter that they are also fine where they are.

"Why have you called us?" asked Azilevu.

There was the scraping of the stool on the floor as Wofemda pulled herself forward. "Your daughter-in-law wishes to discourse with her husband Gbagbladza."

"You mean Sagada?" said Azilevu.

"Yes, your grandson Sagada."

"He is here," Azilevu said. "Sagada, your wife wants to talk with you."

In the ante-chamber, the senses of Ablator and Lucy were on high alert. Their bodies seemed to be suspended in mid-air as their hands gripped the bench on which they sat.

"Ablator, speak!" whispered Ahoga Wofemda.

"What should I say?" Ablator whispered back fiercely.

"Just call him."

Ablator took in a deep breath then said, "Efo Sagada."

"Mhm?" came from the inner room.

Ablator's body jerked on the seat as if from an electrical shock. There was no question that the voice she had just heard was that of her late husband. When anybody called Gbagbladza, his response had always been an impatient "Mhm?"

"Is that you Efo Sagada?" Ablator asked her voice quivering.

"Yes, it is me. What is it that you want with me?" If there had been any remnant of doubt in Ablator's mind, those two sentences removed it. There was no mistaking the deep slow manner of speech of Gbagbladza. Even in death his voice had not lost its slow but cutting-edge impatience.

Tears began to run down Ablator's cheeks. "Is it really you, my husband?"

"Yes, it is me, Ablator," said Gbagbladza. "Stop crying. I am very fine here."

Even the nasal tone Gbagbladza had always applied to the "a" in his wife's name was there. Only *he* called her in that tone and Ablator had always found it special. For some time, Ablator could not speak, she could only weep.

Ahoga Wofemda came to her aid. "Sagada," she said, "your wife wishes to perform her widowhood rites. What cloth do you want her to use?"

"She should use black cloth," said the voice of Gbagbladza.

"How long should she use the black cloth?"

"Four months."

"How many days should she stay indoors?"

"Seven days."

"After the ceremony, what foods should she cook for the feasting?"

"Let her prepare steamed *abolo, dzemkple,* rice, *akple,* rice and beans and *kenkey.* Tell her to use chicken and fish for the stews and goat and fish for the soups. She should prepare groundnut soup, okro soup, palmnut soup and light soup."

"*Yoo*, we have heard you. Is there anything else you wish to tell her?" Ablator could not bring herself to stop sobbing as she listened to her husband's voice.

"Stop crying, Ablator," said the voice of Gbagbladza. "I know all that has been taking place. You shouldn't let anything worry you."

"*Yo-oo*, my husband," sobbed Ablator.

"How are our children, Yao and Sena?"

"They are fine. They miss you."

"Tell them they should study hard at school. Tell them I miss them too. I want them to have very good jobs and ride in big cars when they grow up." That was what he had always told his children.

"How am I going to tell them? Will they believe me?" sobbed Ablator.

"Do you believe you are speaking with me your husband?"

"Yes."

"Absolutely?"

"Yes, absolutely!"

"They will also believe when you send them my message. Tell them even though I am no longer there to punish them when they misbehave, they should be good children. I know you will do your best to correct them when they misbehave."

"Yes, I will."

"How is Lucy?"

"She is here."

Lucy almost jumped from her seat when she heard her name.

"Lucy, how are you?"

"I– I– I am fine." Could she be really talking to a ghost?

"How are Mawusi and her brother and sister?"

"They-they are fine."

"Your husband couldn't come. He said I should tell

323

you he will be ready for you when you come to consult him."

"My husband?"

"Yes."

Lucy also began to sob.

"Do you have any message for him?"

She wanted to ask, is it true that the two of you were killing people for ritual purposes? But instead she said, "Tell-Tell him I will come and consult him very soon."

"He will get the message."

"Ablator," said Gbagbladza, "I am going. Do you have anything more to say?"

"No, my husband," Ablator said. "But isn't it possible for you to just come home?"

"No. Where I am I can't cross over to you. You can come here, but your time is not due. Stay with the children."

"*Yo-o*. Farewell."

"Good bye."

Ablator wiped her eyes with a corner of her cloth while she stifled her sobs.

From the chamber, the leader of the ghosts, Azilevu, spoke. "What do you have with you?"

"Some gin," said the medium.

"Can we have some?"

"Yes, you can."

There was the clink of glasses as the drink was served.

"Thank you... Thank you..." said the ghosts.

After a short while, Azilevu said, "We are going away."

"*Yo-o*," said the medium. "Thank you for coming. Have a safe journey back."

"Thank you," said the ghosts.

"*Fielevi*, take them back home."

"*Yo-o*," said Fielevi.

The temperature in the ante-chamber dropped again as the ghosts left on a breeze that blew through the room. In the darkness, Ablator opened her eyes wide as if trying to see her husband, but she saw nothing.

Then the medium came out looking weary. She sat down on the bench next to Lucy and exchanged greetings with her visitors. "We have finished," she said in a tired voice. "You can now go home and do what you have been asked to do. Ablator, your aunt Wofemda will do everything for you. So don't worry. You are in safe hands."

"Thank you," said Ablator.

"We will go now," said Aunt Wofemda, rising.

The medium saw them off to her gate then came back to sit down to a well-earned meal. Her children had been preparing the meal while she was with the ghosts.

Back at home, Ablator also rushed through the preparation of the evening meal. She was having her indooring rites this very night. The rites would be performed by *Ahoga* Wofemda and another widow, *Ahoga* Tsoeke. *Ahoga* Tsoeke was a short energetic woman, much younger than Wofemda. She was known to engage in no meaningful income-generating activity but her standard of living was well above that of the average community member. Her secret was that she had three of her children in Britain and they sent her regular allowances.

At about eight-thirty in the night, the *ahoga* took Ablator to a refuse dump in the town. This part of the rites is always done on a refuse dump, a clear signal to the dead man that he and his wife are going to part company forever. Before coming out here, Aunt Wofemda had poured libation at Ablator's house, imploring the ancestors to take the widow through this part of the rites safely. She also implored the dead man's spirit to forgive his wife whatever wrong she might have done both before and after his death, and leave her in peace to live the rest of her life. Ablator had earlier on confessed to the *ahoga* that she had not remained pure after her husband's death.

She now stood between the two older women on the refuse dump in the cold night air, her head clean shaven. All other parts of her body except the eyebrows had also been shaven clean and the shaven hair collected in a small piece of cloth held by Aunt Wofemda. The cloth also contained Ablator's nails which had been cut earlier on. Set before her on the dunghill was a pot containing *aditsi*. This was prepared from roasted corn cobs which were crushed and ground into powder, then mixed with water.

Aunt Wofemda was tired. It had been a long day for her. She had taken countless number of women through these processes but never before had she been so hustled through the rites. The night was particularly breezy tonight. The noise of the waves of the boisterous Atlantic Ocean carried on the wind like the continuous rumble of impatient thunder. When you live on these parts of the Atlantic coast you get accustomed to the continuous roar of the sea. It never seems to rest. Day, evening and night, it is a never-ending din as wave after wave crashes onto the beach.

Most people had by now gone to bed so there was little chance of anybody coming upon the three women standing on the rubbish dump. The usual population of goats, sheep, fowls and dogs had also retired for the night. Only the furtive movement of rats could be discerned in the soft moonlight. Aunt Wofemda picked a small stick from the ground and drew a circle of a diameter of about sixty centimetres in the dung. She motioned Ablator to step into the circle and the young widow did so. A circular shallow hole should have been dug for Ablator to step in, but she was not pure — she had been known by a man after the death of her husband, before performing the rites. The shallow hole was made for only pure widows.

Wofemda took off the slip of cloth that Ablator covered herself with so that she stood only in her underskirt. Her breasts were bare and the black nylon skirt offered little resistance against the cold night air. She shivered and crossed her arms over her bosom.

"Put down your arms," said Aunt Wofemda. "I am going to bath you."

Ablator obeyed. Then calabashful after calabashful, the old woman poured the cold *aditsi* over Ablator's head. The young woman's teeth chattered audibly and her body trembled with the cold as she was bathed from head to toe with the *aditsi*. From a rubber container, another mixture was poured into the pot. This was lime fruit juice mixed with water. She was again bathed from head to toe with this mixture. The pot was then rinsed and ordinary water poured in. Then with sponge and soap, Ablator was given a third and final bath. She was bathed from the head to the toes and as the *ahoga* reached her toes, the sponge and soap were left at her feet.

Around them, the breeze had turned into a wind rustling the pieces of papers and leaves on the dunghill. It was the spirit of Gbagbladza angry and threatening to do Ablator harm for having been unfaithful to him, sleeping with a man even before performing the widowhood rites.

327

"*Blewu, blewu,*" intoned Aunt Wofemda. "It wasn't her fault."

The wind died down as Wofemda towelled Ablator dry. She left the towel too at the widow's feet.

"Remove your pants," the old lady said.

Ablator pulled down her pants and stepped out of them. *Ahoga* Tsoeke removed a piece of twine from her wrist and tied it loosely around Ablator's waist. This was the *ahoka.* Then she took a slip of cloth and raising up Ablator's skirt, passed it through the *ahoka* from the front part of her body, slung it in-between her thighs and then over her buttocks and through the *ahoka* at the small of her back. This was the *ahogodi.* From this time onwards, Ablator would not wear ordinary pants again but only the *ahogodi* until she re-married.

From a bag that she had brought to the dunghill, Aunt Wofemda took two large slips of black cloth and a blouse and raising her hands to the four cardinal points of the earth, she counted up to seven. Then she wrapped the cloth around Ablator and pulled the blouse over her head. This was the clothing prescribed by the ghost of Gbagbladza. The widow would now be seen in public during the day only in black clothes for the four-month period of widowhood rites prescribed by the spirit of her husband. In the evening after six o'clock, however, she must not wear the black clothes, she must change into her normal clothes.

Wofemda now took a small shovel she had brought along for the purpose and dug a hole. Into this she put the used towel, sponge and soap and also Ablator's discarded pants and buried them. Then, sandwiched between the two older women, one walking at the front and the other behind her, Ablator made the journey back home from the dunghill. None of them talked on the way, for this was against the regulations of the rites.

Lucy was still up waiting for them. "You are welcome," she said. "Did everything go on right?"

"Yes," said Wofemda. "Where is the room?"

Lucy led them to the door of Ablator's apartment. This was where she would be "indoored" for seven days. Her children had been packed off to Lucy's apartment where they would remain until their mother completed her indooring. Only Lucy would go in to attend to her needs. The rites required that only a widow or a young girl who had never known a man could wait on Ablator during her confinement.

The *ahoga* took Ablator to the inner chamber and there, in the presence of Lucy, a long list of regulations was given her. She must:

— Not shout to attract attention while indoors; she should use a stick to hit the floor

— Bath before eating

— Bath only in the darkness, at dawn or after dark; when she went into the bathroom and found the bathroom wet, it was her dead husband who had taken his bath before her

— Bath three times a day

— Not talk while outside to bath or attend to nature's call

— Use lime fruit in place of pomade

- Use only earthenware plates, no enamel or plastic

- Bath only from an earthenware pot

- Use only calabash as drinking cup and soap dish

- Keep the single stool in the apartment lying down sideways when not in use, otherwise her dead husband would sit on it

- Sleep on only the small mat provided in the room to prevent her dead husband from sleeping beside her; when the mat was not in use, to roll it up and place it on the seat on which she sat

- Not respond verbally to a knock on her door; she should hit the floor with a stick in response

After the indooring for seven days, Ablator would have to go through the outdooring rites. She would be sent back to the refuse dump, taking along one set of new black clothes, a new bottle of pomade, a new tin of talcum powder, a new pair of slippers, new fiber sponge and towel. She would be bathed on the dunghill again and the new clothes put on her. The bath items, sponge and towel would be given to the *ahoga* alongside all the items she used during her indooring. Then she would be led home to begin a normal life.

The fee of the *ahoga* ranged between five and eight thousand cedis. Aunt Wofemda chose to collect a token two thousand.

The feast as directed by the ghost of Gbagbladza

would take place after the outdooring. Ablator would cook all the meals her husband had asked for and entertain any member of the community who cared to come. No musical instruments would be used during the feast; the guests would clap and sing and Ablator would dance in sadness and joy. Sadness at the final separation from her husband, and joy that she was now ready to re-marry if she chose to.

***   ***   ***

Soon after Ablator and Lucy turned in for the night, it began to rain. It began as a light drizzle at first, then the raindrops increased in size and intensity and all nocturnal sounds were drowned in the patter of the rain.

Most people liked a night rain better than a daytime one because your plans and activities were less likely to be disrupted. But on this night someone was fretting and cursing the rain. He was standing at the most unlikely spot in the whole town at that time of the night — the marketplace where ghosts were known to engage in trading activities when people had gone to bed. He had not come prepared for the rain and the flimsy sheds in the market were beginning to prove useless as the rain intensified. The man had a rendezvous. He hated the rain beating him but his main worry was that the rain might prevent the other party from honouring the rendezvous.

The rain suddenly stopped less than an hour after it had begun. The man under the market shed heaved a huge sigh of relief. But he still worried — would the other party honour the rendezvous? He took out a handkerchief and wiped the rain from the little hair on his head. He squeezed the water out of the handkerchief and wiped his

331

head again. He repeated the procedure until his head was satisfactorily rid of the rain. He looked at his watch for the hundredth time. The luminescent face told him it was ten thirty-five. The rendezvous was set for ten o'clock. He told himself if nothing happened by eleven o'clock he would leave.

But at eleven-five he was still under the shed. Like a lovesick suitor who would lay awake, waiting for his lover even until the last cockcrow, he had shifted the deadline to eleven-fifteen. He kept turning in all directions like an airport radar, not knowing from which direction the other party would emerge. At eleven-seventeen, a shadow detached itself from one of the pillars supporting a shed further away from the waiting man. The man's heart began to beat faster as he resisted the impulse to flash his torchlight into the darkness. His eyes peered into the darkness made thicker by the remnant rain clouds that still hung in the sky. The man smiled to himself as the figure drew nearer.

"Over here," he said and the figure made a bee-line for the source of the voice.

The man flashed the torchlight like a radar beacon then switched it off again. "You are late," he said as the figure which was dressed in a dark pair of trousers and a long-sleeved shirt came to a stop a few feet away from him.

"Yes, we took more time than I had expected. And the rain." The man sighed heavily and the figure asked, "What is it?"

"Nothing," said the man. Then he asked, "Have you come to kill me too?"

"What?"

"Like you killed *Huno* Dunyo?"

"Who are you?" the figure asked as it began to back away.

The man shone his torchlight into the retreating figure's face. "Davi Ablator," he said, "the game is up."

The light revealed the frightened face of a woman and sure enough it was Ablator.

"Davi Ablator," the man said, "I am not the man you came to meet. I am Corporal Bena, the police detective." He took some steps after the retreating figure of Ablator. "And I am arresting you for the murder of Hunɔ Dunyo and the attempted murder of Kobla Adekpitor. Look at the knife even in your hands now." He lowered the light which shone off the shining metal of the kitchen knife the woman held in her hand.

Ablator turned to run.

"Don't run," Bena said. "We will be obliged to shoot you if you do. I am not alone."

Ablator stood still. The knife slid from her grip making no noise as it fell into the soft sand on the ground. Her head dropped onto her chest, then she began to cry.

From the shadows, two men emerged. They were Bena's companions, also policemen. One of them was Sergeant Amlima.

"Please handcuff her," Bena said.

Ablator's arms were limp as one of the men clamped the handcuffs over her wrists. She wept as they led her to the police vehicle parked some distance away from the market. She did not stop weeping even as they handcuffed her behind the counter to the long bar attached to the counter for the purpose. She would spend the rest of the night behind the counter in a sitting position.

CHAPTER TWENTY

"When did you start thinking it was the woman who did it?" ASP Adosu asked as he unsuccessfully tried to conceal the look of admiration in his eyes.

Detectives Corporal Bena and Sergeant Amlima were being debriefed in the District Commander's office. Also present was Sergeant Bansa. The news of their previous night's arrest had already spread like bushfire through the police barracks.

Corporal Bena tried to keep a straight face as he talked. Since the previous night, he had not been able to control the inner glow of intense satisfaction that his successful investigation gave him. He had taken a long shot and it had paid off beautifully.

"It was when I started believing the principal suspect, Mr. Adekpitor's story. You see, sir, this man told me lies from the beginning. But later he started telling what I believed was the truth. I realised his first lies were not to conceal the crime I was investigating but to hide adultery. On the night of the murder of *Huno* Dunyo, he told me he was out of town visiting his daughter at Half Assini. I made a call to the police at Half Assini to check out his story. The daughter denied that the father had been there. I confronted Mr. Adekpitor with this evidence. It was at this point that he laid his soul bare. He confessed that when he told his family he was travelling, he was actually hiding out with a woman whose husband had travelled out of town. I checked with the adulterous woman and she corroborated his story. That was no proof though that he did not commit the murder. You see, sir, he could still have been with the woman and gone out to kill Dunyo!" Bena paused and looked round the group.

"Then what made you stop suspecting him?" Adosu asked impatiently.

"The night before the murder of Dunyo, both Dunyo and Adekpitor visited Ablator at different times. Dunyo first, and just as he was coming out he met Adekpitor at the gate. There was a brief scuffle between them because they were chasing the same woman. After the scuffle, Adekpitor entered Ablator's house. That was witnessed by Dunyo and a certain town-crier. Ablator admitted that Dunyo visited her that night but she denied flatly that Adekpitor was there. At first I thought her denial was only to hide what Adekpitor told me he had done with her..."

"What?"

Bena's lips tightened in embarrassment. "Slept with her," he said. "However, in spite of my inner doubts, I was inclined to believe Ablator when she said she had not seen Adekpitor that night. But I also wanted to believe Adekpitor too when he said he had been with her. Then what could be the explanation for these two conflicting stories that sounded true? I had a lucky break in answering this question. The town-crier together with whom Dunyo had seen Adekpitor entering Ablator's house on that fateful night, approached me when he heard that I was investigating the murder. First, he told me about the scuffle between the two men that night. Later, I went back to him and over a bottle of gin, he told me a lot..."

"You were corrupting the man!" Adosu said, chuckling.

"No sir. It was only by line of duty, sir."

"Continue."

"In fact, sir, there is very little that goes on at Woe that the town-crier, Gbekle, does not know about. We talked for a long time. He told me a lot about many people especially Dunyo and Adekpitor..."

"That was where your interest lay."

"Yes, sir. The single most important thing the town-crier told me was that Dunyo was in the habit of drugging women and knowing them sexually. Gbekle told me about an instance when a woman reported Dunyo's conduct to the chief of the town. She had been tricked and drugged and sexually assaulted by Dunyo. Gbekle told me Dunyo admitted the crime before the chief and his elders and he was fined heavily."

"Why didn't they bring him to the police station?"

"I don't know, sir."

"The he-goat! Continue."

"Gbekle's story set me thinking. Could it be that Dunyo drugged Ablator and assaulted her sexually? After that it was not difficult to deduce what had happened. This was what happened. When Dunyo visited Ablator that night he bought drinks and somehow managed to introduce a sleep-inducing drug into the woman's drink. The woman fell asleep, then he took her to her bed and assaulted her sexually. He left quietly, but at the gate he met Adekpitor also coming to Ablator. The two rivals engaged in a scuffle and after that Adekpitor went into the house. He knocked on Ablator's door and hearing no response and finding the door open, he tiptoed inside. He found Ablator naked and fast asleep and thinking this was a God-sent chance, he also knew the woman sexually. When Ablator woke up in the morning she found traces of semen in her private parts. Her mind went straight to Dunyo and she realised she had been cheated. She went

336

mad. It was then that she planned her revenge. She set up a night with Dunyo at the deserted durbar ground and there she knifed him to death." Bena paused again.

"Brilliant," said Adosu. "Continue."

"Thank you, sir," Bena said. "Please can I have some water?"

"Fine," said the District Commander. "Help yourself from the fridge. But hurry up."

"Yes, sir." Bena got up and quickly drank the water. He came back and resumed his seat. "I decided to set a trap for Ablator. I told her the reason why she did not know that Adekpitor had also visited her that night. I also told her that Adekpitor had confessed that he also invaded her womanhood. You should have seen the look on the woman's face. Her face went dark with murderous fury. She clenched her jaws and her whole body shook. It was then that I knew that Ablator was capable of murder. She is a strong woman with a large physique. She has large hands and I am sure when it comes to physical combat she can tilt a few men to the ground. When I saw her reaction to my news I knew that she was ready for violence again..."

"Then what did you do?"

"I told Adekpitor that he would soon be receiving a message from Ablator and that whatever the message was he should let me know immediately before doing anything about the message. He was obedient and in the afternoon he told me Ablator had asked him to meet him at the market place in the night. My trap was working. I knew at once that Ablator was going to kill Adekpitor. I told Adekpitor not to go. I would go and meet Ablator in his place. It was difficult to convince him. He thought the woman's invitation was an indication that she was giving in to his love proposals. But finally he saw reason and agreed that I should go in his place."

"Did you have to tell him that you suspected Ablator killed Dunyo."

"Not exactly, sir. But I think I implied it. During the day, that was yesterday, I was told that Ablator was performing her widowhood rites and would be indoored that night. I am sure she wanted that to serve as an alibi. When the appointed time came I went to the market place with Sergeant Amlima and Sergeant Bansa. Ablator was late for the rendezvous, but finally she came. She was dressed like a man in dark clothes. At first, she thought I was Adekpitor. Then I introduced myself and confronted her with my suspicions. And sure enough she had a large kitchen knife in her hand. We handcuffed her and brought her to the station. That is all, sir."

"That was brilliant," said ASP Adosu. "I congratulate you all. But our work is not finished. This case has become hydra-headed. The more we delve into it the more branches it acquires. Now we have solved Dunyo's murder and as an icing on the cake we have busted a drug trafficking ring. But the major case that started it all remains unsolved. Does Komi Tsormanya indulge in ritual murder? Our principal witness is dead and that leaves us flat on our backs. The question now is how do we make the charge of ritual murder stick on Tsormanya? Then there is the death of that poor boy, what is his name?"

"Kofi Legede," said Sergeant Amlima.

"Yes, Kofi Legede. We know with some certainty from what angle that death came. That means when Tsormanya is in custody there are people out there still carrying out his devilish commands. How do we proceed

338

from here?... Any ideas? Yes, Sergeant Amlima."

"Sir," said Amlima, "the way I see it we will have to wait for the pathologist's report, and the forensic expert's findings too. They promised to come last week Wednesday but they couldn't come. After they have presented their reports we might have something to work on."

"Like what?"

"A little clue could present itself and prove valuable. For the meantime, sir, Sergeant Bansa and myself will continue to nose around to see if we could discover something new. We will also pick up Tsormanya's next-in-command for questioning."

"Who is his next-in-command?"

"His boatswain."

That seemed to satisfy ASP Adosu. "Well," he said, "I think that is acceptable. Meanwhile, prepare dockets so that we can send that so-called prophet and his friend and the woman to court tomorrow. You know the forty-eight-hour law."

"Yes, sir."

"You can go now."

"Thank you, sir."

***   ***   ***

The general medical practitioners at the Keta Hospital normally conducted postmortem examinations on bodies at the mortuary, but the police considered the recent occurrences of such magnitude that they wanted pathologists to conduct the autopsies. Just after the debriefing session with Corporal Bena, ASP Adosu was told two pathologists from the Police Hospital, Accra, were waiting to see him. It had taken the two patholo-

339

gists, Dr. Amaning Acheampong and Dr. Delar Darvlo, a long time to fix a time convenient for both of them to come to Keta. When Dr. Acheampong was free, Dr. Darvlo would find himself occupied, and vice versa. Even on Tuesday, they nearly did not come, because on Monday evening Dr. Darvlo's wife sent a fax from Belgium that she would be coming back home on Tuesday. Fortunately, she later telephoned in the night to say she would arrive rather on Saturday.

The two pathologists were friends not only because they belonged to the same profession, but because they had been family friends since their childhood. Dr. Darvlo was a giant, well over six feet but despite his physique he was quick and agile. Dr. Acheampong was also tall but spare of flesh and ponderous in his movement. When the two of them played tennis which they did often, it was almost always the heavier Darvlo who had the upper hand.

By an arrangement with the police, the pathologists brought along with them the forensic expert's report on the two bucketfuls of sand the Keta police had sent to the police laboratory in Accra. Adosu took the two men upstairs to introduce them to the Divisional Commander of Police, Donald Aboagye. The meeting nearly turned sour when Aboagye started complaining about the delay of the pathologists in coming. It almost turned into a shouting match between the Divisional Commander and Dr. Acheampong. Fortunately, Dr. Darvlo managed to calm down his friend. He knew the type of man they had come to meet when, just after the introductions, the Divisional Commander had said, "So you people have managed to come at long last?"

Back in the District Commander's office, the pathologists presented the forensic report on the bucketfuls of sand to Adosu. Adosu read through the report quickly. The sand in Bucket A, the report said, contained two terminal phalanges, bits of human hair and tissue, evidence that a human body must have been buried there and later exhumed and taken to another site. Bucket B, said the report, contained three human teeth, a canine and two premolars. It also contained pieces of human hair and tissue, also evidence that the site from where the sand was collected once harboured a human body. The two buckets also revealed dried liquids from the human body.

Adosu put the report aside and said, "I hope you know what the report contains."

"No," said Dr. Darvlo. "It was not addressed to us so we did not read it."

"Sorry. The report says evidence of human bodies were found in the two bucketfuls of sand we sent to our laboratory in Accra."

"What exactly is happening in your·area here?" asked Dr. Acheampong.

Adosu spread out his hands helplessly. "I don't know, my brother," he said. "We have a few mad men among us. They are causing the trouble."

"As we understand we are to examine four bodies," Dr. Darvlo said.

"Yes," replied Adosu.

"And you suspect all four bodies are murder victims?"

"Yes. There is no question about that. We only want you to tell us how they died."

Dr. Darvlo stood up. "We'd better get to work at once. We have a lot of work to do."

"Wait," said Adosu. "Let me send for the officers in

charge of the cases so that we can all go to the mortuary."

It took less than ten minutes to bring together Sergeants Amlima and Bansa and Corporal Bena. The pathologists left the vehicle they had brought from Accra and joined the policemen in their vehicle. The team was taken to the Keta Hospital Administrator who took them to see the Medical Superintendent. The Medical Superintendent was on ward rounds and sent word that the pathologists could start their work; he would see them later.

The hospital had two mortuaries, Mortuary A and Mortuary B. Mortuary A was the older mortuary and this was where bodies brought to the hospital in a decomposed state were normally kept. The bodies of *Huno* Dunyo, Kofi Legede, Johnny Klevor and Sena Akakpo were all in Mortuary A. The mortuary man on duty took the team to Mortuary A and after knocking on the doors of the freezer he pulled the doors open.

ASP Adosu had never been able to withstand the sight of a dead body without emotions rushing to his face. He quickly excused himself and left for the police station, leaving the crime officers with the pathologists. It took the pathologists about three hours to finish their examinations. The police vehicle came back to take them to the police station where they presented their report. Their findings were as follows:

Huno Agboado Dunyo

On examination he was found to be anaemic with multiple punctured wounds at the right upper abdomen and adjoining chest. Dissection showed haemoperitorium with multiple punctured lacerations of the liver and a

342

single laceration of the transverse colon on the right side. Death was due to haemorrhagic shock from bleeding liver lacerations.

Kofi (Legede) Kluga

He was found to be very anaemic and no evidence of central or peripheral cyanosis. Dissection showed massive haemoperitonium with fractured 10-11th ribs and disintegration of the spleen. The lungs were found to be normal. Death was due to haemorrhagic shock from disintegrated spleen.

Johnny Klevor

He was found to have extensive bilateral subconjuntiva haemorrhage and slightly bluish tongue sticking out of mouth. Laceration at the frontal scalp. Dissection: Skull is intact and no intracranial or intracerebral haemorrhage found. Dissection of the neck showed band of hyperactive soft tissues of the neck. Cause of death is due to asphyxia from possible strangulation.

Sena Akakpo

On inspection found to be very anaemic with laceration through the right internal carotial artery, the trachea and the right internal and external jugular veins including the intervening tissue. Death due to haemorrhagic shock.

Adosu looked through the report perfunctorily. Later, when the pathologists had gone, he would comb the report with a dictionary. "Will you be available to present this report to the court on court days?" he asked.

"If the necessary arrangements are made for us," said Dr. Darvlo, "we will."

"Necessary arrangements like fuel for your car, food and booze, huh?" said Adosu.

All of them broke into laughter.

"And talking about food," said Adosu, "you must be famishing by now. I have made arrangements for your lunch at the Larota Guesthouse. Let's go there now."

After a sumptuous meal, Drs. Darvlo and Acheampong left Keta for their base in Accra. The relatives of the dead bodies were then notified they could collect their bodies for burial.

**   **   **

Two spectacular cases were called at the Keta Circuit Court the next day. In all the three trials, Lawyer Henry Sekle was counsel for the accused. The first case was the trial of Ablator Dzumave for the murder of Huno Agboado Dunyo. Henry Sekle entered a plea of not guilty for his client and Ablator was remanded in police custody to re-appear in three weeks' time.

The second case was The Republic versus Prophet Elijah Patu and Nana Antwi Boateng. The case as presented by the prosecution was that on or about the 27th of June, the accused conspired and murdered Johnny Klevor and hid his body in a deepfreezer. The two men were also accused of possession and trafficking in cocaine. The case presented Lawyer Sekle with a dilemma. With regards to the murder charge, his two clients agreed that

344

only the prophet was involved; Nanā Boateng had no knowledge about Johnny's death. It was the charge of possession of and trafficking in cocaine that presented a problem. Whereas Prophet Patu claimed he had no knowledge that Nana Boateng was carrying the prohibited drug in his brief case, the latter insisted the prophet was an accomplice, a conduit between Lome and Accra. Lawyer Sekle entered a plea of not guilty to the charge of murder and drug trafficking. To the charge of drug possession his plea was guilty with explanation. The accused persons were remanded in prison custody to reappear on the 30th of July.

***   ***   ***

The court appearance of Ablator, Prophet Patu and his friend from Togo was, as to be expected, a virtual crowd-puller. But it was not able to attract as much attention as when Mr. Komi Tsormanya appeared again in court on the 7th of July. The date was marked on the calender of many people for diverse reasons. Those who had lost relatives under suspicious circumstances wanted to see the accused sentenced to death; Tsormanya's family and those who owed their bread and butter to him wanted to see him freed; others focussed their attention on the date for the mere curiosity of witnessing the trial of a monster.

As early as 6.00 a.m., crowds started converging first in front of the police station, then at the premises of the circuit court. More than a few people in the crowd brought along lunch packs — bread sandwiches, *abolo* and fried fish, fried yam and turkey tail, and fruits. Food sellers were not slow in realising the potential for making some fast money. By eight o'clock, the space between the police station and the courthouse was like a market and those who had brought along lunch packs began to regret their action — there was food to buy in abundance.

A few pickpockets were also among the crowd and at least one was caught and given a severe beating. July 7th was a week-day, but many in the crowd were office workers who should rather be in their offices. Most of these were junior government workers; they kept glancing at their watches, hoping something dramatic would happen before they had to leave for their offices. A few senior government officials were also among the crowd and when these met their subordinates they quickly looked away, or when they could not avoid it they gave the subordinates mild reprimands. The subordinates would smile and walk to another part of the crowd, knowing that no disciplinary action could be taken against them.

Komi Tsormanya had been brought from the Ho Prisons the previous day. At exactly nine o'clock, he was brought out of the cells under heavy police guard. There was no chance of taking him through the crowd without a riot, so as on the first day of his trial, he was taken over the short distance in a police vehicle. The crowd milled against the vehicle as the police did their best to keep them away with their truncheons. In the confusion one of the side glasses of the vehicle was broken. ASP Adosu who was riding in the vehicle alongside the suspect gave the order and two warning shots were fired into the air. The crowd turned away in confusion and those in the fore panicked momentarily when they found out they could not break through the human wall and put distance between themselves and the menacing guns. The warning shots sobered the crowd, and Komi Tsormanya reached the courtroom without further incident.

The trial itself was an anti-climax. The judge entered the courtroom and banged his mallet on his table for order. Many in the crowd were hoping that sentence would be passed that day. But after Tsormanya's charges were read again, the judge announced that in view of the magnitude of the case he was compelled to refer it to a court of higher jurisdiction, namely, the Regional Public Tribunal at Ho.

Most of the spectators were very disappointed. They were glad, however, that Tsormanya's case was the first to be called, otherwise they would have wasted much time waiting while other cases were dealt with first. The crowd stood aside, this time behaving itself for fear of more warning shots, as it waited for a last glimpse of the alleged ritual murderer before he was taken away to Ho.

The morning which was very dull seemed to be growing darker and darker. In their obsession with the trial, most people had not noticed rain clouds gathering in the sky. The rain clouds had been gathering for about half an hour now and growing darker by the minute. As the judge turned the page on Tsormanya's case the first mutterings of thunder were heard in the sky. The crowd looked up like one body. Without a second glance at the sinister clouds, it began to disperse quickly. No-one wanted to be beaten by the rain.

As Tsormanya was being led out of the dock, the first spattering of rain began to fall, accompanied by the muttering of thunder. Then long blinding cracks flashed through the clouds as brilliant lightning began to precede the thunder. The lightning crackled across the sky in several places almost at the same time. The raindrops remained just a spattering but the thunder rolled out in deafening roars.

The crowd began to fall over itself like driver ants escaping from the threat of fire. The police hurried Tsormanya through the courtroom to the door. Another police driver, not Constable Alex Atonsu, reversed the police vehicle as close to the door of the courthouse as possible. One policeman who was sitting in the vehicle opened the back door. ASP Adosu came to a stop at the courtroom door and waited to see the suspect put in the vehicle before he would go and take the front passenger seat. Behind him were Inspector Dongor and Sergeants Amlima and Bansa. Two policemen accompanying Tsormanya both held the suspect's arms to help him into the vehicle.

The intensity of the ligntning and thunder had reduced somewhat and only a small portion of the crowd remained outside. Those seated in the courtroom left their seats to see Tsormanya taken away. Suddenly, the lightning returned with a huge crack that merged with the deafening retort of thunder. The brilliant light momentarily blinded everybody. Those in the courthouse ducked behind the low walls and those outside covered their faces with their hands and clothing. When visions became clear again there was immediate consternation. The two policemen who were helping Tsormanya to enter the police vehicle had been flung by the lightning several paces away from the vehicle. Tsormanya had also fallen down. He had fallen into a sitting position with his head on the step of the vehicle like someone whose head had been placed on the block awaiting the executioner's axe.

ASP Adosu was the first person to rush to Tsormanya's aid followed closely by Sergeant Amlima. He lifted

Tsormanya by the shoulders but the man's head fell forward as if there was no more bone or muscle in his neck. Nobody needed to tell the District Commander that Tsormanya was dead.

The dead body was immediately bundled into the vehicle and taken to the Keta Hospital mortuary. The police moved with such speed that even the rumour machine could not beat them. It was only after the mortuary men had put Tsormanya's body in the freezer that word reached them that the man had been killed by lightning. The mortuary men who were no strangers to the cult of fear surrounding *Torhonor*, the thunder god, raved and fumed for having been deceived into handling a contaminated body. They left the hospital immediately to seek professional advice for remedies against the anger of the thunder god, for they knew they had wronged the god by handling a body that had not first been purified.

The hearts of the policemen who handled Tsormanya's body were also full of trepidation — would the thunder god punish them too for touching an unclean body? It was only ASP Mark Adosu's heart that was filled with a glow. He had at long last been able to score a point against the *Yeve* cult. He had defied them and not allowed them to perform their rites before removing the dead body from the spot of death. He had thumbed his nose at them and they dared not touch him. To make assurance double sure, he gathered all the policemen who had touched Tsormanya's body and took them to his pastor for prayers of fortification.

As for Cathrina who had called on *Torhonor*, the thunder god, in the hour of extreme danger, wherever her soul lay, it would be comforted in the knowledge that the god did not fail her.

EPILOGUE

After numerous court appearances at the Ho Regional Public Tribunal, Ablator Dzumave's charge was changed from premeditated murder to manslaughter. Since Ablator could not afford the services of a counsel, a young lawyer was found for her under the government's Legal Aid Programme. The lawyer argued forcefully that Ablator killed Dunyo and attempted to kill Adekpitor during a spate of temporary insanity brought about by a deep sense of loss when the two men raped her. On Wednesday the fifteenth of October, Ablator was sentenced to five years in prison with hard labour.

Reverend Prophet Elijah Patu was tried at the same tribunal. He was found guilty of drug trafficking and murder. He got ten years in prison with hard labour for drug trafficking, and in addition all his property including his two cars and two buildings in Accra were forfeited to the state. For the murder of Johnny Klevor, he was sentenced to death by hanging.

Nana Antwi Boateng, the man who was ferrying the drugs across the Ghana-Togo border to Prophet Patu also got ten years in jail with hard labour.

The Ghana Police formally notified the Togolese authorities about the involvement of François, alias Boxer, in the illegal drug trade but to date, no-one knows what action has been taken against him and his cohorts.

Constable Alex Atonsu, the police driver, was dishonourably discharged from the Police Service and tried for abetment of crime, viz, the murder of Johnny Klevor. He got ten years in jail with hard labour.

Corporal Francis Dekornu and Constable John Atiku

were both discharged from the Ghana Police for negligence of duty. They appealed to the Commission for Human Rights and Administrative Justice (CHRAJ) for wrongful dismissal, but the decision of the Police Service Disciplinary Committee was upheld and Dekornu and Atiku left the service in disgrace.

Leve Akpai, the boatswain and right-hand man of Komi Tsormanya, was questioned on several occasions by the police. They would pick him up one day and release him the next day after vigorous interrogation, but the man stuck to the same refrain — he knew nothing about Tsormanya's ritual murders. After this had been going on for some time, his lawyer, the ubiquitous Henry Sekle threatened to take legal action against the police for harassment of his client. The police backed off, making some noise about bringing charges against Leve soon, but the man is still a free man on the beaches of Woe, assisting the children of Komi Tsormanya to carry on with their father's fishing business.

Lucy Kporsu became the sole breadwinner of Nani Hordzo's household during Ablator's arrest and trial. Apart from caring for her own children, she had to feed, clothe and pay the school fees of Ablator's children too. She also had to send meals to her father-in-law at the Yeve shrine. It was a burden she was ill-prepared to bear. But just as all hope seemed to be lost and she had begun to totter under her heavy burden, salvation came from a most unlikely source.

Through the instrumentality of Detective Corporal Richard Bena, a charge of rape was brought against Kobla Adekpitor. But despite several attempts by the police to make Ablator testify against Adekpitor, she refused to do so for reasons best known to herself. It was at this point

351

that Corporal Bena heard about the financial difficulties Lucy was going through. Bena approached Ablator with a proposition and this time the woman needed little persuasion to go along with the policeman. Under Bena's plan, Ablator would not testify against Adekpitor and in return Adekpitor would provide financial assistance to Lucy. When Ablator agreed to the plan, she insisted that Adekpitor should also pay the fine imposed on the family by the *Yeve* shrine. The choices were put before Adekpitor — to go to jail or pay up and skip the ordeal. Adekpitor chose the second option and Lucy's financial woes were brought to an end. Soon after Ablator commenced her jail sentence, Lucy started her widowhood rites.

Adekpitor kept his word and paid the one-million-cedi fine imposed on the family of Nani by the *Yeve* shrine. In addition, he provided one hundred thousand cedis for the other items necessary for Nani's outdooring after his initiation.

Six months after Nani had been brought to the *Yeve* shrine, the ultimate rites were performed for his final outdooring on a Saturday. The night before, *vevenyanya* took place again at the shrine. As on Nani's first day at the shrine, seven white and seven black hen were provided for the rite. One white and one black hen were slaughtered and the blood collected in a basin. The *Katidao* touched the blood to the mouths of the idols in the shrine. The two fowls were dry-plucked and placed in two bowls containing corn flour, one in each bowl. Then with his bare hands, the *Katidao* mashed the fowls together with the corn flour. To the mixture in one bowl he added red oil. He then counted one up to seven and touched each mixture first to the mouth of the idols, then to the mouth of Nani who was on his knees, his head shaven clean again.

The *Katidao* placed his hand on the head of Nani and christened him. "From this time onwards," the *Katidao* said in a sonorous voice, "you will be known by no other name than Hutorwohoe and your surname. You are now Hutorwohoe Hordzo."

Early on Saturday morning, Hutorwohoe was dressed in colourful livery. He wore *tsaka* and *avlaya*. *Ese* made of multicoloured parrot's feathers adorned his forehead and two *dakpla* criss-crossed his torso. At about eight o'clock, he emerged from the shrine, holding two rattlers. There was drumming, dancing and singing. The old man, whose body now looked very lithe, danced very vigorously despite his advanced age. He enjoyed especially the long distance dancing, a dance at a fast pace from one end of the yard to the other, with arms flailing.

Later in the afternoon, Hutorwohoe finally went home, the last song of the occasion still on his lips:

Mega yi bo o,
Amekuku ta egla mele nu o he.
De me be mayi boo,
De me be mayi boo,

Xedewo tsi amlima he.

353

GLOSSARY OF WORDS

Words foreign to the English Language appear below in alphabetical order. The page on which a particular word first appears is indicated in brackets.

1. **abolo** (p.5): a steamed food made from corn

2. **aditsi** (p.3 26): roasted corn cobs, crushed and mixed with water, used for a ceremonial bath during widowhood rites.

3. **adzei** (xi): a cry of pain

4. **agbadza** (p.6): a popular form of dance among the Anlo ethnic group of the Volta Region of Ghana

5 . **ago** (p.318): a call to attention or a knock at the door

6. **ahoga** (p.265): a widow who specialises in performing widowhood rites for other widows

7. **ahogodi** (p.328): a slip of cloth used as pants by someone undergoing widowhood rites

8. **ahoka** (p.328): piece of twine tied round the waist of someone undergoing widowhood rites; *ahogodi* is passed through this to serve as panties

9. **akpeteshi** (p.260): locally prepared gin

10. **akple** (322): a type of food made from corn flour and cassava

11. **ame** (p.318): a response to someone knocking at the door

12. **amegashi** (313): a medium

13. **ao** (p.58): a cry of distress or mourning

14. **asɔ** (p.21): an interjection showing disappointment or distress

15. **aʋlaya** (p.353): several loose rings of cloth worn around the waist of a male *Yeʋe* initiate like a skirt and puffed up to show a circular girdle around the waist

16. **aʋle** (p.37): members of the *aʋleketi* unit of the *Yeʋe* cult; they are women and behave informally, engaging in antics that are considered taboo to other members

17. **aʋleketi** (p.126): one of the three divisions of the *Yeʋe* cult; its members join the cult through reincarnation

18. **blewu** (p.328): softly

19. **bozua** (p.137): boatswain

20. **dakpla** (p.225): two lines of marks crisscrossing each other, tattooed on the back of a male *Yeve* initiate; they can also be two rings of cowries and beads worn across the torso to crisscross at the back of an initiate

21. **dashi** (p.126): a member of a unit of the *Yeve* cult called *vodu da*

22. **dasi** (p.88): a female member of the cult of *Yeve*; even though she belongs to the cult, she is not formally initiated into it; she is an associate

23. **davi** (p.192): a form of address showing respect, used for women

24. **dza** (p.32): welcome

25. **dzemkple** (p.322): a type of food made from corn, red palm oil, etc.

26. **dzimakpla** (p.79): an insult, someone not well brought up by his/her parents

27. **efiashi** (p.319): "the wife of the chief", a term used by ghosts to address a medium when she summons them

28. **efo** (p.20): a form of address showing respect, used for men

29. **ese** (p.353): a band worn around the head by *Yeve* initiates into which are stuck parrot's

feathers on the forehead

30. **Esrui hade** ... (p.129): *Yeve* cult language meaning, "Take off your clothes."

31. **etsi** (p.227): black powder prepared from herbs and other items, used for rituals and magical purposes

32. **eyo** (p.318): see *yoo*

33. **fielevi** (p.316): a medium's spiritual messenger to the spirit world

34. **godidzi** (p.268): a strip of red cloth worn by women as panties through beads on their waists

35. **gɔni** (p.130): *Yeve* cult greeting meaning, "morning"

36. **Hogbetsotso** (p.208): a festival held annually by the Anlos to celebrate their migration to where they live now

37. **hunɔ** (p.38): the male counterpart of *dasi*

38. **katidao** (p.125): a high-ranking *Yeve* cult member who carries out punishment on erring cult members

39. **kenkey** (p.2): a steamed food prepared from corn and wrapped in corn husk

40. **kpoea** (p.232): an interjection to call attention or

show scorn

41. **Kporkpor** (p.186): someone under initiation at the *Yeve* shrinè

42. **Kutsiami** (p.117): in Anlo mythology, the boat-man who ferries the spirit of a dead person across the river separating the living from the dead

43. **liha** (p.267): a sweet drink made from corn

44. **mama** (p.315): grandmother

45. **Midawo** (p.38): the head of a *Yeve* shrine

46. **so** (p.126): one of the three divisions of the *Yeve* cult; it draws its membership from the exploits of the thunder god

47. **soshi** (p.126): a member of the *so* division of the *Yeve* cult

48. **Somlatɔ** (p.226): a magician of the *Yeve* cult

49. **Torhonor** (p.xx): The thunder god, the principal god of the *Yeve* cult, otherwise known as *Xebieso*

50. **tsaka** (353): a pair of shorts made from the kentey cloth; the shorts reach down to the knees and frayed at the seams at the back of the knees like spurs; they are worn by male *Yeve* initiates

51. **tsiami** (p.20): person who, traditionally, plays the role of an intermediary in a formal conversation, conveying what one person says to the other and vice versa

52. **Tsoe a lo doe nya ngor** (p.187): *Yeve* cult language meaning, "I don't understand."

53. **tsun** (p.35): an interjection showing disgust or low esteem

54. **Tukpayidakpa...** (p.128): an invocation of the *Yeve* cult

55. **vevenyanya** (p.128): a *Yeve* ceremony during which one black and one white fowl were killed and mashed in corn flour; it is done for someone about to be initiated into the cult

56. **vodu da** (p.126): one of the three divisions of the *Yeve* cult; its members join the cult through illness

57. **wotemehe** (p.127): cult language meaning, "Get closer"

58. **wudi** (p.127): a ceremonial drum of the *Yeve* cult

59. **Yeve** (p.xvii) The name of a cult widespread in the southern part of the Volta Region of Ghana, West Africa

60. **yoo** (p.25): a form of response showing agreement with something said

61. **zhɔkli** (p.127): cult language meaning, "kneel down"

GLOSSARY OF SONGS

1. p.6   *If you bring a gun*
I will ward it off
If you bring a dagger
I will ward it off...
Dare the short man throw the danger
Adzogba!
Dare the short man throw the dagger
Adzogba!...

2. p.57   *There is something inside the anthill,*
It is a dwarf inside the anthill.
There is something inside the anthill,
It is a dwarf inside the anthill.
Let the thing inside the anthill
Come out for a duel with me;
Let the dwarf inside the anthill
Come out for a duel with me...

3. p.59.   *We are coming to Afegame,*
Let the Afegamites prepare to receive us.
We are coming to Afegame,
Let the Afegamites prepare to receive us.
Oh, prepare to receive us,
Alelele, prepare to receive us.
We are coming to Afegame,
Let the Afegamites prepare to receive us...

4. p.130 *Dangoe, what you did,*
It is not good.
Did you not ridicule the god Hebieso

So that non-initiates mocked him?

6. p.353   *Don't go too far*
A skull does not have a jaw
I want to go far afield
I want to go far afield
The folk of Hede have accomplished the
   impossible.